Love Remains

Glen Duncan was born in Bolton and now lives in London. This is his second novel. He is currently working on the screenplay of his first novel, *Hope*.

Also by Glen Duncan

Hope

Love
Remains

GLEN DUNCAN

Granta Books
London

Granta Publications, 2/3 Hanover Yard, London N1 8BE

First published in Great Britain by Granta Books 2000
This edition published by Granta Books 2001

A CIP catalogue record for this book is available from
the British Library.

1 3 5 7 9 10 8 6 4 2

ISBN 1 86207 400 3

Typeset in Berkeley by M Rules

Printed and bound in Great Britain by
Mackays of Chatham PLC

For Louise, Mark and Marina

Part One

LOVERS

When the future ended, Nicholas discovered, you left London and went to New York. Even at Christmas.

Now, five Bloody Marys and eleven cigarettes in, he sat at the bar in Arcadia encased in noise, pencilled by the club's lasers and jet-lagged into physical peace.

On the flight over, a red-haired British Airways stewardess had encountered him in the aisle and said: 'Are you all right, sir?' Details of her had rushed at him in bright fragments: large face, Celtic green eyes and sepia freckles, burgundy lips, black eyelashes, nails the colour of chocolate mousse, navy blue skirt tight across a menstrual abdomen.

'You look a bit lost,' she had added.

Nicholas had squeezed past her and strapped himself into his seat.

There was a collective agreement in Manhattan, apparently – to *be* Manhattan, to look like it looked on television. Nicholas's cab driver (Salim Farouk, medallion number 1168230) had honked and yelled out of the window and smacked the steering wheel and sworn in butchered English. Threadbare down-and-outs drank beer out of brown-paper bags; a fat, bored-looking traffic cop umpired two screaming drivers; mahogany-faced bike messengers flashed past blowing whistles; white steam tore upwards from grids in the roads; the signs said WALK. DON'T WALK. Nicholas had watched from the back of the cab, surprised in a corner of himself that it was all exactly the way he had imagined it – or at least the way he remembered having imagined it.

And so to a hotel he couldn't afford, with three ugly, glamorous receptionists and a liveried crew of contemptuous and meticulously polite porters, whom he forgot to tip, every time. Thank you. Thank *you*sir.

Then the snow had drawn him out. For an hour he had sat on the edge of the tub in the surgical bathroom not wondering what to do next, and when he had walked back into the bedroom had found the dark window cross-hatched with urgent snow.

A bald porter with black nostril hair had said – with a pause, as if hinting at a corrupt allegiance – 'Arcadia,' when Nicholas had asked. 'Third and Twentieth.'

Three more Bloody Marys and eight more cigarettes. A silent rapport with the chiselled bartender. Then an approach from his left. Nicholas looked up.

'Hey.' A smile-smirk, a reflex giggle. 'Hi. Got a light?' Then, over Nicholas's shoulder to the bartender: 'Best single malt in the house, babe. Just ice.'

Nicholas had noticed her earlier. She looked forty, perhaps forty-five. Small, glittering eyes and dirty yellow-blonde hair. Golden tanned skin with lines around the eyes and mouth. She had the porcine version of American attractiveness, the slightly pug nose with wide, full cheeks and a hard jaw. There was older-woman flesh at the throat, hands and underarms. All collarbone, cleavage and bare midriff in the sheer black vest, she looked finished; years of being scrutinized by men had sculpted her into exhausted voluptuousness. Her face's mobility – the greedy smile, the expanding and contracting eyes – showed how much time and energy she spent distracting herself from herself. Arresting motion in her mind or body would create a queasy focus, a clear sight of herself which must be avoided at all costs.

He had noticed her, since he was condemned to notice everything now, indiscriminately. She'd been dancing with her wrists crossed above her head, her nose wrinkled and her bottom lip held in her teeth. The lasers had scribbled all over her.

Now she stood next to him with one hand on her hip (black

leather trousers, open-toed stilettos) and the other waving a white cigarette, exaggeratedly waiting for a light. While Nicholas went through his pockets for the lighter that was on the bar, the bartender leaned past him and lit it for her.

The back of the limousine had seats facing each other and a neon-lined mini-bar. She sat with her bare feet stretched across into Nicholas's lap. At the stop signs dark bodies hurried past through the fast-falling snow.

Her name was Mickey, and with her golden toes gripping his thigh and a drink tinkling in her hand she said, turning her head to indicate the streets: '"The poor you will have with you, always." Hey, if it was good enough for Jesus it's good enough for me, right?' Again the injected giggle. 'Sure you don't want one of these?'

Nicholas looked down at her foot in his lap. Veins showed in the ankle. Her toes gripped and released him repeatedly, as if performing a strengthening exercise. Her hands and feet had the same sun-aged quality. The parts of her meant for work had been looked after instead.

She took a sip of the drink and said: 'Some first night in New York, huh?'

Nicholas dropped his hand on to her shin and felt its long, old, hard bone through the leather. She smelled of the club's dry ice and cigarette smoke.

'Do you ever think about the future?' he asked her, quietly.

She seemed deliberately abstracted, content to have his hand there, but with her attention somewhere else, like a cat. At that moment he wouldn't have been surprised if she had looked at him, suddenly, without any idea of who he was or how he had got into her car.

She did look back at him – smiling, though. 'Sure I do,' she said. 'All the time. Don't you?'

Mickey's apartment looked out over Central Park, and was luxuriously furnished. Small objects on tables and shelves turned out to be made of things like silver and ivory and jade. There were places of red parquet and other places of deep carpet the colour of champagne. In the bedroom there was a thin Persian rug of gold and blue; beyond it – solid, imperial, white – the bed.

For an hour she ignored him. She moved around the apartment, in and out of rooms, doing whatever she was doing. Nicholas stood at the long window with his hands in his pockets and looked out at the park being outlined by the snow. The trees' bare branches were lifted in frail shock. Hours and miles flickered around him in an agitated swarm, then settled, defining his own outline.

'OK, British guy. Playtime.'

Slowly, as if tearing his aura from where it had found rest, Nicholas struggled to the bedroom and stopped in the doorway.

One soft, topaz-coloured lamp lit the bed, where Mickey had undressed and stretched out, her hands crossed again above her head. No hair between her legs. Breasts like appalled witnesses, blonde hair a smashed aureole on the pillow. A thread of white powder from navel to swollen mons.

'So what do you want for Christmas?' she said.

◆

Six years earlier Nicholas had married Chloe.

They met on a wet Wednesday afternoon. Nicholas was supposed to be at a Victorian Literature seminar. Instead he was in a greasy spoon café not far from the university, drinking hot chocolate and reading *The World According to Garp*. After a while he looked up and saw that Chloe had come in and was sitting at a table across the room. She saw him and waved, hesitantly. They had noticed each other over the preceding weeks, but had never spoken.

Eventually, Nicholas went over to her table.

'Where should you be?' he asked her after he had sat down.

'Agrarian Revolution,' she said. 'Couldn't face it. Townsend's crop rotation. Jethro Tull's seed drill. All I can think of is that mad bloke with the flute.'

Her hair was wet from the rain and her lips looked cold and fresh.

'I don't know about you,' Nicholas said, 'but I've been sitting here working myself up to the idea of a full English breakfast. Does that sound obscene to you?'

'No,' Chloe said. 'It sounds like a fucking brilliant idea.'

They took a tube into town and spent the afternoon wandering around the shops in the drizzle, then went back to Chloe's room. When they kissed for the first time, Nicholas felt their mouths as a tropical nucleus in all the world's chilled, swirling rain. At that moment – decoded breath, scents of her wet hair and cold-chastened skin, the sudden nearness of her eyelashes and mouth and breasts – simply kissing revealed itself to him as a shocking intimacy.

'There's something I have to warn you about, first,' Chloe said. She had stopped him, gently, at the third button of her blouse. Nicholas leaned up and back so he could see her face.

'What is it?' he asked.

All afternoon it had rained. In the years that followed he never forgot this moment: the pewter darkness of early evening; the room's objects like devout witnesses; the rain's static; Chloe next to him, trying to overcome her fear – whatever it was. Her eyes glittered in the half-light.

'Burn scar,' she said. 'I fell into a fire when I was small. It's on the left, from the outside edge of my breast up and under my arm. It's pretty vile. So if it's the sort of thing that's . . . If you're going to throw up or something, you'd better stop now.'

Everything after 'scar' delivered in a deadened voice. He didn't know what to do. He did know that whatever he said would be wrong. The words themselves warned him as they formed in his mouth. So, saying nothing, he laid his head down on her shoulder and held her, rigidly, in silence. He was terrified that the scar would disgust him, and at the same time knew he must go on with her.

Slowly, holding her, he undid the remaining buttons.

'And please . . .' Chloe whispered, 'not with pity. I'd rather have detached – I'd rather have just fucking curiosity . . . Oh I'm sorry, I'm sorry, it's not your fault. It's just that I can feel—'

'Why don't you shut up?' Nicholas said. He said it without premeditation, politely; he offered it to her as a genuine question she might consider. It silenced her.

He couldn't see, but he could feel it. The damaged area was perhaps the size of a hand, and the skin there was both silken and rubbery, unevenly healed, in places puckered, in places satin. His touching it anaesthetized her. She went dead and distant in his arms. But he felt nothing beyond a blank determination not to lose the contact, not to have his own will averted. Perversely, he felt leaden, disinterested lust rising for the first time in the encounter. Her deadness engendered it, obliterating his pity. Gradually, as he continued to kiss her mouth, his desire filtered through to her. It satisfied her because it was stripped of sympathy. Opening her limbs, feeling the alien hardness and leanness of his body insinuating its purpose against her, Chloe knew that there must be this callousness, first, if she were ever going to let tenderness follow.

◆

Nicholas lay with his face between Mickey's thighs. He was sure he could feel the snow adding its weight to the world. The bedroom was hot; if he pulled his face away, their separating skins would make a soft tearing sound.

'Everyone said I married him for the money,' Mickey said. 'Until he died. I guess because it was too late to do anything about it then. They kept *telling* him, the assholes. Thing they didn't get was, he didn't care. He was just lonely. He saw something *in* me, you know? I mean it's not like there weren't women who *were* after the money.' She lay on her back with the bedsheet down around her ankles. 'Well, now they'll never know for sure.'

Nicholas hadn't been able to fuck her, which had interested her.

'You're not a fag, are you? Come on, I *know* you're not a fag.'

Eventually she had become annoyed: 'Can you just get me *off*, for Christ's sake? I mean you can get me off or you can get *out*, you know?'

So he had. He responded because going out into the snow and back to his hotel had revealed itself as something he didn't want to do. This was how decisions made themselves, now. Mickey had grabbed him by the ears and shoved his head down to her cunt, where, after a pause, he had begun to kiss and lick her, like a mechanical toy. It seemed a long time since he had done anything like this, though he knew that was an illusion. When she started to come she lifted his head by its hair and looked down at his face with what seemed to Nicholas an expression of perfected hatred – lips curled, nose wrinkled, teeth bared – then slammed him back down and held him there for the remaining five, six, seven spasms. Only at the moment when she had looked at him, when he'd intuited some feral anger or loathing, only then had he felt the faintest flicker in his cock, a ghost-fish of the blood. It had passed in an instant, but the memory of it resonated.

Now Mickey stroked his hair. A ring on her index finger had turned and its stone scraped Nicholas's scalp.

'You better stay here for a few days,' she said, as if having arrived at the decision after long deliberation. 'Since it doesn't look like you've got anywhere else to go.'

◆

The possibility of love revealed itself to Chloe immediately, in a shock. When they sat opposite each other that first Wednesday, with rain streaking the steamed windows and the delicious reek of frying bacon in the air, she felt (thinking, stunned, of the billions who had felt it, down the long bloodied canvas of history) the first murderous utterance of romance: *It's him*. In an instant she knew that her own name – Chloe Anne Palmer – might be added to the scrolled history of love. Love. It revealed both itself and the fact that she'd been waiting for it. In the moment of knowing that it was going to begin with Nicholas – that if she let it, it *could* begin with Nicholas – other truths of her nature uncovered themselves. I'm a romantic, she thought. Oh, God. I must be. Only romantics meet someone and think they know, immediately.

She went with Nicholas through that first afternoon at a pitch of excitement that was almost nausea, because she knew that if they went back to her room they'd have sex. And since, in her life before London (a Devon village, Elm Coombe), she'd been the odd girl who knew that Julius Caesar had had a passion for roast duck, that Alexander the Great probably died of syphilis, that Imhotep designed the Step Pyramid and that the Crusaders sacked Constantinople in 1202, she was still a virgin.

The nearness of the new paradigm – the possibility of love – recreated London for her that day. The fear of what might happen between her and Nicholas invested all the city's spaces and solids with inarticulable meaning: the Thames passing slowly under the Hungerford Bridge; rain darkening St Martin-in-the-Fields; Trafalgar's wet stone lions and derelict pigeons – all of them added their own silence to the city's sudden chaotic significance. The thinking part of her stood to one side, seeing the process for what it was – the romantic's idiotic, shameless imagination let loose. But the rest of her was queasy with fear and hope. She kept having to stop herself from bursting out laughing. A bus passed and she thought of throwing herself in front of it. She had an image of her own body, naked, being seen by him, the shocking contrast between the white flesh and the dark inverted triangle between her legs. People's faces were suddenly unique inscrutable symbols. Inwardly, she listed historical facts to herself to avoid passing completely into surreality: the Vikings invaded Ireland in AD 620; Charlemagne was crowned Holy Roman Emperor in AD 800; the Reformation began with Martin Luther in 1517; the English fleet defeated the Spanish Armada in 1588; Napoleon was defeated at the Battle of Waterloo in 1815. Here I am walking down Tottenham Court Road in the rain on Wednesday the 17th of October, 1987.

It gave her something to do with the part of her that was feverish with scepticism – but simultaneously she had the ludicrous sense that she was only now stepping into a time that was connected to the past, because love had always been in the world, and now it might belong to her, too. Nicholas stopped to look in a shop window, and when his back was turned to her, she mouthed This is ridiculous, to herself, inaudibly, while his dark reflection in the glass and the diesel engine sound of a passing taxi threatened to decode her entire life as a motion towards this moment.

'I spend half my fucking life in here,' Nicholas said to her, in a bookshop called Bibliographia in Covent Garden. 'All the time I *should* be spending reading set books, in fact.'

'Why isn't there a BA in Browsing?' Chloe said – but inside she was still reeling from all of it, the size of possibility. This is how it happens, she kept thinking. This. A café. Rain. Breakfast. Books. Chloe Palmer. Eighteen. Covent Garden. The dumb components have always been there – then one day they cohere and insanity becomes reason.

She went to the shop's toilet to calm down. In the cubicle she took her coat and blouse off. Her armpits were tropical. On the back of the door someone had written: They put a man on the moon – why not ALL of them? Which, through the impenetrable formulae of association, made her think of her scar.

A compact pain opened in her like a flower. She stood still, breathing slowly, letting herself measure the impact of the sensation. For as long as she could remember the scar's scrupulously detailed history had been building, quietly. Self-consciousness in the showers at school. Moments alone at a mirror. The signature in flesh that wasn't her and which defined her to herself, privately, awkwardly. Beyond the fear and excitement a detached part of her registered weariness, a stone weight in her heart. The scar was someone else's unwanted hand on her, permanently.

She let herself suffer the compressed, exhausted sadness, buttoning up her blouse, thinking that when she got to the top button she'd stop herself feeling it. She knew that if she didn't stop feeling it she'd feel nothing else; the delicious physical sensitivity she'd been feeling – wrists, throat, eyelids, thighs – would be gone.

Nicholas was in Fiction when she came out. He was sitting on a footstool reading *The French Lieutenant's Woman*. Walking towards him was like forcing herself into a cold sea.

'Why don't you shut up?' he said to her. It satisfied her because it ended the possibility of pre-emptive explanation. It relieved her of the responsibility. It relieved her of pain, because the pain was hoping that something she could say would soften the scar and knowing that it wouldn't. Nicholas's option freed her, took both of them out of the realm of words.

She knew he wasn't prepared for her virginity, however. Nor did he know, until afterwards: one dark leaf of blood on the warm sheet that still carried their impress.

'Oh,' he said – then, after five, six, seven heartbeats, rested his palm on her abdomen.

'Thought you might have already had enough to cope with,' Chloe said. 'What with me being a mutant and everything.'

'Oh,' Nicholas repeated. 'OK. Jesus Christ.'

'Which is it?'

'What?'

'OK or Jesus Christ?'

He didn't answer straight away. His left shoulder pressed against her. Through it and the flat hand on her stomach, she could feel his calculations, the struggle to work out whether he'd been gulled or honoured.

'Did it . . . Did it hurt?'

'A bit. At the beginning.'

'God. Sorry. I didn't know.'

'It's all right.'

'Christ, I'm really sorry if I hurt you.'

'It's OK. Really.'

He got up out of the bed, confused, standing moving his shoulderblades, not knowing what to do. It made Chloe laugh, which confused him further.

Echoing his earlier intonation, she said: 'Why don't you go and make us a cup of tea?'

For Chloe, the question was whether she *should* love Nicholas. The love she might release was there, a reservoir held *in potentia* – but she knew that releasing its force would leave her open to complete destruction. If you loved someone, you gave them the power to annihilate you. It was a simple equation no one seemed ready to recognize. Loving someone – falling in love with someone – allowed for two possible narratives of your future: in one your love was returned; in the other it was betrayed. That was all. You couldn't create one possibility without the other.

Therefore the question. It came to her in moments away from him. Throughout the first weeks she heard herself speaking quietly, inside: If you let this happen you risk everything. Your history, your identity, all of it. You'll never be one of those people who can love sensibly, in a jigsaw of compromise and half-truth. You won't be able to keep anything. You'll lay it all out in front of him. What will he do with it? Is it worth it?

She had come early to the understanding that she would never be a woman who had her pick of men. She wasn't beautiful, and men wouldn't see beyond beauty. Or sexiness. Or attractiveness. It didn't matter how she labelled the abstract quality – she knew she didn't have enough of it. At sixteen she had stood naked in front of the full-length bathroom mirror at home and thought: I'm ordinary. Not ugly. Not fat. Not without symmetry. But not noticeable. If I'd committed a crime and a witness was trying to describe me, he'd say: 'I don't know. About five-four. Brown hair. Sort of average-looking. You know?

Maybe brown eyes. I can't remember. Ordinary.' She had
decided then, with a perverse force of will, not to enhance
whatever positive features she did have. No make-up, no trendy
hairdos. It had staggered her dismal handful of peers at home in
Elm Coombe. Christ, Chloe, just a bit of bloody lipstick'd do
wonders for you! Let me just do your eyes. Go on, you've got
nice eyes. They'd look proper *mysterious* with a bit of eyeliner.
Just a bit of mascara then. Go *on*.

But she'd resisted. She *was* mysterious. Let someone take the
trouble to discover it. She wasn't going to advertise. Mysterious.
They didn't know the half of it.

But the resolution hadn't held. Periodic capitulations: a black
Lycra skirt and lipstick at a disco in Torquay; a pair of high
heels forced on her for a cousin's wedding reception; a red cocktail dress, plucked eyebrows and eyeshadow for a friend's
seventeenth birthday. The trouble was it had worked. Boys had
gone after her – unsatisfactorily. Either undesirable boys – dull,
brainless, humourless, not good-looking – or desirable boys
who used her as a kind of light seduction exercise, as if limber-
ing up for the real performance with someone else. One such
boy made a date with her for *One Flew Over the Cuckoo's Nest* at
the Royal in Paignton, then turned up with someone else (a
pretty, black-eyed blonde girl), having genuinely forgotten that
he'd even asked Chloe out. Chloe had laughed (also genuinely)
in his shocked face, then caught the bus back to Elm Coombe.
On the bus she'd started crying – let herself feel it for a few minutes, hot and bitter in the pit of her stomach – then stopped.
She could stop. She could always stop crying. At home she'd
made herself a cup of sugary tea and gone up to her room,
thanking God that her older sister Liz was out. ('Chloe got the
brains,' her Mum often said, implying that Liz had got the
looks, such as they were. Chloe didn't think Liz had got anything, in particular, beyond a nice voice and a generous heart –
and it was the generous heart that Chloe was afraid of encountering in the bedroom.) She'd sat on the edge of her bed in the
dark, listening to the rain, and known that Elm Coombe would
never offer her a lover. Not even that: Elm Coombe would never

offer her anyone who could actually *see* her. That's what I want, she had thought, her face speckled with rain-shadows – just someone who can fucking *see* me.

Before London and university her intelligence had alienated her. She wasn't brilliant, but by Elm Coombe's standards she was a phenomenon. It carved her out a default identity: that weird girl who knows everything.

'Ooo'd you choose, Chloe?'

Summer, a sixth form beach party, a campfire, the cold sea, dusk.

The question was who you'd choose to spend twenty-four hours with. Anyone.

'Fuckin' Sam Fox,' someone said.

'David Bowie.'

'That bird off *Dallas*. Victoria Whatserface. The one with the tits. Christ Almighty.'

'Living?' Chloe asked. 'Or from any time?'

'If it's from any time I want to change mine to Jim Morrison,' one girl said. 'When he was alive.'

'Living *or* dead,' the original questioner said.

'Queen Elizabeth the First,' Chloe said.

'What – the *Queen*?'

'That's Elizabeth the *Second*, dickhead,' the Jim Morrison girl said. 'She means as in Shakespeare and that lot.'

'Is that right, Chloe?'

'Yes.'

There was a pause in which Chloe wondered why she'd bothered answering truthfully. Then they all laughed.

'What are you – a fuckin' *lezzer*? Jesus Christ, woman!'

It wasn't very malicious. They all found it incredibly funny. Chloe watched them for a few seconds before joining in the laughter herself.

Then, at university, Nicholas, who had, it seemed, seen her. Before the day in the café, she'd waited for him. Looks of recognition. Then actual recognition. The sudden grasp of the scope of her own passion terrified her. Every morning for days afterwards the question of whether she should love him asked itself. The alarm clock went off, and as soon as her mind hauled itself up to the first rung of consciousness, the question of love was there to meet it, a glowing presence amid all the clutter of Solon's reforms and medieval politics and the Roman Republic.

She and Nicholas spent every night together in her tiny room in halls, though Chloe knew that if they were going to endure it would be an endurance based on something over and above fierce sexual attraction. There *wasn't* fierce sexual attraction. Their shared sense of the possible emotional depth between them precluded it. Very early in their relationship Chloe saw that the hovering shadow of love frightened them both into reticent sex. There was too much at stake to be free with each other in bed. She intuited the consequences, the corrosive ramifications of a wrong sexual turn, the discovery of an intolerable fetish, for example; she knew their love was terrified of incompatibility between the sheets. Therefore they played safe with each other – and worried in silence. She wondered, too, whether she'd hampered them by giving him her virginity. She knew that in his mind she had forced them to start with him taking something from her. She could tell he felt guilty about it. The ribbon of blood on the sheet was a simple statement in cipher: this is serious.

Blood, she wrote in her diary, *is the colour of love.*

One evening when Nicholas was at the library Chloe put down her Herodotus and went and stood in front of her room's one mirror. They had been together three weeks. Now, in the mornings, she woke not just to the question of love, but to the thrilling, visceral fear that the question had been answered. The desk lamp was the room's only light, and her face in the mirror was half shadowed, one dark eye visible, the other a glimmer. Nicholas's seeing her – his *seeing* her – both confirmed and changed what she saw herself. It was still her face – the ordinary face, the eyes that let no one in without resistance, the straight, shoulder-length frame of dark hair, the small jaw and lineless forehead – but it had acquired a new power. He desired her. She saw him looking at her and being drawn in. She saw, for the first time, her own irreversible gravity. It stunned her. She felt ashamed – gleefully caught out – at having waited for this to happen.

Very quietly, knowing that she wouldn't be able to convince herself later that it didn't mean anything, she said, in rehearsal: 'I love you.'

Neither Nicholas nor Chloe had any real friends at university (they made no effort to acquire them), nor, for that matter, any sustained interest in their academic life. Chloe was studying European History, Nicholas English Literature. They worked erratically, with occasional mutant bursts of passion for something – the Florentine murals, *Middlemarch*, Boadicea, *The Rainbow* – but nothing engaged them for very long. They fought it, but they were really only interested in each other: histories, dreams, fears, memories, ideas, tastes. They recognized the obscenity of such mutual absorption, and sometimes panicked and tried to tear themselves away. Nicholas found someone to play squash with, twice a week; Chloe joined a life drawing class. But it didn't help. They fell back to each other, the squash partner abandoned, the classes dropped. Chloe knew that people thought them freakish. It disturbed her. But then a night would come when she couldn't sleep, and would study Nicholas's body beside her in bed, his arms, hands, chest, throat, mouth, eyelashes – she would spend some secret hour in the darkness confirming her ownership of him and would worry herself with the thought of how little everything else seemed to matter. You can put the small things aside, a voice inside her said, you've found him now.

She had a car – a rust-bitten Ford Escort in metallic purple that her Mum and Dad had bought her for her eighteenth birthday. It was bliss for Nicholas to be driven by her. He delighted in her body's gestures of control and in her chin raised because she was short and struggled to see the length of the bonnet. Watching her feet on the pedals or her hand shifting the gearstick invariably gave him an erection – from which followed another bliss of contained desire, of aching to bury his face in her lap but resisting doing so. Chloe, unaware, would inflame him further by saying something like: 'I wish this fucking idiot would stop weaving around like a pigeon.'

In all the weeks leading up to the day in the café, her eyes had offered a kind of recognition to Nicholas every time he had seen her. She wasn't beautiful, he thought – certainly not 'pretty' – but her features were at imperfect peace with themselves. Hidden between two stacks in the library, Nicholas had once studied her where she sat at a window desk with her head leaning on her hand, staring down at an open book but plainly not taking anything in. She was smiling, thinking or remembering something. She'd looked like a small, fearless deity.

He was so curious about what was going on inside her that lust only followed along afterwards, like an obligatory bit of luggage. Before they met properly, he had tried to think about her when he masturbated, but had failed, dismally. The sense he had of her – intuitive, almost telepathic – resisted any reduction; he could only fantasize about a woman pornographically, by freezing and framing her, and somehow Chloe kept moving. It had bamboozled him for weeks, while he had become more and more attracted to her.

After they had been together for a couple of months, Chloe risked the car on a trip up to the Brontë museum in Yorkshire. The weather co-operated: a sky of dull silver with dark, torn clouds hurrying low along the moors like the smoke from a battlefield.

She had become obsessed with people's last words.

'Oscar Wilde,' she said to Nicholas, while the car ran into a sudden thin curtain of rain.

'What about him?'

'Took a last look at the wallpaper in the room and said: "Either that wallpaper goes or I do." Then died.'

'Bollocks,' Nicholas said.

'It's true,' Chloe said.

'It's not true. It's just what Wilde would have liked.'

'No, no – he really did say that. Just like that.'

'Well I don't believe it.'

'Matthew Arnold,' Chloe continued. 'There's a disappointing last utterance for you. "Have you brought the chequebook, Alfred?" Dear oh dear. A lifetime spent pondering the big questions and that's how he leaves us.'

'I don't know,' Nicholas said. 'It sounds fitting to me. Have you brought the chequebook, Alfred? Who was Alfred, by the way?'

'God knows. Anyway, it's easier to believe than Wilde's. And Voltaire's.'

'What did *he* say?'

'"I go in search of the Big Perhaps. *Je vais chercher le Grand Peut-être.*" Cool, eh?'

'I go in search of the Big Perhaps,' Nicholas repeated. 'I'm not going to be capable of anything like that. I'm just going to be lying there plucking at the bedsheet and begging for morphine or something. My last words aren't going to be words at all. Just pathetic pipping and whimpering. My last words are just going to be *sounds*. Of terror.'

'Better than sounds of regret,' Chloe said. 'Do you know what D. H. Lawrence's last words to Frieda were? "Why did we fight so much?"' Her voice cracked a little as she said it. Tears came to her eyes, quickly, absurdly. Things like that often made her choke up suddenly. Nicholas hadn't noticed.

'I know what I'd *like* my last words to be,' he said.

'What?'

'Thank you all. You've been a wonderful audience. Goodnight.'

'It's probably already been done,' Chloe said. After a pause, she added: 'I don't think I want any last words. I don't think I want to be in a position where I know I'm going to die and I have to think of something to say. I think I'd rather just slip away quietly. Like an animal that goes off somewhere and then just doesn't come back.'

'Charming,' Nicholas said. 'What about the poor buggers you leave behind?'

'I know, I know. It's just I fucking *hate* saying goodbye. I *hate* it. Whatever skill it is you're supposed to have acquired by the time you reach adulthood that means you're not a blubbering idiot about these things – well, whatever it is, I haven't got it. It's disgusting. You should see me at train stations. Pathetic. I think I inherited it from my Mum. She's the blubberer to end all blubberers, honestly.'

'Charlotte Brontë died in pregnancy,' Chloe said, later.

They had spent an hour in the Parsonage museum (where could be found preserved, among other things, a pair of Charlotte's ridiculous pointy black shoes) and now, with the light fading, they stood in the little graveyard, looking beyond the building out on to the moors. One bare black tree was pressed against the sky, like the cross section of a lung.

'I know,' Nicholas said. 'My subject, remember? And why is it that you know so much more about it than I do?'

In the diminishing light, Chloe's eyebrows and mouth were dark crescents. Nicholas wanted to be away from the place now, somewhere warm and private with her. He wanted his hands up inside her clothes, feeling the utterly alien softness, the differently encased life of her.

'Her husband was with her when she died,' Chloe said.

'Whose?'

'Charlotte's. Obviously you're not listening.'

'I am, I am.'

'They hadn't been together very long. Before she died, she looked up at him and said: "He's not going to part us so soon, is He?"'

That night they stayed at a very small, dark-bricked country pub which had guest rooms.

'It's an inn,' Chloe said. 'A proper old inn. There's probably horses stabled in the back.'

They were made a fuss of by the landlord and his wife. She was a jolly, flushed, round-shouldered woman with permanently surprised eyebrows and meaty, Popeye forearms who oohed and aahed and tutted as if they must be mad to go driving around and visiting museums and staying in country pubs in the middle of winter, and who eventually served them a supper of savoury beef stew and boiled potatoes. She set the plates down in front of them, then stood with her fists on her hips for a moment, shaking her head as if in doubt that they had ever eaten a solid meal in their lives.

'I want her to be my Mum,' Chloe said, after she'd gone.

Their room was small and cold with a stodgy white bed, Prussian-blue walls and one leaded window. They undressed quickly, slightly drunk, and got under the blankets in the dark.

There was something untranslated about their bodies, moving against each other. At moments they were unsynchronized, hurrying, bumping jaws and noses, as though afraid that the longer the encounter lasted, the greater the likelihood of some irreparable mistake. And though Nicholas felt her breasts close to him and her waist soft in his hands, though he was humbled by the heat and urgency of her cunt when he went slowly into her, though, when he felt her breath against his mouth, a voice inside him said, without emotion: Stay with her for ever and he knew it was right – there remained in him a stubborn nugget of dissatisfaction. The presence of the voice itself appalled him.

Afterwards, they lay together, silent, reduced to this incompletely worked out conundrum. He knew she was awake.

'Chloe?' he said.

'Yeah?'

The room was dark and still. Together under the blankets their bodies made a silent furnace. Nicholas felt empty and certain, as if he was giving himself over to something.

'I don't want anyone else.'

'Neither do I,' Chloe said. 'I just want you.'

An image flashed in Nicholas's mind – Chloe screaming as he tore her breasts to blood with his nails – then it was gone.

'I know this is ridiculous,' he said, after a pause, 'but let's get married.'

◆

Though Mickey told Nicholas to stay in her apartment, he saw
very little of her over the next few days. The morning after
Arcadia she sent him to the hotel to check out and told him to
be back at her apartment by eight in the evening. But when he
arrived, she let him in and then told him she was on her way
out. She came back that night, late, and told him he should
sleep on the couch.

'Don't get any ideas,' she had said. 'I'll tell you when you can
sleep in my bed and when you can't. Understand?' She had
stared at him icily for a few seconds, then her face had relaxed
into the glittering smile. Nicholas had said nothing, but a movement over by the bedroom door caught his eye; a tuxedoed
young man with shoulder-length black hair and green eyes
stood there, trying to achieve a look of sophisticated cynicism.
He was perhaps twenty-five years old.

That night Nicholas lay awake on the hissing, elephantine
couch thinking of slow cars snapping and crunching down the
Fifth Avenue snow. The dividing walls in Mickey's apartment
were solid, and he heard nothing from the bedroom, but he
was aware of the two of them; he felt them as a conspiracy of
flesh, radiating heat somewhere close by.

An hour before dawn the black-haired young man came out
into the lounge with a drink and a cigarette and dropped himself into the armchair opposite Nicholas. Its leather gasped and
the ice in the young man's glass tinkled. He had on the tux
trousers but his chest and feet were bare.

'I'm Zack,' he said. He delivered the name as if it were the satisfying summation of a long tally of positive qualities. 'Mickey's
told me all about you.'

Nicholas, lying curled on his side, facing Zack, said nothing.

'Told me you couldn't get it up for her.'

Nicholas's hand was by his face, and he could hear his wristwatch ticking softly. Briefly, he wondered if he was afraid – but
then found that he was more acutely aware of the white,
unbreathing park outside than he was of Zack only a few feet
away in the dark.

'What are you, man? Mute?' Zack said, then smiled and took

a sip of the drink. The smoke from his cigarette was a soft, invisible presence between them. 'She says you're her little project. Her English patient. I've got to tell you – because I know you're the kind of guy who'll appreciate honesty, right? – I'm not sure I'm comfortable with this. With this situation. *This* situation. You catch my thrust, Nick? I mean situations of this . . . ah . . . *ilk* have a habit of getting out of control. And when situations get out of control . . .'

Nicholas remained silent and motionless. Zack smiled again and his eyes and teeth glimmered like traces of a precious lode. He sank himself lower in the armchair and stretched one leg so that its foot came to rest on the edge of the couch, inches away from Nicholas's face.

'Main thing is,' Zack said, 'is that we both make an effort to keep a sense of what the, ah . . . you know, *parameters* are here. You know? That we don't get the pieces of this out of *perspective*, right?'

Zack's foot smelled of something like aftershave.

'Good,' he said, and took another gulp of his drink. 'I can see you're not the kind of guy who lacks the ability to maintain a sense of *boundaries* – which, let me tell you, Nick, is a useful fucking ability in situations of this ilk. I think things can be kept under control here. That's what I need. I do need that. I don't need much, but I do need that.'

Zack removed his foot and stood up, slowly. It was apparent that he was laughing soundlessly. When he had finished, he said: 'Nice talking with you. Sweet dreams, Shakespeare.'

◆

In their second year Nicholas and Chloe moved out of halls and into a studio flat in Shepherd's Bush. All the woodwork was painted glossy white and the worn red carpet didn't reach the edges of the floor. There was a minute kitchen with a paunchy, companionable little stove and a treasury of chipped and

unmatching crockery, and a similarly cramped bathroom with a
white tub that would have been a squeeze for a dwarf. All the
ceilings showed green and brown coastlines of damp. The radiators were moody and voluble, sometimes chuckling and
clanking, other times cold and silent, then suddenly giving out
a compressed hiss and shudder, startling Chloe. At the front of
the building was a main road along which leathery tramps staggered and red buses groaned, and at the back was a small
threadbare garden with a balding lawn and one anorexic tree.
Beyond the garden was the back of the next terrace: washing
lines, bits of old plumbing, more grey gardens. Nicholas spent
hours staring out there instead of working.

It made them laugh, this new place, since its optimism and
ugliness echoed some metaphysic or aesthetic they both
believed in. So they put posters and pictures up and painted the
bathroom blue and gold and didn't particularly care if they
spilled cups of tea on the red carpet.

They lived dualism, functioning adequately in the prosaic
world – study, housework, practical decisions, money – but
with an intermittent awareness of the love that was developing
between them, which, though never spoken of, assaulted them
in moments of blunt epiphany. It troubled Nicholas. When he
realized how much he loved Chloe he felt his romantic imagination as a giant anachronism. London's buses and hoardings,
the ferment of the Underground, the city's amalgam of breath
and lies, the ache of its buildings and rushed-through spaces –
all of this combined in an inevitable derision. It made the intensity and scope of his feeling for Chloe shamefully childlike. It
wasn't that they never quarrelled or irritated each other; it was
that at random moments Nicholas would see her head from a
particular angle, or a smudge of ink on her wrist, or would
hear her sneeze in the kitchen – and would feel the pure, quietly breathing centre of their relationship like some small
creature lost in an abandoned warehouse, dwarfed by planes
and shadows. It filled him with dread.

'What's your most significant memory?' he said to her one

Sunday morning, when the two of them lay side by side in bed.
(The bed, when they weren't in it, folded up into a couch, but
they were both so domestically lazy that it often stayed a bed for
weeks on end.)

'Tongue,' Chloe said.

'Tongue?'

'The discovery that the meat, tongue, was in fact, tongue.'

'Fucking hell,' Nicholas said.

'My Uncle Bernard had a farm a few miles up the road from
us. He was this weird, slightly mythic member of our family
who was very rarely visited. He was enormous. Completely
bald. Head like a potato. Mum's oldest brother. I could never
believe they were related, but they were.'

It was early summer. Their room had one rectangular
window with an ivory-coloured curtain which was now filled
with pearly light. This was deeply satisfying to Nicholas, to lie
with her, naked, listening to her talk, the rest of the world gone
to hell.

'Anyway, we went up for Christmas, once. Uncle Bernard's
wife was Aunty Audrey, and they had a daughter and two sons.
Only the younger of the sons was still at home by that time –
George, his name is. I was about eight that Christmas, George
must have been about fourteen.'

'You had an unpleasant sexual experience with George in
the barn,' Nicholas said.

'Well, yes, of course I did – but that's a different story.
Nothing to do with the tongue – well, *this* tongue, I mean.
George's eyebrows met in the middle – which should have been
warning enough, I suppose. He was strong, too; he picked
heavy things up as if they were made of cardboard or something. He had a sort of . . . *gravity* about him . . .'

'Where is he now, this yokel with gravity?'

'Still on the farm. He inherited it when Uncle Bernard died a
few years back. He's married to a woman called Roz. No kids. I
think they're into sado-masochism.'

'*What?*'

'Oh, I don't know. But there's something murky there.

Satanism. I don't know. They're just very dark and thick with each other. And like I said: no children. They're probably both werewolves.'

Nicholas was so happy that he wished, with the cretinism of first love, that their life were a television programme millions could share and enjoy.

'Er, the tongue?' he asked, after Chloe seemed to be dozing off.

'The tongue. See, the thing is, I had eaten tongue, from time to time. On sandwiches. My Mum used to say, "D'you want a tongue and mustard sandwich, love?" and I'd say yes, because I liked the way it sounded. Tongue and mustard. I *quite* liked the taste, but it was really the taste I imagined it having because of the *sound* that got me going. Tongue and mustard.'

'If you keep saying that I'm going to have to have sex with you,' Nicholas said.

'Shut up. So anyway, we were there one Christmas. Uncle Bernard had got the idea that I enjoyed doing what he called "real farm chores". "Let's us two go and have a look at that fence up in the front field, shall we? That's a real farm chore for you!" So off we'd go in the fucking snow to fix the fence. He didn't want to take me and I didn't want to go, but somehow we just kept on in the same stupid habit. Anyway, one afternoon he sent me out to fill the water trough for the bullocks in the barn.'

'Bullocks. I see. Did you see their genitals?'

'They didn't *have* genitals. They were for slaughter, not breeding. The poor buggers had had their genitals lopped *off*. Or at least their testicles. I think they leave the penises on. Not that I would have even known where to look for a bull's penis in those days.'

'Before George sorted you out in the barn.'

'Exactly. So off I dutifully went to fill the trough. I was scared stiff of the bullocks, actually, and I think Uncle Bernard knew that – but him and Audrey thought I needed bringing down a peg or two, what with me only being eight but still able to spell words like "consequences" and "demonstration".'

Nicholas smiled to himself. He had seen photographs of

Chloe as a little girl: the dark hair and eyes, the features not yet in their alignment. She always looked slightly sulky or secretive, in some pictures ugly with resistance to being looked at. One photograph of her aged about fifteen in her school uniform (white blouse, burgundy blazer and tie) had flukishly caught her at the edge of womanhood; her breasts had come, and the mystery of her bare throat and clavicle. Her face had almost arrived, a contained intelligence, a look of being always beyond you, whoever you were. Nicholas looked at this photograph in secret from time to time, surprised and thrilled by the lust it inspired in him. He would look at it without Chloe's knowledge, and congratulate himself like a little king.

'There was a low bit in the corrugated iron where you reached over and filled the trough with water from a hose that hung there,' Chloe said. 'You didn't actually go into the shed at all, but when you started the water all the bullocks would shuffle over to you, curious. I'd seen George and Uncle Bernard do it a couple of times, and I knew they'd come. God, I was shaking!'

'And when you turned the hose on, over they all came,' Nicholas said.

'Yes! I dropped the hose and half bolted at first – but then I realized that the water wasn't going anywhere near the trough, so I had to come back. When I did come back, they were very close, you know, their big heads and eyes? But they were lovely. Really beautiful, their eyes – gorgeous long dark eyelashes. And they didn't seem threatening at all – just incredibly fond of me. I wanted to go in with them and be among them. They were nice and warm.'

Nicholas saw the image: Chloe in wellies and an anorak, a small dark figure in the pocked snow, her face white and cold, her hands struggling with the hose. Then the cattle, their breath falling upwards in languid signals, their heavy heads lifted. He believed he saw something archetypal: the child and the animals; the cold rope of water; snow; earth.

'Then one of them licked my hand,' Chloe said, shuddering. 'Have you got any idea how big a bullock's tongue is?'

'I'm pleased to say I haven't,' Nicholas said.

'Well I'll tell you: it's fucking *enormous*. It was like a separate creature all on its own. That's when it suddenly struck me: tongue. The "tongue" of tongue and mustard was in fact . . . the tongue of one of these animals. I don't know why I realized just then. It was just one of those intuitive leaps. For years, that's what I'd been eating. I couldn't believe it. I just could not believe it. I threw up in the snow.'

They could be dangerous, these images, Nicholas knew. They conditioned the way he loved her, if they were vivid enough. After she told him her story he loved her as – among the other shifting projections and metaphors – a child bringing water to beasts.

'What's yours?' Chloe said to him that same night. The room was dark, redolent with candle smoke and the ghost of the evening's cheap red wine. They had barely left the bed all day.

'What's my what?'

'Most significant memory.'

He knew he was going to lie. He had known he would have to lie from the beginning, when he had asked her. He had asked her in the first place partly as a test of his own truthfulness should she return the question. And now she had.

'I think I was about five,' he said – and as he began he had a detached sensation of his larynx making the sounds which were lies. He thought of his mouth and lips moving like an anemone in the dark, then of his head on the pillow, then of the bed, the room itself, the building, London, the intricate web of streets, the leafy trees and succulent fields of the countryside – all the spaces and solids of the world – he thought of all this and was overcome by a feeling of tiredness; lying there next to Chloe, beginning his story, he felt as if each atom of his flesh had its own fixed heaviness, that he would never be able to move again.

'I was about five. There was this place near where we used to live – a kind of rubbish tip. It wasn't really a rubbish tip, it was just one of those odd bits of land between other things that people dumped stuff on. Prams, old cookers, mattresses, tyres. We used to just call it "the Place". At one end there were the backs of these huge advertising hoardings. On the other side of the hoardings was the main road. Which was why I wasn't supposed to be there.'

It was a lie because it wasn't his most significant memory, but not because it never happened. Nicholas could see the Place clearly, despite his paralysis. The remembered sense of childhood prickled in his blood. Chloe, very quiet beside him, stretched her ankles; one of them cracked, softly.

'It was summer. I'd gone there alone. Given my Mum the slip somehow. It was incredibly exciting. I could hear the traffic beyond the hoardings, you know, and it was like hearing the Actual World or something. The air was thick. Bitter.'

'Summer bitter. I know.'

'Yeah. Anyway, there was no one else around. I picked up a stick and spent a few minutes poking around in old paint tins and bits of litter and whatnot – then I saw this black cat lying on its side in the sun, asleep.'

'Oh dear,' Chloe said. 'I hope this isn't what I think . . .'

'I went over to it with my stick. There was something funny about it, about the way it was lying. It looked weightless, like it was made of cardboard or stiffened leather or something. Its top lip was pulled back in one place over a tooth, as if it was giving a little snarl. I could see the gum there and it was black.'

'I don't know if you need to tell me the rest.'

'I touched it with my stick, lightly at first, but when it didn't move I poked it harder. Its fur was stiff and dusty and its legs were rigid. I don't know how I knew to do what I did next. I don't know how I knew the answer was underneath – some movement, I suppose . . . I put the tip of my stick under the body and began to slowly lift it like a lid . . .'

Now Nicholas shuddered. Chloe, whose grip on Nicholas's arm had been tightening as the narrative progressed, felt the memory of revulsion ripple in him. Headlights from the road climbed the wall and then leaped across the ceiling and disappeared. 'The other half of its body was missing,' Nicholas said. 'Completely gone. Instead there was just this writhing mass of maggots—'

'OK, stop.'

'I'd never seen anything dead before. I don't think even *then* that I realized that was death. It didn't strike me that the animal wasn't alive any more – just going through some sort of change . . .'

'That's a fucking horrible story,' Chloe said.

'I know,' Nicholas said. 'But it really happened.'

'I discover tongue, you discover death. Charming.'

'Sorry. I don't think I've ever eaten tongue.'

'Since I found out what it was,' Chloe said, 'neither have I.'

Later that night, while Chloe slept, Nicholas allowed himself the memory he should have given her.

He had been about seven years old, playing across the street at Michelle's house. Michelle was eleven with fine, silky chestnut hair and eyes of dark plum, and Nicholas worshipped her. She knew the words to songs on the radio and frequently put her hand into his pants and felt his little penis. 'Just checking, pervert!' she always said, and though at first Nicholas had had no idea what she was 'checking' for (or what a 'pervert' was), by the time of this particular afternoon at her house he had intuited that it was connected with when it went hard and stood up, and he got the funny feeling.

That afternoon Helen was with them. Helen was Michelle's age but backward in some way. Her top lip was twisted and her eyes moved strangely. She had her own mutant version of English, which most of the local children understood. She was supposed to be at a special school, but she never went. Instead she scoured the streets for pennies and ha'pennies, and when she found them went directly to the corner shop for a bag of sherbet or a liquorice stick, which she would then consume in a languid dream. Some of the street's children bullied her and some of them were kind to her. Nicholas was indifferent, though he was put off by the way she looked and smelled.

Helen was drawn to Michelle, hopelessly, so Michelle was cruel to her. (Once, Nicholas had been with Michelle when she had thrown an unopened can of Pepsi through the air at Helen, who was walking away from her in tears. The can had spun in the sunlight for what seemed a very long time before dropping through the last arc of its trajectory and cracking the back of Helen's head with a terrible inevitability. It was such a long shot – Helen had been yards away – and the sound of the can's impact was so distinct in the silent street that for a few seconds Michelle had just stood with her mouth open in delighted shock. Then she had begun to laugh. It had astonished and thrilled Nicholas that Michelle's laughter had been unequivocal. It fascinated him that she felt no shame. It drew him closer to her. It drew Helen to her, too.)

For a while that afternoon (the afternoon Nicholas should have described to Chloe), Michelle had tolerated Helen – but all three of them had known it would just be a matter of time.

'Spastic,' Michelle said, apropos of nothing, then looked at Nicholas for collusion. He kept silent. Helen forced herself to giggle, awkwardly, refusing to accept that *her* collusion was not being sought, that she herself was the object of abuse. Michelle chuckled, too – then, annihilating all possible ambiguity, leaned right into Helen's face and said, with quiet precision: 'You fucking *spastic*.'

The absoluteness of her own power disgusted Michelle. By the time she sat astride Helen's belly, tickling and poking at will, she seemed irritable, contemptuous and bored. Helen, now utterly conquered, with dirty tears falling in continuous threads from the outside corner of each eye, hummed to herself.

Their three bodies had generated a chrysalis of heat around them. Nicholas's mouth was dry. He had watched Michelle's buttocks rising up and dropping down heavily on Helen's stomach; he had seen Michelle's boredom – had been given an intimation of the vacuousness of cruelty – but he wanted Michelle to check him with her hand, because from nowhere the feeling was shaping itself. If Michelle put her hand there the feeling would come, he was certain. He was certain because of the weight of Michelle on Helen's belly, and because she leaned forward and rubbed noses with her in a parody of friendliness. Nicholas moved himself closer to Michelle's bent knee. Her white sock had slipped halfway down her calf and revealed the elastic's print on her skin like a fossil.

'I could do anything to her,' Michelle said to him, grinning. It was true. Helen wasn't struggling, though she turned her head from side to side, repeatedly, as if searching for a way out. 'I could spit in her face,' Michelle said. 'Oi, Nick, shall I? Shall I groz in her face?'

'Check me,' Nicholas found himself saying. The utterance arrived in his mouth like something that had scurried up from deep inside him. He made himself giggle with grotesque artifice. 'You know . . . that thing . . .'

A detached part of him noticed that Michelle understood immediately. In this matter of the checking for the feeling a universe of telepathic recognition had been revealed. He saw, too, that it empowered her. Her nostrils opened slightly; her back straightened. Quickly, deftly, she put her hand to the front of his shorts and then withdrew it again, half satisfied. Nicholas felt the aura of heat around the three of them solidifying, holding them in place, as if unseen powers had achieved this particular arrangement of atoms and now must struggle to keep it correctly aligned.

Michelle leaned forward holding her hair away from her face and let a thread of saliva drop from her mouth down towards Helen. Helen moved her head violently, but there was nowhere for it to go.

Chloe woke long after Nicholas had fallen asleep. Their one window was a rectangle of smoke-coloured light. She sat up in bed and looked down at him. The bedclothes were down around his waist, his upper body faintly illuminated – one arm bent behind his head, the other down by his side. His hair, eyelashes, nostrils, nipples and navel were small areas of darkness, like unknown musical notes.

An early bus crawled past beneath the window. In its wake of silence, someone in the street coughed wheezily. While Chloe watched, Nicholas rolled over, away from her, cleared his throat, then sank back into deep sleep.

Chloe got up and very quietly made herself a cup of tea, then stood next to the bed, drinking it. She often woke in the night and watched him. Then the love was pain, seeing him reduced to the dress rehearsal for death. These hours awake while he slept were torturous, all her thoughts illicit because they existed in a time when he couldn't see her having them. She was tender with guilt. Alone in the small hours her history seduced her into reclaiming it as a possession that was nothing to do with him. She would compensate when he woke up – make him breakfast, tell him something she'd never told anyone, put her hand over his mouth as a signal that he mustn't ask anything – no explanations – then suck him, selflessly, till he came. She would see him wondering, afterwards. Pleased – but wondering, none the less.

Sipping her tea, agitated, tingling with a wakefulness she was only ever capable of when she was supposed to be asleep, Chloe moved silently around the flat. She went into the bathroom and stood with her face bathed in its window's cool twilight. The tokens of their shared life – toothbrushes, towels, a pair of her knickers and one of his socks on the floor – amazed her. She thought of her years as an outcast in Elm Coombe, watching her female friends going out with and breaking up with boys. She saw herself in her bedroom's bay window in the summer, the afternoon's green light reflected on the page of the book bent open in her lap. *Britain in the Dark Ages*. She had given herself to history because she was invisible to it. She had watched trade routes opened, cities stormed, treaties signed. She'd seen Alexander with his chin in his palm while Aristotle's mouth talked on, endlessly. She'd seen Ann Boleyn, small and distinct, kneeling under the blade's shadow; Galileo at the Inquisition, telling them what they wanted to hear. She'd known them while they couldn't know her: an ideal relationship. 'I'm interested in dead people,' she'd written in her diary, years ago. 'Probably not a good sign.' Now that she was

interested in a living person the present had staked a giant
claim for her, and her response to it was here, surrounding her:
their inherited crockery, the schizophrenic radiators, the smell
of the bed after sex. Now love had cornered her; moreover, it
made her wonder how she could possibly have ever understood
the past without having considered it. Now she sat in lecture
theatres – Causes and Consequences of the Punic Wars – and
found herself wondering what it must have felt like for a soldier
to touch his lover's sleeping throat in the early hours of the
morning, then take that same hand and place it around the hilt
of a sword that would find its way into the liver of an enemy by
midnight of the following day. In that very lecture, in fact, only
a week ago, she had written in the inside cover of her ring-
binder: *There are only two forces in history: love and fear.* Then
she had scribbled over it, afraid that a fellow-student might see
it and take the piss. It sounded at best a flippant reduction and
at worst simply pretentious. She knew it was true.

Their flat was by now overflowing with ragged books. Every
level surface hosted its own weird miscellany. With the reader's
sixth sense, Chloe closed the bathroom door and turned the
mirror's shaving-light on. She had discovered a long time ago
that reading at night wasn't the same as reading by day. Reading
by night – out of real time, while the world slept – was a cosy
infidelity. Passages of formerly impenetrable language finally
yielded their meanings, as if they had only been awaiting her
willingness to meet them in tryst to give up their truth. She
never read history at night. At night, guided by a pure and
illicit quality of consciousness, she read on instinct, like a
hound following the scent of the question of love. Day reading
was for the question of history. Night reading was for the question of love. She never told Nicholas, and though it would have
been of no consequence even if she *had* told him, it still felt
subversive. It was as if she were having an affair with a
succubus.

Two dozen paperbacks on the bathroom's one cramped win-
dowledge, dog-eared and water-buckled. *Sons and Lovers. The
Bell Jar. The Marx and Engels Reader. The Naked Civil Servant.*

Catch-22. The Faber Book of Parodies. Let's Go Italy 1983. She ran her eyes over the fractured spines, not knowing what she was looking for. Then she found Dylan Thomas, asking himself why he wrote poetry.

> Not for the towering dead
> With their nightingales and psalms
> But for the lovers, their arms
> Round the griefs of the ages

Nicholas had read it to her months ago, and she hadn't understood it. But the line about the lovers had seeded itself in her and was now – here, at four in the morning, in the silent bathroom – achieving its humble gestation. It had resonated for her, quietly, because it had articulated love's terrifying promise: that it could expand to contain all imaginable grief. It had resonated for her because she had known that in deciding to love she had set a challenge to her own future: she had set up a sign in her heart that said 'I choose love. Do what you will.'

Back in the bedroom, Chloe looked down at him where he slept.

It's too late to turn back now, she thought.

◆

'Do you know what it feels like to know that no matter how much you spend your money'll never run out?' Mickey said to Nicholas. She had just returned from a shopping trip, and smelled of perfume and the city's snowy air. Her driver had brought her purchases up to the apartment, then been dismissed. Now Mickey lay on the couch, shoes kicked off, rubbing her silk-stockinged feet against each other. The bags and boxes sat in a glimmering heap in front of her; they seemed to give off a faint light of their own. 'I'll tell you,' she continued. 'It's like that's the way it always should have been, your whole life. Being rich – I mean really fucking *loaded*? – makes you realize that you didn't know anything before. You know? Because before, it's all, like, *supposing*. Suppose I could do so-and-so. Would I do it? Blah blah blah. When you've got money – *big* money, I mean, like now? – you don't *have* to suppose. You can just *do* it. You don't have to wonder about anything. It's like . . . everyone else has to *care*. But you don't. D'you see what I mean?'

'Yes,' Nicholas said. He was transfixed by the dark red talking mouth, the glimpses of teeth and tongue. He imagined himself as a tiny creature clinging at the corner where the lips joined, peering into the wet, convulsing cavern.

'What *I* discovered?' Mickey said, as if he had asked her, specifically. 'It was like I'd been living trapped in all these weird *rules*. Like someone had been watching me all the time and I was afraid that something would *happen* to me if I did something. Then when Connell died and I got the money, it was like this huge eye that had been watching me was suddenly turned away. I remember I felt it instantly, as soon as the attorney read the will. It was the strangest thing.'

There was snow everywhere in Manhattan, and more in the sky, like a held breath. To Nicholas, walking downtown in the late afternoon, the city's spaces and solids seemed traumatized into a fresh humility and stillness. Small sounds were distinct and unique, as if making their first appearance in the world. Cars moved uncertainly, like newly blinded creatures. The air was a hollowed space of cold. The smells of food – doughnuts, falafel, hot dogs, fried onions, caramelized nuts – stretched, suspended, overwhelming and ferocious when he passed through them.

Mickey had sent him out for the day, and he had two more hours to occupy before she wanted him back at the apartment. He had some money, but nothing else, so he walked.

On Second Avenue down in the East Village he went into a bar and ordered a drink. The entire interior was black, with the exception of the bar stools, which had red vinyl seats. There were white lights set in the walls in fixtures designed to look like portholes, and on looking more closely Nicholas discovered other *faux*-nautical accoutrements: nets on the low ceiling; glass floats; a helm. But these were vestigial. More than anything, it looked as if the owners had tried to eliminate the maritime theme by painting everything black.

'English?' the bartender asked. Nicholas nodded. 'Hey, Lancelot!' the bartender called to the end of the bar. 'One of your countrymen here, man. Heh-heh.'

Nicholas looked down the bar and through one horizontal skein of cigarette smoke saw a large, heavy-bodied man with a silver paintbrush beard wearing a wide-brimmed suede hat and a corduroy jacket. Nicholas couldn't quite see, but he knew there would be a paisley cravat there too. As Nicholas stared the man raised his glass and beckoned.

'Check him out, man,' the bartender whispered, loudly. 'Guy's like an ex-lord or fuckin' earl or somethin'.'

Nicholas moved to the end of the bar, where the other now sat in heavy profile. Dirty, tough grey hair came down straight from under the crown of the hat. The hands were cold-looking and meaty, and they trembled. A hand-rolled cigarette, sodden at the lip end, sent up a thin line of cobalt smoke which went straight for a few inches then rippled ecstatically. And there was the cravat.

'You English?' the man asked, without turning to look.

'Yes,' Nicholas said.

'Marty tell you I was a fucking viscount, did he? A retired marquis?' He turned briefly, then, and saw Nicholas's acknowledgement. 'Fucking Americans. D'you know why they call me Lancelot? Eh? D'you want to know?' The accent was Oxbridge, eroded by self-loathing and drink. Nicholas knew it lived side-by-side with a vicious East End parody.

'Why do they call you Lancelot?' he asked.

Lancelot turned towards him slowly, like a gun turret aligning itself with a target. For a moment, as he was regarded in silence, Nicholas wondered if violence was coming. Since the future had ended the imminence of violence suggested itself perpetually. Lancelot was hefty and pendulous. His beard was rimmed with nicotine; his jowls and the whites of his eyes showed tiny, livid capillaries, long since detonated. There was a strained bulbousness to him, as if his insides had been swelling, incrementally, for decades. He stared at Nicholas now with the alcoholic's classic and sinister potential for either dismal sentimentality or brutal assault.

'I'm sitting here one afternoon,' Lancelot began, acidly, precisely, 'talking to this bloke about King Arthur. I've been talking to him for twenty fucking minutes. When I pause to order another drink, he says: "So this was . . . what . . . like . . . Princess Di's great-*great*-grandfather?"'

Lancelot stared at Nicholas angrily for a moment before looking down to relight his roll-up from a worn brass Zippo, which he clacked shut and repocketed with a theatrical flourish. Then the two fingers holding the cigarette pointed directly at Nicholas's face; the fleshy tip of each was ochre with nicotine. 'You think I'm joking. I'm not. You really think I'm pulling your fucking leg. I'm not. Christ, I wish I was. Do you think I'm making this up?'

'No,' Nicholas said.

Again the drinker's pause; the double potential, as if every one of Nicholas's utterances might be either laudatory or snide.

'When he asked me what my name was, I told him I was Lancelot. D'you know what he said? Eh? I'll tell you: "Nice talking with you, Lancelot." *Fucking* country.' Again the raised two fingers. 'I'm Lancelot and King Arthur's Lady Di's great-great-grandad. Right here. Man-fucking-hattan. Cheers.' He drained his glass then knocked the empty on the counter. 'Marty? Oi, Marty, yew fackin' khant. Johnnie Red in there please – *one* cube of ice, mate, all right? Not your usual fucking avalanche.'

Nicholas drank mechanically with Lancelot, who seemed sometimes intensely aware of him and sometimes deep in oblivious soliloquy. Other customers came and went, though the bar was patronized chiefly by borderline or committed alcoholics. One small, old, wide-eyed black man in a red beret stood close by and consumed his drinks with a faultless rhythm. There were half a dozen vacant stools, yet he chose to remain on his feet, swaying and buckling from time to time. A big-boned biker in a corner under one of the porthole lights fed coin after coin into an electronic quiz game, swearing and shaking his head incessantly. Black, dreadlocked and bearded, with a long torso and a pot belly, Marty the bartender served all of them with easy and indefatigable cheer, standing in the slow moments with his weight on one leg, beaming, beneficently. Nicholas lost track of time.

'What *are* you here for, anyway?' Lancelot asked him. 'Since you're obviously not a tourist. Since the tourists poke their heads in then turn around and leave immediately they discover the fucking clientele.'

'I got on a plane,' Nicholas said.

Lancelot looked at him. His reflex response to everything Nicholas had said so far had been irritation – terrible impatience, followed at length by self-absorption, then self-disgust, then self-pity, then the empty rapped on the counter and a call for another Johnnie Red. 'You got on a plane,' he parroted, with compressed annoyance. 'Well con-fucking-gratulations. You got on a plane. We all got on a sodding plane, you silly cunt. Oi, Marty, Laughing Boy here got on a *plane*. Whatever next, eh?'

'I ran away,' Nicholas said – but Lancelot shook his head and slid heavily to his feet. A wooden walking-stick had been propped next to his stool. He took it and gasped slightly as he put his weight on it.

'Sorry, old thing,' he said. 'Got to go and empty what's left of my bladder. You can tell me what you ran away from when I get back. *If* I get back, what with me pissing molten fire these days. It's your round, by the way. I'll have a double.'

For a few moments Nicholas sat still at the bar. His last utterance had upset him. For some time now there had been a cluster of flies in his stomach. Certain things stirred them into a buzzing cloud that spiralled upwards into his chest and throat, obstructing his breathing. Certain things – arbitrary things – had this effect.

Carefully dismounting from his stool, aware as his feet touched the ground of the flies' hard whisper under his ribs, Nicholas crossed the floor of the bar to the door, pulled it open gently and eased himself out into the fresh-falling snow.

◆

'Was it OK?'

  'Yes. Good.'

  'Did you come?'

  'Yes. Couldn't you feel it?'

'Sometimes I can't tell.'

'Well I did, and it was yummy.'

This was a bad time for Nicholas, immediately after sex with Chloe. The dark spaces under the quilt were alive with tiny signals that there was an intractable difference between them, no matter how deeply they looked into each other's eyes, no matter what boundaries of each other's bodies they blasted; there was still something unattained. Somewhere, sexually, they were afraid of recognizing each other. Since the night in the Yorkshire pub Nicholas had been certain that Chloe was his. She had settled on him like a last layer of himself and obliterated all alternatives. He still desired other women – in London he saw a hundred women every day he'd gladly have gone to bed with – but the search for *the* woman had been over almost from their first encounter in the café on a wet Wednesday all those years ago. She was his. They were together, for life. It was revealed in the usual banal phenomena: her hand on his shoulder while she lifted one leg to shake a stone from her shoe; her shoulderblades relaxing into him when he came behind her, quietly, and cupped his hands over her breasts; 'Let's get out of here' passed without words from her to him across the crowded room of a party. He *was* certain. There was no room for doubt.

Except that, hanging above her after he'd come, he would see her eyes asking their question: What? What *is* it? Why isn't it right?

It was because he demanded something of her, inarticulately. He felt the demand insinuating itself through his every touch – yet he didn't know what it was. He knew, somewhere beneath or behind his brain, that this imperfection grew because he was asking her to join him in something (*what?*), and she couldn't do it. It wasn't a particular act; it was something else. Nicholas felt it in him like a nascent darkness, a thickening or clouding of blood. But that was nothing. That was just metaphor. He couldn't raise it to language, whatever it was.

Chloe closed her eyes when she came. Or she turned her face away. She tried to disguise it, to present it as an effect of sheer pleasure, but Nicholas knew – again, a long way beneath the scope of language – that it was an aversion, an attempt to escape what she sensed in him. It was as if sex displayed a set of sinister premises – and though neither of them would have been able to articulate the conclusion, it came as naturally to Nicholas to move towards it as it did to Chloe to resist. For him it wasn't enough that she fucked him, and came, and derived satisfaction from it; it wasn't enough. He wanted something more.

Chloe, too, knew that sex revealed a disparity. When he came, his eyes tried to find and pin hers. She looked away, reflexively, knowing that it tormented him but unable to stop herself. She couldn't help it. Fucking her, he sometimes said (looking away): 'I love you. Chloe, I love you . . .' But when he came, when his eyes tried to fix hers and she avoided them, he never said a word. Chloe avoided his face at that moment because she was afraid that he would stare into her and say: 'I love you,' and she would hear the voice in her head countering with: He hates you . . . He hates you . . . He hates you.

It shocked her that she so often felt his fucking her as an act of contempt. That was the first layer of shock. The second layer was the shock of her own clear and disinterested understanding: sometimes he fucks me because he hates me. He hates me for not making him love me enough. He's incomplete. He wants me to complete him. He wants love to complete him. It doesn't. Sex with the person you love is supposed to be the point of fusion, the place where you're relieved of being imperfectly yourself, the place where the gap between you and the other is closed. And if it isn't . . . If it isn't then you're left with yourself, alone, and the knowledge that the other's love is no escape. He wants to disappear. Into me. He thinks I'm whole. He wants to hide in me. But at the moment when all the barriers are supposed to drop (maybe they do drop?) he's still aware of himself. I don't destroy him. Sometimes I see in his face that he wants to destroy me because I can't make him disappear.

They never talked about it. It wasn't present in daily consciousness. Only in these moments of extremis for Chloe, or, fucking, in Nicholas's suspended imagination. Chloe wanted to grab his face, to force him to look at her and *tell* her. It tormented her. It was a third party with them when they fucked, like an inscrutable spirit, hovering between them. One or both of them sometimes pretended to fall asleep immediately afterwards – anything rather than acknowledge its presence, whatever it was. They sensed that it had to be kept out. They knew it had the power to ruin everything. Neither of them was under the illusion that this was something that could be negotiated. It was elemental and potentially lethal; they drew together in silence and dumbness against it, but sometimes it broke through.

'What's the matter?'

'I can't. I'm sorry. I just can't.'

She kept insisting that they be in the dark. Some outside light was always present. They were deep blue shadows to each other in the warm bedroom.

'Christ, Chloe, it's been two weeks.'

She couldn't answer this. Wouldn't. At such times Nicholas felt himself as a distinct, isolated cluster of atoms in an icy void.

'It's not that I don't want to have sex with you.'

'The classic double negative. Well, what is it then?'

'I don't know. It's that – it's just that it's always *there*.'

'For fuck's *sake*—'

'It's that I know you *always* want to. There's no room for *me*, *my* wanting to. Don't you see?'

'The truth is you've gone off me. I'm repellent to you.'

'Don't be idiotic.'

'When was the last time you initiated it?'

'But that's just it. I *can't* initiate it. There's never the opportunity. You're pre-emptive.'

'What do you want me to do? Pretend that I *don't* want to?'

'I don't know. Yes. Maybe.'

'But you'd know, anyway, wouldn't you? You'd *know*.'

This was true, of course. Chloe let out a slow breath. 'You don't understand what it's like, Nick.'

'I understand that I disgust you in some way. I understand that I'm the fucking Elephant Man.'

'Oh, for God's sake.'

'I mean do you *enjoy* it, even?'

'Of course I bloody enjoy it. What do you think I'm doing? Faking it?'

'It's crossed my mind.'

'Now you're being perverse.'

Also true, Nicholas knew. Chloe's body wasn't lying when she came. Nicholas felt her working through the calculus of pleasure, felt her bodyheat rising, her breath carrying soft, half-formed vowels, felt the sudden clutch of muscle, the suspense, shudder, the giant capitulation. He did know she wasn't faking it.

And yet. Her body wasn't lying, but her body brought only its own portion of truth to the encounter. There were other portions, hidden, elsewhere. There was one familiar portion in the space to which Chloe turned her head when she came – away from him, in fear of the unspoken conclusion. There was another behind her closed eyes, locked inside her. 'Open your eyes,' he had hissed, God knew how many times. But she couldn't. It was a reflex, a will to something – protection, maybe. It was the denial of him, of what he was asking of her.

But what *was* he asking? Not the mere actions; Chloe wasn't

remotely prudish. One night not long after Yorkshire, she had
guided his cock to her arsehole – not giggling, not in any way
obscuring the magnitude of what she was doing, but breathing
deep sibilant breaths of genuine, brutal desire.

'Are you sure?'

'Yes. Slowly. Just slowly, Nick. Ahh . . . fuck . . . that's it.
Slowly!'

He had been shocked. And, rank with male hypocrisy, somewhat deflated, because he had imagined she wouldn't want this.
Her lust disempowered him; he had barely been able to stay
hard, that first time. Afterwards, she had lain with her back
pressed into his front, softly curled, like a flower that had closed
after a day of brash sunlight full on its face. He had thought she
was upset.

'All right?' he had whispered.

'Ummm.'

'Are you sure?'

Then she had laughed, quietly, because she knew she'd
shocked him. 'I *liked* it, Nick,' she had said. 'Shattered all your
romantic illusions now, have I?'

'Christ, no,' he had said, lying. 'I'm just . . . Well . . . I dunno.
Just wanted to make sure you're OK.'

'I'm fine,' she had said, quietly, pressing into him. 'I'm a bit
bloody sore, though. Vaseline next time, please. About a gallon.'

He had walked around afterwards in a daze.

So it wasn't that Chloe drew physical boundaries. It was
that . . . Nicholas didn't know – but something separated them.

They got married in the winter of their graduation year.

'I want the Day,' Chloe had said. 'The whole shebang: dress,
flowers, ring, church, pageboy, drunk uncles, all of it. Of course
it's all bollocks – but it's *good* bollocks, if you love someone
enough.'

Nicholas didn't feel one way or another about it, except that
his sense of their connectedness, their sovereignty, immunized
them against anyone's judgement. If they decided to get married
(with the whole shebang, as Chloe put it), then that was simply

a necessarily right thing, a unique event wholly outside the rest of the world's prattle about whether or not one *should* get married, in the abstract.

This moral exemption amused Nicholas no end, privately. He could engage energetically in debates about abortion or euthanasia or capital punishment, he could formulate reasons in support of his public positions on such questions – but as far as himself and Chloe were concerned, he simply didn't care. If Chloe chose to murder someone, well that was fine, because it was Chloe. That was all. There was the social world – people arguing earnestly about what 'one' ought or ought not to do – then there was his and Chloe's world, which was transcendent, and in which the presence and opinions of other people might as well have been grains of sand for all they mattered.

This perception struck Nicholas as, by turns, absurd and delusional, and inevitable and absolute.

The wedding was on an icy November morning at a small Protestant church in Elm Coombe. The sky was high and bright blue, beaten thin by the cold. The wedding party milled and shivered in the graveyard before the ceremony, while in the short grass gleaming starlings hopped and stabbed between the headstones. To Nicholas, who had grown up in London, the smell of the nearby sea elongated the boundaries of the day itself, stretching his sense of the future to something infinitely distant. Standing outside the church (accosted every five seconds by hand shakers or cheek kissers or shoulder grippers) he found himself acutely aware, too, of the chipped and shattered dead beneath his feet, folded, awake, in the rough quilt of earth. It seemed inappropriate that they were not acknowledged in some way. At the same time he was painfully hungry; he had refused breakfast, and now his stomach yowled and chirruped like a troop of monkeys. The air lay flat against his face and his left eye kept watering. At last the usher called them in.

The church was small and high-ceilinged with a crimson carpet, pale, cold-looking walls and a dark, heavily ornamented

pulpit. The altar was of plain stone, and above it an etiolated
Christ in crucifixion looked down with a face like the Tragedy
mask. It seemed lurid to Nicholas, and nothing to do with his
getting married to Chloe. Thinking this and other wisps of
thought, he stood in his suit with his hands clasped in front of
him, like a footballer protecting his groin from a free kick, and
waited for Chloe's entrance.

For sheer number, Chloe's contingent put Nicholas's to
shame. As well as her immediate family – mother, father,
grandmother, older sister – there seemed an endless horde of
aunts, uncles, cousins (including the fabled George of the
barn, with whom Nicholas and his parents were staying),
nephews, nieces and peripheral in-laws, all decked out like
exotic birds. There seemed to be more of them in Chloe's half
of the church every time Nicholas glanced over his shoulder.
His own crew looked skeletal by comparison. His older
brother, Stephen (whom Nicholas felt he barely knew, since
ten years separated them), was his best man; Stephen, too,
stood as if guarding his groin, and said: 'It's in my top pocket.
Don't worry. I've done this before,' every time Nicholas looked
at him. Nicholas wasn't remotely concerned about the ring. He
simply couldn't believe that he was standing at a church altar
with his brother, waiting to get married. And like every bride-
groom before him, he was repeatedly struck by what an
extraordinary thing it would be to turn around, walk from the
church and never set eyes on his intended again. Having built
this edifice of expectation, the desire to blast it into oblivion
was almost irresistible.

That morning he and his father had met in the bathroom. His
father had been shaving; Nicholas had gone in for a pee.

'How're you feeling, boyo?' his father had asked him.

Nicholas (having to practically wring himself out because
he had forgotten that he had trouble peeing in front of another
man) had wanted to reply: 'Utterly empty,' but had known that
would upset the old man. Instead, he had said: 'Pretty good, I
think. Nervous. Bloody starving, too, though I don't think I
could swallow a crumb.'

Against all Nicholas's expectations his father saw through him immediately. He stopped shaving (a third of his jaw clean, the rest still foamy), rested his hands on the edge of the sink and looked at Nicholas in the mirror. Nicholas, having failed to empty his bladder of anything more than one hot javelin of piss, stood with his hands in his pockets and realized with surprise that on this occasion directness was possible between them; the imminent ritual made it possible. Now they were two men alone with each other, one married, the other about to be.

My face will become my father's face, Nicholas thought to himself, the pores will yawn, the skin will thicken, I'll get those pronounced lines between the corners of the nose and the ends of the mouth, my hair will thin and go grey. Discovering this, he discovered too that he didn't mind, that he felt a sudden piercing love for his father, who had always been strong, and who had laughed, generously, and who often (still) sneaked up on Nicholas's mother and wrapped his arms around her and fondled her breasts, much to her delighted outrage.

'Do you know what I thought the morning I married your mother?' Nicholas's father said.

Nicholas smiled. He could still see the young man in his father, the will to adventure, indulgence and amusement. 'What?' he said.

'I thought: At last there's something solid in my life. At last there's something I know for certain. It felt like I'd come home.'

For what seemed like a long time the two of them stood still and silent, Nicholas with his wrists trembling, his father with all his upper-body weight on the heels of his hands, staring at Nicholas in the mirror.

At last he said: 'Do you love her, son? Truly love her?'

And Nicholas, allowed for an instant to transcend embarrassment and the habit of prosaic idiom, feeling his bones settling as if for the first time in his life, had exhaled, slowly, once, and said: 'Yes, Dad, I love her. I truly love her.'

Relieved, grinning, Nicholas's father had picked up his razor, put it to his chin and said: 'That's all right then. She's a good girl, Chloe. Now bugger off and leave me in peace, will you, else your mother'll think I'm trying to talk you out of it.'

That same morning, Chloe, in her parents' cottage, had woken with daylight still two hours away. In the dream that had woken her she'd been standing with her mother and her sister in the living-room, trying on the wedding dress for last-minute alterations. There was a small fire in the hearth filling the room with a disproportionately large heat that pressed against her face and hands. Liz and her mother were agitated, orbiting her, then alighting on some pleat or button needing adjustment. Every touch of theirs, every movement of the fabric against her skin hurt. She was convinced that there were still dozens of pins in the dress, tearing her skin each time something was pulled or hitched or tucked. It was impossible for Chloe to get her mother's or Liz's attention. They kept giggling, thinking she was jumpy. Stand still, Chloe, for *heaven's* sake! Do you want to get married looking like a rag doll?

But it grew unbearable. She began to dread their hands coming near her like wasps. Dizzy from the sensation, watching the living-room rug turning gently under her white shoes, she thought of Gulliver bristling with Lilliputian arrows. Hold *still*, Chloe, will you? She kept trying to tell them she was in agony, but they wouldn't listen. The longer she stood still, the busier their movements became, until she was no longer feeling individual pricks and scratches but a layer of hot pain all over her body under the stiff material. She was terrified that she was bleeding, staining the dress with blood.

She opened her mouth to scream at them (the fire's heat entered between her lips like a quickly inflated balloon), when Liz suddenly stopped and froze. 'Mum!' she said. 'Oh, Mum, *look!*'

Chloe followed their eyes. The edges of the white sleeves, darkening, where the first dribbles of blood were creeping quickly down her hands, dropping in beads on to the rug.

She'd woken with her lungs filled with a huge inhalation, ready to scream.

But she stopped herself. Liz was asleep in the single bed next to hers, mouth open, a slight frown on her face. For a moment the dream-heat lingered, then she realized that the bedroom was cold, and that through a gap between the curtains a hard, clear night sky was visible, stone-coloured with moonlight.

She got up, quietly, and dressed. Her skin still felt tender when she pulled her sweater and jeans on. For a moment she hesitated, standing at the gap in the curtains. Then she tiptoed from the room, down the short flight of stairs, through the listening, moonlit kitchen and out of the back door.

Outside it was frozen and still. Beyond the streetlamps – of which there were no more than a dozen – the moon's light was pale on the boles and branches of the trees. The silence was palpable, and rested on her cheeks and lips like a cool salve. Capillaries of frost glimmered on the main road.

She walked slowly, hands tucked into her armpits, to the church, where, in a few hours, she was supposed to marry Nicholas. The gate was unlocked and half open. She stepped into the tiny cemetery and stood looking up at the spire's single illuminated isosceles.

Was this what happened, the night before? Was everyone given a last chance to retreat from the formalization of love? Nicholas was eight miles away at George's. Was he awake in bed, or standing bewildered in the yard, or at this very moment being drawn to the church so that he, too, could consider what he was about to do and choose not to do it? Chloe stood among the gravestones and wondered how other people discussed their weddings so casually – but then checked herself. She and Nicholas had discussed their own casually over the preceding months: bridesmaids' dresses, flowers, reception menus, music. Now every detail of her surroundings – the canted gravestones, the brittle grass, the dark, downreaching flanks of the church – joined in an articulation of the question she had subconsciously feared asking herself for weeks: Do you really want to do this?

It was, she also realized, only an extension of the question of love. If you were a romantic (and she had long ago accepted, with horror, that she was), then the declaration of love to each

other was only a postponement of the question of whether you
were willing to declare love publicly, with every utterance
inflated by ritual. She had said to herself and to others hundreds of times that she didn't 'believe' in marriage. She had
superficially imbibed her generation's contempt for archaism in
any form. 'Being married or not has got nothing to do with
love,' she'd argued with Liz. 'No one can tell me I love Nick less
now than I will if we get married.' But somewhere deeper (she
had suspected this, queasily, in odd moments of honesty with
herself) there had been a substratum of darker certainty, the
need to take part in a lovers' tradition with the weight of history behind it. Revealed to her now, in the churchyard, was her
own faith in the scale of the marriage gesture – both the
courage (or naïvety) it required, and the cost incurred should
time bankrupt the declarations of permanence. She didn't
believe in God, but she did believe in the cumulative force of
history, in the collective ghost of lovers – all the millions down
the centuries – who had passed through a ceremony like the
one she'd assigned herself to a few hours from now. (And
meanwhile, she thought, here I am at fucking five o'clock in
the morning more or less guaranteeing that I'm going to look
like a *corpse* at the altar rail.) She believed – almost laughing
out loud at herself, standing among the buried dead – that history was watching her. Not just watching, but confirming the
raised stakes.

It's ridiculous, she thought, tightening her armpits around
her hands. It's ridiculous to think of the history of love if you sit
on the couch with your boyfriend and watch *Brookside*. But she
couldn't help it. Love insisted. Love insisted on this preposterous miracle which transformed the incessant mundane
(*Brookside* together, cups of tea, him going off to the launderette
and her titillated by the thought of him folding her skirts and
blouses) into a world of occult emotional resonance. Nothing
was exempt. It was obscenely greedy; it must reach out and
contaminate every detail of life with the beloved until there
was nothing left to resist it.

And since I'm here, Chloe thought, since I'm here, freezing, wondering if I'm going to go through with it, then presumably there is something left that's resisting it.

Me.

'You scared?' Liz had said to her the night before.

'No,' she had said.

Liz had been sitting opposite her at the kitchen table, cradling her elbows in her hands.

'I was scared stiff before me and Tom got married.'

'Were you?'

'Petrified. I remember thinking: What if he . . . You know, what if it's a mistake?'

'But you knew you loved him?' Chloe had asked.

'I did,' Liz had said, wide-eyed. 'But that was what was so frightening. I kept thinking: There's nothing left of me. I've gone. There's just him. Then if he stops loving me, I'll have forgotten how to live. If he stops loving me it'll be like I'm . . .'

'Dead?'

'Yes!'

'Bloody hell, Liz,' Chloe had said.

Because not getting married had, in some final corner of herself, preserved her. It had allowed Nicholas to remain something in her life. Marrying him, standing up in front of everyone and announcing their unity, would mean that her life – her life with him in it – was over. From then on, somehow, it would be *their* life.

Shivering, she stared at the church's black windows. *If you do this and he leaves you*, the night said, *you'll die.*

She had remained standing there for perhaps five minutes. Everything had been still and distinct around her: the moonlit flank of the spire; the glittering grass; the thin shadows of the gravestones. She had had an almost painful awareness of the substance and shape of her body.

At last she had turned and walked quickly back to the house – then lain awake until daylight.

The vows went by Nicholas in a blur, except for Chloe's full

name – Chloe Anne Palmer – which fell from his lips and startled him awake for a moment, as if he had unwittingly
pronounced part of an incantation. Some unattended to part of
his consciousness registered that she looked exquisite, like
a snowdrop beside him, but mostly he thought of the scar
stretched from her breast under her arm, which, in their first
encounter, she had been afraid for him to see, and which he
now loved, brazenly, as the thing that uniquely identified her
and her willingness to be vulnerable to him. When he put the
ring on her finger, their eyes met, briefly. Nicholas saw her fear,
excitement, tentative delight, loss and, with relief, her certainty
of him that went beyond all other surface feelings. He wanted to
laugh out loud. His father's pronouncement repeated itself in
his head: She's a good girl, Chloe . . .

They went through the ceremony in a shared delirium. In the
wedding car they could barely look at or speak to each other.
Chloe took Nicholas's hand – but like someone in shock. It
had only been a marriage ceremony, but it had concussed them.

Chloe sat, exhausted. The walk out to the church last night
had been a dream – hadn't it? There *had* been a dream. Hadn't
there been a dream that had woken her, suddenly, in the night?

'Christ,' she said, after minutes in the car had passed in
silence. 'Did we just get married, Nick?'

And Nicholas, who, at some point in the church had raised
his eyebrows, and who had not yet lowered them, could only
turn to her, bemused, laughably reborn (still thinking of his
father telling him that Chloe was a good girl), and say: 'Err . . .
yeah. We did. Bloody hell.'

That evening they stayed in a cottage that belonged to
George's farm and which had been vacated for their wedding
night. It was a clean, compact place with natty nooks and cran-
nies, but freezing. The bed was a slab of ice when they got in,
but the gradual thaw as their bodyheat built beneath the quilt
was a slow, erotic enchantment.

Still raw from the ceremony and feverish from the familial
overdose of the reception, they made love tentatively, with
moments of awkwardness in the dark. They were both

bewildered by how much it seemed they must now learn a new language. Chloe moved his hand away from her scar, as if the last three years hadn't happened. It hurt Nicholas, but he understood. For once, after they had both come, he didn't feel the distance between them – or rather, the wedding had so unformed their identities that he couldn't tell whether something still divided them.

For a long while afterwards they lay awake, exhausted, struggling with the aftershocks of the day's violence. This was the countryside, therefore the room's darkness was absolute. It felt tangible to Nicholas, something he could wash his hands in.

At last the reverberations of the preceding hours subsided, and comfort with each other returned. As if by mutual consent, they remembered that they did in fact know each other.

'Nick?' she said quietly.

'What, love?'

'Are you sure?'

'About what?'

'This. Us. All of it.'

Nicholas was feeling the wedding ring on her finger. It was the only ring she wore. He was thinking of the bone, laced with nerves and veins and tissue, wrapped in flesh and now circumscribed by a hard band of gold. He clicked his own ring against it.

'My Dad said something to me this morning,' he said.

'What?'

'He said that when he married my mother he finally felt that there was something solid in his life, some certainty. He said it felt as if he'd come home.'

Chloe digested this silently, gently rubbing her foot against his, which was what she always did when they lay naked together.

'He asked me if I loved you,' Nicholas said. 'If I *truly* loved you.' Now she lay absolutely still in his arms. 'He told me you were a good girl.'

Chloe laughed at this and relaxed against him. 'I can't

imagine you two having this conversation. Are you sure you're
not making this up?'

'Don't underestimate my old man,' Nicholas said. 'Big occasion
and all that. He was very specific: "She's a good girl, Chloe."'

Again they let silence return for a few minutes. A sheep
coughed, wetly; it sounded like it was in the room with them.
Nicholas listened to the cottage's ticks and whispers. George
had told him the place was three hundred years old.

Finally Chloe, who had tensed again, spread her fingers out
on Nicholas's chest and shook him, lightly. 'And?' she said.

Because he could, Nicholas reached out in the darkness and
clenched and unclenched his fist; the action was invisible
to both of them, but he felt guilty, because he knew it had
happened.

'And you *are* a good girl,' he said, lowering his arm and
pulling her closer to him. 'And yes I am sure. And it does feel
like coming home. And I do love you. I do truly love you.'

◆

'Connell's body was kinda disgusting,' Mickey said to Nicholas.
'I used to have to do this weird head-trip thing where I focused
on the most disgusting part – sometimes his last two toes,
sometimes a big liver spot on his throat, sometimes his little
shrivelled-up ball bag – and then force myself to see it as beautiful. You know? Just by sheer force of will? I was doing a lot of
yoga at the time, which seemed to help. Hand me that, will
you?'

Mickey was neck-deep in crackling foam in a triangular
sunken bath, talking to Nicholas, who sat with his back against
the base of the sink. He got up slowly and handed her the
margarita.

'If I could pick the yuckiest bit of him and put it in my
mouth for a minute or two? The rest of it was a pushover. Poor
old Connell. He wasn't so bad really. Kinda sweet.'

'Why do you want me here?' Nicholas said. The pattern of their exchanges was becoming evident: Mickey would talk, Nicholas would listen, sometimes for hours. Then he would ask something vast and simple.

Mickey didn't reply immediately, but lifted one golden shin from the foam and smoothed her hand over the skin, bending at the knee to reach the ankle.

'Zack told me he talked to you,' she said, eventually.

'Yes,' Nicholas said.

'You afraid of him?'

'I don't think so.'

'Maybe you should be.'

'Are you afraid of him?'

'Zack? Are you kidding? He's a *baby*.'

They fell silent. After a few moments Mickey, smiling directly at Nicholas, said: 'OK, you can get out of here now. Go on into the bedroom.'

Mickey's apartment smelled of clean surfaces and complicated perfume. It was desperately beautiful, as if constantly struggling to erase the memory of a murder. The bed breathed a double history of apocalyptic sex and flawed sleep. Nicholas lay belly-down on it, his face turned to one side, one knee bent.

Since the future had ended he was having problems with his perception of space and scale. The bed, when he looked along its surface, appeared to stretch away from him for twenty or thirty feet. Moments earlier, when he had been dismissed from the bathroom, he had stood and looked down at Mickey in the tub and discovered that her head was no bigger than a grape, while the walls of the bath reached all the way up to his chin. When the green-eyed British Airways stewardess had encountered him in the aisle, he had been standing and looking up towards the cockpit, at a vanishing point half a mile away.

At first these perceptions had paralysed him. Now he was getting used to them. Sometimes several hours would pass without any distortion. Other times he spent a whole day negotiating thousand foot drops off the pavement, or ceilings high enough for aircraft to pass under. It didn't seem worth telling anyone about – and in any case, who would he tell?

'So where'd you go today?' Mickey said. She stood in the bedroom doorway, massaging her hair with a thick white towel. An ivory silk kimono hung, open, from her shoulders, revealing the bronze, tampered-with body still rosy from the bath's heat. Though her hips were heavy, and the short thighs showed flecks of brooding vein, her stomach was exercised grotesquely flat and her breasts (cosmetically engineered, she had told him neutrally) were big, taut and restive. 'Hey, get up. I said where'd you go today when I sent you out?'

Nicholas got up immediately and stood by the bed, facing her. 'To a bar called Scrimshankers,' he said. 'It's in the Village.'

'*That* place,' Mickey said. 'Jesus Christ, that's where drunks go to *die*. What the fuck did you go there for?'

'I met someone called Lancelot,' Nicholas said. Something stirred in him when he told her this, the flicker of something achingly familiar. Almost immediately the flies in his chest began to twitch and lift – only in ones and twos, but if she didn't give him an instruction soon he knew they would stir quickly into an unbearable frenzy.

'I didn't ask you who you met,' Mickey said. She stopped drying her hair and let the towel drop to the floor. 'Come here.'

The flies stopped. From the moment he had first seen her face in the nightclub Nicholas had intuited Mickey's ability to bring him, if not peace, then a blissful eclipse.

'On your knees,' she said quietly. 'Look at me.'

He could feel it approaching, the craved emptying of consciousness, the miraculous draining of every ounce of self. Her face absorbed him. The small, bright eyes were gem-like, the mouth still. Her own will was held in front of him like a grail. He wanted only this, now. He hung on the edge of himself; in a moment he would fall and become nothing more than a set of responses to her. It was the freedom he had known she would have the power to give. In a moment he would be gone. Even the sense of his own need would be gone. And until she returned him to himself he would not know he had been gone;

then he would realize, and feel desolate, and continue through time (occasionally wondering why he was still here) until she gave him again the unique amnesty she had at her disposal.

'That's right. Look at me.'

Her nostrils dilated slightly, the corners of her mouth flickered. A single drop of water fell from the end of her hair and rolled part of the way down her chest. She breathed deeply and evenly. Finally, seeming to settle into herself, she drew her hand back, palm stiff, raised her eyebrows as if at a pleasant surprise, then swung and struck Nicholas full force across the face.

She sent him out again later and told him to come back the next day.

More snow had fallen and frozen. The evening news had shown the white bodies and black cockpit windows of planes on the ground at Kennedy and La Guardia. They had looked like trapped ghosts. Sombrely, as if communicating the first stages of Armageddon, it had been reported that only twenty cabs were running in the city. With Christmas only three days away and more blizzards predicted across the eastern seaboard, Manhattan was at a virtual standstill. Travel trajectories and planned family gatherings were destroyed. At a stroke the entire infrastructure of New York had become trivial, a matter of indifference to the shifting forces of air and water. The city's inhabitants were reduced to confused childhood, having been robbed of reality in the space of a few days.

Nicholas walked through the straight spaces. The air was thin; each indrawn breath icily measured his nasal passages, throat and lungs. His face froze. In midtown the buildings rose sheer on either side of him. Looking straight up to the sky at the intersections he saw crossroads of dark space, the city's street plan in empty negative. On Broadway a car slithered gently, affectionately, into a streetlight. People were scarfed and hatted, trudging and mincing as snow or ice demanded, talking, always talking. It drew Nicholas's attention every time someone laughed; he found himself focusing on the sound, reflexively, then struggling to tear himself away.

In Alphabet City there were strange community gardens in the dead, drab spaces between the brownstones. Nicholas was surprised. The gardens were tall oblongs of darkness, flanked on three sides by dirty buildings and on the wire-fenced fourth by the oblivious street. AVENUE D COMMUNITY GARDEN PROJECT one sign said. Nicholas didn't understand. The rest of the environment was so hopeless that the gardens seemed no more than gestures of grim urban irony.

None the less there they were, with frozen bird-tables and black flowerbeds. There were bare bushes and empty sweet-pea frames. Benches, statuary. Sometimes a snow-covered picnic table. In one, a chicken coop. In another (a narrow, bedraggled place, overhung by two trees that choked out the light), a goat pen of corrugated iron. A goat's silver, oily-haired head peeping out. A goat in the middle of New York.

While Nicholas stood on the street side of the chainlink fence, watching, a girl came into the garden from a door in one of the brownstones. She wore a dark, zipped-up rain jacket and grimy jeans tucked into a pair of red wellies. The boots crunched in the snow, and she moved tentatively, as if any step might detonate a mine. She looked about twelve or thirteen, with a small, freckled face framed in stiff, unwashed dark hair. She carried a blue plastic bucket – not by its handle, but held in both hands at arm's length, like a sacred offering. Each step required tremendous concentration. It took her several minutes to cross the ten paces to where the goat's sleek head reached out above the door of the pen. When she arrived, she stood as far away as possible, arms at full stretch, while the goat plunged its snout in and began to eat.

Nicholas didn't know how long he stood there. At a certain point the pitched sky and black buildings righted themselves, and he was returned to himself. The garden was empty. Her footprints were dark tacking-stitches in the blinding snow.

'So, you gonna be our newest regular, or what?' Marty asked him, pouring a Scotch.

'A friend told me people come here to die,' Nicholas said.

Marty's geniality never wavered; there was a permanent smile at one side of his mouth. At Nicholas's remark the half smile stretched into a delighted grin, through which came first one long wheeze, then ancient laughter. He shook his head, still smiling, and knocked twice on the counter. 'That's priceless, man. This one's on the house, OK?'

Nicholas took a sip of his drink and felt warmth spreading through his throat, chest and gut. Since it hadn't been instructed otherwise, his body still reported physically pleasurable sensations, some of which, as in this instance, his brain acknowledged before shutting down again. He took another sip. At his side a red-haired woman with a porous, greasy face and thickly applied make-up sat slumped forward on the bar, her face turned towards him. Her mouth smiled slightly (one canine showed prominently); her eyes were almost closed, a faint glimmer between the lids. Once or twice she lifted her head and opened her eyes at him, seeing nothing, then returned to her stupor.

'First the infant, mewling and puking in his nurse's arms,' Lancelot growled, coming out of the shadows to join Nicholas at the bar, 'then the sixty-seven-year-old fat bastard mewling and puking in the toilet in this rancid shithole. You back again then, sunshine? Couldn't keep away once you'd discovered Manhattan's number-one centre of cultural exchange and philosophical whatsit?'

Lancelot rapped the counter with his solid knuckles and Marty delivered two more clinking tumblers of Scotch. Lifting his glass up to one of the bar's weak overhead lights, Lancelot inspected its contents, coldly.

'Doesn't work now, you see,' he said. Nicholas looked up at him. 'Used to shut me up. Booze. Stopped talking. Words used to go backwards, down the gullet . . . used to fucking *retreat*, see. Booze used to see 'em orf. Like a guard dog. Like one of those geese they train to be guard dogs. Know that, did you? Geese for guard dogs?'

There was a place or invisible person Lancelot addressed when he was in this state, Nicholas had observed.

'See, there aren't any people in this city,' Lancelot continued.
'It's just talking. It's just *talking*. Mouths opening. Words. See, the
mouths have taken over. Mouthhattan. New Talk. You think you
can shut up. You think . . . Like Sadie there. Go on. Wake her up.
Ask her how she got here. She doesn't know. Hasn't a fucking
clue. She used to know, before her mouth started talking, telling
her story. Now she doesn't . . . now she can't remember. Ask her
mouth, mind you. Don't ask *her*: ask the mouth and the fucking
mouth'll tell you all sorts of wondrous tales. Astonishing stories.
Weird Tales Monthly, as I used to read when I was shortly after the
mewling and puking incarnation. You come here, sunshine –
I'm warning you. You come here and let your mouth get the
better of you . . . you give it fucking *licence* – you let it go and
pretty soon you'll be gone. Booze, on the other hand, used to
shut me the fuck up. Me. The fuck. Up. Which is about the size
of it, now that I come to think of it. Where was I?'

'Shut up, man, for Christ's sake,' Marty said, smile bright
and intact. 'You're gonna drive your countryman away goin' on
like that.'

'No, I like it here,' Nicholas said.

Lancelot, who seemed, after his last swallow, to be savouring
his irritation rather than suffering inside it, turned to Marty
with a squint. 'I like it here,' he mimicked. 'Now there's a *real*
talker,' he said.

Marty beamed and laughed, silently.

'Garrulous,' Lancelot said, pulling his silver beard, rhythmi-
cally, as if trying to mould it into a point. 'Fucking Loquacious
Larry. A real motormouth. You must give your wife a headache,
ducks.'

'I lost my wife,' Nicholas said.

For a moment no one spoke. Nicholas wasn't looking at
either Marty or Lancelot. He was looking at the reflection of the
bar's horseshoe of bottles on the black counter top.

Marty leaned forward and squeezed Nicholas's shoulder. 'Hey,
man, shit, that's awful. I'm sorry. He didn't mean nothin' by it,
you know. He's just . . . Shit, Lance, you're fucked up, man.'

Nicholas shrugged and looked at Lancelot, who sat now with

his head bowed and his bones gone heavy. Speaking to the floor or into his glass, Lancelot said: 'I'm very sorry. My apologies. I had no idea.'

'It's all right,' Nicholas said. 'Come on. Drink.'

Lancelot looked up and fixed Nicholas with the bulbous, pickled eyes. For a moment he seemed to achieve a span of unpoisoned consciousness; the eyes communicated a flicker of gratitude – and more: an acknowledgement that they shared (however distantly remembered or eloquently reviled) a scheme of things, a culture, a place, a set of codes. They were two Englishmen, after all. In Manhattan. But then it passed, and Lancelot's toxins flooded back in. He grimaced and swallowed the remainder of his drink in one excruciating gulp.

'Jesus Christ in space, Marty, what was that? Fucking *petrol*?' he asked, shuddering.

'Johnnie Red, man, same as always,' Marty said, untroubled, delighted.

'Yeah,' Lancelot said. 'With a fucking gasoline top on it. Fuck my *dog*.'

'You ain't even *got* a dog, man. But if you *did,* I wouldn't want a damn thing to do with it.'

'Get out of it,' Lancelot said, whacking the empty down on the bar. 'You wouldn't get a look in. You'd have to *bribe* the fucking creature. And it'd need fucking *counselling* afterwards I don't doubt. Go on, give us another, you ugly bastard.'

Again Nicholas drank, slowly, steadily. A group of university students came in and began playing Metallica songs on the jukebox.

'If you don't have a word with them, Marty,' Lancelot said, and left it at that.

Marty smiled brilliantly, wiping a pint glass.

After an hour, Lancelot passed out with his head resting on his forearms. His suede hat remained in place, but as Nicholas watched the seam holding the right sleeve of the jacket tore slowly, smoothly apart. The fat and muscle of the collapsed shoulders had forced it, after years of strain on the fabric.

Nicholas and Marty shared this moment without speaking. What should have been funny was in fact unsettling – ugly, even. 'May as well let him sleep,' Marty said, to no one in particular. 'May as well let the man sleep.'

Nicholas's mouth was cut on the inside, from where Mickey's blows had driven the flesh against the teeth, and there was a precise, cold pain on the top of his scalp where she'd grabbed (and uprooted) a small tuft of his hair. So far these were the only indicators. Nicholas assumed there would be more. When he had come back to himself he had felt dismal, as if returning to a cruel Monday morning from a night of deep, blissful sleep. He had come back to himself and been confronted by his identity like an offensive suit he must wear and walk around in. He had come back to himself with the certainty that he wanted to leave again, as soon as possible.

After each blow Mickey had presented her cunt for him to lick. It was clear that the tenderness with which he licked her each time must increase in direct proportion to the escalation of the violence of the blows: the harder she hit him the more delicately he caressed her with his mouth. She would let him stimulate her for a little while, then make him stop; she would rest, stop herself from coming, then hit him again, and the cycle would repeat. Nicholas had fallen into a robotic freedom after the third or fourth blow.

When he had come back to himself, he had been convinced that only seconds or minutes had passed, but his wristwatch testified otherwise. The room was anxious. Mickey had been dozing on the bed. She looked at him sleepily when he stood up.

'Go and shower,' she had told him. 'Don't come back here tonight. Come back tomorrow. If you try 'n' come back tonight I'll tell Bill to keep you out. Got it?'

In the shower he had looked down at his body, his imagination redefining it as a space for the physical text of Mickey's will. When he soaped himself, it felt like touching someone else's flesh.

'Come on, guys,' Marty said, jostling Nicholas awake. 'Even

Scrimshankers closes come four-thirty. Get up and get your asses home.'

'Buggering hell,' Lancelot said neutrally. Then he looked down his nose at Nicholas. 'You fell asleep, you pussy,' he said, again without any audible emotion.

'So did you,' Nicholas replied.

When Lancelot hobbled off to make his last visit to the bathroom, Marty came back to Nicholas's end of the bar. 'Walk with him,' Marty said. 'He's been mugged twice in the last six months. Fucker only lives two blocks down. I normally do it myself but I got somewhere I gotta be the minute I get out of here. OK?'

'OK,' Nicholas said. 'If he doesn't mind.'

'He'll mouth off like he does,' Marty said. 'But don't buy it. It's bullshit. He's scared. Just go with him two blocks.'

It was a long two blocks. Lancelot was slow, and was slowed further by his habit of stopping every few paces to test the depth of the snowdrifts with his walking-stick. He wheezed horribly and his breathing was shallow, though he seemed impervious to the cold. He wore no overcoat, just the corduroy jacket and the suede hat. The sleeve was hanging tenuously. Nicholas had decided not to mention it.

By the time they reached their destination – a five-storey brownstone between a pizza parlour and an all-night deli – Lancelot seemed pent and bitter. They had walked the last five minutes in silence, Lancelot contemptuous of his own audible struggles for breath.

'All . . . right, sunshine . . . this is . . . me . . .'

In the light from the building's lobby Nicholas could see a stringy clot of dark phlegm hanging from Lancelot's beard. He was about to begin a subtle hunt through his pockets for serviceable tissues when Lancelot collapsed – straight down on to his buttocks, as if in an act of political defiance. 'Oh fuck,' he said, quietly. 'Fuck it all.' His head fell forward on to his chest and the suede hat tumbled off into the street. It happened in less than a second. Nicholas had reached out to help him, then something had stopped him, and he had drawn back. He had actually taken a step back by the time Lancelot had dropped. Now he stood bent slightly forward, his hands arrested, the help impulse overridden by something.

Lancelot sighed and looked up. A thread of dark blood had run from his nostril and come to rest in the grey moustache. Another little bulb of blood was peeping from the other nostril. Still Nicholas stood paralysed, with Second Avenue's wall of cold air at his back. Lancelot's face struggled for a moment, as if its internal logic was about to collapse; his mouth trembled and his eyebrows moved first down, hard, then flickered up again, quivering. Suddenly Nicholas realized that Lancelot was crying. For a second or two the face revealed an unendurable anguish – then almost immediately recovered and became contemplative.

'Can't get up,' Lancelot said flatly. 'Not asking for anything, mind you. Just pointing out a fact. I think the coon put something in that last one.'

It defied belief, but Lancelot lived on the fourth floor in a building without a lift. The stairwell was wet and boot-printed and smelled of cat piss. After every third or fourth step Lancelot had to stop and get his breath. At the top of the third floor, he stopped and put his head in his hands, swaying perilously. Nicholas, feeling a vast distance between the two of them, put his hand between Lancelot's mighty shoulderblades.

'Need somewhere to kip tonight, do you?' Lancelot said. His voice was appalling, a falsetto parody of itself. Where his hand touched, Nicholas could feel the effort the man was making not to buckle, to sink to his knees, to surrender to the weight of his past. He could feel it, but as if from a long way away.

'Yes,' he said. He took his hand away. Lancelot gathered himself. Again Nicholas could sense the struggle to reconstruct the habit of Englishness.

Without taking his hands from where they covered his face, Lancelot said: 'Good of you to help. Welcome to stay here. Up to you. No need for palaver. All right?'

'All right,' Nicholas said. 'Thank you.'

'Assuming you're not a psychopath. Assuming I'm not going to wake up tomorrow and find I've been . . . Although . . .'

'Thank you,' Nicholas said. 'Are you ready for these last few steps?'

Part Two

BLOOD

They got jobs about which they felt neither here nor there. Chloe went to work as an assistant to one of the curators at the British Museum, and Nicholas's indifference during an interview landed him a job with a literary agency. It was an ignominious position – underling of sorts to one of the agency's rising young stars, Anthony Caswell-Brooks – but not badly paid, and since Nicholas felt that his degree had uniquely disqualified him from doing practically anything, he didn't complain.

'My main responsibility,' Anthony had said one afternoon in his office during Nicholas's first week, 'is to disabuse you of the idea you've probably got that there's skirt to be had in this job. I mean you'd think, wouldn't you? Entire marketing departments. Editorial assistants. *Publicity*, for fuck's sake. I mean you would think, wouldn't you?'

Nicholas had raised his eyebrows, non-committally.

'It's an illusion. Seriously. It's a terrible illusion. More chance of a shag working on London Transport. I know it sounds ridiculous, but believe me, I know what I'm talking about.'

'I'm married,' Nicholas had said. 'Happily married.'

At which point Anthony had raised *his* eyebrows – then grinned. 'Pulling your leg, mate,' he said. 'Seriously.'

Then after a pause he had added, quietly: 'Truth is, there's women coming out of the fucking *walls*.'

Because he had Chloe, Nicholas could stand the formerly offensive notion of 'doing something'. At especially bleak moments during the working day – London's brown afternoon light like dead matter in the office; the reek of the Xerox; the objects on his desk revealed in a conspiracy of ugliness; Anthony's phone-patter of savvy and bent truth – at these times he would close his eyes and think of Chloe struggling through *her* day, and of the tranquillizing pleasure of seeing her when he got home. He would look around at his co-workers and pity them because he was going home to Chloe and they weren't. It was nauseating smugness (it nauseated *him*), but there was a grain of absurd and genuine compassion in it, too: he knew how he stood his life; how on earth did they stand theirs?

So Nicholas worked with very little of his consciousness applied to what he was doing. All he *was* doing, after all, was wading through manuscripts to make sure that (a) nothing that was utter dreck made it on to Anthony's desk, and (b) everything that looked promising did. Initially he gave aspiring novelists pages and pages to convince him. Boredom and the sheer number of hopeless cases soon took their toll.

Leathon was born in Veldinor, west of the River Longwater, beyond the marshes of Drenn. He knew from his earliest years that when he grew to manhood he would not be a farmer like his father, Obsk, but would run away and join the fabled warriors of Largon, who wore the sign of the burning fist on their burnished shields. It was because of the dreams that he knew this

On the rejection pile.

It had been thirty years since I'd seen Caldcote Manor, and there was a misty feeling over my heart as I stood at the once proud gates remembering the glorious days of my childhood before the war. Where were they all now? Stubbing out my cigarette, my foot comfy in its new Gucci shoe

Rejection.

It was a dark, stormy

Rejection.

'First two paragraphs,' Anthony Caswell-Brooks had told

him. 'Either they've got a fucking good hook – in which case they *might* just have a fucking good story – *or* they can actually *write*. Either way you'll know by the end of the second paragraph. And don't hold your breath for the ones with a fucking good story who can also actually write. Christmas only comes once a year. Got it?'

'Got it,' Nicholas had said. The standard rejection note set off remote emotional depth-charges in him for the first few weeks. After that he hardened to it, and got through the afternoons by thinking of Chloe cradling a telephone receiver, scribbling on a notepad, one side of her hair hanging in a dark sickle.

For nearly two years they stayed in the Shepherd's Bush studio flat they'd had since university. They would have stayed longer, since neither of them cared about having a bigger place, but their parents launched a campaign to get them out and into what they (the parents) insisted on calling a 'first proper home'. Chloe's Dad half lent, half gave them the money for a deposit on a one bedroomed ground-floor flat in Clapham, which, when they first paced it out, seemed palatial. To Chloe and Nicholas's surprise, they found they could afford the mortgage, that they had a bit of money in their bank account, that they could buy a few things.

'D'you think we should get a futon, Nick?'

'Why?'

'As a spare bed. You know, they fold out. For over there by the window.'

'Do you think we should?'

'I don't know.'

'Do you *want* one?'

'No.'

'Well, let's not, then.'

'No, let's not. Good.'

They had no consumer vision, nor any domestic game-plan. They painted the walls white, and Nicholas put some bookshelves up, but neither of them could get very excited about decor. It depressed their parents, endlessly.

*

There seemed for ever before they had to think about children.
They talked about it, but only in a fantastical way.

'And we'll make their birthdays fucking magical,' Chloe said.
'You'll dress up as an old wizard and come in with a blackbird
on your shoulder and tell them stories.'

'They'll be playing Nintendo,' Nicholas said.

'Shut up. They won't. They'll be lovely dark urchins, and
they'll love books.'

Nicholas exemplified the young male attitude to children. He
was certain that if he *never* had them there would be deathbed
regrets; on the other hand, the thought of *having* them – really
waking up and finding himself there, *responsible* for them –
was completely repugnant to him. He envied Chloe. For her,
pregnancy and motherhood offered itself as a giant psycho-
physical metamorphosis, a transformative rite that would (at
the very least) realize her biological potential. He imagined
children centring Chloe in her world. He further imagined them
displacing himself in it. The thought of a puckered baby with
dimpled knuckles and yellowish cradle cap sucking milk out of
Chloe's breast made him feel queasy. He had visions of himself
grabbing the newborn by its heels and dashing its brains out
against a wall.

In any case, it all seemed a long way off.

Chloe wasn't sure what level of fear about childbirth was
appropriate, but whatever level *was* appropriate, she was convinced her own exceeded it. She had been in the delivery room
(with her Mum – *not* with Liz's husband, who had remained
outside the hospital's main doors, smoking, feebly) for the birth
of Liz's second child, Christopher. It had both fascinated and
horrified her. Liz's face had moved beyond recognition in the
last stages of labour, as if its muscles were struggling to create a
different identity, one which would be spared the pain. Chloe
had held her sister's left hand – but had to disengage two or
three times because she'd felt her bones being crushed. She
hadn't wanted to, but had been compelled to look between Liz's
legs. An hour before Christopher had been successfully delivered, Liz had dilated to what looked to Chloe an impossible set

of dimensions – but no one, neither doctor nor nurses nor Chloe's mother, seemed alarmed. It had been, simply, unbelievable to her: Liz's extraordinary ugliness when she pushed; the calm irritation of the doctor; the yawning vulva; Christopher's dark-blooded and pulpy head suddenly out in the stark light; his expression of misery and rage; the strange pathos of the cut umbilical. Chloe had been amazed at her mother's composure, the ease with which she had uttered her litany of dumb comfort: 'Come on now, my darling . . . That's it, that's my clever girl . . . Come on now, my angel . . . One more now . . .' Afterwards – almost *immediately* afterwards – Liz had seemed to Chloe to shrink, to close up; the face struggled back to its former alignment – but to Chloe it seemed simplified in some way, as if some giant flake of Liz's memory had dropped away, as if, already, she was forgetting the pain.

Later that night, at home in her bed, Chloe had placed her own hand around the soft hummock between her legs, as small and compact as a fig, and thought, simply: Jesus *Christ*.

Chloe wasn't passionate about her job at the museum, but she was quite content. Britain 800 BC–AD 500. It wasn't her period, particularly – she'd written her final year dissertation on the monarchy in medieval England – but even had it been her period it would hardly have mattered, since she had started as a glorified departmental secretary and had only recently got involved in the creation and textual support of actual exhibitions. Like Nicholas, she thought of her life as elsewhere (with him), so her expectations from her job were low. If she had things to do that even mildly interested her – which most of the more recent work did – she was satisfied. On the other hand, the museum provided her with her first close friend: Jane Cooper, also known as 'Bolshy Jane', from Egyptology.

It was a strange closeness, established between them as if at the arbitrary insistence of a hidden deity. They met one afternoon, unspectacularly, in the cafeteria, and discovered that they liked each other. Jane was long-boned with a hard, equine face and soft dark eyes. She had large, vampiric fingers, the tapered nails of which were always painted in predatory reds. Chloe didn't consider her mad, exactly – but there was an intensity with which Jane consumed her own mental and emotional energy that seemed self-destructive. After a while – in delighted, grumpy cahoots – they abandoned the museum at lunchtimes in favour of a small sandwich and pastry shop in Russell Square, where Chloe would stun Jane by ordering gâteaux and cappuccino after her sandwich.

'You're one of those people whose bodies never fucking change,' Jane said the first time they went there.

Chloe, fork poised, guilty, said: 'Sorry, yes, I am.'

Jane inhaled deeply through her nostrils, measuring her own tolerance.

'OK,' she said, after a few moments. 'All right.'

Chloe thought: It's all right because she thinks I've got bugger-all else going for me. Chloe wasn't sure why it didn't put her off. Possibly because she felt sorry for Jane, who had been married, and now wasn't.

'It's the lying,' Jane said, one lunchtime. 'You think it's the sex – you know, you think it's the actual disgusting image of your husband fucking someone else. It's not, though. It's the lying. It's the being reduced to an idiot because of someone else's lying.'

It was raining. Chloe was thinking of the other café, the other rain, years ago. She tried for a moment to visualize Nicholas fucking someone else. She tried to imagine herself listening to him, seeing his eyes and not knowing he was lying to her. It was impossible.

'I trust Nick,' she said. 'With my life.'

Jane looked away for a second, irritated, then back at Chloe, saying nothing.

'I can't love him if I don't trust him,' Chloe said. 'It doesn't seem like I've got a choice. I think loving him and trusting him are one and the same thing.'

Jane lit a cigarette, then sighed the smoke out through her nose. 'That's the point,' she said. 'That's what's fucked up about it. If you're going to love someone, you're going to trust them.

You're going to put the bullet in the gun yourself. A bullet with your own bloody name on it.'

She paused. Inhaled again, blew a fat, shuddering smoke-ring. 'Anyway,' she said, 'never again.'

It left Chloe moody. Every now and then the world would reopen the question of love. Every now and then she would startle awake, suddenly reminded of all that she had to lose.

'Stop,' she said to Nicholas that night.

'What?'

'Stop. Stop it.'

He held himself up off her for a moment, then withdrew and rolled over alongside her.

'What's the matter?'

'I don't know.'

'You don't know?'

'No.'

He exhaled, heavily.

'And don't do that.'

'What?'

'Act like it's the end of the fucking world.'

'For fuck's sake, Chloe.'

'For fuck's sake what?'

'What's the *matter*?'

'I don't know. I don't know. Hold me.'

She could feel the anger in every muscle of him, though she knew he was making a superhuman effort.

'Will you tell me what's wrong?' he asked her after they had been still for a few minutes.

'I really don't know,' she said. 'I'm sorry. I'm sorry. Just hold me, will you?'

She waited – the two of them breathing in the dark, saying nothing, aware of danger – until Nicholas fell asleep. Then she got up and went to the living-room.

Jane had let fear in. The fear that if love failed there would be only two options: death, or a return to what she had been before. Before Nick she had withheld herself from the world. Falling in love had thrown the hardness of her previous self into sharp relief. She was afraid of what she would become – what monstrous, inflated version of that former self would be revealed – now if love failed. She knew, with the romantic's certainty, that if love failed this time she would never embrace it again. She knew it just as she had known that she would love risking everything in the first place.

Dylan Thomas wasn't in the bathroom now. He was on a small bookcase in the kitchen. Chloe, barefoot, stood in the dark with the book unopened in her hands. She felt the collective nocturnal awareness of the kitchen's objects, watching her. On another night, long ago, she had thought to herself: It's too late to turn back, now.

She went back into the bedroom.

'Nick?'

A gap in the curtains let in an inch-wide slat of light from the street.

'Nick, wake up.'

He woke on an in-breath, as if having broken the surface of water that had been threatening to draw him under.

'Jesus Christ. Chloe? What's the matter?'

Now she held herself above him in a precise copy of his position earlier.

'Chloe?'

'Shshsh,' she said. 'Make love to me.'

They were still in love – though the love was insinuating a demand for transformation. The world, of course, had crept in. Work. Bills. *Things*. Weeks – sometimes months – would go by without them having anything like a real exchange; routine was a constant, hard, pressing shape that eroded the exquisiteness of intimacy and turned it into nothing more than the irritated need for comfort. It would dawn on Nicholas, from nowhere, that he had somehow forgotten Chloe, that they had been reduced to a set of domestic functions and habits, that she had become the worst kind of stranger: the stranger about whom there is nothing left to know. It would suddenly come to him that he had lost her, that there was nothing between them

now but reflexive dependency. Sometimes a particular conversation would throw this up at him.

'I didn't sleep very well last night.'

'Didn't you?'

'No. I've got a fucking headache now.'

'Shame, love. There's Nurofen in the bathroom cabinet.'

A horror would surge through him, as if he had just been
granted a subliminal image of his own death.

They suffered, periodically, the ache of familiarity. A morning
would come when Chloe would catch sight of Nicholas coming
out of the shower, and she would know, instantly, that she
should get away from him for a few days, unlearn him, let the
distance and her own company reconstruct him. She knew not
to ignore the intuition. It was never false. If the days accrued to
weeks or months she would find herself repelled by the sight of
his kneecaps, or nauseated by the touch of his hand in the
small of her back, or suffocated by the sound of his breath
escaping through his nostrils while he chewed his food. She felt
demonic at such times, as if she could jump up suddenly, and
lay open his skull with a plate. At these times she tasted the
closeness like oversweetened milk, sickening with goodness.

For Nicholas, too, there were times when he hated her for
having finished the shape of him so early in his life. For
revenge, he allowed himself to consider – with clinical disinterest – whether she was pretty enough. He thought of the days
when her eyes seemed dull and dead, or her breasts half empty.
He stood alone in the bathroom and whispered the possible
truths with awed relish: She's plain; I don't fancy her. She dis-
gusts me.

All somewhat nonsense – but not *complete* nonsense. It didn't
stop them loving each other, in the bigger picture, but it forced
them out of the idyll from time to time.

Still, they endured; their love retaliated. In the kitchen, in the
midst of cake-baking, Chloe had asked him to pass her another
egg. 'Throw it to me,' she had said. 'I'll catch it.'

'You'll miss it.'

'I will not. I'll catch it. Go on.'

Before he had thrown it she had stood in exaggerated readiness – then as soon as it had left his hand she had straightened up and turned away. The egg had simply sailed through the air, dropped, then exploded on the kitchen floor. These slapstick digressions were so at odds with the way the world saw her that they titillated Nicholas into a sort of drunken lechery. When the egg smashed she had looked at him, mildly surprised, and continued mixing the ingredients in her bowl. Then he remembered her, that she was magnificent. Then nothing mattered except that he had her; the whole fucking world could go to hell.

They had their measure of certainty. They were sure of each other. They would concede, intellectually (to friends), that no, one could never know or trust one's partner *a hundred per cent*. They would defer to the consensus, grinning ruefully at the dinner table, and pay lip-service to the cynics – but they would secretly consider themselves the exception.

'If your *life* depended on it,' a colleague of Nicholas's said, incredulous, insistent. 'If your actual fucking *life* depended on your wife's fidelity – would you bet your *life* on it?'

To his horror, Nicholas knew that he would, though he didn't admit it on this occasion – partly because the colleague's neck veins were already practically bursting with disbelief.

At the literary agency Nicholas had begun representing clients of his own. Anthony Caswell-Brooks became a director (the youngest in the place's history, apparently), and he and Nicholas became odd friends. Odd, because Nicholas couldn't decide whether Anthony – good-looking, unmarried, viciously intelligent, with a genius for casual wear – was truly, unselfconsciously cynical, or whether he adopted the pose as an apology for making the sort of money he made.

'I just sold *The White Places*,' Nicholas told Anthony in the pub after work. 'Faber bought it for eight and a half.'

'Not that piece of crap about the guy who's obsessed with bathrooms?'

'It's not a piece of crap, you moron, and he's not obsessed with bathrooms.'

'Bloody pages and pages about "the bowl's long yawn of abuse . . ."'

'But you remembered it,' Nicholas said. 'It's got resonance.'

'I know all the lyrics to the first five David Bowie albums too,' Anthony countered. 'You're not going to make any money flogging that small-but-perfectly-formed drivel.'

Anthony mystified Nicholas. The sexism, the cynicism, the clipped pitch, the refusal to flinch at anything was turned on and off like a comedy routine. It was a persona he was attached to in the way a ventriloquist might be neurotically attached to his dummy. That same evening, several drinks later, he had said to Nicholas: 'Nobody cares about ordinary human novels any more, you know. Publishing's turning into an imperative to discover definitive mutation and deviance narratives. The definitive anorexia novel. The definitive E novel. The definitive coprophilia novel. Claustrophobic little closets we can have a quick poke around in and . . . Sorry. No point in going on about it. Specially since I'm one of the fucking villains.'

Nicholas wasn't bad at his job. He had an eye for exactly the sort of small-but-perfectly-formed drivel that Anthony pretended to deride. It was true he wasn't going to make money – not Anthony's kind of money – but he didn't care. As long as he and Chloe earned enough to keep their flat, decent clothes and a few agreed luxuries, they considered it a waste of energy to work any harder. Their life was elsewhere.

They believed in the importance of humble rituals. On Sunday mornings Nicholas would go and make breakfast and bring it back to bed for them on a tray. After they had eaten it, Chloe would read the Sunday papers, always in the same way: lying on her front with her chin in the heel of one hand, occasionally moving her shins up and down through the air. She would read bits to Nicholas, who would be lying on his side at ninety degrees to her, with his cheek resting in the small of her back, just above the curve of her bum. He could lie like this for hours; his eyes and hands never tired of the line and smoothness of her buttocks and thighs, stretching down the bed away from him.

Often, he'd get an aching hard-on and be forced to start caressing her less ambiguously, in which case she might respond, but more usually would break off from what she was reading and just say: 'Oi,' very quietly. If the latter, Nicholas would exhale heavily, and wait to try again later.

'Someone survived for fifteen hours buried in an avalanche,' Chloe said. 'Cher's won worst-dressed woman of the year . . . That football bloke's going to do four years for tax evasion . . . Oh, God, they've found another woman's body. Third one. *Fucking* hell. The new London Ripper, he is now. Oh Christ, Nick, she was nineteen.'

Chloe stopped reading. Nicholas said nothing. Beyond the ugliness such stories brought into their view was the tacitly pondered question (tacitly pondered by Chloe; sensed in her by Nicholas) of how much Nicholas had in common with violent rapist-murderers merely by virtue of sharing their gender. Nicholas had discussed this with Anthony Caswell-Brooks on one of the not infrequent occasions when Anthony had startled Nicholas by suddenly appearing at his desk and commanding him to join him in the pub for the last hour of the working day.

'All men are potential rapists,' Anthony had declared when Nicholas had brought the subject up over a pint of Boddington's. 'Point-of-view exercise. Try it.'

'What do you mean?' Nicholas had asked.

'Next time you read a rape case in a newspaper, or hear one on the news, ask yourself whose point of view the narrative gave you. Always the rapist. Blokes. Always the rapist. Even if all the details are about the victim – where she lived, how old she was, whether she was blonde or brunette, what she was wearing, what route home she was taking – even if the facts you're actually given in the story relate to the victim, you piece those facts together from the rapist's point of view. It's his heart you feel beating in your chest. Never the victim's, if you're a bloke. Point of view, mate. Try it. 'S why men can't fucking write about rape except in distastefully titillating ways: cos they've all got it in them.'

'They'll get him,' Nicholas said to Chloe. (*Men* will get him, he'd wanted to add. Because they'll be able to *think* like him.)

The room was golden with sunlight, the bed a nucleus of almost obscene comfort. But Nicholas could feel the deflation in her; he could sense the misery in her spine under his cheek.

'They might not,' Chloe said. 'Why do we assume they'll get him? There are plenty they *don't* get. It's just that we don't hear about the ones that get away. Did you remember those other two girls? I mean, you remember them *now*, because they've been brought back to your attention. But until this newspaper today, you'd forgotten all about them. And you probably assumed . . . well, that they got him, whoever he was. But look: they *didn't* get him. There's probably hundreds they don't get. We just don't hear about them.'

Over the three years of his marriage, Nicholas had been sharpening his ability to recognize the times when remaining silent was the best course of action. This was one such time. He lay very still. This moment wasn't helped by the two of them lying naked together. It wasn't helped, either, he knew somewhere at the pit of his gut, by their shared sense that this conversation would distantly – oh, very distantly – turn out to be related to that inscrutable ghost that hovered between them when they fucked.

Minutes passed in silence. The heat from their sunlit bodies throbbed. Chloe had stopped turning the pages.

Very gently, Nicholas peeled himself away from her and went over to the window. The bedroom looked out on to a tiny square garden of bright green grass with a thin border of crocuses. One blackbird stood absolutely still and open-eyed in the centre of the lawn, as if hypnotized. Nicholas could see its glossy breast pulsating. In his imagination, the garden squared itself in size repeatedly; within seconds it was a thing without visible boundaries, himself here at the window, Chloe somewhere beyond the horizon.

The bed twanged and groaned slightly as Chloe got up. 'I'm going to run a bath,' she said.

◆

'Oi!' Lancelot shouted, pounding on the bathroom door. 'Oi! You dead in there, sunshine, or what?'

Time had passed – that was obvious – but Nicholas wasn't sure if he had slept. He couldn't keep track of whether or when he slept. It was more that time passed. It was more that other people's behaviour indicated that time had passed – as Lancelot's pounding on the door did now. To Nicholas it seemed only a second or two ago that he had come into the bathroom to pee.

'*Karm* on,' Lancelot said, in pain. 'You stay in there any longer and I'm going to dial nine-one-one. Actually, you stay in there any longer and *I'm* going to fucking need nine-one-one. Come on!'

Nicholas uncurled from beneath the sink. He had been folded in on himself under there. His body felt like a fist being unclenched slowly. He remembered coming into the bathroom. He had stood over the toilet and unzipped his trousers – but at that moment had seen the hollow space under the sink, and had been drawn to it as if it offered a doorway to an alternative universe. He remembered the feeling of relief when he found that the space could contain him, if he doubled up. But perhaps he hadn't peed when he'd intended to – because now there was a cold wet stain in the front of his pants. He got up and observed the bathroom's details as if seeing them for the first time: furred tub, bare bulb, dull white tiles. One step took you across the entire floor. It smelled, faintly, of vomit – and more immediately of ruthless disinfectant. Nicholas's body was sour inside from the drink. His stomach housed a small meteorite, the heat from which was corroding him from the inside out. He opened the door.

'Well for fuck's *sake*,' Lancelot said, rushing past him, pushing him out and closing the door behind him all in one move. 'Christ on a *bike*. My fucking bladder's bursting.'

Lancelot's apartment. One small living-room with a roachy kitchen in a corner. One small bedroom. One bathroom. It looked like a team of furious poltergeists had stormed through it. Cupboards and drawers were open, with their contents partly disgorged. Empty glass bottles – brown, clear, green, blue – were everywhere. Clothes, cushions, shoes, coins, old newspapers, plastic bags. The living-room was close and murky, reeking of the male life lived alone, a smell with a weight to it. Every breath Lancelot had breathed in here was present in a stale, tangible ether. The light was a bloody amber, except where a gap in the curtains let in a sliver of blue-white brilliance, bounced from the snow outside. Furnishings were by default; every item in the room had known happier times elsewhere, from the thin-legged dining-table to the stopped wall-clock in its red plastic frame. The couch, too, was on short, frail legs. Nicholas imagined it splintering like kindling the moment Lancelot dropped down on to it.

He had taken some of this in last night, drunk, watching Lancelot fumbling around the living-room purposelessly. Then, when Lancelot had finished, Nicholas had gone into the bath-room to pee.

Now here was a new block of time.

'You don't ask any questions,' Lancelot said, an hour later, when the two of them sat with cups of tea. 'You on the lam?'

Nicholas didn't understand.

'On the run,' Lancelot said. 'Fugitive, in deep shite . . .'

The swarm in Nicholas's chest stirred slightly. 'I ran away,' he said. 'I couldn't . . . everything . . .' but the cloud hummed under his ribs; he was afraid to open his mouth in case they began spiralling out into the room. He covered his lips with the palm of his hand, then found himself crossing the floor (which now canted at an angle of thirty degrees) towards the bath-room, knowing suddenly that he was going to vomit.

'What the—?' Lancelot said. 'You all right?'

Nicholas missed the door and slammed into the wall on his first attempt; the doorframe cracked sharp against his bowed head, making him stagger two steps backwards. Then the floor pitched again and rolled him into the bathroom. He fell to his knees and grabbed the outer rim of the toilet bowl with both hands.

Lancelot came behind him and stood, maternally, with his hands on his hips. 'Oh dear oh dear oh dear oh *dear*,' he said. 'Go on, get it all up. They open in an hour.'

◆

'I've got Nina Cole in reception,' the receptionist said.

Nicholas remembered, and his heart sank. For the last two weeks he had been interviewing candidates for his old job. He had resisted even *having* an assistant, but it had gone beyond a joke: with the expanding list of clients, he had less time to look at new material, though that was still his favourite part of the work, and things were starting to overwhelm him. He had realized, with dread, that he needed a dreck filter.

'Come on, you'll love it,' Anthony had teased him. 'Get some hungry little tart with a two-two from Oxford Poly. Make her your protégée.'

'*You* didn't,' Nicholas had said. 'You got me.'

Anthony had winced. 'I know. Christ knows what I was thinking. I must have been impressed by your don't-really-give-a-fuck posture.'

'I really *didn't* give a fuck. It wasn't a posture.'

'Come on,' Anthony had said. 'How hard can it be? She's only got to be able to *read*.'

Nicholas had already interviewed four candidates. Two of them had been Anthony's ideal, the other two had been earnest, terrified young men with Firsts, not quite sure what to do in the world, having thus far done everything the world had expected of them.

'Just ask yourself if you could stand seeing them every morning at nine-thirty,' Chloe had said. 'Just give the job to someone you think you'd at least *like*.'

But he hadn't much liked any of the people he'd seen – certainly not enough to want to be confronted with them at nine-thirty every morning.

And now here was Nina Whatsername, whose existence he had completely forgotten until Kate buzzed him and told him she was waiting in reception.

'Thanks, Kate,' he said. 'I'll come and get her.'

It was a warm Friday afternoon in the first days of summer. A swirling blue genie of cigarette smoke had leaked out of the staff room and now hung, suspended and mysterious, in the open-plan part of the office. (Much to his delight, Nicholas had Anthony's old office, which looked out into Piccadilly's sluggish whirlpool of traffic.) The agency was sleepy; some of the women had their shoes off. A work experience lackey sat in his chair in a shaft of sunlight, his hands clasped behind his head, and stared into space as if he had lost all hope. Everyone was gradually yielding to the seduction of the approaching weekend.

Nicholas was tired. When he had married Chloe he had done so with an intimation that he was moving closer to the possession of a core of happiness, a quiet centre of internal peace which could be referred back to, ultimately, when the world threw its irritants at him. But still, walking from his office to reception, feeling his bones not quite at ease with each other, he felt uncertain, unarrived. His life up until Chloe had been searching for its shape, then he had met her and the shape had been realized. None the less there remained an ethereal horror: that there endured strange spaces of blank potential, that he was more than his life had given him. The part of himself that recognized such spaces was as cold and innocent as a corpse.

The agency's reception area had two vulgar leather couches, but Nina Cole wasn't sitting in either of them. She was standing with her back to him, looking out of the window, framed by the afternoon's bleached light.

'Crap, mostly. Escapist rubbish, when I do at all. Mostly I rent videos.'

'When you *used* to, then,' Nicholas said.

'Back in the days,' she said, with pain that had been force-sculpted into grim hilarity. 'Oh, all the good stuff. Lawrence. George Eliot. Rilke. *Shakespeare*, believe it or not. At Bristol I read everything I was supposed to and pretty much everything else. It's a miracle I'm not blind.'

'Contemporary writers?' Nicholas asked her, thinking of Anthony Caswell-Brooks, who had told him that contemporary writers were just dead writers who hadn't died yet.

'Well, not many, these days. There are a few novels I've liked, I suppose, though I can hardly remember them. *The Bone People*. The Norman Mailer Egyptian one. Stuff with a bit of gusto. None of that magical-realism guff. Anyway, isn't it the idea that contemporary writing isn't about writing, it's about publishing?'

However much he had been discomfited by the prospect of this interview, Nicholas had at least assumed he would be able to conduct it by rote. Are you computer-literate? Can you speak any other languages? Does the prospect of fairly lowly clerical tasks quite a lot of the time bother you? Now here was this woman. He had thought at first that she was drunk. Then he had thought she was mentally ill. Finally he had decided that she was neither; she just didn't care what he thought about her. She refused to make any effort. Had she been unattractive, he would simply have brought the interview to an early conclusion.

'It seems pretty straightforward,' she said. 'You need someone with a brain and a critical reading ability to make sure that the wheat's separated from the chaff. No-hopers in the bin, promising stuff on your desk. And you need someone who doesn't mind typing out rejection letters and photocopying typescripts and keeping your appointments book, and God knows what else. But the bottom line is, you need someone who isn't going to get on your *nerves*. You and I both know that I'm rabidly overqualified for this sort of thing, but at the same time I find myself broke and unemployed and utterly directionless. I'm not terribly punctual, and I'll probably call in sick every now and then when there's nothing wrong with me except that like everyone else on the planet I have mornings when just the thought of peeling the duvet off fills me with existential agony. On the other hand, I can certainly do this job as well as anyone else and I can promise you'll never be bored.'

The great betrayal inherent in literature, Nicholas believed, was that it made people seem more interesting than they were in real life. He had never met anyone as alive as Ursula Brangwen or as gloriously wrecked as Heathcliff. No teenager in the world was as likable as Holden Caulfield, no villain as irresistible as Iago. Reading great books, encountering characters who were vibrant and complex, persuaded him to greet the world's actual inhabitants with a renewed openness and a fresh curiosity – only to be disappointed, every time. It was the terrible curse readers lived with, that art held out this dream of possible life – of consciousness as a gripping narrative, of individuals as epic and violent forces – but actual life undermined it. In comparison to literature, life was boring. Great literature was an unsettling revelation; life was just mediocre prose. Exceptions were few and far between.

Fifteen minutes into the interview he knew that life was presenting him with an exception now, in the shape of Nina Cole.

He had his love for Chloe. They had their unarticulated epiphanies. He still thought of her as morally exempt. It was still true that she could murder someone and he wouldn't care, because she was his. But Chloe wasn't *going* to murder anyone. They still operated, by and large, within a matrix of convention. Perhaps that fact was what gave licence to the romantic in Nicholas in the first place. Sitting now in his office, it occurred to him that Nina Cole might well have *already* murdered a dozen people. She might have their heads at home in her fridge. It further struck him that her sense of moral exemption was derived from her own soul; *she* didn't need his allegiance or anyone else's. She would live and do her will and be beyond all judgement because she was her own final judge. She would be impassive in the dock, deaf to the prosecutor's crafted outrage. She would sigh with boredom when it was pointed out that she showed no remorse. She would look at her watch and wish they would get on with beheading her or whatever it was they were going to do. He thought, too, of the distance between himself and Chloe, of her face turned away when she came. It was fear that turned her away from him, he knew, cloudily. He also knew (again cloudily) that Nina Cole would never look away. She would sense it, whatever it was, his penned corruption, and stare straight into his eyes, at worst merely curious, at best radiant with intuition.

All of this while the bulk of his consciousness went on in the familiar ways: there is no way on earth I'm giving her the job. She's fucked up. An alcoholic. Damaged. Chloe would hate her. Appointments diary? Christ, it's a miracle if this woman bothers to put her shoes on before walking out of the house. No wonder she's unemployed and broke.

'Well?' said Nina Cole.

'Madder than Rochester's wife,' Nicholas said.

Chloe sat opposite him later that evening in Difalco's, an Italian restaurant in South Kensington. They went there occasionally, whenever they felt entitled to luxury. Nicholas felt the first seduction of the evening's wine in his belly and chest, though as yet it had failed to dissolve the week's gathered tension.

'But capable?' Chloe said.

'Capable of murder. She's a sort of stream-of-consciousness phenomenon. Either a complete lack of dissemblance, or a complete indifference to what anyone might think of her.'

'You're going to give her the job.'

'I am *not* going to give her the job.'

'Sounds like you wouldn't be bored at least. Sounds like she's *real*, if nothing else.'

'I wouldn't be bored with Hannibal Lecter, either,' Nicholas said. 'I'm sure the Marquis de Sade was *real*.'

The waiter came with their food: chicken and spinach fettuccine for Chloe, salmon tagliatelle for Nicholas. He downed three-quarters of his glass of house red in a long swallow.

'Christ, Nick,' Chloe said. 'Try *tasting* it. It's only eight o'clock.'

'Sorry,' he said. 'I'm not interested in the taste tonight. I'm interested in the effect.'

Chloe raised her eyebrows. 'Fair enough,' she said, and swallowed her own drink in one. 'Refill, then, if that's the way you feel about it. I could do with getting smashed myself. It's been National Pain in the Arse Day at the museum today.'

Difalco's didn't work for Nicholas. He tried. The food was good, and the wine completed its blood seduction. But there was some fragment of bored selfhood lodged in his soul.

Chloe had dressed up a bit: a soft grey woollen dress and a choker of tiny amber stones that made her throat white and vulnerable. She still seldom wore make-up, but tonight the eyes and lips were dark and vampy. Ornamentation made her uncomfortable with herself, Nicholas knew – but he knew too that she knew he liked it, and sometimes surprised him by mischievously embracing its power. Usually, the lust that Chloe's surrender to sexy clothes and make-up inspired was fractured in him by a sense of guilt that she was only really doing it to please him. His desire was always undermined by tenderness, by his understanding that she was silencing something in herself purely for his sake. It was undermined further because Chloe wasn't pretty enough to fully carry it off. Tonight, though, the lust was pure. He found himself – drunk, forcing down the regulation cappuccino – simply wanting her because she was female. He wanted her, bullishly, for the accumulated force of the feminine tokens, and he was contemptuous of himself for it; he was contemptuous of Chloe, too, for making it possible. Most of all, he was contemptuous of sheer reality as well, for reminding him at odd, banal angles of time that nothing, *nothing* was enough.

So he drank on after the coffee, and Chloe followed him. Something of his destructiveness had communicated itself to her, and she was afraid. She knew he wanted to fuck her. She knew *how* he wanted to fuck her, too – without feeling, or with a smear of hatred. That in itself was no disaster. Sometimes she wanted to be fucked in that way. But very rarely. *Very* rarely. Not tonight. So she followed him drink by drink into awkwardness, hoping enough alcohol would take the edge off both of them, knowing it wouldn't.

'Is she attractive?'

'Who?'

'Rochester's wife.'

Hesitating, Nicholas knew there was only one, excruciatingly difficult to calculate amount of hesitation that was appropriate. He knew he'd missed it.

'Not particularly,' he said.

'Well she's obviously gorgeous,' Chloe said, smiling.

'Why obviously?'

'How long you had to think about it.'

'Christ, Holmes, that's brilliant. How do you do it?'

'Well *isn't* she?'

Lies lay around Nicholas like gems – so many that he didn't know which to reach out for and snatch.

'Look, if she's fucking Aphrodite why not just go ahead and say so?' Chloe said. The lightness – what there had been of it – was draining away quickly.

'What's the matter with you?' Nicholas said. A part of him really did wonder if there was something *else* the matter.

'Nothing's the matter,' Chloe said, brightly. 'It's just that you'd come out of this so much better if you stopped dithering and admitted that she was . . . you know . . .'

'What?'

'Attractive. *Very* attractive. Gorgeous. A sex-kitten. A fucking bombshell. Whatever it is you all want.'

With a last, superhuman effort, Nicholas hauled his love for Chloe back into his chest. 'Listen. She's *quite* attractive. That's all. Not a bombshell. Not a head turner. Not a *stunna*. She's *all right*. Quite nice. That's all. Her skin's a bit greasy, if you want the truth. She's a bit thick in the hips and I suspect she's got slightly banana-ish breasts. OK? I mean you're missing the point, somewhat. The point is I think she's *mad*.'

'Would you sleep with her?'

'What do you mean?'

'You know what I mean.'

'You mean if I wasn't married to you? You mean if she was available and I was free and she was up for it? You mean if she wasn't mad?'

'Yeah. That's exactly what I mean. Is she attractive enough for that.'

Chloe's cheeks and chin had reddened from the wine. Her eyes looked sleepy. It still wasn't settled between them that this was a fight. Part of it was still just painful play.

'I don't know,' Nicholas said. 'It would depend on whether she had banana-ish breasts.'

For a minute Chloe looked at him without saying anything, working through the degrees of need for proper conflict. Then she, too, drawing on some reservoir of stored love (and sensing, with the undrunk part of herself, that she was afraid of something huge in all this), decided to leave it.

'Get the bill, wicked creature,' she said, rising, unsteadily. 'Then get a bloody taxi and take me home. If you're especially nice to me on the way I *might* consider letting you have it off with me.'

They were drunk enough to be rough and cold. Nicholas grabbed Chloe the minute they were inside their hallway. There was a small shelf for the telephone and a few uncared-for ornaments; Chloe put her elbows on it and arched her back, sticking her arse out towards him. Hating her, hating the potential she left unrealized, the spaces she left empty, he yanked her knickers down and went into her as quickly and violently as he could. It wasn't anywhere near enough, though he heard her cry out, shocked. She almost turned and slapped him. She did half turn, her forearm accidentally swiping a small ceramic jar from the shelf, then stopped when she heard it hit the floor and softly burst.

They exchanged not a word. Instead the hall was filled with the muffled argument of breath – indrawn in hisses, expelled in gasps – and the small sounds of unspoken combat. Their love rested between them at this moment like a giant irritant. There weren't words enough in Nicholas; no outpouring of obscenity would be sufficient expression of this great rage and boredom and desire. He could see beyond it, too, to where he loved Chloe in the old, deep, timeless way. With even a slight effort he knew he could shift into love. But he resisted, knowing that to sidestep this violence would be a betrayal – though a betrayal of *whom* he didn't know.

Chloe returned his hate, but only because she was afraid. She was afraid of what would happen if she met it with love. She believed, in fact (even as she felt his fingernails digging at her breasts), that it was only through this that they could return to love – to a newly delineated love, a love that could contain this. She rose up against him like a snake. He grabbed her hair and forced her head around to look at him. She knew that he wanted her to see him hating her. With a great effort she withstood it. With a great effort she summoned her own loathing to meet him. But it wasn't whole, and he could tell. He could see her adopting this posture because she knew it was the perverse route to survival, and even though he knew she was right, it disgusted him further. He thought of his father's question on the day of the wedding: Do you love her, son? Truly love her?

He pulled out of her cunt and brought his hands down to her backside, pulling the cheeks apart. She twitched, seemed about to straighten and pull away from him. He reached up again and held her neck, felt her yield, not wanting this, merely knowing that this violence was necessary; he felt all of it in her.

Yes, Dad, I truly love her.

He didn't think of Nina Cole. He jammed his cock into Chloe's arse and felt her body's reflex retreat, all the muscles pulling away from him. But he held her. Now she wouldn't look at him. Now each of them was alone. Now both of them were subservient to whatever was demanding this from them. Chloe held on to the sense that love – something – was visible beyond this, but she held on to it alone, desperately, knowing that now (the rhythm established, silence winding itself tighter around

them) they were mutually occult, that her holding on was an
act of faith or fiat.

He came. She didn't, though he tried to make her, nagging
her clit until she couldn't stand it any more and tore his hand
away. They slid apart, said nothing to each other. They were
frightened to turn on a light. Fucking had inflicted a fierce
sobriety. Now their blood was leaden with alcohol again. Chloe
felt almost destroyed, but she knew she had been right, that
love was possible now – or soon, at any rate. None the less her
body was traumatized. She stepped out of her knickers, left
them on the floor in the hall. She was dehydrated. Looking
back from the kitchen doorway she saw Nicholas on his knees
in the dark, his head leaning against the wall. She knew to say
nothing. She moved softly across the kitchen floor to the sink,
where, after a minute of staring out of the window into the
night, she poured herself a pint of cold London tap-water and
began to drink.

◆

Rain came and began the gradual destruction of the snow.
Nicholas hadn't slept for seventy hours. It was as if an electrical
force was keeping his eyes open. There was a continuous pain
behind his upper eyelids; his temples throbbed. Hallucinations
blossomed and faded: a beer mat detonated its atoms like a firework; Marty's hand had dark, flickering wings; a small reptilian
creature with a serrated spine scurried across the sidewalk on
the way back to Lancelot's apartment; the rain mewled and
flashed colours. Melting snow moved in slithering chunks
through the waterlogged gutters. Street intersections were
miniature lagoons.

The downpour crucified Lancelot, who still scorned an overcoat or an umbrella. By the time he and Nicholas got indoors
they were heavy and freezing with rain.

'Have a shower if you want,' Lancelot said. 'I'll put the kettle on. 'Bout time you changed your clothes, if you don't mind my saying so.'

The water hurt. Nicholas forced his face and scalp under it and felt his skin's ache of neglect. He didn't recognize his own smell. For half an hour he became preoccupied with the dirt under his fingernails, which he removed, meticulously. A large sty had formed under his left lower eyelid. He let the water drum against it.

Lancelot was lying on the floor with one arm twisted under him when Nicholas emerged from the bathroom. For a moment, Nicholas thought he had passed out, but then saw that Lancelot's eyes were open, and that there was a small thick pancake of dark mucus on the carpet next to his mouth. The mouth itself was moving.

'Pills,' Lancelot whispered. 'Bathroom . . .'

For a moment Nicholas was paralysed by the clarity of fear in Lancelot's face: the wet-lipped, quivering mouth; the torn-open eyes; the grey, porous cheeks and glittering beard. Then he straightened and went back into the brilliantly lit bathroom. There was only one small plastic pill bottle in the medicine cabinet. Digoxin. That and a rusty, bladeless Gillette razor.

It was a moment of purity between them, looking at each other: Nicholas depositing the tiny pill in Lancelot's mossed mouth; Lancelot holding on to time, shaking; Nicholas calm and disinterested; Lancelot's eyes seeming to search for his own history, a perplexed attempt to connect everything in the past to this moment.

The minutes that followed were a disappointment, as if for an instant life had revealed a beautiful intensity, then withdrawn it again. Lancelot's steadied breathing and slowly blinking eyes were a betrayal of the urgency his body had expressed only seconds before.

'Doctor?' Nicholas asked, quietly.

Lancelot shook his head.

◆

'The problem is that life irritates me.'

'I see,' Nicholas said.

'But the irritation makes me fuck things up. My own things. Other people's. And I don't *like* people.'

'The majority, I'll grant—'

'All of them. Paradise is the world swept clean of people. Just trees and animals.'

'And you.'

'No,' Nina Cole said. 'Definitely not me.'

Nicholas had started having a drink after work with her – always with Anthony as chaperon. But tonight Anthony had been called away at the last minute. Nicholas was febrile and afraid. Nina had been at the agency for six weeks. He had spent every day in fear of her. He was terrified of her because, when she decided to, she could look at him in a way which disregarded every strand in the weave of lies that allowed them to function close to each other without cataclysm. She could look at him and force him to see what was there between them. To Nicholas, she seemed consummately in control. She would go days without doing any damage; then, without warning, would find a moment to confront him with silence. Without doing anything identifiable, she would reveal herself, her intention, the strength of her will.

He knew she had to go. But the days had stretched into weeks, and now it was her second month.

'I saw your wife, yesterday,' she said, now. They sat at a corner table in the Wheatsheaf, Nicholas with a pint of Guinness, Nina with a vodka and tonic.

'Did you?'

'She met you in the lobby downstairs. I watched the two of you walk up towards Eros.'

Nicholas, with raised eyebrows, lit a cigarette. His hands were shaking. The pub was filling up with the office crowd. Suits, briefcases, smoke, high heels and navy-blue skirts, London breath and cracked make-up.

'She's not very attractive,' Nina said, looking directly at Nicholas, who immediately glanced down into his pint. 'Plain, in fact,' she added, unsmiling.

'Not to me,' Nicholas said. It was a struggle to get any words out at all. He realized, too, that even answering her had been a collusion. He realized that anything other than getting up and leaving implicated him. Meanwhile, there was a reservoir of certainty that he wouldn't betray Chloe. There was a great store of love for her, which he knew he could call on. It was to be used frugally, like a miraculous cordial.

'You don't think I should talk to you like that?' Nina said, not releasing him.

Nicholas was paralysed. What could he say? The time to object had been immediately after she'd said that Chloe wasn't attractive. But he hadn't objected. Now the genie was loose.

'I wonder why you feel the *need* to talk to me like that,' he said.

'What are you? A psychiatrist?'

He inhaled from his cigarette, twisted his mouth to exhale so that the smoke would bypass her. 'No,' he said. 'But your opinion of my wife's merits isn't something I'm desperate to hear.' A part of him was outraged that she dared; another part worshipful of her contempt for pretence of any kind.

She raised her glass and took a sip. The noise in the pub had increased. A fruit machine in the corner whooped electronically and spat out three one-pound coins as if clearing its throat.

'I'm curious to see how long you'll go on like this,' she said.

'Like what?'

'Knowing it's there and hoping it isn't. Because it's too much for you. Because you daren't.'

A pause. Nicholas was thinking of Chloe's scar, of how sometimes, even after all these years, she flinched when he touched it. Habit offered him the image of the eight-year-old in the snow, but he resisted it; he wasn't ready if it didn't work.

Nina, leaning forward slightly, said: 'At least you're not going, "What on earth do you mean by that?" or "I haven't the faintest blah blah blah." I thought you might. Truth is you're tired of talking in that way. *Ergo* me. In your office. I'm ready for another, by the way.'

Then she would leave him alone for a while. Days, a couple of weeks. Speak to him only when it was absolutely necessary. She would leave it just long enough so that Nicholas himself began to look to her for something, some confirmation that his memory wasn't deceiving him, that there had, in fact, been some recognition of each other. Then, like the night in the Wheatsheaf, she *would* confirm it, brutally, sending him into retreat.

She had short, straight, forward-cut auburn hair and a thin mouth. Narrow green eyes and black eyelashes. Her breasts were not, as Nicholas had speculated, banana-ish, but small, hard and pleased with themselves. Her body's great triumph (which she knew) was the high, full backside and long legs, which virtually any skirt or trousers flattered.

'It's not that it's a mouth-watering arse,' Anthony said to Nicholas. 'It's that she *knows* it's a mouth-watering arse.'

'That's projection,' Nicholas said. 'It's not that she knows, it's that she's more desirable to you if you suppose that she does know. Has anything actually matured in your sexual imagination since you were fourteen?'

'No,' Anthony said. 'Should it have?'

It helped Nicholas, the nice-arse banter with Anthony. Through it he could delude himself into reading the whole thing as a mere sexual attraction.

After the night of Difalco's a quiet came between Nicholas and Chloe, like a city after a great fire. Somewhere distant was the giant, delicate, enduring edifice of their shared history. They were aware of it, revealed at moments in certain shifts of light. But Nicholas had forced a truth: that they weren't everything to each other, that there were spaces like unwalked streets.

They were mysteriously tender with each other. The violence of imperfection had been revealed to them and they had been laid low by it. Over the months that followed they evolved a mode of being together which tacitly accepted their ability to destroy each other.

Chloe let her old version of their love go; her imagination was subtler than Nicholas's. Nicholas clung, secretly, to bitterness because their separateness couldn't now be undone. She, after the initial pain, was willing to go forward with him. He couldn't wholly accept that the old way had failed. He saw the new spaces around him in his life and cringed. He was afraid of what he would discover about himself if he moved into them.

Nina Cole existed in such spaces. Nicholas knew that she had never entertained the old version of love – or that, if she had, she had sloughed it long ago. He imagined her crossing streets with her eyes closed, merely curious about whether today would be the day she died. Put a breadknife in her hand and she would consider (with a neutral, aesthetic curiosity) sticking it into your throat. Or her own. That would be the way with her. He didn't know where her indifference came from. Some early, devastating betrayal, he supposed. Whatever the origin of her current psyche, its effect was clear. She observed no rules. She dared life to annihilate her. So far it had not.

'You've got the marriage shadow,' she said to him, one afternoon in his office. He had just put the phone down after a conversation with one of his least favourite publishers (who had dully, acidly turned down a first novel Nicholas was trying to place); Nina, who had come in to hand him faxes, stood by the window with her back to the light.

'Not the time, I'm afraid,' he said.

'It's under the eyes. It mutes them, takes the edge off. Because that's what marriage does, takes the edge off.'

'Some days, Nina, it's charming eccentricity. Today it's not. Please leave me alone.' He had intended it to sound light-heartedly long-suffering, but it had come out dark.

She waited a few seconds, then came and stood behind his chair and put her hands on his shoulders. It was the first time she had ever touched him. Her hands smelled of apricot hand cream. He had a rapidly blossoming image of himself leaping up from under her touch, rounding on her and delivering a demonic denunciation, loud enough for the entire agency to overhear. It was cinematically clear, this image.

Instead, as the air took on the weight of water, he sat staring at her warped reflection in the sunlit screen of his computer. She said nothing, just very lightly squeezed the base of his neck, once, twice, three times. Then drew her hand against his cheek and jaw, cupped her palm over his mouth. He thought of saying: Yes, there's excitement, but it's a hackneyed excitement, and far outweighed by sadness. He thought of saying it, as Nina released his mouth and drew the tips of her fingers across his lips.

The phone rang. He didn't move. Nina backed away, walked out, closed the door behind her. Nicholas stared at the phone knowing it would be his young author whose novel had just been sourly turned down. He let his voicemail pick the call up.

At the end of August Nicholas and Chloe went to Turkey on holiday. Not because they had a passion for that country, but because it was what they could get and what they could afford. They bought a cheap flight to Dalaman and took a bus west to a village called Patara.

('I want to go away, Nick,' Chloe had said. 'I can't take fucking London all summer. Let's for God's sake go and lie on a beach somewhere. Somewhere old. Let's go at the end of the season, after everybody else's already passed through.')

So to Patara, where everybody else *had* already passed through. The place was practically deserted. They sensed the Turks struggling awake for them, barely remembering to double their prices on cigarettes and drinks.

They took a room at a small family-run hotel at the dusty centre of town. Breakfasts were giant black olives and vivid red tomatoes, cheese, live yogurt, oranges; and in the evenings spiced meat and rice. Even as victims of the double economy they found it hilariously cheap. After the first two days they relaxed into the place. Very soon they settled into its rhythm of heat.

They spent time apart. Chloe would leave after breakfast
with her minimal beach paraphernalia: straw hat, sun cream,
towel, sunglasses, *I, Claudius*. Nicholas would 'potter around
the village', which in reality meant that he would select one of
the dozen bars and sit in a shaded corner reading out of date
copies of the English newspapers. They'd meet in the afternoon
for a nap, then showers before dinner and what was left of the
night on their hotel balcony with a bottle of wine.

It hadn't been that Chloe couldn't stand London, Nicholas
knew. It was that she couldn't stand the two of them *in* London.
He knew she was following her intuition that a new context
would relieve them of their guardedness and allow them to be
candid with each other. She didn't want the old love back. She
just wanted an acknowledgement that they could move on from
it and yet be together. Her instinct was to remind them both
that the world was large, that accepting imperfection didn't
entail losing each other. At home it had been impossible.

Because while there had been no outer dialogue between
them since the night of Difalco's, they both knew that something had changed.

Chloe didn't suspect Nina Cole. She had assumed that the
argument in Difalco's had merely made use of her, that the real
trouble was elsewhere. She wasn't afraid that Nicholas would
have an affair – and in any case he had since then successfully
characterized Nina as a comedy neurotic with whom everyone
at the agency was voyeuristically fascinated. But soon after the
night in their hallway, Chloe had realized that she wanted a
baby. She hadn't told him.

One night the muezzin woke Nicholas in the darkness. The
room smelled of sand, stale incense, sun lotion and mosquito
spray. Chloe slept, deeply, a curled question mark next to him.
For a while he lay listening to the weird, undulating, nasal
harangue. Sometimes he heard the beauty in it: the voice on the
minaret unfolded its song like a pennant that flickered all the
way back to Muhammad; but the beauty itself was a disturb-
ance. It shrank Christianity, reason, London, his marriage, his

life – everything. Listening to it troubled him, and there was no escape. It was as if time had stopped, replaced by the elemental force of the voice, the darkness, the room's smell of holiday, the itch of his own open eyes, seeing nothing.

Very gently he drew the sheet off Chloe and put his face close to her. On their wedding night she had smelled of perfume, shampoo, cigarette smoke and wine. He remembered that the day had recreated both of them, so that they were mutually unknown by the time they found themselves alone in the bed. Six years ago. And three years before that she had come into the greasy spoon café and let him know with a look that it would be all right, that he wasn't awry in his attraction to her. Now her skin smelled of absorbed sun and the sea's salt. He pressed his nose against her flesh, felt the comfort of how well he knew her body's shape and heat. He was too old now to say it aloud, but he thought (while the muezzin encased the moment): That's my wife. This woman is my wife.

Like the song from the minaret, the words 'woman' and 'wife' seemed revealed to him as ancient essences. It didn't overwhelm him; a part of consciousness was occupied with the ludicrousness of it. He imagined trying to describe it to Anthony Caswell-Brooks, who (if sober) would have said something like: 'Dear oh dear oh dear. Opium, was it?' and who (if drunk) might have broken down in a completely genuine crying jag.

Then the singer stopped, and the new silence was tangible.

He got up and went out on to the balcony.

The sky was cavernous and teeming with bright stars. Close by, too, he could feel the pitched weight of the sea. He forced himself to think of London, the office, Anthony, Nina. It almost made him laugh. As it was, he felt the muscles in his face moving into a smile. It humbled him, that all one had to do was leave one country and go to another for the sounds and shapes of one's life to diminish to the squeakings and jiggings of a puppet show. 'There's all these millions of people,' Anthony had said to him once, drunk, bitter. 'And the idea is that you find one of them and cling to them in the mayhem. You solve yourself with someone. It's a fucking stupid, disgusting lie of an

idea. And it's the biggest idea we've come up with. It's a vile, idiotic perversion.'

He had found Chloe. He was clinging to her, she to him.
Together they were one immeasurably small event in chaos. It
was absurd. It *was* a perversion. But what was the alternative?

'God's the only alternative,' Anthony had said, fishing for a
cigarette then almost breaking down in tears because the pack
was, inevitably, empty. 'And God's not there. I think He was,
once. But He's not fucking there now, the selfish cunt. He's
pissed off to the Bahamas.'

Nicholas smiled again at the memory.

It wasn't about Nina Cole, any of it. She was just the representative of everything he thought he would be relinquishing by
accepting that Chloe was his insufficient lot in life. It was nothing more. His instinct to marry her had a fluked purity – but
its rightness hadn't aborted the doubts, just suspended them.
They were only now, six years on, coming to the end of their
incubation.

Something *had* changed between them. The old love, the
love that had constituted their youth, had been based on the
assumption that they, together, in themselves, were a certainty,
that they were mutually, essentially visible. Their combined
imaginative ability had rendered a vision of their love as
utterly sufficient, a vision that was only possible because they
were so young. Now, standing under the black, glittering sky,
Nicholas understood: Nina Cole, Difalco's, that streak of
hatred – it was nothing more than a juvenile anger that life
was in fact larger than love. That they were, in part, *in*visible
to each other. That love was not sufficient, even if it was his
love for Chloe. He had hated her and himself that night
because he had understood that loving her would never be
enough, that there would always be something left over. The
discovery had felt like a terrible betrayal. That night it had
seemed that anything other than a perfectly sufficient love
was a loathsome fraud.

Nicholas leaned on the balcony's rail and felt his arms taking
his weight, solidly. A calm had come over him.

They were so much older now. The passing of one's life was the simplest mathematical subtraction, he knew, but the knowledge was no antidote to amazement, when, at moments like these, he understood that a great deal of time had already been taken away. When he remembered the greasy spoon or the church at Elm Coombe, or the afternoon spent painting the bathroom at the flat in Shepherd's Bush, the images were in the fantastical, pristine colours of childhood, or they had the fragmentary quality of recalled dreams. He had met and married Chloe before adulthood had really begun for either of them. The dregs of childhood had allowed them to see their love as both exclusive and exhaustive. They had married without any wisdom, just with a profound intuition. Their world view had been restricted by their youth, so their love had seemed huge. Now that age had expanded that world view, they were discovering that love too had its boundaries. That was all. Surely that was all?

But he wondered, still, how Chloe had been able to assimilate all this so easily. It had been evident to him ever since that night in the hall that she knew the old vision of love had failed. It had been evident too that the failure wasn't apocalyptic for her, that she had a view of her future which was already large and subtle enough to accommodate it. How was that so? What had she been able to see that he hadn't? Why wasn't the insufficiency of their love a devastation to her?

This was part of Nina's appeal, that she demanded, as a starting point, the belief that he would never know her, nor she him. She insisted, *a priori*, on the insufficiency of love.

She disgusted him. Now, standing with the warm air against his skin and his arms locked, he saw that her cynicism (which was all it was, wasn't it?) came not through the usual route of failure, but as a pre-emptive defence against the challenge of even risking failure. Her recklessness wasn't courage; it was cowardice. The nihilist's cowardice. The retreat from morality because one was afraid of trying to be good and failing. It was a sham, a retardation. He would have nothing to do with her.

A dog barked in the distance, three times, like a signal, ir-
rationally reminding him of Peter denying Christ.

He stepped back into the room and stood in the dark by the
bed. He could barely discern his wife, but he could sense her
as he had been able to sense the sea, beyond what could be
seen.

The following morning Nicholas went with Chloe to the beach.

'Love me again then, do you?' she said to him, when they lay
side by side on the sun-beaten sand.

'Yes,' he said. 'I do.'

A minute passed. Nicholas was trying to look at the sky, but
the light was blinding. Instead he turned his head and looked at
Chloe. Eyes closed, all-but-naked body golden and glimmering.
He was thinking about the muezzin, and of how the words
'woman' and 'wife' had momentarily shed all peripheral conno-
tations and been revealed as luminous archetypes. He knew that
it would all seem preposterous once they got home. He knew
London would smirk it into meaninglessness. But he would feel
it while he could, laughing at himself, somewhat.

''S just as well that you do,' Chloe said.

Her profile showed one closed eye and the corner of her
mouth, smiling because the sun was resting on her like soft
metal.

'Why?' Nicholas said.

Her left hand picked up hot sand then let it trickle out in a
thin stream.

'Because I want to have a baby with you,' Chloe said.

'Welcome back, chocolate drop.'

'Thanks. I've learned, late in life, how to lie on a beach and
do nothing.'

'Well you'll be pleased to know that you've come back in
time to acquire a client who might well make you a good ten
per cent for once.'

Nina handed Nicholas a hefty manuscript. '*After the Party*,' she said. 'Adrian Marlowe. Twenty-eight. Hasn't submitted anything before. We're going to make him rich.'

'What's it about?'

'Are you in love with your wife again?'

'Nina . . .'

'The Turkish renaissance?'

'Look. For fuck's sake—'

'Believe it or not it's about a man who wakes up one morning to discover that everyone's disappeared.'

'What do you mean?'

'I mean that the protagonist wakes up one Monday morning to discover that everyone – on the entire *planet* – has disappeared. He's on his own. Animals, trees, the weather – all as normal. Just no people. Anywhere.'

'Science fiction,' Nicholas said. 'Surely?'

'Beyond that. *Way* beyond that. It's huge.'

'How the fuck does he make . . . what, eight hundred pages . . . out of one character?'

'Memories. Lots of them. It's going to sell millions. It's brilliantly written.'

'It's got one-hit wonder written all over it. How does it end?'

Nina smiled. She was standing with her weight on one leg, hands on hips. 'Guess,' she said.

'He dies of boredom,' Nicholas said.

'He meets a girl.'

'Oh God.'

'The *only* girl. The only other person left alive.'

Nicholas flicked through the manuscript, seeing nothing. 'Are you sure about this?' he asked her.

'If he's good-looking,' she said, 'I'm going to fuck him six ways to Sunday. That's how sure I am.'

Nicholas sat down at his desk. 'Fair enough,' he said. 'That's my day taken care of, then. And my next day.'

'You think you've gone off me,' Nina said.

'Nina, stop it.'

'Why don't you just sack me?'

Not entirely unselfconsciously, Nicholas put his head in his hands.

'Oh, boring,' Nina said, quietly, turning. 'Boring, boring, boring, *boring*.'

Nicholas sold *After the Party* to a big, reputable publisher less than two weeks later. They paid Adrian Marlowe an £85,000 advance. Up until then he had been unemployed for two years. Nicholas met him. He was a small, skinny blond with fierce blue eyes who bit his nails and smoked, incessantly. There was a huge, private, hyperactive intelligence there, but also some neuroses. Nicholas, happy with the deal, still predicted the titanic failure of the second novel (because Adrian Marlowe had clearly said everything he had to say in *After the Party*), with nervous breakdown and suicide following shortly there-after.

'We could do with eighty-five grand,' Chloe said.

'We could do with *five* grand,' Nicholas said.

'Can't you write something?'

'Can't *you?*'

Now that they had both let go of the idea of their former closeness, of course, much of it had come back. They were enjoying each other, at times, in their sloppily furnished Clapham flat.

But sex had changed again. Now Chloe could look at him when she came. Because he had shown her that fucking for him was sometimes an act of violence. If she hadn't now wanted a baby she would have had nothing to counter it with. But now Chloe *did* want a child. She countered the violence with her own contempt – because she communicated to him (he could see it, at last, in her eyes trained on him throughout) that he was merely instrumental to conception. She didn't want *him*. Perhaps she had never wanted *him*. She wanted the thing beyond him. The child. Nicholas understood, retrospectively, why she had been able to accept the failure of the romantic ideal. He understood how she had been able to see past the imperfection (the disease, in fact) of erotic love: because her vision of her future was a vision in which he, Nicholas, was no longer the most important thing in her life.

He saw, too, that it horrified both of them. Him, because Chloe was announcing his secondariness, telling him, in the last analysis, that she wanted him now *for* something, and Chloe because she was shocked by the force of her own biology. It disgusted her, somewhat, that after all it turned out that she was just another woman desperate for a baby.

'He'll hate you for it,' Jane said to her.

The two women sat in a pub in Cambridge Circus on a Saturday afternoon of high blue sky and thin, hurrying white clouds. Jane had just come to the end of another bad-tempered affair. Chloe had known this before Jane had told her, because Jane had turned up with a new, feathery haircut and make-up applied with fiendish accuracy. In addition, she was on her third Scotch to Chloe's one.

'I don't know if I care,' Chloe said, untruthfully.

'He'll hate you because all men see their wives' pregnancies as infidelity.'

'Well, perhaps they're right,' Chloe said.

'Of course they're right.'

'But it's not as if I'll stop loving him.'

'Irrelevant. You'll love your child more. That's all they see. Let's have another.'

Jane was suffering, Chloe knew. This latest paramour had left her a note.

'A fucking *note*,' Jane said. 'Do you know what it said?'

Chloe shrank.

'It said: *I see now that this was a kind of necessary phase. You've known, I think, that I'm in motion. You've known that this would be finite.* A necessary phase,' Jane repeated. 'A necessary fucking phase. I let him move in after a month and then he tells me I knew it would be finite.'

Chloe just looked at her, saying nothing. She had been silently (but probably visibly) sceptical when Jane had told her that she was letting her lover move in with her.

'Do you know why I let the bastard move in?' Jane asked her.

'Because he was getting kicked out of his other place?'

'Yes, yes – but I mean do you know why I *really* did?'

Unfortunately, Chloe knew the answer to this too, but she shook her head.

'Because I'm twenty-nine and I want to be in love,' Jane said. 'It's amazing, isn't it? I mean is there something wrong with me? Should I just not *want* to be in love any more? I mean is it some sort of backwardness to want to be with someone to whom you're the most important thing in their life?'

'Of course it isn't,' Chloe said.

'Are you sure? I'm beginning to think it is. Like wanting romance at my age is a sort of obtuseness – like not seeing that you're too old for ra-ra skirts.'

Chloe smiled, but compressed it. Jane's discovery, at the age of twenty-four, that she was too old for ra-ra skirts had been a terrible epiphany, from which she sometimes claimed she still hadn't recovered.

'I think you'd look fantastic in a ra-ra skirt,' Chloe said.

'I bloody *would*, too,' Jane said, half in earnest. 'There's nothing wrong with my legs up to six inches above my knees. D'you know what he said to me?'

'Oh God what?'

'"You've got the nicest legs of any woman I've ever been with." Lying bastard. *God* what a lying bastard.'

Jane had begun with cartoon wryness, but Chloe could see that simply uttering the phrase 'lying bastard' had nearly made her cry.

Jane lifted her chin up and swallowed and blinked. 'I'm not going to,' she said. 'I'm *not* going to sit in this *fucking* pub and cry.'

Later, the two of them walked by the Thames. Jane had spent about £150 on new clothes. She'd spent it robotically, bitterly, not disguising the mechanism. Chloe was thinking of the day she met Nicholas in the café, of the way in which, after they'd begun wandering around the city, London's physical properties had been translated into codes of first love.

'How do you know you love him?' Jane said.

'What?'

'Nick. How do you know you love him?'

Jane, who throughout the afternoon had kept starting and stopping crying, had just repocketed a ravaged tissue. Her long nostrils were red-rimmed and her eyes looked raw. Chloe wanted to put her arms around her – but it wasn't that kind of friendship.

'Jane, stop it, for God's sake.'

'Tell me. Just tell me.'

They had stopped under one of the Embankment's lamp-posts. Over Jane's shoulder Chloe could see the iron dolphins wrapped around its base. Nicholas always said they looked angry, which was all wrong for dolphins.

A train rattle-crashed across the Hungerford Bridge. The Thames was thick, greenish-bronze, moving slowly. Chloe didn't want to answer, but Jane wouldn't let her look away. The train passed. The Greenwich boat hooted, once.

'Because the thought of sharing my life with him makes the thought of dying bearable,' Chloe said.

'Love lifeboat,' Anthony told Nicholas. 'Once the kid comes, you're out.'

'What, for the love of Mary, are you on about?' Nicholas said.

Anthony stood in Nicholas's office staring down into the street. He was wearing yet another scrupulously casual ensemble. Nicholas marvelled, almost daily, at the blinding whiteness of Anthony's collarless shirts, the silk sweaters, the on-the-cusp-of-fading jeans, the just-showered, just-shaved glamour of him. Especially since, from where Nicholas was looking, Anthony was on the verge of alcoholism.

'Simple,' Anthony said. 'Ship going down, right? Wife has to choose between you and sprog. Only one place in the lifeboat. Has to choose. Guess who's going down with the ship.'

Nicholas contemplated this for a moment. 'That's a fucking stupid thought-experiment,' he said.

'True, though, eh?' Anthony said – then suddenly bent close to the window. 'Christ, I think that was Cindy Crawford I just saw.'

*

Nicholas, though he hadn't told Chloe, still didn't want a baby. He was just accepting it. He managed, generally, by not thinking about it – although the procreative agenda revolutionized his and Chloe's sexual repertoire, thereby *forcing* him to think about it. Frequency escalated, madly. And he had to come in her cunt, every time. It wasn't spoken between them, but Nicholas could feel the compressed rage in her if it looked like he was going to come in her mouth or hand. He *didn't* want a child, and he loathed Chloe for reducing sex to its progenitive meaning. When he went into her cunt, now, his imagination was enslaved by images of the female reproductive organs in cross-section. School textbooks. Gynaecologists. Her cunt joined the likes of her kidneys, pancreas, heart, etc.: just another organ with a job to do. He had to force himself to not think about it. She, meanwhile (legs wrapped around him, tugging him in), stared at him with a new intensity which was embarrassing. She was almost gleefully victorious at these times; her eyes shone when she looked at him.

It did liberate them, perversely, because now they could have sex without feeling the need to like each other while they were having it. It was a war between them, but it freed them from the idea that sex was anything to do with love. It was a dark, grim, galling celebration for both of them.

Nicholas was still unsatisfied and uneasy. If Chloe was with him in combat, she still didn't bring to sex what he brought to it. What he brought to it was . . . *what?*

He wasn't sure, even now. He thought often of the two little girls all those years ago, one heavily astride the other, saying: 'I could do anything to her. I could spit in her face. Oi, Nick, shall I?'

'It's an incredible achievement,' Nina Cole said, having walked unasked into Nicholas's office.

'What is?' Nicholas said, not lifting his eyes from his work. 'Not that it's apropos of anything.'

'That we've made sex friendly. Given that it isn't.' She sat down in the chair opposite him. She looked tired. The hair and make-up had been a hurried struggle this morning, he could see. There was a brittleness about her, too, that put him on his guard. He had learned that she was almost infantile in her tendency to disguise pain with brisk, transparent sparkiness.

'I fucked this guy last night,' she said. 'Twenty-three. Long hair. Incredible body. Studying Psychology at . . . Somewhere. God knows. Picked him up in the George. He thought it was his birthday, poor bugger.'

Very carefully, Nicholas replaced the cap on his fountain pen and sat back in his chair. 'Why don't you just write all this stuff down and flog it?' he said.

'Instead of what? Burdening you with it? You love it.'

She put her hand into her trouser pocket and pulled out a small bit of white paper, folded many times. She began unfolding it, delicately. Nicholas found himself hoping, sincerely, that it didn't contain cocaine.

'What pisses me off is the way we just scratch the surface,' Nina said. 'I mean he wanted me to hurt him, you know? Stand on his face with my heels on. Bite. Draw blood. Nails and teeth and whatnot.'

'Which, presumably, you did?'

'Which I did. But that's not the point. The point is that that was all he could come up with. All these people who sort of half get it.'

She had the paper open now. Nicholas's worst fears confirmed. Back into the pocket, then, sure enough, a slender silver tube.

'Nina . . .'

'Yeah yeah yeah bollocks,' she said, and without looking at him bent and snorted, quickly, half the line in the right nostril, half in the left. Reflexively, Nicholas checked the door. She had closed it.

'Nina, you can't—'

'Too late. Anyway I'm leaving. So you don't need to lose any sleep over finding a diplomatic way of sacking me.'

'What?'

'New Year,' she said, sniffing. 'I'm going to Italy. None of your

business. I've just typed up my notice. See? In four weeks you'll
miss all this.'

Feelings jostled in him. Panic. Deflation. 'When did you
decide to go?' he said.

'Oh, I don't know, do I? This morning. Last week. Can't
remember. Anyway I'm off.'

She got up, suddenly. 'Oooh that's better,' she said.

'Confession's over then, is it?' Nicholas said, numb.

'What?'

'Scratch the surface of what?'

She moved and stood closer to him, staring down. For a few
moments, neither of them spoke. He was looking at the floor,
but was aware of the colours of her, peripherally: green silk
blouse; black corduroys; even the vermilion nails and burnished
copper hair. She was a perfumed blur at his side, radiating, as
she could, at will, the open-endedness of everything between
them. Then she bent forward, close enough so that he could feel
her breath, and whispered: 'Hate.'

That night Nicholas lay stretched out on a towel on the floor of
the bathroom at home. Chloe was in the tub, soaking. The
steam was a soft, friendly narcotic for Nicholas. An hour earlier
he and Chloe had had lengthy, tense, vaginal sex. Now their
bodies hummed with exhaustion.

'Nick, I went to the doctor's today,' Chloe said – then, when
his head came up quickly, she added: 'No. I mean for the results
of a fertility test.'

'What fertility test?'

'It takes a while. I started when we came back off holiday. To
see. You know? To see if I'm functional or whatever. I went to a
private clinic. They don't do it on the NHS unless you've been
trying for ages.'

'And?'

'And it's positive. I mean I *am* ovulating. Which isn't a guar-
antee or anything, but it's good to know.' He knew what was
coming. 'So I thought you should have one, too,' Chloe said,
moving her limbs gently in the water.

Briefly (furious, for no good reason), Nicholas consulted an arsenal of objections – then realized he was too tired to bother with any of them.

'It's only been a few months we've been trying,' he said, as quietly as he could.

Chloe's bathwater rustled. 'I know,' she said. 'It's just that – wouldn't it feel better to you to know at the start that we're actually capable of doing this? I mean is there any point in just taking it for granted that we're both OK? If we're not—'

'If *I'm* not, since we've already established that you're more than likely in tip-top reproductive condition.'

A pause. 'Nick, don't fight. Come on. I'm just saying, I'd rather know now than after trying for months and months, feeling the doubt beginning to grow, you know?'

'You'd rather know now so you'll still have time to find a healthy surrogate after it's shown that I'm a hopeless dud, you mean?'

Deep breaths. 'What's wrong, love?' Chloe said. 'Why do you want to fight?'

Because I don't want a fucking baby. Because it changes everything. Because you're imprisoning me. Because you'll let me go down with the ship. Because our lives are turning out to be ordinary. Because I hate you for not being everything to me. Because I hate myself for not being everything to you. Because being together, now, means fucking *settling* for something. Because Nina's corrupt and you're not, and that's what's always been missing.

At last, rising slowly, unable now to feel the steam as anything other than gentle suffocation, Nicholas took a white towel and draped it over his head, prize-fighter style. 'All right,' he said. 'I'll have the test.'

In the days that followed, Chloe blotted him out. It was as if she refused to see him, though they managed the mechanics of living together (and fucking) as if there was no gap between them. She didn't nag him about the test. She didn't mention it, after that first time. But Nicholas knew that he was on borrowed

time, that there would come a day when, casually, as if it were
a negligible detail, Chloe would ask him if he'd been, and he'd
confess that he hadn't, and they'd have an apocalyptic row.
Domestic life became fascinating in its distortions. To Nicholas
it felt as if there were not two but four people sharing their
lives: the visible Nicholas and the visible Chloe, plus their two
demonic shadow-selves, terminally, inarticulately at war. The
visible couple went about their business of eating meals and
watching films and having sex and going for walks, while the
demonic counterparts circled each other with hackles raised
and teeth bared, aware that at any moment they might be given
permission to begin the attack.

Chloe's vision of motherhood demanded a resolute faith in
their ability to be together. It was a dizzying paradox to
Nicholas that she poured such aggression into the defence of
this faith: there was no limit to how much she would savage
him – not to destroy him, but to convince him that they could
be together. Meanwhile he despised himself. He was afraid of
her. In deciding that she wanted a child she had discovered, for
the first time, a giant will in herself. The will inflated, daily.
Nicholas felt it as an expanding presence whose goal was the
occupation of all available space. He shrank from it.

'Boy, girl or stillborn?' Nina Cole asked him in the Wheatsheaf,
one Friday evening.

'Ha ha,' Nicholas said. 'Ha *ha* ha.'

'It's refreshing to know I'm becoming such a rare and valu-
able commodity,' she said. 'Gorgeous, unattached, don't want
children – ever. Do you have any idea how many millions of
men in their thirties are looking for someone like me?'

It was December. The pub windows looked out on to London's
yellow lights and angled sleet. Inside was cigarette smoke and all
the reek, clink and colour of booze. Without telling Chloe,
Nicholas had made the appointment to get himself tested.

'Gorgeous, unattached, don't ever want children,' he said.
'Lonely, neurotic, volatile, destructive. How many millions of
men, Nina?'

Her eyes widened, feigning delight. 'Goodness!' she said. 'Aren't *we* the nasty boy today! Carry on in that vein and I might withdraw my much-mourned resignation.'

The more unhappy she was the more she caricatured herself, Nicholas knew. It was a glittering, perfected defence system. He sat and drank with her, thinking back to the day he had interviewed her. She hadn't turned out to be literature. She had turned out to be life. Perhaps everything did? At the end of the month, she would be gone.

They got drunk together, and he walked her to her tube station. London was in a dark, hurried chaos. All the surfaces reflected ripples of light. Exhaust fumes and damp overcoats; cold, dirty air.

'Answer me one question,' she said, holding his lapels, lightly.

Nicholas looked up, away from her, to where the streetlamp showed its golden aureole of lit sleet.

♦

'It is an ancient Mariner,' Lancelot said. 'And he stoppeth one of three. Or one of one in your case.' He lay on the frail couch, naked but for a pair of faded tartan boxers: flabby thighs and thick knees; waxy, bulbous gut; meaty shoulders; thin breasts, a scribble of grey hair on each nipple. All the flesh was veined and pale blue. He wheezed softly with every breath. 'Shall I tell you anyway? Since you don't ask? Since you don't appear to care?'

Nicholas sat a few feet away from him in the brown armchair, dressed now in the large shirt and trousers Lancelot had forced on him. Rain pounded the windows, continuously. The apartment was warm and stale-smelling. Up until this moment they had been sitting in silence.

'It's like a sort of club, you see, when you've done something. You recognize other members. They don't have to tell you – no secret handshakes or anything. You just know. You, for example.'

'Me?'

'Are one. Did something. No point denying it. I know. The way you are. Like me.'

Nicholas could hear him struggling for his usual self in the wake of the earlier episode with the heart pills.

'The other giveaway being that you don't ask questions,' Lancelot said. 'Which is what those who don't want to *be* questioned do. You see?'

'No,' Nicholas said.

'He holds him with his skinny hand, "There was a ship," quoth he. Well, not a ship, actually. A car.'

Nicholas was wondering whether Lancelot would have died had he not been on hand to fetch the pills.

'Expecting something extraordinary, aren't you, sunshine. Some incredible twist of fate.' Lancelot looked everywhere but at Nicholas. 'Well there isn't. It's ordinary. All incredible twists of fate are ordinary, for that matter.'

'I don't understand,' Nicholas said. He couldn't take his attention away from the sound of the rain. It was an angry presence with them. It seemed to press on his brain, insisting on something.

'Not remotely interested,' Lancelot said, as if reporting to an invisible third person. 'Good. Make us a drink, will you? You know where it is by now.'

Nicholas, disorientated in the too-big trousers and shirt, went over to a side cabinet and poured two glasses of Scotch.

'Roll the bottoms up for Christ's sake,' Lancelot said. 'You'll break your neck. Cheers. Well. It was a lovely evening in Hertfordshire. Where I used to live. A lovely evening not long before I was due to fly here, as a matter of fact. Money, you see? I worked with money. America wants you if you work with money. They've got all this money. What they want is people who can show them how to . . . I made money into more money. That's what I did. I was terribly good at it. Investments. Science of money. Actions and consequences. You take certain actions with money and certain consequences follow. Most people – you, for example, probably – can't get the hang of it. He, on the other hand, was born with it. Laughably simple. Couldn't see how people . . . It was dreadfully easy. The senior partners opened another office here. Remarkable how co-operative immigration is when you've got the knack of money actions and money consequences. Ah, but I'm boring you. Sorry. You feeling all right? Anyway. He was a young man at his peak, you see, this money consequencer. America had opened its legs for him. He was going to fly here to head up the new office. Very happy. Mightily chuffed. Been in the boozer all afternoon. Wasn't used to it. It was probably only the third or fourth time in his life we'd ever been drunk.'

Lancelot's head was propped on a torn cushion. One hand was down by his side; the other held the tumbler of Scotch on the dome of his belly. His left leg hung off the edge of the couch with its solid, blue-white foot casting a small oval of shadow. As Nicholas watched, a cockroach the colour of treacle toffee ran into the shadow, paused, then ran out and disappeared under a discarded paper bag.

'You know those Home Counties evenings. Summer. It was summer. He hit her going forty. She was about thirteen. Saw it in slow motion. He thought . . . Anyway. It was – her bike was too big for her. Saw it. Chain off. Chain must have just come off. But it was – the frame was too big for her. Boy's bike, with a crossbar. To get off she had to tilt to one side. She had to lean to get her foot on the ground. It's funny how you've got time to see all this. He saw all of it. She tilted the wrong way. If she'd gone to the left, she'd have fallen into the lovely summer grass. If she'd fallen to the left she'd have come down in the daisies and dandelions. But she went to the right. Lost her balance. He watched her hop-hopping sideways away from it, trying not to fall. You wouldn't think you could take all that in, would you, in a second, rounding a bend at forty? You can, though. You're allowed to.'

'An accident,' Nicholas said.

'Yes. Be lovely if it was. Wasn't though. Strangest thing. I had bags of time. I saw her, you see. I saw all of it. I remember thinking: I'll easily avoid that. I remember, actually, thinking how awful it would be if he hit her. I remember thinking how lucky she was that he wasn't going to hit her. But a long time passed while I was thinking it. So I hit her.'

Lancelot paused and looked down at his hand holding the glass, then raised it slowly to his lips and took a long swallow.

'Last two people on earth,' he said. 'Sun going down. Smell the bales and the cow dung. Went and squatted down next to her. She had chipped pink nail varnish. I put my hand out towards her – I don't know what for. But I didn't touch her. Couldn't. He got up and went back to the car. He got up, you see, and went back to the car. Took it home and washed it.'

For a long time neither of them spoke. There was a cacophony of sirens, braying and whooping on Second Avenue.

'You think you'll die,' Lancelot said.

'Yes,' Nicholas said.

◆

The agency had had a good year. Anthony Caswell-Brooks was hosting the Christmas party at his new flat in Ladbroke Grove on the 20th. The day Nicholas got the results of his test.

That afternoon, Nicholas cancelled his appointments and went to St Paul's Cathedral. To the top.

It wasn't raining, but there was a fine, damp mist in shreds all over the city, and it was bitterly cold. He stood with his hands in his pockets and looked out to the horizon. He was thinking of the muezzin, the sound from the high place that had woken him, that had revealed his wife to him. It had revealed, too, the absurdity of attachment. 'God's the only alternative,' Anthony had said. 'And God's not there.' Nicholas had discussed it with Adrian Marlowe, who, smoking furiously, nibbling his nails, had disagreed. 'There are other alternatives,' he had said. 'The embrace of chaos, for example. Or hedonism. Or aestheticism. The truth is it doesn't matter how many of the alternatives fail, singly or in combination. There are infinite gaps between them all. None of the order we impose can map the terrain exhaustively, whether it's the emotional order of love or the metaphysical order of religion or the descriptive order of science. There's always all this weird land left over. We can lose God, we can lose love. The only thing we're condemned *not* to lose is our experience. Unless of course we decide to kill ourselves, in the absence of love. Or God, or whatever. If we *don't* kill ourselves, then we're committed to finding a way through. We're committed to . . . well . . . apprehending our experience.'

It meant nothing to Nicholas. He stood in the cold above the city and thought now of how little there had been in his life. There had been Chloe. Beyond her – what?

'The problem is,' Adrian Marlowe had continued, 'that our experience is narrow enough so that we never even realize that God, love, reason or whatever are not exhaustive. The problem is that for most of us those things *feel* adequate because our experience is more or less uniform. But look at what happens when you disturb the uniformity. There was this woman who had been on a plane that got hijacked. She survived, but during the ordeal she'd twice had a gun put to her head. She came home to her husband and three children. Three months later, she woke in the middle of the night, packed a bag and left. They found her eventually. She was painting abstract canvases at an artists' community in Venezuela. Trauma reaction. Why do we call it that? Why don't we call it the soul's answer to the new question?'

Nicholas didn't understand. Now he loved Chloe, reactively, because he couldn't see how they could go forward.

'What's the matter, Nick?' Chloe asked him, later.

'Dunno,' he said, sitting up. His hearing was painfully sensitive to every movement of the bedclothes.

'Don't you want to?'

He couldn't look at her. Hadn't told her.

'Nick? What is it?'

Chloe put her palm against the small of his back. He felt the unspoken narrative spreading inside him like replicating ice crystals, a delicate, expanding fractal. They were just words – but he could feel them, physically, hardening throughout his body. He was afraid to move.

'We don't have to, you know,' Chloe said, quietly. 'It's not like we've been going short lately!'

He couldn't look at her.

'Nick?'

She wrapped her arms around him, pulled him gently back down with her. Despite the preceding weeks of conflict, she was alive to some terrible pain in him, something that went beyond the dynamic their demonic alter egos had forged. She lifted her arm and cradled his head next to her breast, touching her scar. It was how they used to lie when they were younger, whenever there was a mutually intuited need for allegiance.

Recognizing the gesture, Nicholas almost broke. Now, when he needed her enmity, she gave him gentleness. He was thinking of the night in the Yorkshire pub, the feeling he had had of giving himself over to something. The certainty of it.

'I've got to go,' he said, quietly, his lips moving against the strange, satiny skin of her scar. 'I've got to go to this thing.'

Chloe hugged him. 'I know,' she said. 'You don't mind me not coming?'

'No.'

'I just can't face that lot tonight. Bloody Anthony with some nineteen-year-old fuck-machine. You don't mind, do you? Really?'

'No,' Nicholas said. 'I really don't mind.'

Dressed, he looked back at her, naked on the bed. The unspoken facts were poisoning him. He had to get out immediately, or else his body would eject them whether he wanted it to or not. She looked up at him. Nine years.

'Tell me what's wrong when you get back,' she said.

'I will.'

'Nick?'

'Umm?'
'I love you.'

Later, after Nicholas had left for Anthony's, Chloe tidied up, then sat on the couch with her knees up, painting her toenails. There was no emotional rationale for the calm she felt. She knew Nicholas was frightened of what having a baby would do to them. She understood that she was forcing the issue, driving him with an irrefutable will. The strength of her own volition surprised her. It had been apparent from the moment she'd told him in Turkey that this would be her doing, that it would require her faith. She had seen Nicholas looking at her as if she were a mystery. She had seen him hating her for dragging him into parenthood. She knew it was unreasonable. But she knew, too, beyond argument or thought, that she was right. She could see the world beyond Nicholas's centrality in her life. They would have a child, and Nicholas would follow her into the new arena, initially bewildered, but eventually joining her in certainty. The current dissonance between them was a surface mutation. Nicholas couldn't see beyond it – he had no instinct for the future, but she did. That was the root of the calm: the profound instinct for their future.

The living-room was softly lit. The gas fire exhaled, endlessly. The television was on, but with the volume down. From time to time she looked up at the screen. *One Flew Over the Cuckoo's Nest*. She remembered the date that never was, in Paignton, all those years ago, the boy's shocked face, the dark-eyed blonde girl who should have been her. She remembered letting herself cry for a while on the bus back to Elm Coombe. She remembered forcing herself to stop.

Those days, she knew now, were gone. She wasn't smug. She hadn't blossomed into a swan. But she had found Nicholas – and he had seen her. She realized (finishing the first set of toes, which now gleamed back at her like a family of rubies) that in deciding to have a child she was taking responsibility for three of them: herself, the baby and Nicholas. She was calm now because she knew she could do it. She knew her vision was subtler than his. She had known since Turkey, in the brilliant, golden beach afternoons with the turquoise Mediterranean stretched at her feet and the sun lying on her like an angel. All their life together she had felt her own and Nicholas's strength equal. In Turkey the balance had shifted. Supine on the long crescent of sand, she had known (the knowledge had accrued like something passed into her with each beat of the sun) that she had faith enough in the new version of their love for both of them. Nicholas couldn't see beyond fear of change. She saw, somehow, into the certainty of the future. She knew it would be all right.

Nicholas arrived at Anthony's at ten. Most of the agency's staff was there, along with a dozen editors and publicists – no one Nicholas didn't know.

'Where's the missus?' Anthony asked, handing him a whisky in a fat, heavy glass.

'Not well,' Nicholas said, flatly, without any attempt to disguise the lie.

Anthony rolled his eyes. 'Fair enough. Shame, though. We need someone with more than one fucking dimension here.'

Quickly, with mechanical determination, Nicholas entered a dream of drink. Each empty glass was a bitter achievement. Then the miraculous refill. He conversed, tangentially, through a golden miasma of Scotch fumes. Twice he reached up as if to brush them away from his face. He found himself, between encounters, noticing random details of Anthony's flat – a black ceramic cat, a vase of blue flowers, an elaborate remote control – at which he would laugh, idiotically, then become preoccupied by, until the next person came within range and engaged him. Not that such engagements lasted. With every drink he felt himself surrendering a portion of his ability to pretend.

A fiction editor from the house that had bought Adrian Marlowe's book took Nicholas by the elbow.

'*Very* curious to see what Adrian's going to do next,' she said to him. 'He's definitely a find.'

'He's definitely a fucking *freak*,' Nicholas said. 'He's one of Thatcher's flukes. Pushed so far down in the social scale that he meets high art at the other end. Like being so happy that you're sad. So poor that you're rich. Circularity. Like loving someone so much that you hate them.'

The editor, a stocky woman in her late thirties with a severe haircut and piercing blue eyes, smiled, feebly. 'You think he's a one-trick pony, do you?' she said.

'He'll be dead in two years,' Nicholas said. 'Now why don't you fuck off and leave me alone?'

He was aware of Nina, always. They kept *seeing* each other. They kept seeing each other not paying attention to whoever was talking to them.

It was too bright for Nicholas, after a while. Anthony's entire flat seemed to be made from cut glass. Drunk, he couldn't stop flinching at the brilliance of people's fingernails and teeth. Rings, bracelets, earrings. There was a small white chandelier in the centre of the lounge that presided over everything, like Lucifer. Nicholas went quietly to an empty bedroom and sat down on the carpet.

'I'm not drunk,' Nina said to him.

'I am.'

'I can drive.'

'Leave me alone.'

She had come and found him in the softly lit bedroom.

'You knew this was going to happen,' she said. She stood in front of him; his face was at the level of her knees. He was thinking of Chloe, and all the years – and today's facts. I'll just give you the facts, OK? the doctor had said.

'Perhaps you're right.'

'I know I'm right.'

'No. About the world. Take all the people away. Marlowe's thing. He says there's always spaces left over.'

She sat down next to him and took his hand. 'You knew this was going to happen, Nicholas, didn't you?'

No amount of drunkenness was sufficient, it seemed, though all breathable air now filtered through Scotch. He looked at her hand in his: white skin, slightly risen veins, dark, hard nails. It was suddenly extraordinary, that this was her hand, her actual hand which had touched all the objects in her life. All the people in her life, whoever they were. Her unknown life.

'We should be called to prayer in the middle of the night,' he said. 'Like the Muslims.'

'Is that what you discovered on your Turkish retreat?'

'God should be something that gets you up. Startles. Like a call from the hospital or something. Make you . . .' He was having trouble. 'Make you panic. Make you fear God. Cos it's complacency, sleep. Just another form. We should be woken every night . . . *every* night . . .'

'Come with me,' Nina said, leaning close. Faint wine on her breath, some spice from the hors d'oeuvres.

'Leave me alone, Nina.'

'Come with me.'

All Nicholas's previous moments gathered, formed into their inevitable shape. He felt it as the end of a breath he had been exhaling for ever. Now was the point of non-time between the end of this breath and the beginning of the next. Here, in the place of absolute rest, Nina was nothing more than a shadow to him. Not a real presence at all. It was a pure space, unoccupied, waiting for his will.

'There's no excuse,' he said, gently.

'There's never any excuse,' she said.

The taxi ride home from Nina's was the last time Nicholas knew the old world.

He retained only isolated images of what had happened. He remembered it (already, in the taxi, distracted intermittently by the colour sequence of traffic lights or the left and right glances of his bald driver) as something that had taken place not minutes but years ago.

Nina's flat. He didn't even know where. Somewhere east of Liverpool Street. He had lost track of the passed Underground stations. Nina's flat: small, air dried out by too much central heating; tidy, sparsely furnished; an ancient, threadbare carpet; the blur of a doorway and a light turned on and then off again, quickly; the unmade bed. The first soft bed contact sobered him in a nauseating rush, then he was clear.

It came to him, then, what he was doing. If he failed to embrace it there was a giant fear waiting to engulf him. To embrace it at all there had to be some violently willed shutdown; it was as if there was a third eye which must be blinded to do this. So he blinded it and kissed her, hungrily.

It was disappointing. Then the disappointment was titillating, because it offered scope for his control. At first, as if simply to shatter his expectations, she seemed dull to it; there was no onslaught. They kissed, sometimes with bumped teeth or wrongly angled heads, for a long time, and she made no move beyond it. There was no room for lust; he was occupied with the reconstitution of her in his scheme of things, now that her body was something he touched, now that her mouth was something that didn't merely talk to him. This new assimilation progressed by degrees as they kissed. However much of his time had been spent imagining this, it had been wasted. Not because she surpassed or fell beneath his fantasies, but because in imagining her he had had only three of the five senses to feed off. Now that he was touching her – discovering the alignment of bone, the undulation of muscle, the privacy of pulses, the cracked code of mouth, fingers, ribs, midriff, throat – now that touch and taste were liberated he saw that attempting to imagine them based on sight, smell and hearing had been a doomed project. For all he had thought and seen of her before, now that he held her she might as well have been a complete stranger.

Very slowly. For a long time the kisses. Tell me what's wrong when you get back.

'Why are you doing this?'

His voice in the dark to her. She sat astride him, skirt gone, shirt open, breasts out of the bra's lace cups. It was the first word between them since the party.

'I don't ask questions any more. You knew this would happen.'

She had gone slowly, he now thought, because she had wanted him sober. She was changing gear. There would be many changes possible with her. She wanted him aware of what he was doing. She wanted maximum culpability. Both of them. It was a punishment, for her. All of it was a punishment for something. And it was a confirmation of what she needed to be true: that she – by her ability to prove corruption in others – was exempt from the moral challenge herself.

'Is this hate?' he said, though it meant nothing to him, though it was just his mouth making noise.

'Of course. Of course it is. Shut up.'

Then the clarity of consciousness as they moved through the repertoire. Her forcing the clarity of consciousness so that he could see the pleasure inherent in betrayal.

'Do you love her?'

'Yes.'

Her mouth poised, warm-breathing at the head of his cock. 'Then there's no excuse. I told you: there's never any excuse.'

She wanted him to understand that to embrace this he had not to blot Chloe out, but to keep her in mind. He was appalled, because as soon as he sensed it he knew that he had known it already. He wondered how Nina had learned this – but then remembered the years with Chloe, hanging above her, *knowing* that destruction, a deep force against life, was not part of what she brought to their fucking. It wasn't learned. It was a nature. Michelle spitting into the riven face of her victim hadn't taught Nicholas anything. Her actions had just given him the opportunity to remember his nature. He had proposed to Chloe partly in an attempt to escape it.

His wedding-ring finger buried in her arsehole – a detail she hadn't missed – and the bliss of her weight on him. Again long periods of silence, protracted kissing. Staring at each other in the dark.

Then it was over. Her silence, filled with her unknown history, his somnambulistic dressing. She turned the bedside light on, sat with her knees up to her chest, staring at nothing. Clothed, feeling already the old world's shock through his skin's contact with shirt and trousers, he paused in the bedroom's doorway.

'Do you know what the devil is?' she said.

Nicholas, blank, deadened, trembling at the return to the relic of what used to be, said nothing.

Nina hugged her knees with her arms, her head on one side like a perplexed bird's. 'He's boredom. He's not the force of evil. He's the force of boredom. It's the boredom.'

In the taxi he thanked the God who wasn't there that this was winter, that there were still hours before daylight. Daylight would bring its own leaden cargo of guilt. That was as far ahead as he thought. To think beyond was to think of Chloe. It was to think of language – either the desolate language of confession or the anti-language of maintained deception. To think into language was to think into the changed world. The world that he had changed.

With the wedding ring pressed against her arsehole he had known that this was an exquisite defilement, and that beyond the defilement would be its exact counterweight in shame. Partly, a disinterested curiosity had carried him through such gestures, an amoral spirit of enquiry. He had detached slightly from his body, observing, clinically. It was one of the spaces left over from Adrian's maps. Nina herself was one of the spaces. He had been afraid to go there from the moment he had met her. He had been afraid of finding himself in such a space.

Do you love her?

Do you love her, son? Truly love her?

He had known Chloe that night as his wife. He had known her even before that as his wife, lying warm together under the bedclothes after the cartoon Yorkshirewoman had fed them their supper. He had *recognized* her. And again, after the cries from the minaret. Nine years.

Still thinking backwards, still unable to visualize anything of his future beyond the stale breath and diesel-wheeze of the taxi, Nicholas discovered too late that they were at his building, that the meter had stopped at £14.50, that the bald driver was waiting.

The front door. Which he couldn't think beyond. He couldn't bring himself to think of Chloe, inside, asleep. Key in hand, he rested his head against the cool paint and breathed, steadily. He couldn't remember, afterwards, how long he stood there, while the first broad, surprising flakes of snow began to fall.

The first thing he saw inside was the small, glued-together ceramic pot that had broken on the night he and Chloe had fucked in the hall. It was lying on the floor, still in one piece. One of Chloe's shoes lay next to it. So he knew something was wrong. He heard it, like an orchestra's strings sliding into dissonant minors. With the front door behind him still open to the quickly arriving scent and whisper of snow, Nicholas understood that the gathered moments earlier had been a false alarm; that this, now, was the true end of the long-held breath. There was a new odour in the house, like iron. Feeling no more control over his hand than if it had been a fluttering bird tethered to his wrist, he reached and turned on the hall light. Beside the shoe and the pot nothing was out of place; but when he tried to call out for Chloe he found that his larynx was paralysed. He felt light, as if his insides had been removed and replaced with helium. With each step his body's weight diminished. Halfway into the hall he found himself holding on to the living-room door's handle, convinced that if he let go he would rise, slowly, to the ceiling. He turned and looked back to the open door, where the white, hurrying flakes reached for the earth out of the darkness. Already things were being newly outlined: the lamp-post, a locked bike, two thin-branched black trees across the road.

Again he felt himself at the end of the released breath. The pause between this and the new inhalation could last for ever, if he remained as he was, holding the door handle. His tongue was pressed against the roof of his mouth – the way it had stayed from the moment he had tried to articulate 'Chloe'.

The first blood was a handswipe on the white wall beside the kitchen doorway. The second was a twin print on the wall opposite, closer to the bedroom. The third was a patch under one of his forced-down footsteps; the carpet was marshy with it, squelching once, quietly, as if in gentle warning. It reminded him of long-ago football on a waterlogged pitch.

To enter the bedroom meant letting go of his handholds (all ten fingers gripped a picture rail that ran along the hall). Convinced of his weightlessness, Nicholas shoved himself tight against the wall and descended, by degrees, first to his haunches then to his knees and finally down on all fours. One hand depressed the blood puddle and came up dark and wet with it. The other hand forced its way into the carpet's fibres and held tight, anchoring him.

Cold air came from the kitchen and touched him like a ghost. The door to the flat's square of garden was open. It struck him that the building was a frail, miraculous structure, howled around by empty space. The whole street, London, every city on the planet – all preposterous gestures against the scale of what was outside them. The nearness of the snow-flavoured air arrested him, and he felt his hands' muscles straining to keep him attached to the floor. His legs seemed to float lightly behind him like fins. The temptation to let go – to rise up and feel the back of his head bump against the ceiling – was nearly overwhelming. He moved forward and found the edge of the bedroom doorway.

There was a moment just before the eruption of nausea when he saw with angelic clarity the pointlessness in the human habit of connecting anything to anything else. It was like a vision of God, something wholly other-dimensional which proved the redundancy of all the familiar and fundamental frameworks – space, time, cause, effect. He was granted, in this thing which was neither moment nor state (since motion and normal consciousness dropped away in two giant scales), licence to receive pure, disinterested revelation: his entire life (all life, everywhere) was a succession of habits forced on to experience which was chaotic. Things mattering was a habit, an order worn by chaos like a costume to amuse children. It shone at him from everything like a brilliant light, and he knew that the rest of his life now would be a choice between accepting or denying it. He knew too that he would never in this life be up to accepting it. He knew (all outside time, while he floated at the doorway in the air that was water) that the revelation would pass, that he was wedded to the way of habits, that immediately the old version of the world would rush back in, that all the connections would be viscerally real, that he would shut out what had been shown to him and hold on to what he had seen.

He hadn't known that blood had a smell. A vestigial animal part of him recognized it. Now that the thing which was neither moment nor state had passed or imploded, all his body gave itself over to sickness and shock. His gravity returned in an axe-blow and he found himself leaden, flat on the floor, struggling to get to his elbows and knees. One bedside lamp was on the floor, throwing a long ellipse of yellow light on to the carpet. The room was hot and dry. A pair of Nicholas's jeans had dried stiff on the radiator, and looked now like the protruding legs of someone hidden behind the curtain. A white teacup lay on the rug at the edge of the bed, small, empty, distinct.

The knowledge that she was still alive was in him, come from somewhere – that and the fragments of what he must do, now, immediately, before it was too late. The most familiar concepts, though, were chimerical. Telephone. Ambulance. The words repeated themselves in his head like signals, but he could barely remember what they were, how one related to them, what one *did*. There was an agonizing discrepancy between his inner urgency and his body's ability to move. Now his weight had doubled. It took a tremendous dreamy effort to get to his knees, to get his forearms on to the bed. Telephone. Nine-nine-nine. Telephone. In the hall. Back. With rotary phones it must have taken seconds longer. People must have

died. And why nine? Takes longest to dial. You're wasting time.
Killing her.

But the blood was distracting him. There was a wound under
her jaw that had whistled, softly, three or four times.

Breathing

Therefore

And a great weight of it like a continent to the right of her
leg. Her eyes open.

A voice somewhere was saying: 'Oh sweet Christ. Oh sweet
fucking Jesus. Chloe? Chloe? Jesus fucking Christ help me.'

But it was a long way away.

Part Three

CONTINUE

there's a dark place tight around you then you come out it's an anti-birth you come out to find that you're dead

I think you were there. Weren't you there

I read this thing once it goes grief anger acceptance

Ceiling hospital-blue. Walls hospital-white. Floor hospital-grey. Her throat hurt the most. Two other beds, both with very quiet occupants, one of whom falsetto-babbled in her sleep. Both the other women were old, lint-haired, frail-skulled. Both had learned to not say very much. Their teeth watched over them through the night. Chloe had the window bed. No trees. Just London sky and wet roofs. Nothing. Nothing. Nothing.

You were with me. You were with me you were with me you

I remember

For a long time there was very little organized consciousness. Occasionally perception crystallized in a face she knew or words she understood; but for an immeasurable time there were only two states: sleep, and an unfocused awareness that was like the sea's echo in a deep shell.

But gradually – without any sense of how long she'd been gone – she arrived at the memory of who and what she was. It was as if she had been coerced into identifying a corpse.

She had to ask what the date was, and the day. The Filipino nurse who looked about twelve.

There's no point. Now there's just space.

Her sister, Liz, had said to her: 'I'm so glad you're alive.' Liz had never said anything like that to anyone in her life. Chloe had seen her sister's discomfort, had seen that she was checking herself inside to see if she was feeling what she thought she should be feeling. Liz's face had been baggy and raw around the eyes. Chloe had watched her, without speaking, seeing their mother in her.

What she should have been feeling. Chloe didn't know, didn't care. I'm glad you're alive. The word 'feeling' made her sick. To her stitched-up stomach. Everyone kept talking about feelings. Everyone assumed she had some, somewhere. Everyone talked and no one knew what to say. Everyone knew she was alive and everyone wondered if she had survived. None of them knew. I'm so glad you're alive. Alive.

None of them knew except Jane – and even she didn't really know. It was just her decree: Chloe's going to be all right. Jane had to think that, make that decree, because she was terrified.

Now Chloe saw a million different degrees of fear in people, and knew it was the product of having reached the end of herself and returned. Jane's fear was as vivid as blood. Chloe observed her butching it out massively, heard her fighting with someone in the corridor: 'I don't give a fuck what the visiting hours are. What are you going to do? Call the fucking police? She *asked* me to bring her these. Yeah, yeah. Piss *off*.'

The sort of thing that would formerly have made Chloe think, Good old Jane! It didn't. It didn't anything. Nothing anythinged.

When Jane had asked Chloe what she wanted to read, Chloe had written: *Nothing for the rest of my life*.

She couldn't tell the divisions between days. Hours diffused into one another. Hospital time was aerated, camphorous.

Another discovery: a reservoir of hatred for other people because it hadn't happened to them. Because they still had the luxury of the old thing, the old way. Because they still had the before. A reservoir of hatred because it wasn't their bodies. And they didn't know.

I see lots of things, now, Chloe thought. That Jane is half in love with me. About which I think?

Nothing.

When Chloe's mother came she sat on the bed and held Chloe's hand. Sometimes this returned Chloe to childhood, the cottage at Elm Coombe, to glandular fever and the wallpaper's pattern of heavy roses which in her delirium melted, dripped, coagulated, crawled towards her. The weight of Liz's sleep in the bunk above her. Whistlings in her blood, clangings in her head. All sorts of monsters.

Her mother came and stroked her hand. (She can't stroke anything else, Chloe thought; it's all sewn together in black and red seams.) The touch of her mother's fingers in her palm made Chloe want to scream. It disgusted her that she couldn't tell her mother to stop it. Similarly, she hadn't been able to tell her to stop crying. (Not because there was nothing to cry for, but because it paralysed her – Chloe – with yearning and rage.) Instead Chloe had given her father a look. He must have understood. The next time, her mother controlled herself.

This is not my body.

*

This is not my body. My body's gone.

The Filipino nurse was Toi. How did they take the smell of this place away from their skins when they got home? Hilda was curious. Toi told her fresh lemon. Quartered, rubbed.

Chloe knew that Toi was afraid of her. They were all afraid of her. Her survival was the measure of their imagined cowardice: 'I wouldn't be able to . . . I couldn't . . . I can't imagine . . .'

They couldn't imagine.

Chloe woke Hilda and Moira with her screaming. She opened her mouth and tore the wire from her jaw. You could scream blood. You found these things out. You didn't know such things. Chloe knew that there were only a handful of single rooms – but she saw the doctors looking at her and knew she was a good candidate. *Her?* Jesus Christ, don't even ask. You don't want to fucking *know*.

She didn't want them to move her. She didn't want a room without sky. London's egg and snot. She didn't want to lose Hilda and Moira's teeth, which grinned through the small hours like grotesque guardian angels. Not that it would matter if they did move her, since now she contained infinite space, since now she could assimilate anything. A single room. No window. It would only be more fear. Fear wasn't much, now.

There are all these questions, Nick, and I can't ask them. Even if my mouth worked it wouldn't be able to fit itself around them. You can't ask them with words. You can wake up bellowing blood.

Her face in the mirror, barely recognizable, rewritten. She didn't know if it was hers. Every day it tried out new colours. Stitches: lines crossed out like a tally of days on a prison-cell wall. I've been crossed out, she thought. My face has been edited. Cut and paste. Cut and paste. I don't want to be here. The rape woman says the word 'survival' and I keep wanting to tell her it's just a licence that can expire any day, any moment. *She's* afraid of me. They're all fucking terrified of Chloe Anne Palmer who looks like a map of the fifty states.

Detective Myres came on a wet morning without Detective Keller. In spite of herself, Chloe wondered about Myres. (Then wondering would start to feel like a muscle, tearing very slowly, and she would stop.) Chloe saw lots: that Myres had boredom and anger; that she was the only one who even partly got it, the only one so far who was *ashamed* because no amount of rage and disgust she could show would make the slightest difference; that she was bored by her own anger. She was bored by the gap in the equation, Chloe thought, smelling the rain on Myres who sat, shedding curls of steam at her bedside. She resents having to see me because my fifty states body and edited face ask for a purity and visibility of rage she's tired of failing to express. She gets it because she knows that her questioning me, hauling me back into a world where anything (words included) is connected to anything else insults me. If she could dispatch me to heaven I think she would.

I talk to detectives, Chloe thought. Television language arrives (and finds the exit blocked) in Chloe Palmer's wired-up mouth. I write my answers, slowly, on her yellow legal pad.

But it was difficult to concentrate. Nothing that the world which relied on words (questions and answers) could offer her was anything less than a further degradation, a further insult.

Detectives could wear jeans, apparently. And DMs. Rained-on, Myres's donkey jacket hung like a pelt on the chair next to the radiator. Chloe smelled London on her when she came in. She smelled London on her and saw London in her eyes. All the

London Chloe herself had never seen, all the buried silt it was their lot, now, to dredge.

Myres was over forty and her face was as hard as a winter vegetable. Chloe imagined her shoulders and cheekbones icy to the touch.

All the anger and boredom had stripped the detective's language of frills. The first time she came, she asked Keller to go and get her something from the cafeteria. Chloe observed that Keller was afraid of Myres, that he seemed like a little child next to her (though they looked the same age), because there was a finality in Myres that undermined him.

He's scared of her, Chloe thought. He should be. He should be scared of me. He *is* scared of me.

That first time, Myres had got rid of Keller, then leaned close to Chloe.

'Listen to me,' she said. 'I'll only ask you this question once. When we get him, do you want him in prison or do you want him dead?'

It was the absence of passion that convinced Chloe. She knew Myres was looking at her and seeing beyond the cut and paste, seeing *her.* She isn't offering it to me as anything more than the barest, basest, most cursory compensation, Chloe thought. Not even that. She's just telling me it's in my power. She's telling me it's *mine.*

Chloe wrote *dead* on the pad. She didn't have to think about it.

Myres said: 'I'll do everything I can to make sure that happens.'

That was all. No rhetoric, no intensity. As Myres leaned away, Chloe began to wonder about her for the first time – but it made her mind ache, so she looked out of the window instead.

At the end of that interview, Myres had said: 'There's one other thing I have to ask you – but again, I promise this'll be the only time.'

Chloe kept very still, knowing. Now she knew what people were going to say before they said it.

'Do you have any idea where your husband might be?'

When Liz and I were kids, we argued about the worst way to die. She said drowning, because it wasn't even your own natural element. I said being eaten by an animal, because then you were just meat and blood and skin. Because then nothing that was *you* made any difference. Because to a tiger or a shark or a crocodile you weren't even a person, you weren't even *you*.

To Chloe, it seemed that Myres was ashamed of the framework into which the victim had to be made to fit. Profiles, facts, details, clues. He's been operating for five years. Chloe wrote: *Like a surgeon.* Myres just turned her hard, parsnip face away and consulted the sky.

She knows there's no framework for me. She knows that to me it's not that I'm 'the fifth' or 'the sixth' or whatever they think it is. She knows that to me I'm not 'the one who survived'. She knows those are the labels in her framework, not mine. Not mine. For me there's no framework. For me it's just that I'm someone who used to be me. I'm someone who used to be me. Remember that? Do I?

Myres is disgusted because we have to keep talking the police language. She doesn't believe in the law. Now Myres just believes in blood. Now she's the Old Testament. Just get them. Just get them and *end* them. She's dead and fierce with this conviction. And another part of her knows that she's capitulated to her gut. All the head-language, all the abstract questions are over. Now there's just finding the men who do this and removing them. It's a simplicity she's earned by finding the bodies. More than half of her knows she's earned it. Another part hates the world for forcing her to this point. Another part hates herself because she thinks she's failed to stand beyond blood. Revenge.

There aren't any abstract questions. There's just bone and skin and blood. The body's the last particular that destroys all generals. The concrete that out-argues all the abstract. There aren't ideas. There's just the presence or absence of pain. There's just whether you keep or lose your blood.

If you don't want to read anything, I thought perhaps you might feel like writing instead, Jane had said. She brought Chloe a blank book and a beautiful fountain pen. I thought perhaps you might feel.

Chloe had hated her for it, had wanted to stab her in the eye with the silver italic nib.

But then later had found comfort in the smell of ink and paper, just because it didn't belong in the hospital's palette of odours. She doodled all over the first pages, aimlessly repeating heraldic, leafy designs, or holding the pen firm in one spot, watching the ink spread in a soft black explosion through the paper.

Eventually, she wrote: *All you need to become terrifying to everyone is not to have died when you should have.*

Do you have any idea where your husband might be? Your husband. Might be. Where. Chloe tried to keep the words together but they sailed off from each other. Idea. Do you.

Take this man to be your lawful

Her mother didn't ask, and Chloe intuited that her father had told her not to. At thirty degrees in the cranked bed, Chloe saw all the unasked questions like a rapidly multiplying species behind her mother's eyes. Not just behind her eyes. Everywhere: lungs, stomach, throat, fingertips. Surely she could barely breathe. Soon they'd start straggling out like flies. Chloe imagined her mother at home, hiding the questions in linen baskets and teapots and handbags. There were so many of them. Eventually they'd

There's a part of you that keeps trying to think of worse things. Once there was this story on the news. A woman was driving her husband and two daughters when they were hit by a drunk driver. The woman went into a coma, and when she came out of it they had to tell her that her husband and two daughters were dead.

I remember it wasn't the main story on the news. It wasn't even the national news. It was London. Regional. I remember saying to you: Why wake up? If that's what you wake up to. Why bother? And you said: You don't have a choice about being woken up.

You don't have a choice. They woke me up. They saved me. They saved me to not recognize the woman in the mirror.

They're taking the wires out of my jaw soon.

Funny. At moments hatred of this body. Other moments indifference, clinical curiosity. Other moments (most) sorry for it. For *it*. Parts of it. They won't let me have a proper bath because of the stitches. There won't ever be enough bathtubs in the world. There won't ever be enough water. I dream of baths. In weird places. A recurring one about climbing to the top of an old, three- or four-storey house and finding a white room at the top with a giant old tub set on a platform under a skylight. I fill it with water that's almost scalding and get in. It thaws my skin, my shins, belly, throat. It's salt water. Smell of the sea. Even the sea's not enough.

There isn't enough water in the world.

Toi bed-bathed Chloe and nattered about her life – flatmates, hospital gossip, shoe dilemmas, bank stress.

They've told her to talk to me, Chloe thought; to reassert the world. Nothing's changed. Show her everything's OK. Going to be OK. See? *EastEnders. Coronation Street.* Just like before.

It wasn't Toi's fault, but Chloe could hardly stand her hands on her, insisted on doing as much of it for herself as she could.

There's a big line of stitches across my stomach that reminds me of *The Wolf and the Seven Little Kids* Ladybird book. The wolf eats the little goats, swallows them whole, still alive. All seven of them. (Actually six of the seven, I think. Can't remember – maybe the youngest escapes.) The mother goat waits till the wolf's asleep then cuts his belly open, frees the kids, and replaces them with seven stones. Then she sews him up. The wolf wakes up, bemused, wanders off, then falls in the river, unbalanced by the stones. The nanny and kids live happily ever after.

I'm scared of having my mouth back. Scared of what it'll say. Do you have any idea where

How many times? Eventually you stop asking the question. Eventually it's not a question, it's a state. A new state. Constant. It's a quality of mind through which everything else filters. Like eventually, if it rains long enough, it's not rain any more because rain stops.

One of the auxiliaries was a girl called Vicky. Chloe deduced that Vicky had been told about her, that she woke up and didn't go back to sleep. One night Vicky asked her if there was anything she could do. Chloe thought of her as an old soul. It was something else new, the ability to count people's incarnations. It was easier to see in the ones, like Vicky, who weren't bright. Chloe wrote: *Get me out of here.*

*

Vicky's voice was pure East End, incongruously husky for her small, brittle frame. She was in her twenties but Chloe thought of her as a little girl. Her mouth smelled of Juicy Fruit. In response to Chloe's request, she said: 'When are git me brike. If yaw stiw up.'

She came back at two with a wheelchair. Whispered: 'I'll push, an' you'll 'ave ter owld yer drip. Give yer the tore, innit.'

All the corridors brightly lit, with sometimes buzzing strip lights. Kidney-shaped steel dishes. Oxygen cylinders. Beds on wheels. Plastic curtains. Three undisturbed drops of red blood in a white corridor. Air stinking of medicine, of medicine saving people, stretching their stay, waking them up, keeping them alive.

An old woman with no hair and half her face plum-black with bruises. Vicky whispered: 'Mugged, poor ole girl.' Other insomniac patients standing or shuffling with their drips. Chloe heard a woman moan, one protracted, melodramatic moan that ended in a sob, and then a nurse saying: 'Oh *do* come off it, Mona. You're going to wake everyone up with that palaver.' One fat, frog-like woman in a tartan dressing-gown and slippers stood in a doorway with her fists on her hips and her lips pursed, as if she had come to the end of her tolerance and was about to pounce on someone and give them a thrashing.

Whistling, unshaven porters and thick-calved nurses in flat white shoes. All the porters and nurses riotously cheerful.

Chloe drank her water through a straw, and by the time Vicky got her back into bed she needed it. Her face was sweaty. Hands shaking. Vicky looked at her for a few seconds, then reached out to Chloe and moved her hair off her face.

I want a transplant. A mind transplant. I want my body. The

other one. I want to sink these stitches in the Dead Sea, sink this
flesh that looks now like parts hauled from a lake. Dissolve.
Dissolve in salt water. There isn't enough. There can never be
enough, not all the seas on the planet.

Where are you?

I don't know which is more the fear – that you've gone of your
own free will or that something's happened to you. Parents
whose children go missing. I'm eligible for membership of all
sorts of dark élites.

Wrist hurting. Haven't had that since Finals. That and the smell
of the ink makes my mind slip off, back.

In disgust, Chloe had crossed out her observation about her
power to terrify people and gone back to doodling, inhaling the
scent of the ink. But slowly, thought began to reassert itself. And
there was no one else to talk to about Myres.

Myres is a visitor, not a detective. There's nothing more for her
to ask me, but she was back again this morning. Is there anything more for me to tell? She thinks there is. I couldn't fucking
care less – but I'm *becoming* something to her. What? I don't care.
Survival decreases what you care about. Myres is guilty because
it hasn't happened to her. I can see it so clearly. The hardness and
deadness – even the cold-looking skin and bone of her face – it's
guilt. That she doesn't know the process, only the product. Only
the leftovers. Only the bodies.
    She made some pretence of checking a detail, but it was all a
charade. I don't know what she wants from me. Today we sat for
a quarter of an hour without a word to each other. She's not
solicitous. No grapes or nonsense. She comes because I'm a
unique gravity. She comes because she can't help it. They all do.
Mum, Liz, Jane. I wish they'd stop coming. Stop waiting for me

to give some sign that everything's all right. That's what they're doing: waiting for me to let them all off the hook.

It's disgusting. It's all about them. They love me and it's revolting because it's really themselves. I'm going to ask them to stop coming.

But Myres? Thinking about her tires me. I've got this sickening sense that I'm being offered the opportunity to demonstrate my survival by becoming interested in something.

Every now and then I realize I'm doing this to avoid thinking about you. Every now and then I notice the rain I'd forgotten because it's become all weather.

Myres said: 'Your nights aren't good.'

At the end of a silence, Chloe wrote: *So?*

It was almost impossible to keep the words people said together. She watched them come out of their mouths in bright flakes, drifting away from each other. Good. Nights.

'What happens at night?' Myres asked. Chloe couldn't tell her. There weren't words. (Another by-product: she could see all the world for which there wasn't talk. It was like the discovery of a new colour spectrum or set of musical notes. It shrank the talk-world to laughable proportions. If you could laugh, that was.) She couldn't tell Myres. She couldn't tell her that space – all the space that wasn't her, everything beyond her skin – felt solid and alive. Couldn't tell her that walls, floor, ceiling, the bedsheet, the hospital gown – couldn't tell her that they disappeared at night, that there was just her skin, that all the spaces hurt. That looking hurt. Hearing, smelling, thinking, breathing – all hurt. Touching most of all. Touching anything. Pain. She kept wondering if a nurse was going to appear and say: 'Shall I give you something for the pain?'

* * *

When Liz and I were kids once at Uncle Bernard's, we found
what was left of two rabbits Aunty Audrey had skinned. She'd
just slung them into the stream at the bottom of the yard. What
they were were heads and skins, with all the insides taken out.
Liz threw one at me and it stuck to my shoulder. I wailed. To pla-
cate me, we improvised a funeral and buried them. I remember
the light weight of it in my hand, holding the foot with the head
hanging down. The eyes were open. What its ghost would
weigh. I cried, late at night, thinking of its eyelashes. Your mag-
goty cat.

The surgeon minimizes his contact with me, since it's obvious
that I hate him. We say almost nothing to each other. Women
who fall for their surgeons – the gory intimacy on the operating
table. I'm not one of them. For every part of me that he's pulled
together I'd happily undo ten of his. After he'd gone this afternoon Toi came to change my drip and I knew that she could feel
the disgust around me like an aura. She worked quickly and got
away.

I try not to look at myself. A new horror, if I do, is that some
parts of me are recognizable. The backs of my hands. My toes.
My elbows. Confirming that it was me, still is me – forcing
physical evidence on me. Me. I don't want it. I don't want to
receive it.
    Physical evidence. That's Myres's talk.

There was a full moon. It shocked Chloe when she turned the
bedside light off. She could feel its light on her face like a liquid.
She watched it for a long time. Formerly, things like the sun or
the moon, clouds, trees, had been either friendly or malevolent.
Not just natural objects. Teabags, umbrellas, lampposts, car
headlights – if she had wanted to, or if the situation seemed to
demand it, Chloe could consult the part of her imagination that
endowed all such things with personalities and know whether

they were for her or against her. When she'd been for the interview at the museum a tubular stainless-steel pen holder on
Mason's desk had been absolutely against her. On the other hand
a dolphin-shaped grey cloud visible from his window had been
very much in her corner.

The faculty for judging the bits of the world in this way was
always there. (It was one of the things she and Nicholas had
known about each other, immediately.)

Now it was different. Now they were neither for nor against.
Now they were just there. Now all of it was just there. All of it.
Everyone. People.

Myres gave me faces to look at. A whole ring-binder full of men's
faces. Hundreds of nostrils and eyebrows and ears, heads of hair,
mouths that didn't care about anyone or anything. Lumpy faces,
scarred faces, porous faces, faces eager with sweat in the camera
flash. Horse faces, dog faces, lizard faces. Sleepless, mad, vicious,
ill. I knew I should be looking at the eyes. I knew Myres was
waiting for me to see the eyes I'd seen before. A disinterested
part of her curious: would I vomit? Scream? Shit myself? Break
down, shaking? I knew, with the bit of me that knows these
things now. It's only a bit of me. A calm bit, that just goes about
its business while the rest gropes through the dark, struggling,
screaming. This same calm bit of me knew that I wouldn't be
able to stand seeing the face I'd seen before. So I didn't look at
the eyes. Mostly.

Perhaps I like Myres. Because of her boredom with the gap
that has to exist between us. Because all her police life of trying
to ask women painful things carefully has shown her that there
is nothing that will make it less painful for them, so now she just
asks functionally, without any ornamental compassion. Because
she knows that with me anything less will sicken me. 'If you feel
up to it, I'd like you to look at the men in this folder. Maybe get
an identification.' That's all. If I hadn't known he wouldn't be in
there I don't know if I'd have looked. Myres seemed to know he

wouldn't be. She offered the folder to me because it was a police motion that had to be gone through. Myres knows they don't have his picture, that he doesn't have a record, that he doesn't get caught.

Hard to write. When I write 'he' my skin hurts. A sensation that comes from the nib of the pen scratching the paper up through my fingers and into my arm.

The rape woman, Maggie, said: 'You'll have to make some decisions about how much you're going to let him have taken from you.'

Maybe the word 'he' is one of the things.

So Myres got the artist in.

I'm not writing what I

I don't want to thi

Liz fiddles with the edge of the bedsheet, or her coat, or the hem of her skirt. Easier for her if I'd died. I'm so glad you're alive. Easier because just my still being here shows her the thing worse than losing someone: losing someone but still having to look at them every day. There's a pleading in her: Don't let this have happened. Don't let this have happened because I don't want something this big to have come into my life and dwarfed everything. Don't make me ask myself whether I love Tom. Don't make me ask myself whether this is how I want to be spending my life, given that my life could end at any time. Don't be the same. Don't be different. Just don't.

No Myres today. Trying to wean herself off me. It occurred to me, tonight, hours ago, that I'd been expecting her. Just expecting her.

Wheelabout with Vicky again earlier tonight. We wait till Moira and Hilda are asleep. Vicky isn't pretty, and she's young and un-educated. Therefore ingenuous. Therefore bearable. Just. She's not one of those East End girls wot rabbits. She doesn't over-compensate, nor load her harmless remarks with the weight of reassurance. We're at odd peace with each other. Her forehead's high and spotty and as delicate as a Fabergé egg. Her knuckles are thin and red. She's weaselly. A friendly, peaceful weasel. I don't mind her.

Sitting makes my back ache. Even in the wheelchair. None the less.

The hospital is a machine, a method. Remember when we had that conversation about how you see people through the lens of your job? Accountants see people as anxieties about income and expenses; psychiatrists see people as secret-keepers; airport staff see us as beings in motion, looking forward or back but never at the now. Doctors and nurses. Hospital workers. They see units of flesh and blood. Broken, burned, pierced, punctured, rotting, ripped. They see us leaking, tottering, dazed, robbed of memory, knocked about, terrified, sick. They see us in terms of potential for repair. I see them evaluating my potential for repair. The doctors are simple: can it be fixed? Can it be made to satisfy the criteria of being physically functional? Can we take these two wings of skin and rejoin them, almost seamlessly? Will it walk, talk, eat, digest, excrete, respire, grow, perceive? The nurses see more – or are allowed to, because the physical integration is less their responsi-bility. Is she all right? I mean, is she, you know, all *right*?

And red-knuckled, red-elbowed Vicky goes through it all as a dream, whispering. Her soul's ancient, resolved already, as if this incarnation's a superfluous afterthought, a deliberate regression for one last strouwl darnee owl King's Rowd, a final cheerio before she says hello to Nirvana.

'Assa burns wawd,' she said. 'Rarver not, if it's all the same ter you.'

I looked at her.

'Iss the kids. Can't be doin' wivvit. Summa them kids in there's only free or four years ouwld. I can't be doin' wivvit, Klow, onnist.'

I'm Klow to her. I've never been Klow to anyone. She's no-
nonsense about the burns kids. Not sentimental at all. She just
can't stand seeing them. At an appropriate moment I'll show her
my scar.
    My old scar, I mean. *My* fucking scar.

Parts of the world suddenly and momentarily returned to Chloe
(sometimes intensified) from wherever what had happened had
sent them. Three nectarines, for example, someone brought for
Moira. Chloe had been lying watching the sky (smoky grey with
strands of white, like albumen) for perhaps five minutes; when
she looked over at Moira's side table the brightness and solidity
of the fruit seemed unnatural, as if it had come from some other
realm. It startled her. The nectarines blazed for a minute, then
faded again, became negligible.

She could feel her internal organs at times, in the way she could
feel her own scalp. She was aware of them, dark, viscous, pulpy,
membranous, repacked. She could feel each of them doing its
job – or struggling to, or failing. She could feel each organ's anxiety over whether it was meeting the doctor's criteria. Her organs
trembled, separately, having survived the intrusion of the outside
world.

It's the skin that's not mine. That I don't want to be mine. That I
feel sorry for and loathe, alternately. It's the skin.

The thing with the police artist. Hateful. Could barely co-
operate. Thankful that my mouth was excused, being trussed
with steel and whatnot. Myres told me to pick something
from the ring-binder as a template; the artist would elaborate
according to . . .
    The artist a thin, receding man with an Adam's apple that

bent his gullet like an elbow. Dark-rimmed glasses. As wordless as if he'd had *his* jaw wired shut. Myres interlocuted. Broader forehead? Nose too big? How about now? Sideburns or no side-burns? Meanwhile the artist stroking in lines and rubbing them out, adding shading, detail, definition. Meanwhile me not want-ing the likeness to appear. Kept thinking of St Veronica with Christ's face left on her cloth.

Had to keep being brought back to it by Myres. Not gently. Help me get him, Chloe. Help me *get* him.

Things kept tilting. Felt like Myres was stealing it, shoving it back into the police framework. Then she'd sense me thinking it and freeze, raging, ashamed, helpless, knowing nothing she can do will make it better. The face indelible, miraculous. My stom-ach heaving, with nothing to expel. Nil by mouth. Either going in or coming out. Food, words, vomit, lies. I lay trembling, dis-possessed. Maggie had said: 'You're probably going to go through layers and layers, Chloe. It's a theft, too, rape.' Her earnestness and sculpted gentleness infuriate me so much that I can't even see the truth of her statements until she's out of my sight. I can't stand it because it's just in her head. It hasn't happened to her. Empathy, sympathy, imagination – there are places beyond them. Beyond them for ever, even if they understand the truths that the visitors to those places have brought back. Even if they under-stand, they're not licensed to utter them. They're not permitted.

What I can see in the women it hasn't happened to is the integrity of skin. They still own themselves. Their skin

Once you said to me: 'The curse on us is that, if we ever lose each other, we'll still remember everything.'

Your nights aren't good. No, Detective Myres, they aren't. Do you know how good it is to see the sky cross the cusp that takes it closer to dawn? Do you know how good it is when the dark grey turns its first shade of blue? Do you know how pitifully grateful you can be for the sound of the first tube or bus? Do you know the shame of lying curled under the blanket, packed as tight into yourself as possible, sweating, shivering, crying, aching and aching and pleading for it not to be night? Do you know how big the space under your ribcage can be? Do you know that utterly empty universes can exist in your chest, bent to the shape of all that used to be in them?

Despite everything the prosaic mechanism of life outside the hospital continued exerting demands to which Chloe couldn't respond. Her father brought bank forms for her to sign to pay the bills by standing order. Jane told her that the museum would keep her on salary. After each encounter – some mealy-mouthed representative from the other life shamefully informing her of how things were being, or ought to be, taken care of – Chloe found herself shaking, a state somewhere between rage and hilarity. Jane and her father had brought their quotidian titbits like beggars suffering acute self-disgust. She signed whatever needed to be signed, her hand trembling as she made her signature: *Chloe A. Palmer.* As a child she had agonized over the design of her signature, and spent days concocting something unforgeable. Her father had encouraged her: 'Got to make it so's no bugger'll be able to copy it, love. There's all sorts of criminal minds out there just waiting for a girl like you who's got an easy signature. Then before you know it, *bang.* That's you cleaned out of your life savings.'

Liz brought her letters. Get-well cards – patently from people who hadn't been told what it was she was supposed to be getting well *from.* These cards too unbalanced her, whether they were understated florals, reproduced Impressionists or inappropriately 'amusing' cartoons.

Sorry You're Poorly! Hope You're Back on Your Feet Soon! Keep Your Chin Up!

The exclamatory idiom reverberated in her head. She couldn't shake it; for hours she heard everything as an expression of surprise, encouragement or optimism: I've Come to Change Your Dressing! Wires Out on Wednesday! It's Time for Your Bed Bath!

Myres had told Chloe to make a list of approved visitors so that none of the press could pester her. Still, a journalist snaked through. He was young, but with a widow's peak and hanging jowls. Chloe knew almost immediately, from the raincoat and stale eyes. She was buzzing for Toi with her left hand and with her right had begun her message on the pad: *journalist get him OUT* – all before he had had time to see that her jaw was wired shut; he had asked her two or three questions and was still looking at her mouth, trying to see why she wasn't bothering with 'No comment' at least, when Toi appeared and forced him to leave.

It took no more than two or three minutes but it left Chloe shaking, soaking with sweat, her throat scalding with tears. He had said: 'Ms Palmer, what have you got to say to the man out there the whole nation's calling the London Ripper?'

Even before he had said them Chloe had tried to block the words out. The whole nation. 'The whole nation' loomed like a white shadow when he said it, and Chloe saw herself in a vast open space; the space itself an unanswerable question. Again her skin felt inflamed to an unbearable tenderness. Again she felt herself being forced into another schema – 'the whole nation's' schema, in which she was nothing more than a component, a *role*, in a story. The fragments of her sense of self that had returned and cohered had threatened to disintegrate again; with the asking of a single question from the outside world her identity had almost dissolved.

It occurred to her as if for the first time that she would eventually have to leave the hospital.

She dreamed of Nicholas, once. One dream in which she followed him through every room and hallway of a dark house, trying repeatedly to get him to turn round and look at her. In the end they emerged into a small garden with dead trees and cropped grass, and he stopped and began to turn. Chloe woke with his face still only half turned towards her. Not his face. Someone else's. It had been someone else all along.

* * *

The morning Chloe had her jaw unwired Myres came with a different look on her spartan face.

Chloe still couldn't speak properly. 'Can you say your name?' they had asked her, intoning as if for a baby.

'Khler Pomr,' she'd said – and been reluctant to try anything else. She had got used to writing; now it felt safer to communicate without the intimacy of voice. Her speech was a harbinger of re-entry into the world, and she was afraid of it. Even the almost vowelless attempt at her own name had jabbed her, fleetingly, back into real time. As soon as the sounds had left her throat she had felt stripped and visible, walls, floors, ceilings, doors, all transparent. 'The whole nation' could see her, could scrutinize her, could ask its unanswerable questions. Voicelessness had shielded her, had diminished what might be expected of her. Now she was terrified of what would be expected: that she speak, describe, make sense of, reassure everyone that she was all right, that nothing fundamental had changed.

'How's the jaw?' Myres asked, seeing that the wires were gone. Her eyes flickered slightly, noticing that Chloe was still using pencil and pad.

Weak, Chloe wrote. She knew what was coming, had known it would be soon.

She and Myres stared at each other, Chloe aware that the detective was assessing the extent of the damage her news might bring.

'Your husband went to New York,' Myres said. 'Less than twenty-four hours after he brought you in here. We hadn't tracked his credit card for the literary agency. Didn't know he had one. Stupid. Could have saved us a lot of time. He took a British Airways flight from Heathrow to La Guardia and checked into the Royalton, but checked out again the next day. Could be anywhere.'

The sealed-off part of Chloe was wondering how Myres bore the forced intimacies of her job. Here they were, two women, one dragged back from death, speechless, robbed of herself by the world's new tilt and pitch; the other bringing information in a lethal bouquet. How did it feel to Myres to know that anything she told Chloe might propel her into a new orbit of pain? What was it like, moving through life with poison on the tip of your tongue?

Chloe forced herself to coldness. Since Nicholas's disappearance she had clung, cerebrally, to the hypothesis that something had happened to him – though there had been from the beginning a gut-sense of something worse. Now she was doubly betrayed: by his abandonment, and by their history, which had persuaded her that he couldn't have left her of his own free will. In the moment of Myres's revelation Chloe felt almost exhaustively depleted; she felt the vast space left behind in her chest after all the imaginative energy she'd squandered on the idea of Nicholas's innocence. Meanwhile she saw what Myres was thinking: that this news was, perversely, easier to break in the wake of everything else that had happened to Chloe. If the body was on fire, how much could it feel the amputation of a limb? Myres had seen it before, victims with new hierarchies of pain, people sighing at news which a month earlier would have driven them to suicide.

Chloe felt her voice stirring like an incubus. But she knew that once she used it decisions would shape themselves around her like a circle of standing stones. To speak, to let the inner become the outer, would be to name the new paradigm, to accept the transformation. She remained silent. Myres, who had been standing, reeking of wet London air, sat down beside the bed. Chloe could hear her not bothering with any of the crutches: I know this must come as a terrible shock . . . Try not to be too devastated . . . We don't know anything for certain yet . . . I'm sure there's a reason why your husband . . .

She looked at the dark figure sitting bent forward, knees together, ankles apart, and heard the omissions as if Myres were shouting them one by one.

'One carry-on bag,' Myres said. 'Nothing else.' Then, after a long pause in which Moira coughed huskily and cleared her throat, the detective asked: 'What does it mean to you?'

* * *

Disbelief is a finite hoard of fuel. The certainty of its exhaustion makes lighting the fire redundant.

For once Myres drew back from something. She's not telling me everything. Her face is furnished so functionally that lies show through like patches of damp. It'll come out eventually, whatever it is. Not that it matters. How could it matter? Every why hurts, so I salve by not asking. Your husband went to New York. I think of it as one of Mrs Williams's essay questions: '"Your husband went to New York." *Continue.*' Use nouns and verbs, Chloe. Adjectives are lazy. If you use the right nouns and verbs you'll find you hardly need adjectives at all.

They keep trying to make me talk. Now, inside, I'm the revolutionary tied to the interrogation chair. You'll *never* make me talk.

Mum's almost hysterical because I'm still writing. She wants my voice back. Liz, too. They all want the voice back because then they'll know that *I'm* back. Me. I. Me.

'She'll talk when she wants to, love. Don't force her if she don't feel like it just now, eh?' Dad's face is long-jowled, as if his cheeks have been silting up, these last days. His face is liver-spotted and loose-jawed and rupturing with its expression of everything'll-be-all-right-you'll-see. Inside he's on the verge of violence – to himself, to Mum, to me, to Nicholas, any object that might conduct the crackling guilt. He blames himself, because he's a man and he let another man do this to his daughter. No edifice of reasoning is excuse, no fact of his age, no logic of his not having been there. His blood sends him the same message, twenty-four hours a day: she's your daughter and you let this happen to her. He believes it's his fault. Each of them believes it's his or her fault. Even Jane. I haven't got the energy to tell them otherwise, to tell them that all their noble blaming of themselves is just appalling arrogance.

After this happens, you're forced to believe that you've never actually seen anything before. It takes your skin away. There's nothing between you and everything. Today, Toi drew the blanket over my arm, thinking I was asleep; she might as well have scored me with a wire brush. I startled both of us with the noise that came out of my mouth.

What does this mean to you?

Myres asks her question. Doesn't even sound like a police question. What does this mean to you? It means the discovery of how much you have to lose before you achieve emptiness. It means your voice is a currency you can choose to withhold. It means the confirmation, absolutely and for ever, that you're alone. It means that if you're going to go on you can do so only by never giving your past your full attention. It means that your past will become a petitioner, waiting, knowing it'll never be granted a proper audience.

Same with history. I understand. Exhaustively describing the past prohibits the future. I used to wonder why so little was written about the Holocaust. It's our collective decision: if under-standing the Holocaust is the prerequisite for the future then there is no future. It's the opposite of Freud. We move forward by forcing ourselves to never properly look back.

These hospital phrases. Head trauma. Intensive care. Casualty. Head trauma. Myres is suffering head trauma. I'm a casualty. They want to provide me with intensive care. Your husband went to New York. Continue.

They put you in hospital to recover from the annihilation of your body's integrity. All you've got is time. To consider how simple it would be to heal if it was just bodily integrity.

You quoted Camus to me once, years ago. 'There is only one seri-ous philosophical question, and that is whether or not to commit suicide.'

I think of Maggie telling me that I have to decide how much I'm going to let him have taken from me. If I commit suicide, the answer will be: my life. That's another thing they're all afraid of. For them the retrospective question will be: how much did you do to get her through this? And the answer will be: not enough. It's all numbers in the end. All those math-ematicians and their faith in numerical expression. Maybe they're right.

*

I want to get out of here.

Where?

I can't tell Maggie that I want anything. She'll say: 'Good.' She'll interpret it as a decision to go forward. I haven't made that decision. They'll all think it means something more than it does. Bored. What saved you? What got you out? Boredom. Boredom is responsible for tectonic shifts but it goes utterly unthanked.

If there was no redeemer – and Chloe knew there was not – then all you had was yourself and the world. The world posed itself as a question to her: am I sufficient?

   All the long last days in hospital the question repeated itself. Her face in the mirror repeated it. The quick-moving parcels of cloud in her oblong window. Hilda's and Moira's shut, boneless faces in the small hours. Vicky's tortuous vowels and perfected soul. The reek of disinfectant, the amplified crash of a dropped bedpan. Myres's hard eyes the colour of mica. If there was a geometry of recovery then it was hidden only in herself and the world's components; it wouldn't help to go wailing for God in the wilderness.

   The world had made itself to see if it worked.

Myres came often, blatantly unofficial. It was unspoken, now, between her and Chloe, that their contact had its own occult necessity. In Chloe's new paradigm there seemed no need to question it further, though she still suffered the relationship as an irritant at times, a temptation to admit that she was willing to engage the rest of her life. She still experienced her interest in Myres as an ache, as if imagination were a muscle being called into use after devastating atrophy. She resisted. To capitulate would be to forfeit her right to retreat into death. That option remained with her. The longer she retained it the more liberty it granted her to crawl forward into life.

Myres spoke and Chloe wrote, so to an eavesdropper it would have sounded like the detective was talking to herself. Myres seemed so at home with this that Chloe began to imagine her as someone who did talk to herself, all the time.

They never spoke about why Myres continued to come, though the unasked question was always with them, like a subsonic hum. Chloe knew that Myres herself was afraid of asking it, and sometimes looked at her in obvious enquiry, gratified to see Myres's fear breaking through like hives.

Why detective? Chloe wrote.

Myres sat in the chair by the bed in the evening. She looked exhausted, drained. The eyes themselves gave nothing away; they were as they always were – small, dark, steady, like the eyes of a night driver – but around them the orbits were as blue as snow shadows. Chloe felt the imaginative muscle trying to unpack its blood.

'My Dad was one,' Myres said. 'I never wanted to be anything else. Think it's in the fucking genes.'

How old are you?

'Forty-six.'

Regret no kids?

'That obvious, is it?'

Chloe just stared. Her idiom, her pencil and paper idiom, had become skeletal too. It was one of the things joining them.

'Couldn't,' Myres said – then, seeing Chloe thinking the wrong thing, added: 'Stand the worry, I mean. You know. Even people who aren't the Old Bill think twice about bringing kids into this sort of world. Seeing what I see – couldn't do it. I'd never let them leave the house.'

Chloe's pencil stilled. The wind hurled a prodigal handful of rain at the window, then subsided.

You don't believe in the law

Myres said nothing for a while, then, rolling her neck, once left, once right, said: 'It's just that I'm tired.'

Chloe stared at her, not releasing her.

'Believing in the law takes . . . Believing in the law tires you.
I've been doing this a long time. Seeing things.'

People like me, Chloe wrote.

'People like you. Waking up one morning to find that everything – every last fucking thing – is totally different.'

Snow

Myres nodded. They were both aware by now that it was
more than Myres having got used to Chloe's shorthand. They
shared a grammar of the imagination, also never mentioned.
Chloe had been thinking of the snow of long ago in Elm
Coombe, of drawing her bedroom curtains as a child to discover
that the landscape had been transformed overnight: a shovel
and a stack of fence posts outlined in white; the cuneiform of
birds' footprints on her windowsill; the hills a blue and white
moonscape stretching away to the dark edge of the sky. The
great, uplifting betrayal had been at work while she'd slept.
Waking, discovering the world's power to reshape itself, she'd
been speechless, euphoric.

It snowed that night.

'I know,' Myres said, quietly.

Objective correlative, Chloe wrote.

Myres looked up from the pad. 'Don't know what that means,'
she said.

Chloe just shook her head, dismissing it. She had a headache.
Myres gave her headaches. Because she was honest; because
Chloe recognized that this kind of honesty was where she must
begin, if she wasn't going to end herself. Because she understood that in her state Myres was as good as it got.

Pain still rose up and engulfed Chloe, randomly, but she had
begun to be able to sense it coming. Initially she'd had no fore-
warnings. Initially, she would just find herself curling tight in the
bed, as if her body were contracting every muscle, trying to
minimize the area within which pain could operate. Not physical pain. She would find herself trying to shrink, to implode, to
contort herself into another dimension; she would find herself
failing and feeling the space under her breastbone giantly empty,
like a desert stretched over by a thin skin of sky. She would find

herself unable to breathe out, the last inhaled molecules of air dancing tarantellas in her blood. She would find herself reaching for everything that had spiralled away from her. She would find herself falling, weightless – then suddenly leadenly corporeal again in the hospital bed, her bones and muscles beyond volition. It was in these capitulations that she asked all the questions she couldn't bear asked. Why did you leave me? Why did you leave me? Where are you? Why don't you come back? How can you not be who you are? How—

That had been the way of it, initially. Now it was as if she could see the pain coming. It was as if she stood on a shore with her back to the sea but felt it rising up behind her, blotting out the light. Now she could prepare herself, could will herself not to ask the questions. She had discovered, too, that Myres's presence was some help – if only because Myres's presence forced one to be at least partly aware of it, like an ungainly grandfather clock that would not be ignored.

Chloe felt the shadow rising now, though the room was lit bright yellow and the air redolent of the ward's evening meal. Formerly she would have written *Tired*, and Myres would have got up and left.

'What's an objective correlative?' Myres said.

Chloe looked at her and saw some shame – residual, utterly incongruous – about education. It almost made her laugh. Myres looked away, down at the floor. 'Don't need a degree to be a copper,' she said. 'Everyone knows that.'

The phrase 'objective correlative' had taken Chloe back to university days. That part of her past (along with almost every other part of her past) had been revealed as an edifice intricately constructed out of chatter. She thought back to images of herself: in her room in the first week, handling the term's new books as if they were religious artefacts; sitting at her desk in the small hours, exquisitely alive to the sense of herself as someone connected, through all the long years of documentation, to people who had been dead for hundreds of years; standing by the Thames, letting the miracle of London's ghosts drift through her in a cavalcade – Elizabeth, Johnson,

Dickens, Pepys, Wren, Cromwell – coming to and being deflated by the insistence of buses and black cabs and hoardings; seeing Nicholas in the café, knowing she was about to begin something significant. She thought back to it all and shuddered. Yet here was Myres – who found the bodies, who saw carpets and floorboards and beds mapped with blood – irritated and sheepish because Chloe had access to a language that she, Myres, did not.

The arena for amusement shrinks, Chloe thought. Now it contains only the most warped and distended ironies. This'll be the stuff, I suppose, if I'm ever going to hear myself laughing at anything again.

Like a symbol, Chloe wrote.

Myres read and nodded.

The sea-shadow was rising up behind Chloe. She was afraid of what would happen if she didn't get rid of Myres.

'You thought about where you're going to go when you get out of here?' Myres asked.

Chloe had thought about it. She was going home, to Elm Coombe, knowing it was the wrong thing to do. Going back to the flat was out of the question of course. Liz had offered. Jane had offered. Both women had been terrified that Chloe would accept. Chloe had almost accepted just to see the reaction, to watch the face's struggle to transform horror into delight. In the end, she had discovered that in spite of everything there was a small, inevitable pull to her home – not to her parents, but to the room she remembered from childhood, to the window's square of landscape, the cattle-shadows revolving through the afternoons. The time before Nicholas.

Devon, she wrote for Myres.

'To your Mum and Dad's?'

Chloe nodded.

'You might find . . .' Myres began, then stopped, looked at Chloe. 'You might find it's not the best place to be,' she ended.

I know that already

'So why are you going?'

Where else? Chloe wrote, then added: *New York?*

Myres blinked slowly, then ran her hand through her hair, which was short, battled with and flecked with grey.

'Tired?' Myres asked, not looking at Chloe. Chloe didn't respond. The sea-shadow was long in front of her now.

'Point is,' Myres said, 'there's a place you could stay if you wanted to be on your own.' Now she did look at Chloe, who had let the pad slide away from her, but still held the pencil, loosely. Chloe stared back at her. 'In Cornwall, actually,' Myres continued. 'Which isn't that far from where you're going anyway. My Dad bought a place down there years ago. It's nothing, really – more of a hut than a house. We were supposed to go down for summers, but we never did. My parents rented it out, then I did, for a while, after they died. Couldn't be arsed after a few years. Had a dodgy lot of tenants who virtually trashed the place. Last two years, I've been going down there and trying to put it back together. Still a shithole, mind you.'

The words drifted to Chloe as if from a long way away. Sweat prickled on her forehead. Myres was a formless shadow, a voice, offering something – though Chloe couldn't grasp what it was. She tried to focus. Failed.

'I'll let you get some sleep,' Myres said coldly, and stood, rising in one swift motion from the chair.

Sometimes the worst thing happened. The worst thing was more than pain. The worst thing was having pain inflicted. The worst thing was suffering pain because someone else chose your suffering. The worse thing was looking into the eyes and seeing that the other person's pleasure increased in direct proportion to your suffering. The worse thing was seeing in the eyes an infinite capacity for pleasure and at the same time knowing your finite capacity for suffering. The worse thing was knowing that the limit of your capacity for suffering would be reached long before the limit of the other's capacity for pleasure. The worse thing was understanding from the start that no amount of your suffering was ever going to be enough.

*

Chloe lay awake at three in the morning drenched with sweat and passed through repeatedly by violent shudders. Hilda's and Moira's heads were two black musket balls. A sliver of light from the corridor ran in a straight line across the floor then bent up at ninety degrees and climbed the wall.

It always seemed that the colossal wave at her back must annihilate her when it crashed. The shadow advancing up the shore spoke of a wall of black water a mile high, rising behind her. She never turned and faced it, though she knew that watching its shadow spread in front of her was more terrifying than confronting it could be.

But it never did destroy her. It never crashed at all. It engulfed her and forced her to bear its weight.

Vicky found her awake and exhausted at four, and fetched her a cup of tea. In spite of herself Chloe put her head in Vicky's lap and lay still while the girl gently moved the hair from where it was sweat-pressed to her face. Chloe knew this was a terrible surrender, that she would regret it, that even now she felt a little compartment of herself filling up with shame; but she couldn't help it. Vicky's presence, the starchy, medicinal smell of her uniform, the light touch of her hands (which seemed to Chloe deliciously cool), the humble, solving simplicity of her was irresistible. Vicky's was the only touch that didn't hurt her skin. Chloe pressed her face against Vicky's belly (as small and taut as a grape), feeling the sweat cooling on her own skin, hearing herself whispering, 'Sorry . . . sorry . . . sorry . . .' Vicky sat and rocked, very gently, back and forth, holding Chloe's shoulder.

'I brought you summink,' Vicky said quietly after a few minutes, when the two of them had become still.

Very gradually, Chloe eased herself away, though she was still too weak to sit upright. She lay instead curled on her side.

'In't much or ennyfink,' Vicky said. 'Tella troof, I fink my Uncle Nev come by these in sumwot shaddery circumstances. Anyway. Fought you might like one.'

Vicky reached into her apron pocket and brought out a small, very thin silver bracelet. She lifted Chloe's left wrist and fastened the fine hoop around it.

'In't much, lark I said,' Vicky said. 'Just fought, you know, since Nev give us arf a dozen each . . .'

Chloe, now feeling more acutely the shame of having clung to Vicky, said nothing, but took Vicky's hand in her own and hoped the gesture would pass for gratitude.

'I wannid to tell you, Klow,' Vicky whispered, shoulders forward, knees together, 'that I don't never ask you nuffink about what appened to ya because . . . because . . . not coz I don't care – you know? Coz I mean I *do*, dun I? It's just . . . It's just I don't fink no one's got the *right* to say nuffink about it. Know what I mean?'

Chloe nodded, squeezed Vicky's cold hand.

'There's nuffink to be said about it unless it's you what says it. I just wanted to tell ya. You leavin' ere soon an' whatnot. I just wanted to tell ya, all right?'

The bracelet, reflecting a thin crescent, indicated the degrees of first light, told Chloe how much there was left of the night's sentence. In years to come, waking or awake in the small hours, she would consult it instead of a watch.

In hospital her dreams – during what little sleep there had been – were of a new order. No narrative, just forces, as if giant colours or weights drenched or tore her. She woke struggling for breath or shouting, the shouts telescoped into whimpers. Maggie had asked her if she had recreated that night in her dreams; Chloe had closed her eyes, ignoring the question.

But on her last night in hospital she dreamed of horses. She lay half locked in cold clay. Parts of her – her face, her knees, her fingertips – broke the surface, but the bulk of her body was buried, clutched, a great weight of earth holding her down. She lay looking up into a high, ultramarine sky with an icy wind tearing over her and through the ground felt the thunder of hooves coming towards her. Imprisoned, she could do nothing. All her will focused on lifting her head and shoulders. She raised her head an inch or two, but her hair, woven into the earth, held her. She could see, in a shallow angle down the green grass where her body should have been, movement in the distance, at the far end of a deep valley. Horses. Ten, twelve, twenty – she couldn't tell. Sunlight shone on them. They were approaching at supernatural speed; the hoofbeats rang in the ground, reverberated through her bones in a continuous, explosive percussion. She opened her mouth to scream but produced only empty breath that scorched her throat. She watched, helplessly, until they were almost upon her – then in a final effort to escape trampling pressed herself back, as deep as the earth would take her. Every limb strained to pull the ground over her body like a quilt. At the very last instant, when the shadow of the first animal fell on her, when the phalanx was so close that she could hear the foamy breath, she felt a tremendous relief at the certainty of destruction. She looked up and saw silver hooves like quarter moons above her, lifted against the distant sky, felt herself laughing, then everything changed. She was looking down on them. They seemed not to be moving, like runners on a treadmill. Their backs glowed in the crashing sunlight, their necks plunged up and down like beam engines. The green of the valley rolled under them.

Liz was driving Chloe down to Elm Coombe, four hours from London.

'Ready then?' Liz asked.

Chloe sat, dressed, on the edge of her bed with her back to her sister, looking out of the window. London sky. Rain. The old world. Out there was the smell and engine yawn of buses. Out there were shop windows with angular mannequins. Out there were no allowances. Out there were a billion signposts pointing backwards. To the life before.

The clothes – underwear, jeans, socks, hiking boots, a flannel shirt, a sweater, an ancient leather jacket – hurt Chloe's skin. She'd asked specifically for them, the boots in particular.

(Standing, her feet felt like boneless bags of blood; she wanted as much armour around them as possible.) She had told Liz exactly what to bring, but still, dressed, the surface of her flesh roared with pain. Each item of clothing carried its own portion of force, the force of the old world that would not be satisfied until she re-embraced it.

Without turning, she wrote on the pad: *In a minute. You go down.*

She handed it back to Liz, timed the pause, the calculations her sister was making about what it meant (this not being ready; the hiking boots; *everything*), heard, in the silence, that Liz didn't know what it meant (any of it), then exhaled, slowly, to the sound of her retreating footsteps.

Moira was asleep with a collapsed face and arms straight by her sides – but Hilda looked at Chloe when she passed her bed.

'You off then, dearie?'

'Yes.'

'Lucky, eh?'

'Am I?'

'Luckier'n me, anyway. I'm not leavin' this place now, 'cept in a bleedin' box. Nor's 'er, neither, shouldn't wonder.'

Chloe had never asked what was wrong with either of her roommates. Now she discovered they were dying (or believed they were), it made little difference. Hilda, dying or not, was desperate to be thought of as a good old London girl – was, in addition, proud of having *been* thought of in this way for so much of her life. The bit of Chloe that would have indulged Hilda was part of the petitioning past to which Chloe would never again give full hearing.

'Say 'ello to the world for me will you, love, eh?'

In the lift Chloe imagined Liz rationalizing the decision to come down alone: That's Chloe being brave, that is. Showing the world she's not going to be afraid.

The reality was that Chloe was reeling, drunk with fear. Liz's anxiety would only have added to it.

Her skin was voices. As the lift drew her down the voices

whispered, a swelling agitation that she knew had the potential to become a scream. She wondered if the two doctors in the lift could hear her. She shrank from the rough touch of her clothes.

She hadn't realized how long she'd been away from the world, how distant it had become. The view from her window – the city's pasty sky and deserted roofs – had nothing to do with this world, the one she confronted now, stepping through the glass swing doors into wet air and a sudden blunt blast of wind. The window had looked out on another place, another time, remote, unpopulated.

For a moment Chloe stood on the steps leading down to the car park, breathing through her nose, hands buried deep in the leather jacket's pockets, shoulders up high to protect her neck from the touch of nothingness. She stood still, moving only her eyes, feeling her jaw tight shut, trembling. Wet stone and concrete; black, fine-branched trees bordering the car park; the cars themselves in hard, flat colours. Loving Nicholas had made him a condition of her perception. Now, confronting all the space beyond the hospital, Chloe was given the first real sense that that condition had been removed; objects were peculiarly raw and naked, unexplained. She stood, hair slashed away from her face in the wind, thinking of all the time that stretched ahead. Her life. The rest of her life. Your husband went to New York. *Continue.*

'Chloe.' Myres, with Keller hanging back.

'I wanted to see you before you went,' Myres said.

'What for?' Chloe said, then shuddered at the sound of her own voice in the air.

Myres's stone eyes, unwavering. The thin mouth that dealt language without ornament. 'Wish you luck,' Myres said – then laughed, once, through her nose. 'Tell you we'll get him.'

Chloe looked past her to where Keller stood with his hands ramrodded into his trouser pockets, staring down into the car park.

'And if you don't?'

'We'll get him. I'll get him.'

Chloe saw Liz standing by the car, waiting. 'I've got to go,' she said.

'Funny to hear your voice,' Myres said.

'You know where to find me,' Chloe said.

'There's something else.'

Chloe was thinking: Liz can see me talking.

'We're going to know if your husband comes back into the country,' Myres said. The wind was making her eyes water. 'If he does, do you want to know?'

Part Four

WATER

On Broadway, in the first cobalt light of evening, Nicholas stood in the small graveyard of a Catholic church, shin-deep in the snow. A lattice of dark, stripped trees hemmed the place. Black and white headstones protruded at different heights and angles around him. Only a few yards from where he stood was the unending clamour of traffic and people. The city gave no surface indication that it contained such things as old churches; but they were there none the less, pygmy incongruities in the riot of secular concrete and glass. Nicholas had opened an iron gate and stepped in to escape from the road. He had been standing at a corner waiting for the light when the opposite sidewalk had suddenly receded to a distance of a hundred yards. He had looked up at the green traffic signal to discover that its light was solidifying in a brilliant sheet that descended through the air towards his face like a slow guillotine.

Out of his body, he saw himself from behind and above, standing now on the church's threshold, silhouetted by the vestibule's amber candlelight. Then his flesh and blood recalled him. When he came away from his body in this way (and it was happening with increasing frequency), Nicholas thought of the bat and ball game of childhood: a thin, pancake-sized wooden bat with a length of elastic attached to its face, and at the end of the elastic a soft rubber ball. As a small boy he had never tired of it, the ball's return to the centre of the bat, no matter how hard it had been struck. He always imagined himself as the ball – the illusion of freedom on the outward trajectory; the loss of velocity; the point of full extension; the split second of absolute rest at the end of the elastic's reach; the queasy realization; the return to impact. Now, as if at the full extension of its own outflung umbilical, his consciousness had turned and rushed back to his body in the entrance to the church.

The place was empty. White candles burned in the transept and apse; the arched ceiling contained a space of blue shadow. An ornate black iron grille ran the length of the floor. In the half-light the statues breathed: the Virgin Mary in one alcove, arms out, wrists like broken stems; Christ across the nave, displaying the Sacred Heart as though with resignation. Another Christ above the altar, gorily crucified – spiked feet, bent knees, stretched abdomen and flaring ribcage, nailed palms and uptilted, questioning face. Nicholas remembered the idea, inherited at home and at school, that Catholics were mad. Obsessed with sex, hell and the mumbo-jumbo necessary for avoiding perpetual torment. He remembered hearing of papal infallibility, of the Holy Spirit guiding the prelate in matters of doctrine. As a child he had imagined a secret panel behind the pontiff's bed, concealing a dumb-waiter shaft that climbed all the way to God. He had imagined the Pope waking in the middle of the night to the sound of contained wingbeats: a message brought by the dove. He remembered Chloe telling him that for a while in medieval Europe there had been two popes, one in Avignon, one in Rome, arguing about which one of them was *truly* God's living mouthpiece on earth.

Remembering her, he found that his mouth had positioned itself for the beginning of her name. But he couldn't utter it. The church's incense-flavoured air pressed up against his face, invaded his mouth when he opened it.

'Can I help you?'

Nicholas came to. He was bent over the altar with his cheek pressed against its cool stone. He wondered if he had slept. If he had, he had woken with an agonizing snow-thirst. He rose and turned.

'Is there something you want here?'

The priest was a tall, brown-skinned, handsome man with silver hair and a solid silver moustache. He looked to Nicholas like a veteran conquistador. He stood loosely, hands in pockets, regarding Nicholas from the bottom of the three steps to the altar. Nicholas said nothing.

'I'd prefer it if you came down from up there,' the priest said. 'Would you mind?'

Nicholas fell coming down. One moment his legs were under him, the next they weren't. He got one hand flat in front of him but most of his weight was taken by his chest and the side of his head, to which the iron grille rushed up as if its design were an urgent and intimate message.

He didn't black out. Time and motion slowed for the fall, then returned to normal speed after the great bone howl of his head hitting the floor. Lying with his wrist trapped underneath him, Nicholas knew the priest would be thinking that he was drunk. He wondered if he *was* drunk.

'Can you get up?' the handsome priest asked him, close to his ear. 'Can you get to the seat here?'

The question was so close Nicholas thought he could feel the soft hairs of the silver moustache. He got up on to his elbows with blood singing between his ears. The priest put his hands (which were large, long-fingered and muscular) under Nicholas's arms and helped him to his feet.

'Sit here a moment. You're bleeding. I'll get something.'

'Have you got any milk?' Nicholas asked him. 'It's the snow. You want milk when it's snow.'

'Just sit there for a minute.'

Nicholas's discomfort grew in the priest's absence. His consciousness did its elastic stretching trick, repeatedly, so that he looked at his body in the pew from a dozen different angles in rapid sequence. The statues moved and sighed, as if relieving cramp, then became still again.

The milk was icy and Nicholas swallowed it so fast that it seemed to splinter his skull.

'It'll do for now – but you'll need a stitch or two, I think.' The priest had applied a rudimentary dressing of antiseptic, gauze, lint and two Band-aids to the gash in Nicholas's eyebrow. 'No brain damage,' he said.

Nicholas didn't understand. A red-and-white-frocked altar boy had come in and lit two large candles beneath the crucified

Christ. Now the figure on the cross had a giant shadow stretched out behind it, like the wings of a pterodactyl.

'Just don't sue, OK? We can't afford it. Go to Rome. Crack your head on the steps of St Peter's Basilica. *They* can afford it. Not here.'

'You look like Omar Sharif,' Nicholas said.

The priest laughed – which Nicholas didn't understand, since the man *did* look like Omar Sharif.

After a moment the priest said: 'I have things to do. You should sit here for a little while. How do you feel?'

'I want to ask you something,' Nicholas said.

'What?'

'I want to ask you . . .'

'Yes?'

'I wanted to ask. Forgiveness . . .'

'Would you like me to hear a confession?'

'No no. I mean *about* forgiveness. A question *about* it.'

The priest smiled. It was a source of pleasure to him, for some reason, Nicholas could tell. Perhaps just because it was a break in the routine. Looking at him, it occurred to Nicholas that the man had reached a point of indifference to the particulars of his own religion – the minutiae of doctrine; the idiosyncrasies of ritual. He had moved beyond all that, at last. Nicholas could read it in him – the sense that the serendipity of their own form was what all religions ultimately revealed, the belief that the best religions were fabulous, intricate references to something, something which could not be grasped. Something which *could* only be referred to. But he remembered, too, the moment before nausea at the flat in Clapham. He remembered that all the room's objects had been illumined from within, lit with their own separateness, absolutely denying a relation to anything – the white teacup, his jeans on the radiator, Chloe's whistling, gurgling wound. He remembered (as the statues moved again; Mary in midnight blue adjusted her heel on the serpent's head) the vision of his life and all human life as a sequence of habits, a preposterous, charlatan order sketched on to chaos. He remembered that there was nothing to be referred *to*.

'Why do you insist on forgiveness?' he said. 'On God's grant-ing forgiveness? Are there no unforgivable things?'

'Do you want for there to be unforgivable things?' the priest asked. His smile was thin-lipped, almost wicked. Nicholas took another long swallow of the cold milk while pain hammered erratically behind his forehead.

'God's imagination is too subtle for there to be unforgivable things,' the priest said. 'Do you want some more milk?'

Nicholas shook his head, gently. Inexplicably, he began to believe the man was an impostor. It was the moustache, partly, decorating his mouth in two thick, ostentatious scrolls; it was his size and grandeur, his brown, porous, used skin, as inviting to the touch as the leather of a sun-hot saddle. It was his indif-ference to the salvation of Nicholas's soul, his casual, discerning black-olive eyes.

'God doesn't "grant" forgiveness anyway,' the priest continued, languidly. 'Forgiveness is a necessary consequence of true peni-tence and remorse. It's a condition of the universe, like gravity or stars or rain.'

He didn't bleat. There was no insistence. He might have been standing at a bus stop discussing the weather. He had gone beyond such things, it seemed to Nicholas. His religion had given him a profound instinct for life; he had not begun with faith, but he was ending with it, smiling, less and less concerned, less and less afraid of death.

They sat together without speaking. Nicholas slipped in and out of present time and space. When the priest spoke again, it was unclear how much time had passed between them.

'It would be easier – so very *much* easier – if there were things which, in themselves, were beyond forgiveness, God's forgive-ness, I mean. It would be easier because at least then one could do such things and so once and for all be finished with the struggle to get away from God.'

'But there *are* some things—'

'There is nothing. There is nothing unforgivable.'

The interruption had been forceful but the priest's charming

(almost saucy) smile had barely wavered. 'To speak of the
unforgivable is to compromise God's omniscience.'

Very slowly, as if each of his muscles was capitulating, one
after the other, Nicholas leaned forward and rested his head on
the conquistador's broad chest. He didn't cry. He had not cried a
single tear since that night; nor was this the solace of theology.
He was simply overwhelmed by the heavy, resonant peace of
the other man. It was as if a confidential magnetism had reached
out and drawn him down to the dark breast.

The priest neither welcomed nor rebuffed the gesture, but
sat still, easy in his muscle and bone. They remained motionless
together, staring at the crucified Christ above the altar.

'Do you know what that represents to me?' the priest said
wistfully, contemplating the nailed palms and feet, the averted,
bloody face.

'What?' Nicholas asked.

The priest didn't answer for a few moments, as if he'd either
forgotten what he was going to say, or was searching for its most
concise expression. Eventually, with a slight chuckle, he said:
'Endurance.'

It meant nothing to Nicholas, though he was momentarily
contented in the nearness and solidity of the other man. They
lapsed into silence again, then the priest said: 'How's your
head?'

Nicholas didn't answer. He was waiting for the suspension of
consciousness. The black cloth had seemed to offer it, covering
the broad chest. Here was another version of what Mickey did
for him. Here was another route away from himself.

But he couldn't close his eyes. On the shelf above the kneeler
in front of him was a bright yellow book: *Fifty Good News Hymns
and Carols*. The yellow gave him a peculiar pain, as if a fat insect
were trapped and struggling behind his cornea. Eventually,
having received no physical acknowledgement from the priest,
he sat upright again. Now a tremendous weight of boredom was
on him. He slid to the end of the pew and stood up. The conquistador, unsurprised, glamorous, grinning, looked up at him.

'Had enough?' the priest asked.

'I've got to go,' Nicholas said – then flinched as something dark suddenly winged close to his head. He looked up and around himself, and at the corner of vision every time was movement he couldn't catch. There was nothing to be seen, yet movement everywhere.

'There is no distance so far from God that you cannot turn and walk back to Him,' the smiling priest said, reclining, now. 'That is the curse of salvation, unfortunately.'

Nicholas, backing away, bumped into a cast-iron candle-stand which jabbed him in the kidneys. He stood still, sucking his breath in. The movement had stopped. The air was empty. The priest, taller than Nicholas by a head, stood and brought him the half-drunk glass of milk. 'Why don't you take this with you,' he said. 'In case the snow makes you thirsty again.'

Together they walked the length of the nave, the priest with his large hand flat between Nicholas's shoulderblades. Half a dozen huddled parishioners had come in unnoticed. He saw them on his way out, dotting the back of the church like dark stones. None of them looked at him.

'You promise I'm not going to get a nasty letter from your lawyer?'

Nicholas stood again among the gravestones, all buried deeper than before.

'Come back if you want me to hear your confession,' the priest said, brilliant teeth and eye-whites flashing. Then, with a wave, he turned and went back into his church.

Mickey's doorman greeted Nicholas in the same way every time: with a look of distilled contempt and a flat 'Yes?'

There was a pause after he announced him on the phone. Then: 'Yes, ma'am. Sure thing.'

'She says you're to go up, but that I'm to remind you that you weren't sent for.'

Nicholas turned and crossed the lobby to the elevator. The ascent to Mickey's apartment always made him suffer. The confined space heightened his relationship to himself; his hair and limbs screamed. On more than one occasion he had had to get out halfway and take the stairs, which, deep-carpeted and bereft of other traffic, offered him their own unnerving attendance. Being alone indoors generally was becoming unbearable. Only the presence of another person could sustain him.

He was sweating by the time he reached Mickey's door. Zack opened it, and made no move to let Nicholas in. Instead, replicating the doorman's greeting, he said: 'Yes?'

Nicholas looked past him into the apartment's gilded light. Music filtered out: Sinatra.

'Yes?' Zack repeated. He looked directly into Nicholas's eyes, his face communicating the precise degree to which it was pretending unrecognition. Stressing every consonant, as if Nicholas were a lip reader, Zack leaned further forward and said: 'What do you want?'

And this also was a torment, to be made to speak, to represent his will. Throughout everything Nicholas had found it almost impossible to speak to Zack, to allow his own voice to pass between them.

He could barely make the words now. 'I came to see Mickey.'

Zack let his eyes die and harden, then moved his body slightly to one side so that Nicholas could see into the room. Mickey sat with her knees up under her chin on one of the soft leather couches, smiling. She waved one set of fingers.

Zack moved back to block Nicholas's view. 'Sorry, man, she's not here.'

Nicholas looked down at the floor. All he could think of was the impending horror of the journey back down to the lobby alone.

'Could I . . .?' he said, unable to face Zack. 'I wanted to see her.'

'For God's sake, Zack,' Mickey said, in a trickle of laughter.

Zack reached out and put his hand on Nicholas's shoulder. 'I guess you're really disappointed,' he said – then, squeezing, added: 'Jeez, man, I know. I *know* – you know?'

Nicholas felt the muscles of his face compressing, his lips quivering. Zack pulled him close, within the radius of whisky breath and aftershave, embraced him, rubbed his back. 'I know, man, I *know*. Don't you believe me? You think I'm hiding her somewhere? Look, come inside for a second. You're frozen to the bone! You got no sense to get in outta the snow?'

He hugged Nicholas, left one arm around his shoulders, then walked him into the brightly lit room.

'See?' Zack said.

Nicholas looked at Mickey on the couch. She was barefoot and her cheeks were flushed. The blond hair was piled high and haphazardly. Smiling, with wide eyes, she shrugged, helplessly, as if Nicholas were asking her to reveal the secret location of a hidden Christmas present and spoil the surprise.

'*Now* do you believe me?' Zack said. 'I know you believe me now, Nick.'

Nicholas remained motionless.

'Let me hear you say it,' Zack said. 'Let me hear you say: "You're right, Zack, she's not here. I was a fool to mistrust you."'

'You're right,' Nicholas said. 'She's not here. I was a fool to mistrust you.'

◆

No sirens. Just the soft static of snow splashed by the ambulance's revolving red and blue lights. Two medics in mint green, one bald but with a thick moustache, the other sandy-haired and freckled, with a compactly muscular body and sparkling blue eyes. Together they manoeuvred Chloe on to a stretcher and into the back of the vehicle.

To Nicholas, all of it seemed choreographed. Each of them, himself included, moved in slow motion. Even his own vomiting (once, in the hall, when he saw Chloe's blood darkening one leg of the bald medic's green trousers) was a graceful gesture in a dreamy waltz.

A calm female voice spoke fragments of first-aid-manual phrases in Nicholas's head. Heavy bleeding, or haemorrhaging, is a life-threatening emergency. Bleeding from a large artery can result in death in less than five minutes. There are half a dozen pressure points. Never try to explore a wound to find fragments of. Leads to symptoms of shock. The femoral artery, supplying blood from thigh to foot, passes over a pelvic bone. Less than five minutes.

The ambulance interior was brightly lit and painful. The equipment looked archaic. Brown rubber tubing; a black cylinder; glass. Nicholas had imagined hard white plastic and gleaming steel, LCD displays, beeps, automation. He had imagined everything looking brand new.

'Put your fingers here,' the sandy-haired medic said. 'Look. Where mine are. Like that. Press down there. That's it.'

Now there was a siren.

'Blood pressure's bad. Keep your fingers there until I tell you to stop.'

Chloe's eyes had closed. The skin of her face was a greenish grey around the wounds.

'She's in shock. Talk to her. Come on, man, for Christ's sake!'

There was so much blood. Less than five minutes. Nicholas saw the tourniquet on the left arm. Unless there is no other way to stop blood loss. Tourniquet can result in death of tissues in a limb, and may lead to amputation. Five minutes? Hadn't this been going on for hours, days?

'She's stopped breathing. Get out of the way. Steve, I'm at CPR in here.'

'Almost there.'

'You better start talking to her or we're going to lose her.'

Then an explosion at the hospital. Everything speeded up, like time-lapse film of a flower opening or the sky from sunrise to sunset. Brilliant light and the crash of doors. A busy coven of nurses, a white-smocked female doctor with stethoscope dangling like a long-legged insect. Casualty. Nicholas's screaming redundance. The sharp, stabbing scent of disinfectant. Doors, doors, and a nurse telling him to wait outside. Chloe received into an inner sanctum. White perimeters closed around her.

* * *

No one had noticed him leaving the hospital. For two hours he had sat in the Casualty waiting-room, staring at the signs: NO SMOKING. PATIENTS AND STAFF ONLY BEYOND THIS POINT. THIS IS AN ACCIDENT AND EMERGENCY UNIT. SOME CONDITIONS, THOUGH PAINFUL, ARE NOT LIFE-THREATENING. PLEASE RESPECT THAT PATIENTS ARE SEEN ON THE BASIS OF NEED, NOT ON THE BASIS OF ORDER OF ARRIVAL.

He had sat on an orange plastic chair bathed in the room's fluorescent light and felt his gravity falling from him again in thin, sloughed layers. Images had come to him like faces rushing to the lens of a camera, desperate to be seen: Anthony handing him the heavy tumbler of Scotch; Chloe, naked, looking up at him, wondering what was wrong; London like an intricate fossil, looked down on from where he stood on the dome of St Paul's; the doctor saying, 'I'll just give you the facts'; a doorway with cold air and steps going down into the earth; Chloe watering the trough, a small dark figure in the snow.

Once or twice in his life Nicholas had dreamed that he had murdered someone. Waking, he would feel the guilt like an indelible stain on his chest, and the consequences of crime (the agents of justice) rushing through the world in an effort to pin him down and make him pay. Then would come the realization that he had dreamed it, that in fact no such thing had happened, that he was lying with Chloe in their bed in the morning, that he had nothing more terrifying to face than another day at work, that he was innocent of crime, that he hadn't killed anyone. The relief would come in waves, transforming nausea into happiness. He always wondered (once he was re-established, free of guilt, beyond the aftershocks of the dream) what would happen if the relief never came, if he never woke to reassurance, if he really had murdered someone. He always wondered how long he would be able to sustain that level of fear.

So he had sat in the hospital, discovering. His mind refused the material, and instead transferred all reaction to his body. Therefore the diminishing mass, the steady draining of substance, as if the physical apparatus were struggling to hide itself, far from punitive forces. It was as if the mind was telling the body that it was possible to escape by disappearance, and the body, half convinced, was annihilating itself by degrees.

As in the flat, Nicholas found himself virtually weightless. He gripped the seat of the plastic chair to stop himself from rising up to the room's low ceiling and tubular lights.

But when he looked out of the window, he saw that the day's first light was seeping in. Bars of pale cloud; snow-roofed cars beginning to show dulled versions of their colours; time reasserting itself.

Without premeditation and in silence Nicholas had got up and walked from the building.

Two police cars outside the Clapham flat. Yellow Police Line tape across the open front doorway.

He moved like an automaton unaware of the semantics of its program. At the rear of the building was a small alley separating it from the back of the next terrace. Nicholas forced himself through a gap in the ragged hedge and crossed the flat's small back garden in the silver light. He ducked under the tape across the back door and stepped into the kitchen. There's no excuse. There's never any excuse.

Sounds of occupancy. Voices. The scratch and hiss of a walkie-talkie. A female voice saying: 'Unclear. No more than four or five hours.' In the bedroom. For a moment Nicholas stood still, understanding that the flat had been translated into a different language. Its structure and contents were being rewritten as units in a new system of meaning in which only certain things mattered: point of entry, intruder's movements, position of the victim. The furniture's historical significance – where he and Chloe had bought a painting; which of her relatives had donated a wardrobe – was irrelevant. Now all that mattered was the extent to which such objects could be used to decipher an invisible sequence of events. If a doorframe carried a print, it shifted to the top of the hierarchy. If a green vase hadn't been moved or touched (no matter how much Chloe had loved it), it meant nothing.

Nicholas had no sense of urgency. It neither surprised nor failed to surprise him that he stepped past the open bedroom doorway unseen, walked into the living-room, took his passport from a drawer in the desk, then returned silently to the kitchen unchallenged. On his way back there he had passed within three feet of a police officer who stood with his slender back to the corridor, hands on hips. Nicholas had actually stopped for a moment and stood behind him, staring at the dark uniform, the white collar, the crewcut, the rim of the cap.

'We're going to have to see if all of this blood's hers. Since she survived, we can assume she put up a fight. Maybe she stuck him.'

'You reckon?'

The woman's voice again: 'No, Dave, I don't reckon. But I fucking hope so. I sincerely fucking hope so.'

'We got someone at the hospital?'

'Carlisle's on his way – but she's still in surgery.'

'What are her chances?'

'What do you think?'

Nicholas crossed the garden again and tore slowly through the leafless hedge. The alley was deserted.

◆

When Nicholas moved through the drowning city now he hurried. The streetlights lit long, unfurled banners of rain which swept over him, fresh, cold, heavy. Hardly any snow remained underfoot; the roads were a weave of slush. Headlamps tunnelled through the darkness, showing horizontal columns of rain like static. His clothes carried a new weight of water. Shop awnings released single large droplets that exploded on his head then scurried down the back of his neck. The traffic hissed.

Mickey had told him to come. Had told him in the way that meant he couldn't disobey.

And still the rain wouldn't stop. He was afraid. Something was moving behind him, eroding the distance between itself and him in sure degrees. He knew it was only a matter of time before it found him, and beyond that encounter he could think of nothing, could not imagine himself surviving it.

Not that he thought any of this clearly.

There is no distance so far away from God that you cannot turn and walk back to Him.

The priest's smile, the charming grin of the veteran conquistador, flashed in Nicholas's memory.

Sensing this thing dogging him, understanding that if he stood still or turned it would have him, Nicholas flagged a cab and flung himself into the back seat. Rain pounded on the vehicle's roof. He gave Mickey's address, rolled up the cab's half-open window, then lay back and closed his eyes.

'Hey, sweetie, you made it!'

Mickey opened her door to him with glittering eyes and a hungry, mobile smile. She drew him into the middle of the room. Zack was on the couch, one leg widely crossed over the other, a drink in his hand.

'Shakespeare!' he said. 'Man, I knew you wouldn't let us down! Everybody, this is Nick. Nick's the theme this evening. He's a man of few words, but don't let that fool you. Underneath that . . . you know, *taciturn* exterior the man's a goldmine. Pure gold, you know?'

On the couch facing Zack three people sat and looked up at Nicholas. A Japanese woman of about forty with heavily made-up eyes and short, wet-gelled black hair. Her face, a face beyond any kind of surprise or arousal, was a slender ellipse with a small mouth that looked like a finger-poked hole in her flesh. She sat neatly on the edge of the couch, holding a dark brown cigarette with the very tips of her first two fingers. No jewellery. Just an impeccably cut ankle-length black dress, strapless, revealing thin-skinned shoulders and long magnolia arms.

Next to her a younger man with jaw-length white-blond hair and a scrupulous tan who lounged ostentatiously with a large, complicated cocktail in one hand and a cigar in the other. Economically muscular, he sat with arms and legs spread, smiling and scrutinizing Nicholas in an appalling ease of body.

On the farthest edge of the couch a middle-aged man in a navy suit neither drinking nor smoking but sitting with legs tightly crossed and fingers woven around one knee, as if his posture was an attempt to compensate for the expansiveness of his neighbour's. Grey, short-cropped hair, dark eyebrows and a dark moustache. He examined Nicholas with his head on one side, as if pleasantly perplexed.

'Hey, Nick, how's it hanging?' the blond lounger said, then laughed huskily, eyes twinkling.

'Shakespeare, I gotta level with you, man: you look like shit,' Zack said. 'You gotta stop walking around in all fucking weather, you know? I mean it's not even *logical*.'

'Why don't you take a shower, honey, and I'll find you something to change into?' Mickey said.

Nicholas looked at her, remembering the first night he met her at Arcadia. He was seeing now a version of what he had seen then: her unwillingness to arrest her own motion. What she had chosen – this year, last year, ten years ago – had set her in motion away from herself and now there was neither looking back to what she once was, nor stopping to consider what she had become. To halt, to be even momentarily at rest, was to risk the horror of knowing she could have chosen otherwise.

In the bathroom with Nicholas, she paused at a mirror to repin a lock of blond hair that had dropped on to her forehead. Even then her face remained perpetually mobile, mouth and eyes trying out infinite nuances of levity and delight. She saw Nicholas standing behind her, reflected in the glass. She winked at him, initially refusing to accept the new quality of silence between them, refusing to concede that he had his own view of her. Initially, the smile wriggled and the small eyes glittered. Then she turned on him.

'Don't,' she said, stone cold, flat. Her nostrils dilated, her cheeks coloured. Her throat darkened, the smoke-coloured jugular suddenly visible under her skin. She forced a laugh. Tried not to understand her own doubt. 'I don't know what's got into you lately.' She span back to the mirror, made a final adjustment to her hair, dabbed a speck of something away from the corner of her mouth with her little finger. 'Shower and wait in the bedroom,' she said, not looking at him; then left, closing the door behind her, softly.

Nicholas undressed and got into the shower, afraid of his own body. There was a new text of injury written on it, scattered hieroglyphs of damage, but too much of it still expressed the past: the elbow wrinkles had been traced by Chloe's fingertips; the sternum remembered the precise weight of her head, almost asleep; the knees had fraternized with hers, thawing under the quilt; the palms still knew the warmth of her midriff and thigh. She had touched every part of him. Every feature of his flesh was a signal back to its encounters with her.

It was with him, here, in the bathroom, whatever he had hidden from in the cab. He knew the sense he had had that he could outdistance it had been delusion. It couldn't be evaded. If you took a cab and covered forty blocks in ten minutes, it would be there ahead of you, waiting to show itself. Waiting until you thought you were safe.

He sat down in the tub (the size of a tennis court), closed his eyes and let the water crash down on his head.

He wasn't sure how much time had passed. The door opened and a bubble of music and laughter expanded into the bedroom, where Nicholas lay curled up on the rug. It startled him awake – and immediately on waking he knew he had all but reached the end of his ability to hide. Each indrawn breath inflated his visibility. Consciousness now was the sound of fast-running water, of a reservoir being recklessly drained.

'OK, British guy,' Mickey said to him, a deliberate affirmation that there was nothing new between them, 'time to come join the party.'

White noise. Vulgar salsa and the gabble of voices. Laughter and people shouting to be heard. Everywhere red mouths talked and opened for drink. Cigarette smoke hung in a pall under the ceiling. Fifteen or twenty more people had arrived. Nicholas saw the blond man dancing, shirtless, with a heavy-bodied woman with red hair and bright green eyeshadow. She was naked but for knee-high red leather boots and a black corset that covered her waist. Her breasts were large and deflated, with dark aureoles like shocked eyes. Several other people were naked or half undressed. Those who danced did so with urgency and a concentrated pleasure, their eyes focused on each other in radiant collusion. Their mouths seemed compelled to mobility, snarling and grimacing and puckering by turns.

The room's brightness assaulted Nicholas. As at Anthony's, the light cut at him like slivers of glass. He raised his hand to cover his eyes, but someone (Mickey?) grabbed his wrist and pulled the hand away.

To retreat from this would be to turn and embrace what was pursuing him. He stood in the centre of the room, wearing the white bathrobe provided, unable to move. The familiar desperation was with him, the craving for the space of his own will to be occupied by another's. He didn't know what was expected of him.

The guests moved frantically, like the severed and still-animate parts of a once unified body. One by one they became aware of Nicholas standing motionless among them. Some looked at him with deliberately hackneyed suggestiveness, others with childlike or primitive detachment. The innocence in these looks frightened him, then relieved him – since he understood that for them his annihilation was the annihilation of an object. It satisfied him, anchored him, intimated a vast peace at hand.

The Japanese woman now sat alongside Zack, still on the very edge of the couch, still with a cigarette at the tips of her fingers. Her clothing was intact, though Zack was naked, loosely stroking his own erection, talking to her, receiving short replies from the compressed mouth. She didn't exhale her smoke but let it fall out and upwards with her words.

Pain exploded, suddenly, under Nicholas's ribs. His breath rushed out of him and he sank to his knees, doubled over, rested his forehead on the floor. Hands (strangely cool, as if their owner had held them in an open fridge) manipulated his arms, began to tie his wrists behind his back.

Mickey's face, so close that he could smell her lipstick. Her eyes liquid. Someone was lifting his head by its hair. Mickey was imitating him, facing him on her hands and knees like a puppy trying to engage an old dog. The hand pulling his hair forced his head all the way up, brought him into an upright kneeling position. The blond man was on his haunches next to Mickey, holding the object with which he'd struck Nicholas: a police nightstick, longer and slimmer than the British truncheon, matt black with a short handle two thirds of the way down. The expression on the young man's face was one of happy, quizzical evaluation, as if he had just demonstrated one of a hundred options and was assessing its impact before selecting the next. He smiled at Nicholas, nodded, as if to say, Not a bad opener, eh?

Nicholas sucked oxygen in with no certainty that he would be able to expel it before his lungs tore. He thought of the blood vessels burst in the blow, imagined them as tiny supernovas in a deep red galaxy. Meanwhile the music still played and half a dozen people still danced, glistening with sweat. Nicholas understood he was a diversion, no more. He was aware, too, that there might even now be a small space for his will to reject this, that if he chose he could exempt himself. But even as he considered it he sensed the confrontation (infinitely more terrifying) that would await him beyond this, if he chose to withdraw. It was outside Mickey's front door. It filled the space of her lobby. It was on the stairs; it was out on Fifth Avenue; it filled the park, the streets, the city. It was everywhere: to be conscious and free was to encounter it at every step.

The blond man with the nightstick rose and stepped over to Nicholas. Nicholas looked at Mickey, who knelt upright, now, bright pig-like eyes glittering, lips slightly parted. Nicholas looked directly into her eyes, searching for the part of her that recoiled from this. (He had known, as if picking up a remote and garbled signal, that Mickey hadn't succeeded in erasing her past, that for all the forward motion, for all the blind trajectory, there remained a younger version of herself that haunted her slip-stream. Nicholas had felt it as an entity between them at the times when Zack was absent.) For an instant she saw what he was looking for. Her eyes focused; but the heavy, red-haired woman came behind her and squeezed her breasts, hard, with phthisic, magenta-nailed fingers, speaking something into her ear, staring at Nicholas – and the focus dissolved in Mickey's hurried laughter.

The nightstick, under Nicholas's chin, inclined his head very gently upwards. The golden face beamed down at him. Mickey moved forward on her knees, undid the blond man's fly, grinned as his cock sprang out at her. It was her answer to Nicholas. She took the phallus in her left fist and crammed it into her mouth, forcing her head back and forth up and down the length of it with a violence that made it look as if she were trying to stab herself in the back of the throat. The man yielded to her, dis-tracted for a moment by the sensation of her mouth around him – but the red-haired woman took the stick from him, looked at Nicholas eagerly for a second or two, then struck him, hard, on the side of his throat.

Nicholas felt the two pain locations expanding, desperate to meet each other. But more acutely he felt the pressure of every-thing outside Mickey's apartment swelling in an attempt to break in and embrace him. It sent visions at him: Chloe lying naked, looking up at him, wondering what was wrong; Nina's face across from him in the Wheatsheaf, forcing the acknowledge-ment of what was between them; the snow-light from the open door at home showing the small ceramic pot and Chloe's shoe next to it; his father's half-shaved face in the mirror; the priest's cheeky smile.

He went under and resurfaced many times. The music never stopped. At first it had been possible to focus on individuals. Some of their faces achieved a pure, martial beauty, expressing the truth of their natures. This hadn't helped, since the percep-tion of beauty shackled him to himself, to all his history of perceived beauty. Sometimes the faces were languid, with dreamy eyes and smiles. Other times heraldic, with white teeth and scrolled tongues.

Submerged, there was nothing. Returning, there was a different posture, different hands, feet, faces. Time was a series of vignettes: Zack standing with his arm on the blond man's shoulder, breathing heavily, both men with lean muscles lacquered in sweat; the older, grey-haired man, naked and paunchy, sitting in an armchair and staring into space as if paralysed by boredom; Mickey at two moments – one, watching in a trance while a young Hispanic woman stood masturbating in front of her, the other sitting with her knees up under her chin, tears dragging mascara flotsam down either cheek.

In the moments of consciousness Nicholas discovered that he was wearing pain like a hot uniform. It was impossible to tell which parts of himself had been damaged; now his body was a unified signal of distress. He heard it over the music – and in the spaces between songs his own blood deafened him.

'You flakin' out, Shakespeare?' Zack asked him.

They had taken him into the white bedroom, where he had collapsed on the floor. The music had stopped. Nicholas had the sense that the people with him now were the only remaining guests: Zack, Mickey, the red-haired woman, the blond man, the Japanese woman, still seemingly untouched in the faultless black dress. Whatever had been waiting for him outside Mickey's apartment was now held back by only the bedroom door. He knew it would have him, very soon. He knew it had defeated him. Even now, feeling himself lifted and manoeuvred by warm hands, there were strands of its presence creeping around him like the scent of a potion. He knew it was only a matter of time before it possessed him entirely. Now his chasing after the submission to violence was a sickening redundancy – though he couldn't summon the will to do anything else.

The Japanese woman lay on the bed on her left side, resting on her elbow, staring at Nicholas who stood pressed facing the wall. Mickey lay behind her in an identical position, her bright face carrying confused expressions, struggling always to contort into levity. The red-haired woman sat with her legs primly crossed on the edge of the white bed, her tired eyes focused on him. Zack was alongside him, naked, loose-limbed, twitchy with energy. A forearm pressed the back of Nicholas's neck and though he couldn't see, he knew it belonged to the young blond man.

'Not necessary, Josh,' Zack said. 'Not necessary, right?' he asked Nicholas. Nicholas said nothing. After a moment, the forearm released him and Josh joined the others on the bed.

They were waiting for something. Zack, behind Nicholas now, was tapping him with the nightstick – light blows, tripled in effect because all the flesh they fell on was already bad-tempered with pain. Mickey cleared her throat and draped her arm over the Japanese woman's side. The Japanese woman's eyes were focused, as if her will was the one anchoring them all in a composition. Nicholas, breathing heavily, remembered Michelle sitting astride Helen's stomach, himself suffering the irresistible fall towards her. He remembered the way in which the three of them had come to rest, as if unseen forces had worked to achieve a particular alignment. He remembered the inevitability of it and recognized it here in this tableau.

Slowly and with a delicacy of movement she might have adopted if her body had been covered in burns, the Japanese woman reached down and began to draw the skirt of her dress up over her knees.

Nicholas closed his eyes.

Again, he experienced the time that followed as a series of isolated fragments. The tiny, distinct pain of Zack's cock forced into his arse; the reflex association with needing to shit; the strange inrush of new knowledge and grief that came with the wreck of bodily integrity; his own voice crying out, sounding remote in his own ears, their generous laughter. The carpet scorching his shins in two intimate inflammations as Zack bent him and ploughed him towards the bed. The precision with which the red-haired woman held his chin in her hand, struggling to absorb every detail of him while her face went through the angry gymnastics of pleasure – eyes wide then narrow, lips

loose then pulled tight, tongue slack then curled like an alerted
reptile – while Josh, on his knees behind her, fucking her,
seemed perpetually distracted by the movements of his own
muscles, the amber deltoids and radials, the abdominals like a
clutch of golden eggs, as if he couldn't quite assimilate the miracle of himself, as if his godliness was an irritating impediment
to getting the job done. The translation of pain into sound:
minor cello chords, hysterical violins, clumsy timpani. Then
one cacophonous, almost comic explosion of brass when something broke. Always moments in which he surfaced from the
bliss of hiding to discover that one of them was trying to make
him *see* them, their looks of disappointment when they saw him
slipping away. The sour iron of his own blood in his mouth, then
realizing a canine had gone. It surprised him that these small
details made themselves manifest without any regard for the
overall scale of what was taking place. It comforted him. The
Japanese woman, prodigiously bored, masturbating, desultorily,
with Mickey's finger buried in her anus; Mickey herself with
her face hurrying through every expression of excitement it
knew, arriving at nothing. The knowledge that now he was no
longer supporting himself, that Zack's penetration was keeping
him from collapse, that and a hand holding his hair. The sudden,
deflating intimation that he had achieved nothing more than a
catalogue of distractions.

Because now everything that the bedroom door had held
back was in the room with him. He felt its force tilted in precise equality against the force of his desire for disappearance,
with himself suspended in balance at the apex. There was a
single, infinite instant in which he heard himself breathe in,
once, this solitary inhalation creating space for his body's
announcement of everything it had borne – and in that instant
he knew (feeling Zack's sudden shudders inside him) that it
wasn't enough.

He had thought he had been searching for the worst thing. He
had thought they would help him. But the worst thing had been
with him from the beginning. It had joined him, now, in the bedroom (while the party moved through its last trivial and

redundant motions); it had joined him and made what remained
of consciousness loud and joyous with discovery.

Two images before he passed out: the red-haired woman's
face, convulsed, trying to spit at him and missing; and the
Japanese woman, neither irritated nor satisfied, sitting up, standing, walking from the room.

It was only an hour or two of sleep, but it brought a dream, presented it to him in a bright, truncated utterance.

He dreamed he was back at secondary school on a cross-
country run. It was winter and he was running on a narrow
path through the woods in fading light. No other runners were
visible: he had outdistanced the field. His legs were possessed of
an inexhaustible energy – indeed, the running seemed to require
no physical effort at all. It was merely what he did, as reflexively
as blinking or breathing.

The path wound, overarched by the bare black branches of
trees, but eventually he came to a straight stretch and opened his
stride. Happiness flowed through him. His feet thumped the
footpath in a rhythm that seemed both natural and miraculous.
He could feel his cheeks and eyes pulling into a smile.

Then, perhaps twenty yards in front of him, he saw a small,
white bird, flying very low to the ground, away from him.
Without knowing how, he knew its speed was identical to his
own, and that it was imperative now that he catch it. He ran
faster.

Now a strange thing happened. Joyously, as if remembering
with relief a former incarnation, he realized that he could run
faster on all fours, and in one forward motion he dropped to the
ground and felt his musculature and skeleton fluidly rearranging
themselves; he became a quadruped. There was no horror in
it – only a delight, as if he had recovered a lost talent. It made
him laugh (he felt his chest, close to the earth, laughing) that
now he understood the world that dogs moved through. It
amused him, seeing his arms and hands reaching out in front of
him in long, graceful strides. It seemed ridiculous that he had
ever run in any other way.

He gained on the bird quickly. There was no malice in him, only a friendly desire to catch it. He felt playful, but also infinitely gentle.

But the bird became aware of him and lifted its flight. Now he had to crane his neck to see it flickering under the dark weave of branches, twenty or thirty feet above him. He knew – again without knowing how he knew – that if he could only double his speed he could leave the ground altogether. He knew that if he ran faster – almost unimaginably faster – he would be able to fly.

Now his lungs started to protest. He ignored them, increasing his speed. He felt himself getting lighter, leaving the ground for three, four, five heartbeats. He stared up at the bird through the darkness – and only when he felt the first rush of pain did he look down again to find that his arms and legs were on fire.

Nicholas woke to thunder, lightning and a redoubled, down-rushing force of rain. Canted by the wind, it hammered at the thick glass of Mickey's living-room window. He didn't remember leaving the bedroom.

As if at the end of a long journey, the thought arrived that he was badly hurt. He was divided: a part of him experiencing an encumbrance of pain (laid on his limbs like a fiery suit of armour); another part detached and empty, mildly curious about the changes in his ability to function. He decided to try to stand up, and found that he could, though there were insinuations of wrongness throughout his body – odd weights of blood bottle-necked in his limbs, something that felt like a heavy blade wedged in his left side, forcing him to bend, bits of his face swollen into his visual field, as if mushrooms had grown there while he slept; he kept trying to brush them away. Other pains, leftover fires, negligible given what had been destroyed.

The disarrayed room, shocked into stillness by the events it had hosted, was filled with greyish light and the stale smells of spilled drinks and loaded ashtrays. Nicholas carried tranquillity around him in a forcefield, step by heavy step as he crossed to the window and pulled a curtain aside. Not daylight proper, but the tarnished silver of the hour before dawn. Central Park was a soft cloud of shadow absorbing the rain. Fifth Avenue was naked, as if the day marked not the beginning of a new year but of a new, post-apocalyptic era. Nicholas recalled Adrian Marlowe's peopleless world in *After the Party*, found himself smiling at the thought. It hadn't been so long ago that Nina had presented him with the manuscript and proclaimed that Adrian was going to be rich. Nina. Anthony. Work. London.

Chloe.

He was humbled and astonished at the peace that had descended on him; it seemed tangible, as if he had bright wings folded at his back. His physical incapacitation was ludicrous, since even burdened by it his every movement felt angelic, transfigured.

Naked, tattooed with bruises, tenderly exploring the evicted canine's cavity with the tip of his tongue, he made his way from room to room without any specific design or intention, just abstractly curious, just wondering, without fear, where it had gone, the colossal force that had pursued and eventually crushed him into survival only hours earlier. Throughout everything that had happened last night (and perhaps for days before), he had been aware of its presence. The white-smiling priest had only confirmed it.

But now, moving through Mickey's apartment, he was aware only of clean, empty space around him, its conditioned air thinned to a new purity, all the objects he encountered solved into simple beauty: armchairs, a rolled umbrella, a wineglass, door handles. He had never felt such peace of spirit. Everything belonged. Everything was connected to everything else. He had discovered an ontological grammar – the exact opposite of the discovery he had made when he had crawled into the bedroom at home and found her. Then, the disconnectedness of things had blazed at him, brilliantly. Now the relatedness penetrated him, filled him with silence and a profound delight.

On the other hand, there was something not right. At moments he thought he caught sight of something in the apartment with him. The same thing had happened in the church:

movement on the periphery of vision, the sense of a presence with him, concealing itself.

The bedroom door was half open. Stepping softly across the faintly lit carpet towards the bed, Nicholas heard his own voice repeating, gently, 'Now. Now. Now.'

It was a revelation, a pure articulation of his time. Each whisper made each moment manifest. He had never before grasped the concept of the present, never before understood that life was a continuous expansion of now.

Mickey slept curled tight away from Zack, the blonde hair all undone in glimmering fronds on the pillow. A tiny asteroid of mucus in a nostril whistled. Her shut mouth was a dark seal, her closed eyelids two buds of shadow. Zack slept face-down, both slender arms by his sides, ankles loosely crossed. He lay at an angle, as if he had been carefully positioned as a pointer to a hidden treasure. A perceptible heat rose from their bodies, creating an aura around them.

Nicholas's head ached. He brought his fingers up and pressed the inner corners of each eye socket, but found that the tissue there had swollen: thumb and index finger exploded two charges of pain which sent a white flash through his head and swung the room. He dropped gently to his knees, retching, soundlessly. Bile, sour and hot. He let it dangle from his bottom lip until the carpet took hold and claimed it. The clarity of moments ago had gone. Now he was confused. There was a solution here, he knew, like a familiar object seen from an unfamiliar angle. The strain of trying to identify it almost tipped him back into unconsciousness. For several minutes he remained motionless, breathing deeply, listening to Mickey's nostril whistling, counting the now.

He crawled to the bathroom.

The back of the white door held a full-length mirror. It wasn't that he didn't recognize himself. It was that the assaulted body made a mockery of his previous incarnation. It was that the truth of himself had been there all along and had only needed brutality to bring it out.

One eye was a puce sunset. The other looked surprised. He

tried a grin. Joke heavyweight's face, after the no-hope come-
back. A plum-coloured tumulus grew out of his left cheekbone.
He had thought he had been standing straight all this time, but
the mirror showed him his new posture, shy under the right
ribs, as if in reflex from a violent poke. There was something
wrong there, a large alteration that would have consequences.
He didn't think about it. Instead, he tried raising his eyebrows.
The sunset side didn't respond. He was intrigued. A bead of
warm blood trickled down the inside of his thigh. Gently, he
touched his anus, brought his fingertips away with viscous
blood.

But he was plagued by the infuriating nearness of the answer.

Blank, struggling to see it, he moved around the bathroom,
not knowing what he was looking for. When he stopped and
tore a strip of toilet roll to wipe himself, misery suddenly
expanded in his chest and tears fell from his eyes – then stopped
again, abruptly.

He shuffled around the white space, picking up and putting
down objects at random: a green towel, a plastic bottle of talc, a
heavy-handled hairbrush, a pink conch filled with pot-pourri.

Then hard and cold in his hand an incongruous weight. It was
a slender sculpture cut in sharp planes of matt black stone. He
had seen it before: almost formless, but with the suggestion of a
bird's throat and wing. It stood at one corner of the rectangular
tub, the only black object in the white room. One afternoon,
Mickey's glistening fingers had dabbed a fleck of bath foam on to
it, idly, her head tilted on one side, talking of Connell. Nicholas
had assumed it had belonged to him. It was unimaginable that
Mickey could ever have chosen such a thing.

Holding it, he turned and looked again at himself in the
mirror.

Everything he had feared, the confrontation he had dreaded,
that he had tried to outpace in the taxi, all that he had thought
of as waiting for him in every space that wasn't pain, had
embraced him. It had not only entered Mickey's apartment; it
had entered him. It had come and enfolded and taken possession

of him while he slept. He had been wrong. It wasn't a confrontation at all. Nor was it anything to have feared. What he had supposed would destroy him had in fact illuminated and elevated him. He smiled at how misplaced his fear had been.

He found his clothes (Lancelot's clothes, still sodden from the rain), dressed himself gently, with a new reverence for fingertips, leg-hairs, lips, knees, the tiniest crenellations of a toenail, and felt even the pain of bone and muscle as a contribution to the new corporeal harmony. All with a clarity so sharp it cut at him. All with a grace of mass. He hadn't known himself capable of such grace. Never so inevitable; each atom of his body arrived at its own truth, a perfect concord of the flesh. He saw the air in the bedroom criss-crossed with choices like outlined constellations, felt himself singling out one that glowed, that sang his movements back to him.

Now. Now. Now. Now.

He didn't touch Mickey. Zack didn't move. He had no fear that either of them would wake up. He stood for a few moments, wondering at the transformation, the force of life in his limbs, seeing as God saw, the beauty of infinite relativity. He thought of the conquistador priest telling him that to posit the unforgivable was to compromise God's omniscience – and understood. There had been something else in the church, some other roughly delivered revelation. What was it?

He couldn't remember.

The snow was gone and the rain had stopped. Now only a thin mist hung in the air. Nicholas walked to the sound of chuckling water, everywhere. Discarded umbrellas dotted the streets like the mangled corpses of bats. Litter sailed on thin streams between the gutters. The city was urgent again now that the weather had released it. Cars hissed on the wet-skinned roads; all the surfaces were thin and hard, as if a rind had been pared away.

It hadn't occurred to him not to walk, but after ten blocks the pain in his side became unbearable. He knew with an indifferent certainty that any movement now would only increase the pain. He flagged a cab.

'You got money?'

The driver was a small Sikh with long, obsidian eyes and pearly fingernails. For a moment Nicholas didn't understand, then realized that he no longer *looked* like someone who had the money to pay. He pulled out what he had in his pockets. Twenty-three dollars.

'OK, sir, where to?'

Without snow the church on Broadway looked depressing. For a few moments Nicholas stood among the gravestones, staring up to the segment of darkness beyond the doors. Then he climbed the steps and entered. A dozen candle-flames like static spirits. Smell of incense and polished pews. Halfway up the aisle's iron grille he stopped, listening. The place was deserted. He waited for the sense that the building was aware of him, but it didn't come. He moved forward, stopped in front of the altar, beyond which the crucified Christ hung with his face slightly averted, as if his ordeal had engendered a peaceful introspection.

'What do you want?'

Nicholas turned to his left, where, from a doorway hidden in shadow, a young man was emerging. He was tall, with greasy blond hair and a pair of thick-lensed glasses. A checked shirt, short in the arms, and faded jeans. 'Can I help you?'

'I was looking for the priest,' Nicholas said.

Having noticed Nicholas's condition, the young man had stopped three paces away. Nicholas could see him computing the probability of violence.

'Which one?'

'What?'

'Which priest? Father Fernández or Father Bourke?'

Nicholas looked again at the figure on the cross behind the altar, then back to the young man.

'Fernández,' he said. 'Is he here?'

'Father Fernández won't be here until six o'clock this evening. Is it something – is there a message I could give him? Or . . .?'

Nicholas felt suddenly dizzy. Swaying, he grabbed the pew to his left to steady himself.

'Tell him I'm going back,' he said. 'Tell him the man who spoke to him the other day . . . He gave me a glass of milk. He'll know. Just tell him I'm going back.'

'OK. I'll tell him.'

The young man hesitated, the tips of his long fingers in his jeans pockets. Nicholas knew he was afraid.

'It's all right,' Nicholas said. 'I'm not going to do anything. I just need to rest here for a moment.'

He remembered the Avenue – Avenue D – but he didn't know the cross-street. He found it eventually, but the half an hour searching took the last of his strength. The gate was open. There was even a rotting wooden park bench inside. He sat and smoked the last five of his crumpled cigarettes in the damp air, with Lancelot's trousers soaking up the seat's rain. The boles and branches of the two trees were black and leathery, glossed with moisture. The goat had been liberated from its pen, but was still roped to a stake. Initially it strained towards him, licking its lips. If Nicholas had had the energy he would have crossed the garden to fondle its silver head.

His own inner time was rushing through memories. That first afternoon, long ago in Chloe's room when she had worried that her scar would put him off. Her eyes young and dark, approaching him and retreating, repeatedly, trying to force herself over the fear. At the altar rail, her white, flickering presence beside him throughout the mesmerism of the wedding. The night of Difalco's. His hand gripping her neck. His wife. He thought of the billions of men and women who had become husbands and wives – all the promises. I promise. The moments of idiot peace, lying with her in the sun-struck bed, faintly guilty because he had known he wasn't entitled to such happiness. He thought of the simplicity of pleasure in seeing her; at some level – no matter how short a time they had been apart – there was always a small joy in seeing each other. Coming home from the agency and busying himself in the flat, sheepish, laughing at himself, knowing that his time apart from her was really just a waiting period, that real life began and ended with her. All her countless utterances of his name. Nick, do you love me? Come on, Nick, we're late. Her key in the door: You home, Nick? Always, always, always the simple, tiny pleasure of seeing her, smelling the outside world on her skin, London on her coat and in her hair, her immunity to it, her grudging tolerance of the city's ugliness. Her face under the oxygen mask in the ambulance: grey, clammy, almost resigned to leaving.

I don't think I want to be in a position where I know I'm going to die and I have to think of something to say. I think I'd rather just slip away. Like an animal that goes off somewhere and then just doesn't come back.

Leaving.

He had left her.

Leaving.

He waited for more than an hour, and eventually she came. Again in the rain jacket and the red boots, carrying the bucket at arm's length as if it might explode at any moment. She was younger than he had thought – perhaps ten or eleven – and seemed afraid of the goat. Though the snow was gone she moved with the same careful premeditation, every slow step a unique event. She looked neither left nor right, but stared at the animal, who had turned from Nicholas and now strained towards its food.

He knew she wasn't aware of him, and he didn't want to startle her. He didn't know what he did want – but he wasn't prepared for her reaction when he spoke.

'Hard to imagine a goat in this city,' he said.

It happened in a matter of seconds. He hadn't realized that he had stood up and taken a step towards her – but immediately she turned he knew that he had frightened her. He saw too (before the strange vowels began pouring from her open mouth) that she was backward in some way, that nothing he could say or do – no gesture of reassurance or retreat – could undo her fear.

'It's all right. It's all right. Don't be frigh—' but she had already dropped the bucket and thrown her arms around her own waist. Already the face had collapsed into panic. The bucket's disgorged contents on the ground: potato peelings, a cabbage stalk, apple cores, blackening lettuce leaves.

Nicholas took a step backwards. Her eyes were locked on his, wide, staring. The wordless voice rose.

'Karen?' a voice said from inside. 'Sweetie? Whatsa madder?'

He heard a door open. A woman rushed out into the garden. Nicholas was already backing towards the gate. He saw her face: glacial blue eyes; a thin mouth; greying hair scraped back into a short ponytail. A cigarette between her fingers. He saw her taking in all the information, building a narrative.

'What the fuck you do to her?'

'Nothing. Nothing. I—'

'You get away from here. You get the *fuck* away from here. Did he touch you, honey?' She looked back at Nicholas, hatred and exhaustion in every line of her face. 'Did you put your fucking hands on her?'

Nicholas, shaking his head, backed through the gate into the street. The woman followed, slammed the gate closed, clicked the padlock into place.

'I see you around here again I'll call the fuckin' *cops* on you, asshole,' she said.

Nicholas fell asleep in Lancelot's apartment. He had come in and found new empties and the remains of a pizza on the floor by the couch. He had sat down with the intention of resting for a few minutes.

When he woke up it was dark. Rain streaked the windows. Lancelot hadn't returned.

The pain in his side shocked him when he tried to stand. He sat back for a moment, breathing, deeply, then slowly pitched himself forward and crawled to the bathroom. At the sink he pulled himself upright and examined his face in the mirror. The sunset eye was almost closed now, its vision a mesh of light. Individual pains clung to his face like leeches, each with its own pulse. He smiled. Saw the missing upper canine and thought of all the newspaper teeth he and Chloe had blacked out with biro over the years. The state of bliss had evaporated; in its place was a simple calm. He was still detached from his body, observing it like an undeparted spirit. Even when he looked down into the toilet bowl and saw his piss turbid with blood it didn't disturb him. You think you'll die, Lancelot had said.

'Holy shit – what the fuck happened to you?'

For once Marty's smile was absent. Scrimshankers was empty but for himself, Nicholas and the quiz-addicted biker in the corner.

Nicholas smiled. 'An incident,' he said.

'A *incident*? You better tell me you *killed* the other guy, man.'

'I killed him,' Nicholas said.

Marty leaned on the counter with his weight on the pink heels of his hands, shaking his head in disbelief. 'Jesus Christ,' he said. 'Jesus *Christ*.'

'Where's Lancelot?' Nicholas asked him.

Head-shaking stopped, abruptly. 'What?'

'Lancelot. Where is he. He's not at the apartment. I thought he'd be—'

'Shit, man – you don't know?'

'Know what?'

Marty sat down on his stool behind the bar. 'Motherfucker had a heart attack last night. Right there where you're standin'. No fuckin' *pills*. Went down like a fuckin' *stone*. Never seen anythin' like it. Nine-one-one. Ambulance. All that shit. He's in Beth Israel. 'Less he died since last night. I called at four-thirty this mornin' – they said he was OK.'

'Where's Beth Israel?'

'Five blocks up. Can't miss it.'

Nicholas turned to go.

'Wait,' Marty said. 'Give him this. He's gonna die for sure without it.'

From under the counter, sporting a beer stain and two cigarette burns, Lancelot's hat.

◆

Seeing her that night, the slenderest, most durable thread of perversion in him had realized that it was a liberation. Because what had happened to her seemed to remove all choice. It had flashed the message to him (through the room's handful of upset objects) that life up until that moment had been lived without understanding. At that moment all habits of identity – the habit of being – had dropped away. All roads into a future with her had ended. In the ambulance he had been powerless not to think of what he had done. Nina. He had thought of his wedding-ring finger buried in her arse and felt the world's laboured history, its vast boredom with the finite, repeated human permutations: love; betrayal; pleasure; fear; desire; regret; lies. He had felt it distinctly, the world's exhaustion, its erosion by the same details re-enacted, over and over.

◆

Lancelot was in a small room with only one other occupant, a grey-haired man with a wedge-shaped face and a thick, pockmarked nose, who was asleep when Nicholas entered.

'You think you'll die,' Lancelot said. 'You surprise yourself.'

'Why weren't you carrying the pills?' Nicholas asked him.

'Why do you think? And what in God's name happened to you?'

Nicholas smiled and shook his head. 'How long are they keeping you?' he asked.

'Fuck knows. You've got keys, haven't you?'

'Yes.'

'Well, make yourself at home. Just don't drink the place dry.
You haven't *got* a snort on you, have you?'

'No, sorry.'

'And you could tell that bugger over at Scrims to send me
over a bit of liquid gratuity, you know. I mean I support the
place single-fucking-handed. What *did* happen to you? You look
terrible.'

'I feel better,' Nicholas said. 'I wanted to ask you something.'

'What?'

'Was it true?'

For a second Lancelot was about to pretend he didn't know
what Nicholas was referring to. Nicholas saw the face flicker
towards it – then not bother.

Lancelot said, 'It's funny. I'd been thinking recently that perhaps it wasn't – then this, last night. It's not your whole life
flashing – it's just the salient bits.'

'Didn't you ever think of going back?'

'Cowards don't go back.'

'Then you're a coward?'

'It's not courage that keeps you alive.'

They sat for a while not looking at each other. A nurse came
in to change the other patient's drip. Nicholas watched her. He
was thinking of the other hospital. Some conditions, though
painful, are not life-threatening. He was remembering the feeling
of weightlessness in the waiting-room, the hard rim of the plastic chair in his hands. Now he felt immovably heavy, as if every
bone's mass was increasing with time.

'Do you ever think about being forgiven?'

He had spoken the question to his folded hands. When he
looked up he saw that Lancelot was crying, silently.

'Sorry,' Nicholas said. 'I'm sor—'

'Got to use the loo,' Lancelot said. 'Pass me that, would you?'

*

For a few moments Nicholas sat still, watching Lancelot's slow
progress with the Zimmer. The hospital gown had been tied
wrongly; one heavy buttock showed through the gap. Each step
took a long time. Nicholas listened to the rasping breaths. In the
doorway Lancelot paused.

'I'm sure you've got better things to do, ducks,' he said, without turning round.

Nicholas sat still, listening to the sounds of the ward. He had
the peculiar sense that he could hear, beyond these sounds, all
the distance between himself and Chloe. The wrinkled Atlantic,
bent north and thin-crushed at the edges of Cornwall. From
Cornwall the whole of puckered England like a green garment
shrunken from the wash, cigarette-burned at London. London.

He left Lancelot's key on the hospital bed.

In the cab, he realized that he still had the beer-stained hat in
his hands.

Part Five

NECESSITIES

Maybe change my name. To Cassandra. Since I knew what this would be like. The scrutiny of every detail: whether I eat; when I shit; how long I sleep; whether I wash my hair. Their shared belief that all they need is a number of signs to add me up to recovery.

They've made me a shameless eavesdropper.

''S good she went for that walk again today, eh, love?'

'Jean, I've told you: stop 'overin' over her. She don't need it.'

Mum's reflex, Dad's rebuke. Tennis rally.

'I heard her get up at three, mind. God knows how she stands it. Sittin' there lookin' out the kitchen window. She 'an't taken none o' them sedatives they give 'er, neither.'

'Just let 'er get on with it, Jean. She's strong. It don't 'elp to keep fussin'.'

I collect these out-takes. I use them as soundings for the depth of distance between us.

They live in fear, now.

In the small hours in the kitchen, listening to the mouse, I feel them awake above me, blaming me for having proved that they couldn't protect me. They're dumb with it, as if I'd suddenly slapped them without reason. Because the world has touched me, smudged me with shit, I've become to them the representative of the world. I'm contagious with the disease of the unimagined. I've brought it under their roof.

They're beginning to get it – that they'll never assimilate me, that I've grown into something alien. Mum drowns out her own screams by baking pasties and unearthing drawings I did when I was five – a perceptual assault on the amnesiac's senses. Dad carries his head low in his shoulders, believing the other Chloe will come back and knowing she won't. Believing and knowing. They don't mention Nick – but I eavesdrop.

'I just can't believe . . . I mean I just can't *believe* that he'd . . .'

'Don't talk to me about it. That bastard shows 'is face, I swear I'll put an end to 'im.'

'But I mean—'

'I'm tellin' you, I'll put an end to 'im.'

Sometimes I walk into the room suddenly, having picked the point in the exchange from which it'll be most difficult for them to revert to harmless banter. It's awful of me. I get some deadening satisfaction from it. I get some deadening satisfaction from awful things generally, it seems. That's the way of it when you yourself are an awful thing.

Chloe had known in the car with Liz that it would only be a matter of time before the cottage and her parents would begin to crush the air out of her lungs. But she had known, too, that she must go, if only to establish within herself once and for all that there could be no return to the old world, not to any part of it. In addition there was the weight of love for her mother and father, from which it seemed there would never be relief. It had pressed on her the whole time she'd been in hospital. She had watched them and seen in their faces the terrible faith in their love for her. She had seen so clearly their belief that their love could heal her. It frightened her. It had slowed her recovery, because she had known that they would never forgive her if she didn't let them try. It had horrified her that after all she had suffered there was still this daughterly duty to perform. For an hour she had sat alongside Liz in the car, crying silently, watching London thinning out into Wiltshire and Avon, knowing that the time at home would be a murder in cruel increments. Every detail of the afternoon seemed to confirm it: the hissing lorries, the cramped sky, the chalk hills, the rubbery squeak of the windscreen wipers. Then, gradually, she had resigned herself. When Liz stopped at the Bristol services for a cup of tea, Chloe had found herself eager to get back on the road, impatient to get it over with, since it was inevitable.

The first day home had been almost unbearable. As soon as she had seen their faces she had known two things: one, that they had been preparing themselves, affirming to themselves that they weren't going to suffocate her, that they were going to let her be, that there would be no recovery agenda imposed; and two, that her actual arrival had rendered all such resolutions void. Chloe saw all of it in her mother's tired face, quivering with the strain of holding back love, then breaking, coming to her, hugging her as hard as the injuries allowed, practically carrying her to the sofa and willing her into comfort. Whereas her father seemed to understand – immediately his eyes met hers – that they had already failed, and her presence back in the cottage would be a demonstration of his own redundancy. Chloe glimpsed this in the first instant of seeing him – but then moments later saw that he had forced himself back into faith, that he would resist to the last by sheer strength of will.

Their eagerness that first afternoon and evening had made her skin ache. The television was turned on (by her mother, to show that nothing special was going to be demanded of their time), then very quickly turned off by her father (who suddenly worried that something about rape might appear on the screen). Food she couldn't possibly eat, not pressed on her, but *present*, screaming of her mother's need. The bathroom newly decorated; a subscription copy of the *Curator* at the top of the stack next to the toilet. Her mother (utterly unaware that she was doing so) actually following her into the bathroom, as if Chloe might have forgotten where it was. Her father on the telephone, hissing at someone that they'd been told not to ring today.

In the end, Chloe had called on the only talisman she possessed: tiredness.

'Yeah, you get on up, maid,' her father said. 'Can't go overdoin' it on the first day.'

'I'll bring you up a hot-water bottle,' her mother said.

'I'm fine, Mum.'

'Now, no nonsense. It gets perishing up there when the heatin'
goes off.'

Understanding that she would have to choose her battles in
the coming weeks, Chloe acquiesced. At the top of the stairs, she
stopped and looked out of the landing's one small window. The
land was indigo under a steel-blue sky. Sheep like white stones
in the twilight. A thin flake of moon.

'You all right, love?'

Her mother's voice, halfway up the stairs. It had sounded like
a shriek. It had startled her.

'I've told Liz to come up too. Needs a good night's sleep if she's
been drivin' all day, 'spect.'

And of course, in the ways that they *could* have helped, they
didn't. Liz could have slept on the couch. That hadn't occurred
to them. They'd put her on a camping-bed alongside Chloe.

'Looks weird in here without the bunks, doesn't it?'

Chloe at the bedroom window kept her back to her sister,
making no move to get undressed. Looking at the land calmed
her. The room had been scrubbed into a startled spotlessness.
Her childhood was there, holding its breath.

'D'you want the bathroom, or shall I?'

'You go.'

Chloe found she couldn't undress. She was afraid to expose
her flesh in the room that had known her so well in another
incarnation.

Liz came back in bereft of eyeliner and smelling of tooth-
paste. Chloe was already in bed with the covers up to her chin,
fully dressed apart from her boots. Since Chloe hadn't closed the
curtains, Liz left them alone.

'Night, then,' Liz said.

'Night.'

After perhaps an hour, when her sister was deeply asleep,
Chloe slid her arm out from under the covers, so that the silver
bracelet could reflect the arrival of first light.

That had been ten days ago. Since then she had observed herself and her parents trying and failing. There was an impatience creeping into them. Chloe wondered how long she could last here, how long it would take for this necessary demonstration to have run its course.

The one unlooked-for comfort was the land. Elm Coombe had no more than a thousand inhabitants, and was surrounded by agriculture. Hours, years of her childhood had been played out in the woods and fields, in the cool shadows of the hedgerows – but the land had done her the courtesy of having forgotten her. She remembered summers, flat on her back against the dry, ringing earth, overarched by skies of pure ultramarine, dizzy from the bitter scent of grass. She remembered copses, the wood-darkness, bluebells at her shins. She remembered the profound sense of entitlement: it had all been hers. She had moved through it with regal impunity.

But the place had forgotten her. Now, in winter, she was grateful for its indifference. She couldn't walk far, but she could get out of the village. There was a common that the villagers ignored – that she had ignored herself, when she had lived here; now she claimed it. It was a small hill of dark meadowgrass crowned by a ring of sycamores and birches. She went there in the afternoons (over-clothed by her mother), and sat with her back to a tree and her knees up to her chin. She took a book with her – but only to fool her parents. They wouldn't want to think of her simply sitting, hour after hour, staring at the land. They wouldn't want to know that the common was her respite from their indefatigable love.

From the top of the common she could see the sea. It comforted her. Whatever didn't care about her comforted her.

The villagers all knew. Chloe avoided contact with them, but felt the glances, heard the muttering. Childhood friends had moved away, but many of their parents remained. Their sympathies were with Chloe's parents; they were quiet and aghast at what Mr and Mrs Palmer were now forced to keep under their roof. Because they didn't love Chloe (sullen maid with smart-arse answers, who had shown her contempt for their world by getting into a university in *London*, for God's sake) they were

allowed to see her as a freakish curio; there was no onus on them
to be part of her recovery. None the less they passed words to
her – 'Yes, luvver, what can I get you?' – as if nothing had happened. Chloe didn't care one way or the other. After the first few
afternoons, she was grudgingly assimilated as the madwoman
who went and sat in the cold on the common all day.

I'm discovering that the more something screams to be mentioned, the easier it is not to mention it. A nice relationship of
inverse proportion. No one mentions Nick. No one mentions the
man who did this to me. It's as if there are two giant black
obelisks right in the middle of the living-room, and all of us just
carrying on as if they weren't there. Peering round them to see
the telly. Careful not to knock the edges with a laden tea-tray. On
the common, with the wind chiselling my cheeks and scalp, this
almost seems funny. In the living-room with Mum and Dad, it
almost seems evil. Not that I mention either of them, mind you.

I was dreading Liz going back last week, but it's made it easier.
For one thing the bedroom. Staring at her throat. Listening to
the steady breathing. Seeing the hands at peace. Impossible to
ignore. Impossible to sleep. The integrity of flesh. She thinks
Tom knows her body. In one way he does. Then a man comes
and shows you another way he can know your body. She's wondering about Tom now. Is secretly miserable with wondering.
What would Tom do if it happened to her? That's Liz. Not what
would *she* do if it happened to her. Not what if *Tom* did it to
someone. Not what if Tom did it to *her*. I couldn't stop looking
at her – the full, freckled arms, the nostrils like two apostrophes,
the thick throat – couldn't stop myself hating her for being
whole, couldn't stop myself from thinking that wholeness is
wasted on Liz anyway because all she wants is to be something
for Tom. Couldn't stop wondering if she felt finally compen-
sated for not having been the one with brains. In the wee hours
there's no one to observe the shameful pettiness, the meanness of
spirit, the poison. It's better that she's gone.

For another thing, they don't try as much now that it's just the three of us, with no one to watch. Maybe that's nothing to do with Liz. Maybe it's just that they're flagging. In any case, my personal space has expanded; now the perimeter fence with the KEEP OUT describes a wider orbit.

I miss Myres. Because? Don't know. Probably just because I wasn't new to her. Material, I mean. Because she got it, I suppose – the state of being shorn of superfluities, the new grammar, the paradigm shift. 'What's a paradigm shift?' she would have said. Living with them, daily, having no definitive expression for them. Coppers don't have to go to university. Thank God.

She – or her lot, whoever they are – has told the local constabulary to keep an eye on me. I've seen all of Elm Coombe's half-dozen preposterous bobbies driving by the cottage too often for it not to have been her doing. I know what she'd say if I phoned her to complain: 'He's still out there. You're the only one who can identify him. Makes you a target.' Just the facts, just the blameless equations. She doesn't need to deal subtler currencies.

Still wonder about her. Do you want him in prison or do you want him dead? She was serious.

So was I. Funny: some philosophical questions just dissolve after this happens to you.

I came in the front this afternoon and went upstairs. They didn't know I'd come home. Dad was in the back garden, burning rubbish. I watched from the open bedroom window. He's an old man now. Mottled cranium visible under the remaining candy-floss hair; shoulders shrinking; hand-flesh contracting around the tired veins. He moves more slowly, with less conviction. Things he's done uncomplainingly his whole life (done with pleasure, in fact) now irritate him. Burning rubbish, for example. I watched him trying to break up an old fruit-crate with his feet. He twisted his ankle. In the end, cursing, he went and got a hammer. Mum brought him out a mug of tea. The two of them stood side by side watching the fire. Tufts of flame tore upwards, like spirits rushing to the afterlife.

'Dunno how much more of this I can take,' Mum said. It was apparent that they'd agreed (tacitly) not to talk like this: truth-fully. I saw it in the sudden adjustment in his shoulders, that he'd known she wouldn't be able to hold out, that he'd known it would only be a matter of time.

'Have to,' he said. 'Nothin' else for it.'

'It's like she's not there.'

'I know.'

'But it's like she's . . . you know . . . *gone.*'

He didn't answer immediately. Took a long sip of tea. Something in the fire popped and emitted a little spray of sparks.

'She knows,' he said. 'She knows she's gone. Maid's in two minds about whether she's comin' back. 'S what it is.'

Mum in profile then, not touching him, arms folded, shaking. 'We've to *bring* 'er back, then. Somehow.'

A strange silence between them. The whisper and snap of the flames. Smell of burning in the cold air.

'Remember when she fell in the fire when she was little?' he said.

'Umm.'

'Remember?'

'Course I do! Didn't I scream?'

'Remember afterwards, when she was home, how quiet she was?'

'For days. *Days* afterwards she hardly spoke a word.'

Another silence. He was going somewhere with it, wasn't sure she'd understand. Wasn't sure it would help either of them if he articulated it. She turned back to the fire, only half listening to him.

'I was relieved,' he said.

'Relieved?'

'I remember thinking: No one falls in a fire *twice.* Like she'd used it up, see? One of the bad things that could 'appen. Children . . . burnin'. Like it couldn't 'appen again . . .'

He couldn't finish it. She had turned back to him, was looking up at him, confused, annoyed. 'What you on about?'

Then suddenly she reached out to him, her mouth open in shock, but he put his hand up as if to ward her off. The mug of tea dropped and spilled on the grass.

I've never seen him cry. He fought it, made his jaws hard, held Mum at arm's length as if her embrace would destroy him. He really fought it, but it kept breaking through. His face recreated. My whole life never having seen this – the face crumpling, the lips quivering, the whole frame shaken as the sobs bullied their way through.

'Don't, love, don't. Oh don't.'

He stood bowed with his hands covering his face. Ashamed. Horrified because he hadn't the strength to hold this back. Unmanned completely, he let her put her arms around him. When she pulled his hands from his face the eyes were open, the long cheeks wet with tears and snot. I wondered if she'd ever seen this before, couldn't believe she had.

But then *her* face, hard, determined, a clarity magically conjured by his collapse.

'You look at me,' she said, eyes focused, forcing him to see that she could see him like this, that he had lost nothing, that he was her husband. 'You *look* at me, now.'

'Ah, Jeanie, Jeanie . . . Christ . . .'

'You hush now, come on. Come on now.'

Dull pain in my chest. All the minutes I'd been there with the cold air pressed against me. Skin freezing. I didn't want to see any more. I was ashamed.

The night before she left, Chloe took a long, deep bath, then examined herself in the mirror. The bruises had almost completed their bloom: burgundy, indigo, black, yellow-green, ochre, sepia, faint grey. They had marked the time away from that night like gorgeous organic clocks. Soon they would be gone, absorbed, no trace. Not so the scars; those were for life. She'd be an old woman who was once grazed by a meteor shower. If she got to be an old woman. It wasn't clear to her that her body could carry this new forced message. He had written; she still had the power to burn the book.

Something had changed since the hospital. There, she had felt paralysed. There, it had seemed that there was to be only one effect from his cause: inertia. Now, her own curiosity aroused, Chloe discovered that she was in motion.

In itself this was neither here nor there. Her fear was that it was all purely reactive. She was tempted to remain at rest, if only to deny him the possibility of continuing to act on her – or worse, to act on the world through her. That possibility horrified her. But, again, practical details continued to inter- pose themselves, like idiots: staying at home was impossible. As was returning to the flat in Clapham, which, through the absurdity of signing *Chloe A. Palmer* to certain documents, she had put on the market. The flat had been in her name. Her par- ents had very politely made it clear that that was a condition of the deposit they had half loaned, half given them – her father's insistence, Chloe knew. The plan had always been that they would shift to joint ownership behind the parents' backs, but it hadn't happened. It hadn't happened because when it came down to it neither Chloe nor Nicholas had cared *whose* name was on the deeds. They barely thought of it. They barely acknowledged the concept that the flat was theirs in the first place.

So it was up for sale. Most of the furniture was still there, but Liz had taken the valuables (such as they were) to her place for safekeeping.

She rang the number Myres had given her. Got no reply. Realized – alone in the blue-dark kitchen, her feet dead with cold from the tiles – that it was four o'clock in the morning. Realized that Myres was probably asleep. Or at work, lifting a plastic sheet, angling her flinty face to see under, blinking once, twice, saying: 'Who is she?'

She tried again at dawn.

'Yeah?' Myres said.

Chloe heard everything in the monosyllable: that for Myres the phone ringing meant someone wanted her to do something.

'It's Chloe Palmer.'

'Hello, Chloe.'

No *how are you*.

'Did I wake you up?'

'No.'

She knows, Chloe thought. She knows why I'm phoning. I could be trying to find out if they've got him. I could be seeing if they know where Nicholas is. I could be freaking out. But she knows what I want. Knew what I would want.

'I wondered if . . .' Chloe said. 'I mean I wondered.'

Myres lighting a cigarette: *paff* of match; silence; inhale, exhale. 'Did you want to take me up on the offer of the Cornish shithole?' Myres said.

Chloe shivered with shame. Almost hung up. Stopped herself, forced herself through it. 'Yes,' she said. 'I don't know why.'

'Get a pen and paper,' Myres said.

Chloe took down the details. Camvellyn. She'd never heard of the place.

'Eight miles up the coast from Tintagel,' Myres said.

'King Arthur,' Chloe said.

'Yeah, whatever.'

'Are you sure it's—'

'There's a newsagent's in the village run by an old couple. Frank and Edna. They've got a spare key. I'll tell them you're coming.'

Chloe stood cradling the receiver under her chin, her hands in her armpits. It was almost fully light outside. The kitchen window showed four squares of cerulean sky scored with dark quills of cloud. Last night's washed crockery glimmered on the dishrack. Birds sang. Someone pulled the flush in the upstairs bathroom and shuffled back to bed.

'It's wood-fired,' Myres said. 'Can you handle a wood fire?'

'I don't know.'

'I just want to warn you: it's pretty basic. I mean it's not

decorated or anything. I haven't been there since last spring.
You sure you want to do this?'

'I can't stay here,' Chloe said.

Inhale. Exhale.

'Yeah,' Myres said. 'Understood.'

A long pause. 'Do you want to know anything?' Myres said.

She means Nicholas, Chloe thought. A chasm yawned, black,
freezing, immeasurably deep. The toes of her bare feet gripping
the edge, an uprush of icy air. Nothing.

'No,' Chloe said.

Digested. Not judged. 'There's something else.'

'What?'

'I might need to come down there myself for a day or two,
sometime over the next couple of weeks. Is that OK with you?'

What for? Chloe wondered. But she said: 'Don't be daft, it's
your place.'

Do you want to know anything else? Like God. She knows.
Nicholas. She knows. Does she know?

'I'll phone,' Myres said – then hung up.

'That's ridiculous. You're not well enough.'

Chloe had waited for them to get up. Now the three of them
sat at the scrubbed kitchen table. Her father's hands were trembling, a riotous fury and despair contained.

'Love,' her mother said. 'Love . . . for heaven's sake . . .'

'I've decided, Mum.'

'But you're barely up and about!'

'I'm fine.'

'It's plain stupid,' her father said. 'It's plain bloody madness's
what it is.'

'None the less.'

'None the less,' he mimicked, bitterly. 'Aren't we lookin' after
you? Can't you see—'

'Is it us, love? Is it somethin' we're not doin'? I mean all you've
got to do is *tell* us. All you've got to do . . .'

'Well she's not goin' an' that's an end on it.'

'All you've got to do is *say*, love. Your father an' me, we're just . . . I mean we can't know 'less you *tell* us.'

'It's not you,' Chloe said, staring down at her cup of tea. On the surface she was at breaking-point. On the surface their panic was almost killing her. But underneath there was a dead, clinical resolve. Underneath was the certainty that if she stayed she would destroy them.

Because he had known from the outset, her father fought all the more violently. It was that he hadn't expected it so soon – and that he had known, too, that no amount of time would be preparation enough.

'I just need to be alone for a bit,' Chloe said.

Her mother put her head into the palms of her hands, shoulders shaking.

'Don't upset yourself, Jean. She's not goin' an' that's an end on it.'

'Stop fucking talking like that!'

Her father stood up suddenly. This was what Chloe had feared. The last part of the demonstration. She had tried to believe it wouldn't come to this – but somehow she had known.

'Stop, both of you, for God's sake,' she said. She was trying to calm herself, but all her blood was swarming. A surge of life. Euphoric. She couldn't stop it.

'Don't you *see*?' she said. 'Don't you see? There's nothing I can or can't do now. How can you think – how can you think you could *possibly* know what I can or can't do? Do you think loving me makes any difference? Do you think what happened hasn't changed *everything*? Dear *God* use your imagination. Don't you see your wanting me here is about *you*?'

'How can you *say* that?' her mother said. 'Chloe, love—'

'Mum, stop.'

'I dunno what right you think—'

'No right,' Chloe said. She could feel her face hot and ugly with this liberation. 'No right, Dad. It's not about rights any more. You think I don't know that you love me. You're wrong.

But how can you be so . . . so *arrogant* to think that that'll have to be enough? How can you think it's as simple as that?'

'Look, don't start gettin' clever an' tyin' us up in—'

'Listen! Listen to yourself!'

'Oh please stop it,' her mother said. 'Please, please, please.'

Chloe lifted her hand and wiped the sweat from her forehead. She'd been feeling feverish all morning. But the air in the cottage would crush her if she stayed. She knew.

She stood up slowly, legs trembling, the muscles in her neck aflame.

In the kitchen doorway she stopped and looked back at them. Her father stood with his back to her, silhouetted. Her mother sat with a tissue pressed under her reddened nose, tears in silver threads. Their age and weakness sickened Chloe. The need to comfort them was a deep fracture in her chest. She leaned on the doorframe, feeling a cold pinion of fever wrap and release her.

'It's not your fault,' she said quietly, all the poison gone. 'I love you, and it's not your fault.'

Her father drove her in silence to the station in Paignton. She told him to leave her on the platform, but he ignored her.

It was a terrible time for both of them, the waiting. They sat side by side on a green wooden bench with their collars up against the cold. Scraps of litter blew about them. An empty Coke can rolled repeatedly to the very edge of the platform, then back towards them in a slow arc. A teenage boy and girl stood ten feet away, her with her back against the wall, him kissing her as if he were trying to extract something from her mouth. Occasionally, he detached himself from her, walked away, spat through his teeth, then returned.

A soft rain began to fall as the train's arrival was announced.

'All right, Dad,' Chloe said. But he waited, his face set, not looking at her.

'Put your bag on for you,' he said quietly.

They found her seat, then Chloe walked back to the door with him. The deadness and certainty hadn't left her, but still when he took her hand she cried and clung to him. He froze for a moment, then his thin arms came up around her.

'I'm sorry, Dad. I'm sorry, I'm sorry . . .' Pain had come out of nowhere. She could feel the brittle age of him, the tired muscles, the sense that he didn't have the strength for things. She could feel how much she was breaking in him, how what had happened to her had all but destroyed him.

''S all right now, maid,' he said. 'Shsh, come on now. Come on now, there's a good girl. 'S all right.'

The meaningless comfort pierced her. All her childhood suddenly welled up, all the times she'd heard him say that (a cut knee, a bump on the head, a wasp sting), all these times coalesced in a single moment and for the first time since coming home she felt the true, ancient, dumb weight of his love. 'S all right, now, maid. It almost turned her. She clung to him desperately.

But pulled away before he did. The door closed. She felt the fever wriggling through her, flooding her hot and cold by turns.

'You ring us when you get there, all right?'

'I will, Dad.'

'You telephone and let us know.'

'I will, I promise.'

Doors slammed down the length of the train. Chloe could see him struggling not to cry. His lip quivered. She could see the shrivelled Adam's apple flickering, swallowing tears back. He looked like a five-year-old boy.

The train lurched, halted, then began to draw away. He was crying now. In the last moment, he reached and grasped her hand, held it briefly – then the train's motion tore her away.

Afterwards, Chloe remembered very little of the first day and night in Camvellyn.

The train journey fermented her fever. Her skin's contact with anything – a plastic cup, the windowpane, the cushion of her seat – hurt her. The smell of coffee from the trolley made her heave. She was hot and her guts were sour. She kept thinking of curdled milk – or of her blood *turning* to milk, through all the

shades from red to white. She put her fingertips to her forehead
and they came away wet with sweat, trembling.

Another laughable irony, she thought: She dies of motion
sickness.

She tried to laugh out loud, to prove there was still a division
between her and what her body was experiencing, but no laugh
came. Her mouth flooded with saliva. The knowledge that she
was going to vomit. Breakfast. She'd eaten it as a concession to
them. Eggs. She staggered to an acrid toilet and threw up, holding her scars.

She had to change trains at Plymouth, by which time her
scalp ached and her teeth chattered. She sat in the window seat
passing in and out of consciousness, flickered around by bits of
dream, alternately deafened and cajoled by the sound of her
own blood. Fragments of the landscape: a narrow lake like a
blade of black iron; a cluster of bulbous pines on a hill; a pud-
dled scrapyard, tiers of rust-nibbled car bodies and yawning
fridges; pockets of new, identical houses; a steep, dark green
field with sheep like lumps of meerschaum. She lost track of
time, heard snippets of conversation, suddenly loud when her
body went quiet:

'. . . caramel . . .'

'Hardly the fuckin' point.'

'Fourteen across: vestigial.'

'. . . well you *know* what that daft bugger's like . . .'

'So I said no. I said to her, No. *No*.'

The second train crossed Bodmin Moor and dropped her at
Camelford. The theory was a bus from there to Tintagel, then
another from Tintagel to Camvellyn. A taxi stood in the rain outside the train station. Shivering, Chloe got in, told him where
she wanted to go.

'You know that's about twennie moils frum yur?'

She felt too ill even to be relieved that the driver was old,
beyond harming her. 'I know. I'll pay.'

She gave herself to darkness whenever it came for her. Hoped
it wouldn't coincide with her arrival in Camvellyn, when she'd
have to find Myres's newsagent couple. In her moments of clarity

she wondered what was wrong with her. Flu's a virus. Gastric trouble might be bacterial. Fever can be caused by either. Headache? No, just oily blood and cracked thinking. Skin hurts a lot. Bodyache. Cold. Hot. I'm getting the fucking flu. There's the great thing about having died and come back: you're still eligible for the flu.

So she soliloquized, silently. She felt sympathy for her body, now, for the skin that hurt – but she still hadn't reclaimed it as her own. She didn't want to raise the stakes by taking it back.

The driver tried conversation once or twice, then gave up. Chloe wrapped her arms around herself, passing away, coming to, watching the dark rain buckling in the wind.

The newsagent couple weren't Cornish. They were ex-Londoners who'd bought the shop with his redundancy money. Edna and Frank. Her: pale grey and bird-like with inquisitive blue eyes (each with its own deflated bag underneath), and a thin mouth. Him: balding and paunchy with blond-hairy forearms, thick-rimmed glasses and jowls like two ripe pears. Both very pleased with themselves. Both much more pleased with relative prosperity than with their thirty-year-old marriage. Myres had told them to expect her. Frank had been down to the cottage and left wood for the fires.

'You sure you're gunna be all right down there?' he asked Chloe.

'You look a bit peaky, love. You feelin' all right?'

But she got the keys, quickly, and left. Her scalp froze and blistered by turns. Her skin was a million disorientated ants.

'Can't miss it,' Frank called from the shop doorway. 'Iss the ownee one on the parf downa beach. We left you some basics an' whatnots. Sort it later, yeah?'

Camvellyn sloped down towards the cliffs. Two pubs, a post office, half a dozen bed-and-breakfasts, a Spar, maybe seventy houses. A zebra crossing that looked utterly unnecessary. A car park at the bottom end of the village, then a stretch of sand and gravel, then nothing. The land ended in a short sheer drop

down pale cliffs. White shingle coves below, the thud-crash of
the sea.

A path wound down to the beach. Twenty paces along, a
minute cottage set in an overgrown clearing. Myres's place.

She knew there was a small space of time within which she'd be
able to function before the fever laid itself fully upon her like a
succubus. Instinct made her check the rooms. Two very small
bedrooms, roughly plastered, only one of them containing a
damp-looking bed and a dark wardrobe. One bathroom,
upstairs, with exposed but operative plumbing. Downstairs the
front door opened straight into a sparsely (and randomly) furnished living-room, also with unadorned plaster; beyond this, a
kitchen with a Formica dining-table and four odd wooden
chairs. Tea, coffee, milk, sugar, bread, toilet roll and a copy of
the *Sun* on the table, courtesy of Frank and Edna, to be sorted
later.

Shivering, she phoned her parents and told them the place
was idyllic, centrally heated and virtually next door to the police
station.

She discovered how violently she was shaking when she struck
a match and tried to hold it to a twist of newspaper protruding
from the readied fire. It took her three attempts. Only a very
small and stubborn part of her held to the importance of getting
the fire started at all. The rest of her just wanted to curl up in a
ball and close her eyes.

She could hear her voice – sometimes from a long way off,
sometimes close and distinct – forcing consciousness until the
fire was going:

so this is the coda as in the end piece a bit of leftover madness
because I didn't get through the allotted amount yet send viruses
in when the injuries have done all the damage they're capable of
if there's still work to be done give her the flu and if I don't get
this fire Nick it's not big enough to throw myself into a second
you think the chances of it happening twice children burning
ahh there it's caught wood's a bit damp I've only ever done this

two or three OK flames and she lies down and is finally permitted *finally* I say to get some rest . . .

There was a tartan blanket draped over the back of the couch.
With what energy she had left, Chloe dragged it over herself,
fully dressed, and closed her eyes to the fire's heat.

Ghosts live in Cornwall. They say the writers come for the
ghosts. The land's rough grace, the legion buried dead. The earth
here holds civilizations of smashed bone; the fogs complain of
spirits; the wind keens with the voices of the slain. There's
ancient stone here; it breaks the mounds in white molars and
fangs. There are howling caves in the cliffs. King Arthur – or not,
depending on whether you choose history or myth.

They say. Somewhere. You read these things, they stick.

But there is something here. The people live secretly, with
their backs to the rest of England. It's the lingering spirit of
resistance – Celts forced into the elbows of Cornwall and Wales
by wave after wave of invaders from the east. The spirit of
their contempt still lives here. It's in the eyebrow of the least
significant six-year-old boy, the smile of the feeblest granny.
Even the dogs are Cornish first and canine second. You can
see it when they look at you; you can see it in the slinking
shoulders.

I romanticize. Me, Chloe. The woman who used to be Chloe.
Disgusting.

The first forty-eight hours. Hell. Without Frank and Edna I'd
have died. Of fucking *cold* if nothing else. The next morning
Frank came, I suspect to settle up for the basics. Said he got no
answer, looked in the window and saw me asleep (looked
bleedin' *done* for) on the couch. Went away, came back an hour
later. Same. Tried the door, which of course wasn't locked. Woke
me, discovered my condition, summoned Edna, whom I just
barely managed to prevent from calling a doctor. Instead stayed
herself, overnight. I raved, apparently. Tried to go out. I think

shame killed the fever. By the second morning I was better,
crushed with embarrassment.

Now the two of them wonder about me. I tell them nothing.

The beach is all mine. Kelp, bladder-wrack, tarry white stones
the size of babies' skulls. Reek of brine. A dead gull, one wing
raised in farewell, eyes gone. A shell like a cochlea, which I
picked up and brought back for the empty mantelpiece.

Every day a different sky. Two vast, curdled winter sunsets.
The sea comes thinly finished at the shingle's edge, butts and
explodes against the land's limestone shins. Time moves differently here. Not London's kaleidoscope fragments, but focused
pictures that sit still for hours, then gradually fade. Gulls slide
out and return like slow boomerangs; I let their shadows run
over me.

Ghosts. One ghost, Nick. Yours.

The sea lets you see your life whole. The sea shows you your life
as a root-system of choices, intricate, blameless, all the immeasurably small motions forward to where you are now. To where I
am now. Cut and pasted. A changeling. This afternoon under
lowering thunderheads I sat on the shingle and remembered the
day Dad brought a fossil stone back from Lyme Regis.

'What is it?'

'It's where the bones of a creature used to be. It was in there,
see, like a letter in an envelope. Like a message. A message to us
from long ago!'

'Where's the creature gone?'

'Heaven, 'spect.'

Which I accepted, of course. Then the brief fossil-mania that
followed. Then books about stones. Then the Romans. By the
end of primary school the disease established: Alexander; the
pyramids; Hadrian's Wall; Stonehenge. Firmly established the
greed for being able to see time backwards, to the illusion of
origin. Firmly established the instinct for the present as a series
of clues that led back to the beginning. The fool's creed of begin-
nings. By the end of secondary school messages that were less

fragmentary: the Bayeux Tapestry; the Magna Carta; Marcus Aurelius's Meditations; Leonardo's notebooks. The mutant girl who knew why places were called what they were called. The freak who knew nothing about *Coronation Street* or Duran Duran, but who could tell you how far a Roman foot-soldier could march in a day on half-rations in wet weather, or how long it took to build St Paul's, or when the Church officially declared Mary's perpetual virginity.

The fossil led to books, books to learning, learning to university, university to you. Today I sat on the beach and wondered what would have happened if Dad had brought me back a talking doll, or a slice of rum cake, or a penny whistle.

The sea lets you see the fragile root-system of choices. If there were a sea big enough, a white coast that could accommodate the entire human race, would we be able to see the whole of history in the same way?

We go to the past to lay the blame – since the past can't argue. We go to our past selves to account for our present miseries. When Bolshy Jane asked me what I wanted to read and I bit her head off, do you know what I thought of? Those lines of Dylan Thomas's.

> But for the lovers, their arms
> Round the griefs of the ages.

I thought of them and blamed them, randomly, because they had played their part in my loving you the way I did. When you wake up and find out that the other person's gone, you seize any part of the past that demonstrates your stupidity and despise it. You blame anything that led you to believe in what you believed in. Nothing's exempt: Dylan Thomas, fossils, a scar from an old burn. Anything. They're all guilty. In the search for the place to lay blame, your whole past is a conspiracy of culprits.

You sold words.

Was that a clue? Would Myres have spotted it and warned me if she'd known?

The horror of seeing your past whole is that it makes you

wonder if there were clues you could have discovered. The sea asks you if you should have seen it coming. It shows you the root-system and its culmination: the above-ground plant hacked, decapitated – asks you if you could have grown differently, avoided the blade.

And you don't know the answer. You don't know if you could have read of lovers with their arms around the griefs of ages and yet known that there were griefs beyond any imaginable embrace. You don't know.

The sea asks you if you want to walk into it. Reminds you that it's there every day, should you decide to. So I go to the shingle, every day.

Camvellyn doesn't mind me. I think I'm odd enough to have escaped its mistrust of outsiders. Either that or Myres has threatened them with something. Either that or Myres is secretly the local witch, with power to shape the village's collective mind. People say hello to me. I say hello back. The words feel like moths released from my mouth. I think it's just that the ugliness of my aura fits here. I think it's just that the Cornish recognize someone else who's got her back turned to the rest of the country. The scars fit here. They're accepted coin, somehow. You're allowed here if you're hiding. You're allowed here if they've hurt you and you've turned against them. Them. Whoever they are. The Cornish recognize fugitives. They don't embrace them, but they don't shun them either.

A slave to the Spar's eccentric stock, I eat things I've never eaten before. Mr Kipling's Almond Slices. Scotch broth. Leeks.

The cottage is cold and damp. An hour before bed I light the upstairs fire. We're not allies, me and fire. I haven't forgiven fire for what it did to me. Fire gave me the scar that you touched in a way that made me love you. So I handle it at arm's length, with the longest tongs I can find. Even when I'm on the couch absorbing its warmth there's no gratitude, just a gleeful, bitter sense that I'm clever enough to *use* it, now, while it can do nothing to me. As if in acknowledgement of this, it spits showers of sparks from time to time – but they never get anywhere near me.

The bathroom smells of mould, but its minimalism appeals. Everything's exposed: U-bends, tub base, boiler, floorboards. I sit in hot water up to my neck every evening, listening to the place's repertoire of ticks and moans. When I see Myres again I'll tell her that this cottage is her objective correlative just the way it is.

There's no radio and no television. The passage of time is marked in light.

Now there were two Chloes. One wrote, the other went to the sea's edge. Once or twice in a day they might meet – opening a tin of soup, striking a match, steeping a teabag. Each was suspicious of the other. The writing Chloe knew that the Chloe at the shore could make all the words meaningless. The Chloe who watched the dark water loathed the writer for holding her back. In the moments when the two fused, she experienced a strange stillness of time and blankness of mind, as if neither movement nor thought were possible.

Then, a week after her arrival, a night came when she couldn't sleep.

She had done nothing out of the ordinary. She had woken at first light to a morning of biblically spectacular clouds and light (announced in the first instance by the silver bracelet's slender circle), eaten a slice of brown bread and marmalade, washed in cold water, made a flask of tea and taken her journal out with her to the beach. She had sat and watched the water; her palms had received the impress of pebbles and sand; the gulls had sailed out and returned. Three tankers had crossed the black horizon, slowly. She had come back to the cottage, telephoned her Mum and Dad, made the fires, dozed, eaten a meal of kippers and boiled potatoes, bathed, then crawled into bed when the first stars were showing through rents in the cloud.

But the time had passed (dawn was perhaps an hour away), and physical discomfort – an ache in her abdomen, a hollowness in her chest – had turned into anxiety, then in a sudden lurch into a visceral fear.

It was worse than anything in the hospital. It was worse because it was overwhelming and specific: it was the fear that the man who had raped her knew exactly where she was, had observed her every move, had followed her to Camvellyn and was at any moment about to force his way into the cottage.

Once she had recognized the fear for what it was, it escalated. Became a certainty. It was as if nothing had happened since that night. It was as if that night were all nights, now, tonight. It was as if she had been asleep to the reality that it must happen all over again, as if everyone – the doctors, Liz, Jane, her parents, Myres, Frank and Edna – had been conspiring to lull her, as if together they had mesmerized her into an insane sense of safety. He was coming. He was close. There was nothing to keep him from her.

It took perhaps five minutes for the transformation to complete itself, from anxiety to fear to terror. Tearing herself out of bed, stumbling, pulling her clothes on, she could hear herself whimpering, crying, struggling for breath. With every second that passed she expected to hear the door downstairs crash open, footsteps on the stairs, the bedroom door open, the hands grasping her in the dark.

It was a terrible awakening. Nothing made sense except the certainty that he could get her. Her blindness up to this point was a kind of meta-horror, as if she were only this moment understanding that he had been with her ever since she had left the hospital. It affected her so violently that she had to cover her mouth with her hand to muffle the sounds of distress. He was so close, so *close*.

She could hardly draw breath. Her lungs tightened, her legs were unsteady, the blood in her ears thudded. Every step took an age. The air was thick, the air of nightmare that fought every forward movement, the air that was in league with him. Surely she could be out of the cottage in seconds? But no, hours seemed to pass while she watched her own feet descending the stairs slowly, slowly; her hand on the banister advanced an inch at a time. Time itself was tangible, resisting her – though she knew that for him time was weightless, or a stream flowing with him, speeding him towards her.

One painfully conquered stair. Another. Lungs giant with an unexpelled breath. His face recreated, blooming over and over as if in repeated camera flashes in her mind: the neatly trimmed moustache and beard, the eyes and mouth concentrating, their composure barely disturbed throughout the struggle; the strong eyebrows raised as if in gentle surprise at the first splash of blood on his shirt.

Oh God oh God oh God please – her own voice trapped under her throat, his forearm rationing air to her windpipe; her rage rage rage that her physical strength could be so quickly mapped, countered, contained. All the muscles of her face straining to keep her eyes closed so she wouldn't see his face when he spoke because to see the ownership of the words was worse, worse than anything. Come on you little cunt. Does that hurt? Shame. Now don't make me come yet you filthy little bitch. Don't you dare.

The living-room. The miracle of having got down the stairs. Get out. The front. He came in the back. Get out the front.

She hadn't turned on a single light. How many seconds now? Minutes. Hours. Get out.

And still the face flashed in her mind. A metamorphosis. No words now – just the sound of his breathing; her intuiting that this took him to a realm beneath words, that words would have hindered him. The words had been like a preliminary formula to be got through as quickly as possible. Her understanding that the realm beneath words was worse, further away from any contact with something human. His silence measured the infinite distance between them, as it would with an animal. The terrible realization that none of the resources she had would work because all her resources were human – and now he was not.

The face, the face, the face. The police artist's results were a lie because the face they showed still met the human criteria. The descent into the place beneath words had transformed the real face into something no itinerary of features could ever reproduce. They would be looking for something only she had seen.

Her whole life torn open, everything exposed. Nothing left that was hers. You'll have to decide how much you're going to let him have taken from you.

Everything. Everything. Everything. I didn't *let* him take it. He just took it. I'm not me. Anyone. Erased. Nothing.

Her hand found the front door latch, turned it, flung the door open. For an instant she saw him standing there. All the world's air rushed into her, burst her lungs in an explosion. One second. Then she knew he was not there, not real.

She ran, feeling the slowed time membrane tearing at last, and the cold night flowing over her like fire.

There wasn't much left of the night.

She had crashed on to the shingle and seen almost immediately that she wasn't alone. Three teenagers – two girls and a boy – were disposed around a small fire, drinking and talking, quietly. An old couple were standing waiting for daylight while their dog sniffed and scuffed around the stones.

For a few minutes she stood catching her breath. The run had exhausted her, but had lifted something from her too. She felt clear and empty.

When she walked away from them towards the far end of the cove, each step was a precise gesture with its own unique necessity, the crunch of her feet on the pebbles a steadily evolving expression. The emptiness behind her expanded with every step. A calm had come over her limbs.

A narrow spur of dark rock ran out into the sea. She steadied herself with her hand against it.

She didn't remove her shoes. The water was colder than she could have imagined. She thought nothing – only noticed the advance of cold over her ankles, stopped for a while, got her balance, then took three more steps. Shins. She stood still. Knees.

They saw each other simultaneously. She heard a voice to her left and turned. A small boy in a bright yellow oilskin and wellies standing next to his father, who sat on the very edge of the spur, fishing rod in hand.

'Daddy, look!'

''Old on a minnet, Mattie.'

'There's a lady in the water!'

At which he turned, saw Chloe up to her waist now, ten feet below him.

'Jesus Chroist, woman – what you playin' at?'

For what seemed a very long time Chloe stood perfectly still, looking up at them, the man on his feet now, the boy's small face filled with curiosity. The water lapped and gurgled against the spur. The sea stretched away, its offer of unimaginable weight held, indefinitely.

Finally, with no explanation, she turned and slouched back through the water towards the shingle.

When she got back to the cottage, Myres was standing in the doorway, smoking.

'Just about to send out a search party,' Myres said.

There wasn't enough light for her to see that Chloe's bottom half was soaking wet. Chloe calculated this, stopped five paces away from the door. She didn't want Myres to see how close she'd been. She stood still, wondering if Myres could smell the sea on her, amazed that minutes separated suicide from embarrassment. Daddy, there's a lady in the water. Detective Myres, I was trying to drown myself but unfortunately a small boy fishing with his father interrupted me – so I've come back here.

Myres smoked agitatedly, as if she resented the cigarette. Her face looked drained of blood and her small eyes were alert with exhaustion. Chloe was wondering how she was going to get past without Myres seeing what she'd been up to. She was wondering if Keller was here, with his lardy chops and sagging shoulders. For an instant Chloe pictured him in the back garden, having been set to weeding by his partner.

'You OK?' Myres said.

'Fine. Yeah.'

'Need a dog if you're going to walk this early.'

'Yes.'

She's trying to figure it out, Chloe thought. Seeing with police
eyes. Causes. All the *other* causal explanations. It's compulsive.
The world we see isn't the world she sees. She sees motives and
secrets and lies. It's her business, her job. Chloe returns to the
cottage looking weird. *Continue.*

They stood looking at one another for a moment, surrounded
by an anarchy of birdsong, Myres leaning in the doorway, Chloe
with her jeans dripping on to the grass. Then the kettle began to
whistle.

'Cup of tea,' Myres said, as if naming a phenomenon Chloe
might never have encountered, then turned and ducked into
the cottage.

Chloe changed and came down to the kitchen. Myres, smoking
another Marlboro, sat at the bare table. A pot of tea and two blue
cups. No questions about why Chloe had changed her clothes.
Now the windows showed dull winter daylight.

She looks worse than I do, Chloe thought.

It was true. Myres's eyes were bright with sleeplessness, her
face's skin translucent over the angled bones. She had the most
neglected hands of any woman Chloe had ever known; the fingers had years ago resigned themselves to a life without care or
glamour. They did what they were told, and when they were told
nothing, rested. Now two of them held the cigarette on its
parabola to and from the bloodless lips. The grey in Myres's
hacked-at hair seemed to have doubled since her hospital visits.
Under the detective's flesh, Chloe imagined a mechanism of
overdriven steel and wire: no soft tissue; no fat. With their arms
round the griefs of the ages.

'Gave up the pad and the pencil then,' Myres said.

Chloe sipped her tea, waiting – but got the sense quickly that
Myres was the one waiting for a cue.

'Thanks for letting me use the place,' she said.

'Ugliest fucking house in Cornwall.'

'It suits me. It's quiet.'

'Met the East End Thatcherites?'

Chloe wondered if Myres had heard of the fever fiasco, decided not. 'They've been sweet, actually. Think Frank's regretted leaving me the *Sun*, mind you. Think he thinks it's an irreparable *faux pas*.'

A funny little silence, then Myres's odd, lipless smile. 'Yeah, I know what a *faux pas* is.'

No bitterness – but Chloe was a long way from levity. She did her best to return the smile.

'Things rough with your Mum and Dad?' Myres asked.

'Not great. It's hard for them. They think there's something, you know, they should be *doing*.'

'Yeah.'

'They're old. It's weird: they probably thought all the bad things were behind them. Then this. They feel helpless. They are helpless. It was best I came away.'

What *is* it? Chloe was thinking. There's something. What is she – examining me? What does she want?

She'd never seen Myres nervous. Tired, angry, robotic, precise – but never this tightness, this uncertainty. Again Chloe thought back to herself standing in the sea, the turbid water sending its message of cold through to the bones in her legs. She had felt so distinctly her own weight in comparison to the endless weight of water. She had felt the exact distance she would need to pace before she would be out of her depth. Walking out had been an act of remembering, as if each step had been rehearsed long ago, then forgotten. Now she sat opposite Myres, drinking a cup of tea.

'I never thanked you for the visits in hospital,' Chloe said.

Myres looked aside at the long ash of her cigarette.

'It helped,' Chloe said. 'You don't know what'll help.'

Myres dragged deeply, suddenly, then mashed the filter in the ashtray and stood up. She wouldn't quite look at Chloe.

'What's the matter?' Chloe said.

Myres stretched her arms, slowly, made her scapulae meet. 'Nothing,' she said. 'Sorry. I'm very tired. I haven't slept in a while. Do you mind if I just get a couple of hours upstairs?'

*

Chloe hadn't cleaned or tidied the cottage the whole time she'd been there. It took Myres's arrival to make her realize. She had used every piece of crockery she could find, and now it sat in an ugly heap in the sink. When she had run out of clean dishes she had resorted to eating straight from cooking-pans or tins. The kitchen's one bin was overflowing. Noticing the smell of rubbish for the first time, she began to clean.

On the landing upstairs she gathered up the wet clothes she'd dumped there and went to hang them in the bathroom. Looked in on Myres.

She was asleep on her back, fully clothed, one forearm dashed across her eyes as if in grief or passion. She had taken her boots off. Thick black socks, one with a hole at the ball of the foot displaying a pink moon of flesh. Her mouth was open, but her breathing was silent.

It was horrifying to Chloe, though she didn't know why. The utter vulnerability – even of detectives who spent their days gathering the evidence of damage. Sleep's egalitarian reduction. All the thoughts and utterances and actions, all the root-system of choices meant nothing in sleep. While Chloe watched, Myres's top lip flickered, then was still. She wondered, watching the ribcage rise and fall, seeing the soft pulse between throat and collarbone, whether Myres had watched her sleep in the hospital. She wondered what Myres's idea of her had been. For a moment, she felt compelled to lie down beside her. For a moment all her own body's weeks without human touch expressed themselves like a chill over the entire surface of her skin.

She turned and walked from the room, holding her elbows.

It'll never be over. The sea stopped asking questions and instead gave me an answer: it'll never be over. Only you can be over.

You keep living, and for a while – the product of shock – allow for the idea that there can still be other things in your life. Not even good things, necessarily – just things. Then, one night, you realize that's just a survival delusion. There can be no other things in your life. There can be no other things. I saw the fishing boy's surprised eyes and realized that it wouldn't be any different if you were still here. If you hadn't disappeared. Even you wouldn't have been big enough to find room in my life now that it contains this. There wouldn't have *been* room. How could there have been? Did you know that? Is that why you went?

My life. Joke. There isn't a life. There's just this event that takes up all the available space. If there's a life, that's all it is: a fully occupied space. *I* am an occupied space. I've seen them all looking for me: Jane, Liz, Mum, Dad. I've seen them all looking for *me*. But I'm not there. Something else is there – the thing that occupies my space. You would have looked too. I don't know if I could have stood seeing you looking for me and me not being there. So you spared me that. A small mercy for which I'll never forgive you.

I don't miss you. You need a context for missing someone, something within which their presence would make sense. I don't miss you. I wouldn't have anywhere to put you if you were here. You would have gone anyway, sooner or later. Sooner or later I would have told you to go.

Chloe stopped writing. The fire whistled and snapped. The room was warm and very still.

When she turned and saw Myres standing in the doorway, she knew. She had known all along.

'There's no easy way of saying this,' Myres said. 'We think we've got him.'

There was a moment before the dream began. Myres got into her car and Chloe stood looking back over the car park down to where the land ended in a gulf over the sea. While she watched, a tern sailed from the edge and caught an updraught, tilting out

over the water. She knew the pattern: the bird would drift out
twenty, thirty, forty, fifty feet, bank, and return to the cliff.

She watched and waited. If I stand still until it turns, I won't
go. This is how the world reveals its leylines, its logic of action.
If x, then y. We don't need to toss coins. The apparatus for decision is all around us. It's everything.

Twenty feet out.

A light rain began to fall.

If I'm still watching when it turns.

Thirty feet.

The cat's-cradle of cause and effect is everywhere.

Forty. Fifty.

Another updraught. One wing dipped.

Chloe turned and got into the car.

'You don't have to do this,' Myres said.

Chloe listened to the rain, harder now, on the roof and
bonnet.

'Yes I do,' she said.

Then the dream began.

They drove three hundred miles. Everything Chloe wanted to
know was given to her in separate pieces, utterances passed to
her one by one like stones. Myres didn't look at her. There were
a thousand questions Chloe might have asked. She asked perhaps two dozen in three hundred miles.

'How do you do this?'

'By breaking the law.'

'How many of you?'

'A handful. Not often. It's almost always impossible.'

They drove through billowing curtains of rain. Roads cut
through hills. Bridges. Black and white cows like beautiful
carvings in the green grass. A new perception, of neither time
nor space. Individual and perfectly formed memories lifted
from and settled upon her like butterflies. I know this sounds
ridiculous, but let's get married. A message to us from long
ago! Vicky fastening the bracelet around her wrist. Her father's
face crumpling into tears. The primary school classroom with

its stretched squares of sunlight, her thin-lined drawing of a brontosaurus. A page in a science book naming clouds – nimbostratus, cirrus, cumulus – all depicted in the same unnaturally blue sky. Looking down her body and seeing, gauzily, tributaries of her own blood, feeling the lightness of her limbs. Kissing Nicholas in the rain. Alone in front of a mirror on a dull afternoon hearing her inner voice saying: I love him. I love him. I love him.

'What if it's not him?'

'It's him.'

Every detail of the world revealed itself to Chloe with a new purity. An RAC emergency telephone box. The giant wheel of a lorry that passed. A single bare tree in stilled ecstasy. She felt a buoyant indifference to everything. At moments it seemed this was the happiness she had been searching for her whole life – that everyone searched for, always. She looked across at Myres in profile: the face of planes and angles, no curve, no grace, no yielding; eyes dreaming the road; mouth that had become final years ago, moving now only to form the stone words.

'Where is he?'

'Basement of a council block that's coming down next month.'

'How many times have you done this?'

'Once before this.'

It didn't matter. Chloe sat in the passenger seat unfolding into lightness. In a break between showers she saw half a rainbow, knew that Myres had seen it, shared with her the act of saying nothing about it.

London reached out for them, dark, tentacular – but still didn't break Chloe's sense of dream. Her childhood had come with her unasked, a ghost in the car. She remembered moments in the afternoons studying the whorls of her own fingerprints while the sun dropped perpendicular heat on her head. A time when her body was still trying to get her to see that it was hers. Then the paradox of puberty: the caress of a blood droplet sudden and intimate on her thigh which for an instant made her alien to her own flesh, then drew her into it as into an ancient

allegiance. Masturbation: an inarticulate tracing of a previously
unseen design, suddenly ignited pleasure, the radical, forbidden
knowledge that her body was something she could give to herself – an unearned sufficiency. Then, by degrees, the adult
package, neglected, sometimes shared with others: the pathos of
elbows and knees; the ordeal of absorbing desire; the finite
vehicle.

Then love. All of love. Love's divinely unreasonable demand
of the body – that it find a way of speaking love. And the strange
time after love, the bruised friendliness, touch worn to comfort,
a hand in the small of the back, crossing a road.

Finally this. The broken boundary. The admission the body
struggled to avoid through all its years of hurrying blood and
shucked cells. The admission that it could be stolen, sacked,
emptied.

London was a dark, complex presence around them – but separate, like a film projection. It still felt to Chloe as if she were
seeing everything from within a wholly other realm. She heard
car horns, watched lights change, read road signs and hoardings – but none of it connected; she and Myres were inside a
hollow globe that revolved around them, all points equidistant,
failing to manifest the passage of time. And the consciousness
she possessed now – heightened, indifferent, sensitive – made a
mockery of anything she had experienced before. She knew
Myres was in a similar state. Didn't know how she knew, except
that the skeletal questions and answers they had exchanged had
bred a telepathy of sorts. They were in motion together.

Hammersmith. Earl's Court. Charing Cross. Liverpool Street.
East. Myres never took her eyes from the road, even when lighting her cigarettes, which she smoked bitterly, aggressively, with
the driver's window down letting in the wind and the city's roar.

She realized they were off the main road. She had lost track of
where in London they were. It was dark. The rain had thinned to
a suspended mist. Myres's eyes were wide and bright, all her
body's slight movements the product of an intense concentration.

To Chloe, nothing had passed between the tern and here; the events of the last few hours were like distinct sounds, resonating indefinitely.

Freight containers, deserted forklifts, a warehouse. On one side a high wall of black concrete covered in illegible graffiti. They drove across a scarred demolition site, the car bumping over flooded ruts and potholes. Beyond the black wall was a sprawling pile of rubble. Two council tower blocks: glassless or fanged windows with blackness behind. Chloe wondered about the people who had lived there, about the spaces that had contained their lives, about where they were now.

'Dave, come in.' Click-scratch of a walkie-talkie. Myres with one hand steering, crawling the car alongside the building. Chloe saw a wheelless bike frame, tin cans, torn bags of rubbish.

'Go ahead, over.'

'We're coming in, OK? Over.'

'She with you? Over.'

'Yeah.'

A pause. 'All quiet. Come ahead. Out.'

Outside the car the air smelled of refuse, dirty rain and cold metal. Chloe closed her door and leaned against it, suddenly nauseated. Myres came and stood next to her.

'You OK?'

'Queasy,' Chloe said.

Anyone else would have touched her, rubbed her back. Myres stood still. Chloe spat out sour saliva. Breathed deeply, straightened. 'OK.'

Chloe found it increasingly difficult to speak. In the world she now inhabited there was no place for words, only the cumulative sound of everything – the sky, mud, light, blood, grass, tarmac, skin – a din so intense it equalled silence.

'Does he know you're the police?' Chloe said. The nausea had passed. Now she felt a return of the lightness, the perfection of objects. She realized her bootlaces were undone, and that her breath tasted sharp and oily. She followed Myres through a door next to the building's gutted lift-shaft.

'He doesn't know who we are,' Myres said. 'He won't know who you are. He won't have to see you.'

'What'll you do if it's not him?'

Myres didn't answer. They were under the building. Pipes. Dirt. A short corridor. Two doors, one on either side, Keller in the winded suit standing outside one, drinking a can of Pepsi. He was wearing surgical gloves. Myres said nothing to him, opened the other door.

A small room with a plastic table and chairs. A gun in the centre of the table. Chloe had never seen a gun before. It looked as if it had fallen there from the sky.

Two other people sat at the table. A man in his thirties asleep with his head on one side and his mouth open. A woman opposite him with her arms folded. The wreckage of a McDonald's meal littered the floor. The air in the room was old. Both the man and the woman wore gloves like Keller's.

The woman looked up when they entered. Same quality of exhausted hyperawareness. She looked Myres's age, possibly older. Steel-rimmed glasses and large, glaucous blue eyes, grey-blond hair pulled back in a tight, short ponytail. Her skin was tight and dry, the lips chapped.

'Tell her,' Myres said.

The woman studied Chloe for a moment, then unfolded her arms and exhaled slowly, placing her palms on her thighs.

'The man in the room opposite is Lawrence Verne. White, thirty-four years old, unmarried. His fingerprints match those found at the scene. We can't access the blood or semen samples without it being known. We need you to identify him.'

'How do you know he's . . . How do you know he did . . .'

'Circumstantially we can only tie him to one of the other crimes.'

Which left a silence. The sleeping man woke up. Said nothing. Looked at Chloe.

Time still hadn't reached her. Her entire life was with her. She had never felt it before. Every self she had ever inhabited flickered inside her, lambent, shivering, a fire of identity. The worst way to die, she had argued with Liz, was being eaten by an animal. She thought of the distances she had travelled: from the fossil to university; from awkwardness to love; from the possession of a scheme of things to this racket of silence. A part of her was thigh-deep in the Cornish sea, looking up into the boy's surprised eyes.

'I'll say this one more time,' Myres said. 'You're under no obligation. You want to turn round and walk out of here, that's OK. No one's asking anything of you.'

Chloe looked down at her undone laces. The man stood up slowly and stretched, twisting his upper torso from left to right, cracking the vertebrae.

'That doesn't make any difference,' Chloe said.

Keller was standing with one hand in his pocket, the other squeezing the now empty Pepsi can. Myres gestured with her eyes, and he shuffled to the end of the corridor, climbed the stairs, disappeared.

'I don't want the others here,' Chloe said.

She didn't know why. In this state she was discovering unique necessities everywhere, relations between things that held for a moment then passed away. At this moment, she knew that the presence of the two other officers was prohibitive. She had acquired an apparatus that graphed and deciphered the invisible, told her, infallibly, what went where. Myres understood. It was a version of the ability she possessed herself.

They didn't look at her as they filed past, the man with his jacket slung over his shoulder, hooked on his bent-back index finger, the woman with eyes shrunk by the removal of her glasses. In one fluid movement Chloe was not meant to see, the gun passed from the man's hand to Myres's, then to her jacket pocket. The exchange had a softness to it, an affection – two magicians sharing a trade secret.

The door had a flap of black masking tape at head height. Myres lifted it, peered through the hole underneath for one heartbeat, two, three – then stood back and looked at Chloe. The two women were absolutely still. Chloe felt her history shrivelled, a thing that had been brought out and bleached by the

sun. Around it now was a dry space of light. A strange happiness, too, the buoyancy of pure disinterest. Her childhood,
girlhood, womanhood, every inhaled scent of her own identity
and the whole world's history of argument was present, observ-
able, an unfinished and laughably inadequate attempt at
wholeness. Books teemed on shelves. Words multiplied, expo-
nentially. Millions of people collected their own memories and
desires and ideas, wove them, wrapped themselves, believed
they knew themselves. Chloe saw it all: a small, reflex movement
in a cavernous space of darkness. She was detached from it.

But her body remembered. As if the gesture had been previously agreed between them, Chloe lifted her violently shaking
hands slowly in front of her for Myres to see.

◆

It had been impossible to grasp that what was in him was contained and expressed by just his body. It had been impossible to
understand that the body didn't revolt, that it had no will of its
own to refuse what drove it. They were, after all, arms, hands,
teeth, knees, fingers; up until that moment Chloe's definitions of
them had been functional or friendly: for eating, for shaking
hands, for playing the piano, for seeing, for talking. Her life had
brought her to such definitions. Her life hadn't shown her
others.

There had been (in the separate, out-of-body part of her, for a
handful of liberated seconds) an inability to understand that
this was a person acting through his body, that the body was for
him a neutral implement, that there was no necessity in her
definitions of hands and eyes and mouth, that he could recreate
them, was recreating them.

Then the seconds had passed and she had been sucked with a
finality back into her own body.

Her own body had consumed its fuel of resistance so quickly.
She had expended it, reflexively, without choice. The assaulted

body had no choice: the compulsion was to create escape. There had been a finite store of fight, ignited, instantly, first with the forced belief that it could free her – then very quickly with the certainty that it would not. It had been fire, an inevitable, limited combustion. Then the terrible incarceration within her own skin. The skin suffering and incapable of letting her go. Tissue, blood, flesh, bone, neurons, capillaries, the senses' quintet conspiracy – all colluded, helplessly, in her imprisonment. Only her eyes could help her, shut tight. At least not seeing, at least with the power to disembody the voice.

But only for moments. There had been the conditioned belief that survival must be enhanced by information, by opening her eyes and seeing. Dead-ending because each time the sum of information was the same: the ceiling; his face; the static angles and colours of the room.

She had hated her body because it encased her in suffering. Every cell had betrayed her. She had felt her history cut to a stump, her life (the root-system of choices) as a simple, final failure because nothing she had chosen had prevented this. Her past and her body revealed as binaries in a giant infidelity; she had wanted rid of them. In a matter of moments, dying had become a pure and craved sacrament.

But she had had no control over that, either.

Before the words had taken him to the place where no words were, he had spoken to her, had unravelled the litany of hate mechanically, quickly. She had known, somehow, that he needed to get beyond personhood (his own and hers), but that to get beyond it he must first assault it, must first force her to see that *he* was doing this to *her*, the actual human being she was. He had kept telling her to look at him, to force her to see him. He had wanted her to see that even before the animal level, even while language still kept them within the human realm, there was no hope. So he had continued to talk to her, to insist on her personhood, until her suffering as a person took him to the lower level of being, at which the heavy, blind blood dream could play itself out.

Once the lower level had been sounded, once she had understood that he was beyond all reach, that he was no longer seeing

her as *her*, that she was freed from the doomed imperative to
make the person in him stop – then she had known that he
would kill her, and even that small certainty of the release from
suffering had brought her a fragment of calm. The appearance of
the knife, strange and brilliant and unfamiliar against the white
of the bedroom, had enhanced her sense that there would at
least be a release from her own flesh and blood. That and a
burning sadness that she wouldn't be able to say goodbye to
Nicholas.

◆

Chloe, shorter than Myres, stood down off her tiptoes.
  'Is it him?'
  'Yes.'

Another layer fell on the dream in a golden flake. Chloe saw
Myres's face as if for the first time. The exhaustion was a veil.
Underneath was fear – of what she had committed herself to.
Fear of herself, looking back to where the belief in the law used
to be. How many times have you done this? Once before. Chloe
could see what it had added to Myres, what it had taken away.
The hard face was alone. A faint version of her smile, betrayed
by the eyes. The face was scored by icy courage. But she was
alone.
    There was no telling how long the two women stood there.
Chloe could hear him breathing beyond the door. Myres was
doing something with her hands. When Chloe looked down she
saw her fitting a silencer to the gun. Now the gun looked familiar, again as if Chloe had seen these movements before, a long
time ago, had forgotten them until this moment. Myres's hands
that morning, carrying the cigarette to her mouth. Her hands'
history, the gestures that had written them into unloved plain-
ness. Myres asleep, lips parted, the appalling humanness of the
flesh revealed by the hole in the black sock.

'Wait in the other room,' Myres said.

Dreaming still, Chloe stepped across into the room opposite. The door swung slowly shut behind her. Everything was as before – the ugly table and chairs, the food refuse. We need you to identify him. Chloe thought of television police. The police. An abstraction. Not people. Crime – another abstraction. Not his forearm under her jaw, not the fire blown into her. Not his voice, hurrying through its incantations: dirty little cunt come on move that's it that's it feel that open your eyes open your eyes and look at me does that hurt good eh does that hurt you filthy fucking cunt – all abstractions. They had all been abstractions. Then her own body had rewritten all of it.

A terrible weight of space around her, not measured by the room. Her life was over. Now she could hear the scream of infinite space, the emptiness of time. Her life was over and the old world had been sloughed; history was a shrivelled skin in sunlight. Each moment of consciousness created the present, where nothing was known except that she was alone.

The persistence of her body – reconstituted, imperfectly remembering itself – left her blank. Moving through spaces had felt different ever since the hospital. The journey from London with Liz. Her bedroom at Elm Coombe. The village. Only the cold Cornish water had defined her outline in an offer of final confirmation: this is who you are.

Do you want him in prison or do you want him dead?

She remembered Myres asking her in the hospital. She remembered sensing the detective's disgust at the necessary gap between them. I promise I'll do everything in my power to make that happen. Driving from Cornwall, Chloe hadn't asked Myres for any of the details. Hadn't cared. Still didn't. He was a few feet away, cuffed to a bolted chair, breathing.

You fucking sewer cunt, he had said. You fucking open *drain*.

Sometimes her chest, abdomen, pelvis – sometimes all seemed to fracture. Half a dozen times since she'd left hospital. She would find herself with her own arms wrapped around her middle, holding herself together.

She moved back to the door and pulled it open.

Opposite her, in profile, Myres stood bent double, hands down by her knees, one set of fingers loosely clasping the gun. The gun hand shook. Myres looked up. Chloe saw the will stammer: Myres had opened her mouth to say something – Get back inside – but had stopped, arrested by what was made known between them. It was around them in the dead air like an awaited conjunction of stars – though Myres shook her head, no.

Chloe felt a deep tiredness – and at the same time a lightness of being that made her smile. The lightness made her movements fluid, perfect. Myres still fought it, but weakly. The gun hand lifted for the exchange like the morning's tern on its updraught. Chloe took it smoothly, without pause, knowing (remembering) its weight.

She could feel her own beatific smile when she stood in front of him, her face a rose of fire. She saw his eyes remembering her, saw a light come into them and then disappear. He hadn't had the time to compute all the information. His breathing was still escalating, the adrenalin still racing to its sites. Chloe raised the gun to the level of his head. She felt her own radiance. The new space and time around her history was beautiful with cold and emptiness.

He said: 'You can't do this.'

She pulled the trigger.

Myres drove Chloe to her own flat in Bethnal Green.

'What'll happen?' Chloe asked.

Myres's look had changed. The hyperawareness had receded; now only the physical weariness in her face's flesh remained. The city's lights crawled over her.

'Nothing,' she said. 'People disappear all the time.'

Chloe looked down at her hands. The gun's weight and kick had finished their old life. Now touch was starting again from scratch. People disappear all the time.

The flat was above a row of shops, all closed for the night. Chloe followed Myres up two flights of stairs, smelling cat litter, cigarette smoke, newspapers.

'How long have you lived here?' she asked.

'Eight years,' Myres said. 'Time to get out, I think.'

The flat's interior surprised Chloe. For one thing, it occupied the whole floor. A living-room, a big bedroom, a third room with a desk, chair, computer and filing-cabinets, a very small bathroom, and a spotless kitchen. There were rugs and bare floorboards, houseplants, two stripped wooden chests, a large leather sofa, floor-length ivory curtains. Not what Chloe had expected. She'd imagined bare rooms, functionality, the tokens of existence rather than life.

'Bought it cheap after a fire,' Myres said. 'National Front used to own it. Kept getting fire-bombed. I think the word finally got out that a copper was living in it, so they left it alone.'

'It's very nice,' Chloe said – then almost burst out laughing. Myres was sheepish, ashamed of herself for the concessions to comfort.

'Sorry,' Chloe said. 'I feel funny.'

She was very calm. In Turkey late one night she had got up and walked to the sea for a solitary swim. Twenty yards out from the shore she was surrounded by blackness, body submerged (treading water, gently), head tilted up to the stars, hair spreading on the surface in soft fronds. In the first few moments she had been afraid – of the scale of emptiness, the dark water dropping away beneath her softly kicking feet – but then a calm had come over her. A paradox: she had felt both utterly inconsequential and supremely important. The night and the water around her reduced her to nothing; yet at the same time she felt she was a pin holding the entire universe together, suspended, vertically, in the Mediterranean Sea, alone, at night. In the end these two conflicting senses of herself had created a calm that was beyond thought. When she eventually left the water she had no idea how long she had been there. She walked back to the hotel, slipped into bed behind Nicholas, then slept, deeply, late into the next day.

This calm was the same – the pure tiredness of a child. She knew a long draught of sleep was coming.

'I'm really sorry,' she said to Myres. 'But I think I need to lie down.'

The next day, on a National Express coach back to Cornwall, she drafted her letter of resignation to the museum.

There's neither regret nor triumph. There's just time, restarted.

Liz came to Camvellyn that weekend to see her. Chloe hadn't asked her, but she'd brought various bits and pieces from the Clapham flat. Clothes, a few books, some of the letters that had still found their way there.

'Bloody hell, Chloe,' Liz had said, on seeing the cottage's minimalism. 'Bloody *hell*.'

'It's fine, Liz.'

'But how can you *live* here?'

'Easy.'

'I mean is there electric and stuff?'

'Of course.'

Liz had shuddered, hunched her shoulders, as if afraid the walls might spit something at her.

'Do Mum and Dad know it's like this?'

'No,' Chloe had said. 'And you're not going to tell them either.'

They went through the two days awkwardly. Chloe could see that Liz thought she was losing her mind. Chloe herself could see all around Liz's life, the smoothed-down edges, the hidden knots, the contained fractures and plugged holes.

'Liz,' she said, in the afternoon on the beach. 'You're not happy, are you?'

'What?'

Chloe stared out at the water.

'What d'you mean?' Liz said, with a little laugh.

'You don't trust Tom.'

'I do.'

'You don't trust him and you're afraid of him.'

'Chloe! What's got into you? Course I trust him.'

In the space of a few seconds, Chloe saw the way the rest of the conversation would evolve. She decided she didn't want to hurt her sister.

'I'll tell you something,' she said.

'What?'

'I think Nick was with someone else that night.'

'*What?*'

'Don't make me say it again.'

She hadn't known until that moment that she was going to say it. Saying it had been her mouth testing itself. Silence, then another wave hissed on the shingle.

'Don't be afraid,' Chloe said, not looking at her sister. 'It's all right.'

'Chloe, you've got to—'

'I think I've known for a long time. Detective Myres knows. She hasn't told me.'

'But how do you know? I mean . . . I mean . . .'

'Imagine it.'

'Chloe, don't. For God's sake don't.'

'Imagine it,' Chloe repeated. 'History's full of unimaginable coincidences. Life's full of them. We just don't imagine them, because if we do, we can't live.'

'I think you're being silly,' Liz said.

'Of course you do,' Chloe said. 'You want to live. You can't afford to be silly if you want to live.'

They sat in silence on the tartan blanket. Chloe could see that her sister was getting cold. She herself was impervious to cold, it seemed. She sat with her shoulders back, the breeze making her face's scars speak. All the scars spoke from time to time, describing the flesh's new argument with the world.

'Are you too cold?' Chloe asked her sister.

Long pause. You're scaring me, Chloe. Don't talk like this. There's something wrong with you. Don't, don't, don't. But I won't say any of that.

'Well, it's a bit nippy,' Liz said, knees under her chin, fingers wrapped around them.

'Come on then,' Chloe said. 'Let's go back and have something to eat.'

History is, among other things, the story of people killing each other. You think of the number of people who've killed other people. You think of it as a small number. It's a huge number. A sprawling fraternity that stretches all the way back to sticks and stones, teeth, claws. You don't know the dark élites to which you'll graduate, to which you'll descend. You don't see that your time, the bronchioles of choice, expanding, every moment, is carrying you towards membership. I've joined. Soldiers, pharaohs, assassins, psychopaths, wronged lovers. The contexts are myriad, the act is the same. The moment is the same. Whether I want it or not I share something with all of them: the instant of crossing over. I've crossed over. Cross over and, regardless of what else follows, for a second the world reopens its calyx and corolla in a new bloom where all previous relations pass away. Cross over and for an instant you know that writing commandments on stone is a preposterously optimistic fiat – because you can break them and live. Rain still falls, clouds still sail their shadows over the sea. TV commercials still try to persuade you with happy jingles and beautiful faces. Chocolate still tastes good. Water still comes when you turn the tap on. You still cough, sneeze, scratch your head. Wonder if you'll make the train. The human condition is the persistence of the ordinary. That's one of the things Myres was trying to spare me, no doubt, though she wouldn't have put it that way.

There's a residue from the old world, even now. Last night while Liz slept, I woke mumbling, whimpering, dripping with sweat. Staggered to the bathroom and threw up the evening's Heinz tomato soup and Findus shepherd's pie. Afterwards I looked in the mirror at the face I've acquired. The new look. The new me. The me who reopened the world's seal in the instant of pulling the trigger. I wondered what would have happened if I'd missed. I could have missed, buried a bullet in the bare brick, been left standing, stupid, unresolved, forced to make a decision where before something other than decision had carried me forward. I wouldn't have fired a second time. I know I wouldn't have been able to. Me. Chloe Anne Palmer, whose Dad brought the fossil stone home from Lyme Regis.

But I didn't miss. My dreams tell me I didn't miss. Myres hurrying me out. Keller shivering with the other two outside, away from the two white lights. The car waiting to take us away.

Myres put me in her guest bedroom. I got up in the small hours, saw the living-room light on. She sat at the window drinking, smoking slowly now. There was nothing to say. Myres and I move into moments where there's nothing to say. I turned and went back to bed. Slept deep again.

It's time.

* * *

There were three days to pass between Liz's departure and
Myres's arrival in Camvellyn. Chloe spent them simply: making
easy meals, sitting on the hard beach; improving her fire-making
skills. Twice, in the early mornings, she had encountered the
fisherman who had interrupted her walk into the sea. They said
hello to each other, but nothing else.

She felt herself getting physically stronger, muscles coming
awake. The smell of the sea was comforting.

Myres arrived on a cold wet evening. Chloe was sitting by the fire
with a cup of tea when she heard the car and saw the swung beams
of headlights cross the ceiling. Myres came in with a duffel-bag.

''S all right for some, then,' Myres said, deadpan.

'I'll make you a cup of tea,' Chloe said.

In the kitchen it began to dawn on her that there was a familiar shape here, in Camvellyn, with Myres, in the cottage. It
struck her that she hadn't even asked Myres if it was OK for her
to come back to the place. In the flat at Bethnal Green the morning after, Myres had asked Chloe what her plans were, and Chloe
had said: 'Go back to the cottage for a while, I suppose,' without
a second thought. Telling the truth, bluntly and without premeditation, revealed all sorts of things that could be taken for
granted. Even now, realizing that she was in fact staying in someone else's property rent-free without having asked their
permission, Chloe had no misgivings. It was what Myres
wanted. There was a body of mutual knowledge between them
that made the old formal ways redundant.

But still (and Chloe was shocked that she had noticed this at
all), there was an awkwardness between them. Myres had
watched Chloe reopen the world, and yet they were physically
clumsy if they both tried to pass through the same doorway, or
started a sentence at the same time.

Stirring milk into Myres's cup, Chloe realized that even with
the new clarity of vision certain things had been withheld from
her. Now that she knew, she wasn't sure what to do with the
knowledge.

*

'I want to know everything,' Chloe said to Myres. They sat opposite one another with the hearth between them, Chloe with her knees tucked up on the couch, Myres in the unmatching armchair with her legs stretched straight out in front of her. The flames whispered and buckled. Rain battered the windows.

'Why now?'

'Because I can take it. Whatever it is.'

Myres lifted a cigarette to her lips and lit it from a book of matches. Tossed the spent match into the fire.

'Where do you want me to start?'

'Was he with someone that night?'

'Yes.'

In spite of everything it thudded into her like a bolt. Nicholas. Nick. With their arms around the griefs—

'Who was it?'

'Nina Cole.'

After the first fact this was less of a shock. It wasn't a shock. It was a precisely measured and contained disgust. A small piece of dried shit. What pain there was for Chloe came from the feeling of Nicholas shrinking to ordinariness. She felt it inside her, physically, as if he had shrivelled to a small, tough nugget, knocking around in her heart.

And in a moment something is finished. Something that ran through your blood – something that *was* your blood – reduced to an artefact, imperfect, petrified, ended, so much smaller than you'd dreamed.

No 'sorry' from Myres. She sat and slowly smoked and drank her tea. Something was over for her too, it seemed to Chloe.

'Where is Nina Cole now?'

'She's in Italy. Doing we're not sure what.'

'Not New York?'

Myres shook her head. 'There wasn't a relationship,' she said. 'It was a one-off. There was no plan to run off together or anything.'

'How do you know all this?'

'I spoke to her.'

'What?'

'On the phone. Before she left.'

'You didn't try 'n' keep her here?'

'What for? She hadn't broken the law.'

Chloe took a sip of her own tea. The wind blew a sudden extravagant attack of rain at the living-room window, then subsided again. She couldn't help remembering Nicholas's repeated characterization of Nina as comedy vamp, someone who ruined what appeal she might have had with obviousness. Chloe had only met Nina once, briefly, at the office. She had come to meet Nicholas for a drink and dinner after work, and while she waited in reception Nina had come out to leave a stack of post with the receptionist. Chloe had felt it even then, the flash of knowledge, the sense that however farcical a person Nina might be she none the less had a version of the nasty-looking sexiness that men desired, invariably. In that moment Chloe had heard a small voice say once, quietly and clearly: He fancies her. Then Nina was gone, and a few minutes later Nicholas was with her, and she had forced herself not to start a fight with him.

Now, sitting opposite Myres, she imagined Nicholas fucking Nina. Because she could. It was one bruise she could press. She conjured the most explicit images, let them flick through her mind like a sequence of film frames. Each one burned her, separately, quickly. Then it was over. She had been staring into the fire. Myres had waited.

'Do you know where my husband is?' Chloe asked.

Myres leaned over and threw the cigarette butt into the flames. 'Yes,' she said.

'Where is he?'

'He came back to London more than three weeks ago. He was in hospital for ten days. He's staying with Anthony Caswell-Brooks. I haven't spoken to him.'

◆

'Come on, mate,' Anthony said to Nicholas. 'You've been

standing there for an hour now. Come and sit down at least. Have a drop, for God's sake.'

Nicholas stood at the window, looking down through rain on to Ladbroke Grove's cavalcade of headlights. His memory – his life's memory – was compressed, now; it inhabited a much smaller version of himself, a child version. Around the child version of himself was a vast, empty space. He was afraid that any movement – to the couch, a drink, an exchange of words with Anthony – would send the child out into this new unknown vacuum, where nothing would resist it, where it woud travel in one direction, *ad infinitum*. A heavy calm was on him, though he was afraid to move.

'I'd consider having a shave if I were you,' Anthony said, lighting a cigarette.

Nicholas stood with his hands by his sides, his back to Anthony. The tube station entrance across the street released another stream of disembarked passengers. Umbrellas sprang into being like buds opening, suddenly. Lights shimmered on the wet-skinned road.

'My advice is, say as little as possible,' Anthony said. 'My advice is don't say a fucking *word* more than you need to. Not that it's any of, etc.'

The child version of Nicholas's memory refused to go forward into the new spaces until certain conditions had been satisfied. The child version of himself was still waiting for something. The time of using words premeditatedly was passed. Now words sprang the trap of his mouth independent of his volition; they had momentary, incandescent meaning, then were gone, and forgotten as soon as they were gone. He wondered if he would meet them out there in the new spaces around himself. He was waiting for her. For what she would say. That was all.

'After tonight,' he said to Anthony, 'I'll be gone.'

Anthony buzzed Chloe in and met her on the landing outside his door.

'Chloe,' he said.

She stood still, out of time.

'Look, Chloe, he's—'

'Just go.'

He froze. Then: 'Right. Right. I'll get out of your way.'

She let him pass her, listened to his footsteps down all the stairs, heard the front door open and shut.

Nothing except the knowledge of her own blood's pulses. One soft white light burned on the landing. Anthony had left the door to the flat ajar.

Ten years ago she had come into the café and let Nicholas know he wasn't mistaken. It had been raining then and it was raining now. Her hands and face and hair were wet with it. She had taken the tube from Liz's in Hammersmith, then walked from Ladbroke Grove without an umbrella. She'd been unable to believe that each step was bringing her to this moment.

For what seemed a long time they stood opposite each other without speaking.

'You look different,' she said at last.

Despite everything (she heard her own voice in her head saying it: 'Despite everything') she felt a detached horror at how bad he looked. Emaciated. The hands, half reaching out towards her, shook. A terrible economy to all his movements, as if there remained only a few precious reserves of life, not to be squandered. The eyes were wide with exhaustion and wouldn't stay on her.

Love. I still.

'You know everything,' he said. Statement.

'Yes, I know everything.'

Chloe walked over to the window. No traffic noise. Just the silent cars and headlights.

'I thought I'd come and find you,' Nicholas said. 'When I got off the plane. I went to the flat. I thought . . . But then I had to go to hospital.'

'Which one?'

'South Western.'

'I was there.'

'Yes.'

'That's where they put me back together. That's where they raise the dead.'

'They were kind to me.'

'I know. They were kind to me, too.'

She turned and looked at him again. He had looked at her, once, briefly, when she had entered, then kept his eyes averted. She moved across the room, reached up slowly and pulled his face around to her.

'Look at me. You haven't earned the right not to look at me. Different, isn't it?'

It was a tiny, bright firework of rage – but it burned out in seconds. She recoiled from the deadness of his flesh, the absence of their history when she touched him.

'It's not you,' she said. Neither surprise nor sadness; just the clarity of her perception. 'It doesn't even feel like you.'

She walked back to the window. 'I was wrong,' she said. 'I thought I could come here and . . . But it won't be, now. You can't swallow all of it in a single goodbye. I'll be saying goodbye for years. For the rest of my fucking life.'

Nicholas didn't reply. Chloe decided she would speak again after the fifth car had passed.

'What was wrong with you?' she said. 'In the hospital.'

He was confused. 'I can't remember. Something in my side. Blood. I can't . . . I don't remember some of the things.'

'Didn't you want to see me?'

'I didn't know where you were. I couldn't speak to anyone. It's . . . I couldn't speak to your Mum and Dad. Liz. I phoned Jane at the museum, but when she came on the phone I couldn't get my voice to say anything. I didn't think you'd—'

'Why did you do it, Nick?'

She turned and looked at him. Her husband. All the thousands of minutes and hours and days. He stood in Anthony's clothes that were too big for him; it seemed to Chloe that he was shrinking, visibly, even as they spoke. His arms hung dead at his sides, his palms turned slightly towards her. Her husband wasn't here. This was a changeling.

'I don't know.'

'Come on. Why?' She heard the words coming out of her mouth and already felt exhausted. Little noises. The worn currency she was forced to use, no matter what, if she was going to do this at all. She wished she hadn't come. She remembered Myres's face when she had told her she was going to do this. She remembered what the hard eyes had said: Don't, because you'll have to speak, and it won't be enough.

He stood perfectly still. It was a continuous pain for Chloe to see him, the face a surprised parody of Nicholas's, the eyes all wrong.

'I don't know,' he repeated. 'She . . . she—'

'Oh not *that*, for fuck's sake. You did *that* because you're fucking stupid. You did *that* because that's what people *do*. I'm not interested in why you—'

But it wasn't that easy. The images did come again. She had trusted him. Loved him. Despite everything. She had been betrayed. It astonished her – it jumped out at her suddenly, though she thought she had done with it very soon after Myres had told her.

'I mean why did you leave?' Why did you leave *me*? she had nearly said.

Nothing. Just the horror of his stillness. Mouth open, lips moving slightly, saying nothing. She stood and looked at him, seeing the memory of language; the gap between the memory of words and the ability to use them.

'Why did you leave?' Repeated. And the knowledge that he wouldn't be able to answer.

Eventually she couldn't stand the pain of it. Eventually she couldn't stand the pain of her own survival.

'I'm different now,' she said. 'Funny, isn't it, how you become different?'

'Everything's different,' he said. A whisper. Tears fell quickly from his eyes. Chloe watched. Not a man crying, every tear grudged. Different. A physical mechanism to which he remained oblivious.

'You think you'll die but you don't,' he said. 'Everything becomes different.'

'You get a choice,' Chloe said. 'Between dying remembering things the way they were, or not dying and having everything different. Everything's different. You should die – but you find you don't.' Then, thinking of the hospital: 'Or they don't let you.'

It was surprising to her, the way his eyes continued releasing tears, copiously, him unaware and completely still.

'I was afraid,' he said.

'So was I.'

She couldn't remember what she had imagined this would be like. It hadn't been this. It hadn't been anything. It had been an empty space. He was very far away from her, whoever he was. She could feel language evaporating between them. She wanted to leave.

'Our life,' he said.

Our life. They had had a life. The day after the wedding. Him making a fire in the hearth. Her making tea, flirting with the role of being a wife, laughing at herself inside, a bit shocked because it titillated her. Twenty-one years old. The other faces from the other life. All the nights of love and sleep; she saw now how much she had believed they would add up to something in the end. Because she hadn't known the end would come before the end, when there was still life left over.

Standing with her back to the window, seeing his thin hands almost covered by the unbuttoned cuffs, she realized she was in pain. A great, empty pain she had never prepared for over all the preceding weeks. She had thought this meeting might finish her, might once and for all help her to give up on the rest of her life. It was the real reason she'd come, in the hope of something to help her to death. She knew now that she had been holding on to the idea of seeing Nicholas so that he could tip her over the last precipice.

But even this had failed. It had failed because this wasn't Nicholas. Now that she saw this she was impatient to get away.

'There's a lot of stuff,' Chloe said. A sweat had broken out on her skin. Small, dislocated anxieties made themselves known to her: that she'd told Liz she was here to see Jane and to wrap things up with the museum; that she'd left their bathroom in a mess; that she'd forgotten this week's telephone call to her Mum and Dad.

'Chloe—'

'I mean about money and the flat and things.'

She wondered what he'd been about to say.

'It's over,' she said. Now the nausea was because she couldn't extricate herself quickly enough. Nicholas hadn't moved from his spot in front of the couch.

'In the ambulance,' he said.

'What?'

'Your heart stopped.'

It shocked her. Not that she had died and been brought back, but that he had seen it. And once again, despite everything, she felt a piercing pity for the body she remembered, the old body that had been allowed to pass away, that had been replaced with this new contrivance of unease, this instrument that had been turned back from the sea, that was dissonant, that had pulled the trigger and restarted time.

'Your heart . . .' He had stopped crying. She didn't move. She could see the state he was in (that his damage, like hers, was structural, paradigmatic), but she couldn't unlock herself from the image of him seeing her death.

'I don't remember,' she said. 'No bright light or tunnel or anything.'

'I couldn't do anything,' he said. 'He kept saying, Talk to her, talk to her or you're going – going to lose—'

She watched him, his stillness. He seemed now both calm and disinterestedly curious, as if the scene he was remembering fascinated him. She knew she could summon hate if she chose. Or, if not hate, then the rage of loss. It was a constant option – had been an option from the first moment she'd seen him. But he was so far away. To hate she needed Nicholas, the other Nicholas, not this ravaged simulacrum.

'I couldn't do anything.' Each word an unexpected discovery.

A strange thought came to her. To feel sorry for him. Which almost made her laugh. Suddenly the whole world – the whole of history – offered itself as a perpetual choice between hatred and compassion. She didn't *feel* sorry for him; it was just that she had become aware that she could, if she chose. Despite everything. A lightness like the lightness she had felt in the car with Myres, driving to murder. Another liberation from the old framework of feeling. If life was offering her anything, it was offering the novelty of previously unknown states.

None the less, this wasn't Nicholas, and that, perversely, angered her.

'Stop this,' she said. 'It's disgusting.'

He looked up at her slowly, the face alien and perfected.

'Stop it,' she said. She crossed again to where he stood still on Anthony's *faux*-Moroccan rug. 'Couldn't you have been stronger than this, Nick? You used to be strong.'

He was seeing her face for the first time. For a few seconds the only thing he saw was the new face, scarred, an identity they'd scrambled to recover. Very slowly, he lifted his left hand. Whispered: 'Chloe. Chloe.'

She let the fingertips come so close to her face that she could feel their heat, then drew away. Nicholas dropped his hand, stared at her, emptily. Chloe saw everything: that if their life together could be set for ever at this pitch of honesty and nakedness, they could share it; that no shared life – even theirs – *could* be like that; that ordinariness (the persistence of the ordinary) would seep back in; that there would be minutes, days, years of ordinariness which would demand that they live as if nothing had happened. There would be cups of tea made, walks taken, hoovering done, weather observed, meals eaten – simplicities that would insist nothing had happened between them. They wouldn't be able to stand it. Eventually (quickly, in fact), sharing ordinariness would send them mad. Chloe was only able to bear him now because the moment between them was pure and original. She knew that to repeat any experience with him would destroy her. She could come to him now because this territory (seeing him again, after what had happened) was unknown and singular. Were she to arrange to meet him tomorrow the first sight of his face in the tube station crowd would force her to turn

away from him. Dispassionately, solely for convenience, she
wished that he had died.

'There's an irony,' she said. 'You saved my life.'

'I killed you.'

'You saved my life. You were there to call the ambulance.'

'I killed you.'

'I would have died if you hadn't been there. Funny.'

She saw that he had gone past something, too, that the
urgency in the air had diminished.

'I'm going,' she said.

'Don't go.'

'I can't see you just now,' Chloe said. Oddly, she realized that
she meant it as it had sounded: like she was busy with other
things. 'I'll phone you about the stuff. The flat and whatnot.'

'Chloe?'

'What?'

'Do you wish I was dead?'

He was motionless, looking at her. For the first time Chloe
noticed that Anthony's living-room was dotted with manuscripts. Words. All those people who wanted their words heard.
She remembered hospital, discovering all the world that escaped
language. She had a fleeting vision of the earth spinning in
space, thinly woven around by an atmosphere of tiny trapped
voices. Then space.

'No,' she said. 'I don't wish you were dead. Not now. Things
would be easier if you hadn't come back.'

'I love you.'

For a few moments she just stood and looked down at him.

'Do you know who I am?' she asked him.

'Yes. It's you. Chloe.'

'And who are you?'

'Nicholas.'

It solidified the silence between them. It solidified and
expanded it until Chloe realized she had walked away from him,
backwards, to the door.

◆

Myres isn't here. No note. Just all the crockery washed and put away. The one bed still pressed to my last shape of sleep. A week on the couch must have permanently realigned her bones. The sudden sense when I opened the curtains this morning, ground mist peeling back to the clouds in torn curls, that my licence for paralysis has expired. Inexhaustible ordinary thoughts knocking like dogged police: I need money; I should think about a job; establish an address; sign on. God knows what all else. Every day I say to myself that I'll start. Every day I go to the rough beach of skulls and live in the weather, whatever it is. The weather, like ordinariness, is condemned to persist. Afterwards, you're left with things like the weather: clouds writing their oblique messages on the sky; rain like a hail of arrows shot straight down in anger; God moving his shoulders in the sea; a night of brilliant constellations like diagrams of an eloquent mathematics; wind tearing through the dark grass. The weather makes an effort to speak of the world beyond language. When so much has been taken away from you, you begin to make the effort to listen.

I've done with the diagonal between here and London for a while. I've got a concrete sense of where I am here, on England's green ankle stuck out to test the Atlantic. It's appropriate, God knows why.

Celts were killed here. Romans, far from home. Saxons. I know what's underfoot: the dark strata flecked with bone, copper, iron, hair; bogs have drunk blood, stones have sealed kings and queens. The land's broody with the buried dead, confused with the lives it's swallowed. It doesn't sleep; it tosses and turns and sends its ghosts trailing and whispering above the ground. I hear it all when I wake in the small hours, Vicky's bracelet lit by the moon. We share sleeplessness, me and the land, the cold comfort of each other's muttering.

I didn't know who he was.

He said he knew who I was. Chloe.

I told him it would have been easier if he hadn't come back – but knew even as I said it that he hadn't come back. That I hadn't come back either. Myres, warning me silently, was right

about the words. I should have just looked at him. Said nothing.
The words only measured the silence. Since I've been back here,
I've caught myself wondering about another Nicholas altogether.
The other Nicholas, mine, lost.

Fairy stories. It's Cornwall, with its back turned and its hoard
of sleepless dead.

One evening a week later, Myres returned. Chloe had been sitting watching the light fade from the chalky path, a packet of
Bourbon biscuits unopened on her lap.

Different car. The other had been a brown Sierra. This was a
green Metro, and looked in no state to have been driven from
London. Chloe watched from the living-room's sash window
while Myres got out, finished her cigarette, then stood for a
moment with her hands at her sides, considering the sky. The
day had been cold and bright. A wind from the sea had
unpacked brilliant white clouds over the coast, then torn them
apart by degrees. Now the sky was darkening from gun-blue to
black. A high quarter-moon like a silver hoofprint. Faint stars.

Myres only brought one thing in with her from the car: a
bottle of Scotch. Barely acknowledging Chloe's hello, she went
straight to the kitchen and returned with two glasses.

'I'm not sure I can drink that,' Chloe said.

'Why not?'

'My insides.'

Myres poured anyway, handed her the glass. Chloe hadn't
drunk since before hospital; now the golden scent of the whisky
touched her nostrils like gentle flames, igniting a world of
memory. She closed her eyes for a moment, inhaling.

'What are we celebrating?' Chloe said.

Myres sighed, drew her hand down her face from forehead to
jaw, then let it drop back to her side. For the first time since
she'd known her, Chloe had a glimpse of the woman who wasn't
a police detective. The eyes. The usual hard focus was struggling. Thinking was going on, beyond the need to find answers

to questions. It struck Chloe that Myres had once been a little girl. She imagined her on the front step of an East End terrace with her chin on her knees, scowling out at the world, troublesome, immeasurably beyond understanding. She imagined hard skinny shins and the dirt dragged by afternoon tears.

'I packed it in,' Myres said. 'The force. Resigned.'

'Fucking hell,' Chloe said. 'Why?'

Myres shook her head gently, raised her glass to Chloe's. *Clink*. The unfailing intimacy of the ritual.

'Cheers.'

'Oh well, fuck it, cheers,' Chloe said, and swallowed a large sip.

Warmth, a down-reaching fire. She'd forgotten.

Myres drank half hers in one gulp.

'It was over,' she said. 'You get to a point – I saw it in my Dad. It's just over. You know. You just know.'

'I'm sorry,' Chloe said.

'Don't be. Christ knows what I'll do now, mind you. Sell the flat, I suppose. No point in being there.'

'I can clear out of here,' Chloe said. 'It's been good of you to let me—'

'Leave it out,' Myres said.

They couldn't look at each other. Chloe felt a great tiredness. She remembered that from the beginning Myres had felt like a challenge to her imagination; she remembered that thinking about her in hospital had seemed a concession to going on with life.

'Is there anything to eat?' Myres said – then very quickly added: 'I'll just be here for a few days. It doesn't affect . . . I just had to get out of fucking London. Sorry. I didn't even phone.'

Chloe watched her patting her pockets for cigarettes, saw her realize she'd left them in the car. Myres took a couple of steps to the door, stopped, swallowed the rest of her drink, looked back at Chloe. It's you. Chloe. His face beneath her, transformed by grief. A forearm pressing on her windpipe. You can't do this. The boy looking down at her in the sea. A shuffle of images. The tiredness because she understood that this was how it would be

for a long time. 'There's Spar chicken drumsticks,' she said. 'And
Bourbon biscuits. And bread and butter.'

◆

Nicholas sat at the bar in the Blue Boar on Westbourne Grove,
surrounded by afternoon cigarette smoke and the smell of
spilled beer. The woman next to him was heavy, with round
shoulders and a glossy face. Blonde with black roots like dark
flames, all the hair scraped back into a greasy ponytail. One eye
was bloodshot, and she smiled, incessantly. She had been drinking with Nicholas for three hours. All her fingernails were bitten
to the quick. She looked to him the most lonely person he had
ever seen.

'What'd you say your name was again?'

Nicholas looked down at the hat on his lap.

◆

After Myres fell asleep on the couch, Chloe left her a note:

Gone for a walk. I've changed the bedclothes. You sleep in the
bed tonight, I'll take the couch. I insist. This is your place. I
might sit on the beach for a while.
        Chloe.

She didn't sit on the beach. For once she went the other way,
up on to the cliffs. Her hair had grown longer than it had ever
been. The weight and novelty pleased her. The wind, which was
irascible, sporadically bullying, tugged it out from under her
collar and blew it wildly behind her. The madwoman of the
cliffs, she thought. The murderess of the cliffs. The mad murderess of the Cornish crags. Ridiculous. And true.

She didn't know where the levity had come from. Attributed it to the Scotch, of which she had eventually sunk two glasses. Myres's generous measures. Myres.

She didn't know where the levity had come from, but she knew it hid something fearful. She had got through the hours with Myres by not talking about anything of substance. A previously unseen dynamic between them – both of them slightly shy of it, both of them edging around the absurdity. They had discussed practical things, vaguely: the possible sale of Chloe's flat; Myres's place in Bethnal Green; Camvellyn's dread of summer and tourists; Frank and Edna's good-hearted greed; the handful of relic-freaks who scoured the cliffs with metal detectors, dreaming of swords and gold; the sadness of the Spar. Both of them had seen the need for this distraction. Myres had drunk a lot of Scotch. Chloe had watched her in the latter stages, fading in and out, trying to keep her eyes open, until eventually they had closed and stayed closed.

Chloe hadn't lost the hospital vision, the ability to see fear on faces. Myres's face, at moments, had revealed not fear but a kind of compact trauma – as if only at moments was she realizing that her old life was over. Chloe had felt distantly sorry for her.

It came, eventually, like rain that had been approaching in a faint shadow.

One moment she was sitting looking out at the preposterous beauty of the thin moon over the sea, the next she was crying, bitterly, in silent sobs that seemed to crack her chest.

She had thought: Like the ordinary, beauty persists. It's got no choice. It's just there.

Then she had broken. It was as if she had survived everything that had happened to her so far only by a monumental aversion of consciousness; as if all the former clarity – the brutally spoken truths, the nakedness of other people's fears – had been both desperate and cunning, an elaborate distraction of which the only function had been to carry her from one moment into the next, breath after breath, hour after hour, until it was safe to stop and actually realize what she had lost and what she had become.

That was where the levity had come from. The Bourbon biscuits, the clink of her glass – the last strokes in a master-plan of
avoidance. Now it was finished. Now there was the full, unal-
leviated weight of loss.

Crying for the body that was gone, for the fingertips and eyelashes, for the moment of recognition in a café long ago, for her
father's life tapering to the grave, for the grotesque doppelgänger
who had been returned to her in place of her husband, for the
sound of a silenced gun, for everything she had ever held and for
everything that had been taken from her, she dug her fingers
into the turf and held on to the buried, sleepless dead.

For life.

A long time had passed, but it was still dark. Two or three hours
of the night remained. On the landing outside the bedroom door
Chloe stood still, empty. The small hours.

She sat very gently on the edge of the bed. She was a space
where pain had been and would be again. The scars were quiet,
astonished. The flesh didn't believe, wanted no part of this. She
had no idea what she was going to say.

But Myres's wet, agate eyes were open in the dark. For ten,
twenty, thirty heartbeats neither spoke. Chloe almost got up.

'I don't know if I can be here,' she said at last.

Myres lay very still, but with her face turned to Chloe.

'I can't . . . I mean I'm not . . .'

'No. I know. That's not it,' Myres said.

Silence. They didn't move. Chloe swallowed, terrible knots of
tears. She couldn't swallow them. It was so quiet in the room
that they could both hear the little *putt, putt* of the tears that fell
on the bedclothes.

'Sorry,' Chloe said, in the air-speech of crying. 'Sorry, sorry.'

Myres's hand came to her in the dark. She took it, remembered it lifting the gun to her, irresistibly.

'I know you're alone,' Chloe said. But it didn't mean anything.
Nothing she could think of to say meant anything. She stopped

crying. Knew nothing. Took her shoes off. The mattress twanged. The words were over, at least.

Very slowly, Chloe, fully dressed, pulled back the sheets and blankets and lay down on the bed. Myres rolled on to her side to face her, not touching.

For further information about Granta Books
and a full list of titles, please write to us at

Granta Books

2/3 HANOVER YARD

NOEL ROAD

LONDON

N1 8BE

enclosing a stamped, addressed envelope

———————

You can visit our website at

http://www.granta.com